The Kingdom Below

By

Maggie White

The Kingdom Below by Maggie White
Book 1 of the The Kingdom Below Series
Story Copyright 2024 Maggie White
Editing by Jenny Raden
ISBN: 979-8-9876093-7-8

Content Warning
The book you're about to read includes the death of a characters on page. The Kingdom Below contains sexual tension and mature thoughts and language. It may not be suitable for readers under eighteen.

My mom said you can come play mermaids if you want to....

With Gratitude

This book would not have been possible without the support of all of these amazing backers. Thank you so much.

Nicola Thompson
Sherry Mock
Kourtney Randall
Ruthenia (Ruth) Dillon
Justise Briones (That/Them)
The Creative Fund by BackerKit
Billye Herndon
Elizabeth Spisak
Alice Hanov
Erica Bosko
Cara Beth Fishback
Claire Lee
Joy Stacey
Anna O'Brien-Smith
Alexandra Corrsin
Ashlyn Barnes
Crystal Vasalech
Chanel Holm
Vicky Salas
Tanya Young
Alyssa Partin
Jensa
Laura
Alesha
Jess Wolchesky
Colleen Farrall

Becca Epstein
Nekia T
Ika
Elisha Bryant
Bianca Tatjana Višić Ritorto
Kelly Stirling
Amy
Annette McElroy
Rachmarie
Kristin
Amber
Nena Yochim
Deborah Leland
Jessica
Katie Zimmerman
Samantha Case
Deborah Cooke
Tomaya smith
Chloe Ruggieri
Samara Hull
Jessica Rea
New Door Media
Ariel S
Amanda Balter
Jayme Johnson
Kamalloy
Krystina R

Frank Rosellen
Danae
Caitlin Millsaps
Maike ten Dam
Katrina Gilles
Azra Markham
Nicole Sanders
Taylor Elrod
Crystal Palumbo
Katy Collier
Abby Richardson
C.M. Hawken, Author
Celosia Starfall
Giselle Trejo
Nikole Clow
Jenny Saunders
Samantha G
Victoria Psomiadis
S
Elizabeth Morgan
Qavee
Juliette Krainess
Andie Andrews
Elise Crowley
Kaitlyn Sterrett
Kailey Boyan
Rachel Rasmussen
Monica Arsenault
Angela Morse
Megan Herrin
Gianna Christopher
Katie Skinner
Stacy Ward

Chloe
Meghan Edwards
Liza Clarke
Leah Barr
Brittany Barboza
Lisah Frankland
Jessica
Brandy Hartley
Tracey Angle
Megan Kell
Christy
Elizabeth
Felicitas
Jaye Viner
Anna Mucci
Laura McWilliams
Laurel tr
Alicia Lux
Tracy Kretsch
Alexandra
Rebekah Margaret Doss
Courtney Arnold
Summer
Lisa
Nikki Mathis
Jenna
Maria Mejia
Nikole Ghirardi
Sue Frecker
Hannah Wilkinson
Amber
Sebastian Olano
Genna Carlin

Kati Bennett

Carly Dore

Elizabeth Decker

Katie Dice

Shannon J

Aubrey Dickson

Lindsay Ross

Rstaley8

Susannah1998

Vannessa

Nyphera

Hailey Lawson

Samantha Rozmarynowski

Lauren Gordon

Table of Contents

Part One

Chapter One

"Your father is going to kill you. You know that, right?"

I glanced over my shoulder, wrinkling my nose at my best friend as he approached, every tremulous step across the ship's prow making my smile wider. Rhoe hated the water, hated ships even more. The fact he was here, aboard the massive battleship made its way out into the Great Sea, told me absolutely everything about the seriousness of our venture today. Even with his joking tone, there was an underlying anxiety twisting Rhoe's handsome face as he joined me along the taffrail.

Turning to lean against the polished wood near the stern of *The DeArtinan*, I was careful not to jostle my far less sea-faring companion. "I imagine he'll have to try. Objectively disobeying his royal commands has that effect on any Adrialian. Princess or not." I shrugged as the enormous sails filled and began to pull us out of the pale-blue shallows and into deeper water.

"But then, I guess that's the unexpected pleasure of being his sole heir and daughter. He can't really kill me. At least, not yet. I mean, can you imagine the spectacle?"

Rhoe leaned back from the spray of the water that whipped from the brow, making me smile a little. "Perhaps you're right, but he will want to."

I sighed. "You and I both know that I had to be here. When it's one of our own, Rhoe, I need to be here. A man I've trained and served beside for years." My dark hair blew around my face. "I couldn't let him go alone, no matter what my father would've said."

Rhoe sighed, tall body sagging a little under his lightweight leather armor. No metal today. It wouldn't do any good in this environment. But I could tell he was still uncomfortable without his usual attire. As my father's Chosen, Rhoe spent even more time within the Adrialian court than I did. And he enjoyed that, thank the gods, because it meant that I could continue to avoid the court at all costs.

Rhoe had a rare gift for the politics that I couldn't compete with, even when I really tried. As the King's Chosen, he was specifically trained to not only defend the royal family from physical attacks, but on the political battlefield as well. He was a fine-tuned weapon, pure and simple. More deadly than any sword could be when he stepped into the King's court. It didn't hurt that every woman and a good number of the men north of Port Sol were vying for a drop of his attention.

"I know what you mean. Pierse is a good man. Hopefully we can find whatever it is he needs. Or at the very least, we can find him some level of peace."

I eyed Rhoe's expressive face again, curiosity growing in the pit of my belly. I'd known for some time that my friend often knew more than he was allowed to say, and at times those secrets seemed to tear away at his chest. It hurt to see him like this, but I had learned long ago that to ask was only begging more problems for the both of us.

I may have been the heir to the throne, but he was my father's blade.

Perhaps that's why I preferred the ocean, even with its dangers. Sitting silently beside my father at court did nothing to free our people from their fears. I was needed here, where I could do something good with my training.

Whereas most of my people feared the water of the Great Sea, I found myself only growing more intrigued by it as I grew up. And a few years ago, after becoming frustrated with lack of progress with my kingdom's greatest enemy, I enlisted in this elite group. My father was initially disappointed then furious, but in the end he allowed me to fight alongside these select few as much as my schedule allowed. He knew more than most how important what Captain Linus Sheldon aspired to do was for the future of Adrial.

Our mission, led by Captain Sheldon, a weathered, stone-faced military man, was to assist the Adrialian people with the one thing that no one on land could manage. With something so twisting and confusing that oftentimes the crew went home feeling the all-consuming weight of failure.

But on other days, rare as they were, we succeeded. I swallowed hard, tearing my eyes from Rhoe's worried expression to the trap door to the small jail they'd created on board *The DeArtinan*.

We were far into the sea now. It was almost time.

"Bring him out!" our captain called, his gruff tone carrying easily across the waves.

I stepped forward, taking my position. I was a lucky Adrialian. My ability to resist the calling of the curse made me perfect for the last stage of our process.

At a jerk of the captain's stubbled chin, the latch was undone and two familiar faces lurched into the sunlight, dragging behind them the creature who had once been Pierse Vallide. Whereas Pierse had always offered a kind smile, a quick wink when we were training together, now his body flailed about the deck, twisting and turning as he lunged and fought against the men who held his ties.

It sounded as if he wanted to speak, but the noises from his lips had devolved into a series of high-pitched squeals and grunts of pain as the men he once fought side by side with struggled to guide him forward.

I hadn't seen a cursed one this far gone in a long time. "When was he cursed?" I whispered to Rhoe, who I knew stood behind me.

"Only the night before last."

Cold sweat dampened my palms, and I wiped them against my pants. For the curse to be this advanced in only two days did not leave much hope. But we had to try. Pierse would've done the same for us.

As our former compadre was brought up the stairs, each positioned soldier offered him a sharp salute. No matter what happened today, Pierse was a sacrifice and a loss in the war against the God of the Sea and his devastating curse.

For generations, madness had plagued my people, sweeping through the city picking off people who dared to touch the Sea God's waters. And Trayon showed no mercy. One day people would be going about their daily business. The next they would begin to display odd behaviors. Often they would mention the Great Sea or the cursed waters that surrounded the castle and our thriving port.

From there it was only days before they would begin to plead to be let in. Beg for the water's touch. Going as far as to hurt or attack those who kept them from the frothing water. And all it took was the barest touch of the cursed sea.

The cravings, they wouldn't let up. Not until the victim found a way to scale the expansive walls that encircled all of our shores and leap into the waves. Those who survived the worst of the cravings on land were often changed forever, even once they gave up their desire to leap into the ocean.

I felt nothing but pain and pity for them. Courtier or sailor, the god below the waves had damned them all equally when it came to his curse. My own mother had passed due to Trayon's curse upon Adrial. I was too young to remember most of what transpired but often wondered. Had my mother thought the same wild things? Had she screamed and cried out for the bite of the cold water on her skin as I had seen so many others do?

I watched as the soldiers finally got Pierse walking the direction they wanted. My heart rose in my throat, uncomfortable tears pricking at the backs of my eyes as Pierse thrashed on the stairs. This was the worst part, getting them into position.

I shivered as Pierse's wild gaze rose to the edge of the deck. He had seen it. The water.

Pain twisted my gut as his face changed, for a second transforming that into Pierse the man, not the damned creature before me. He walked straight, tall, almost human once more as he drew closer to the rail, now dragging his captors, unaware of their shouts of dismay as he got dangerously close to the churning sea.

Pierse suddenly froze, every bulging muscle still. Goosebumps raced along my skin as I watched Pierse lean his head back, his nostrils flared wide, huffing in the brine-filled air in huge gulps. When he opened his eyes again, I flinched away. His eyes were glowing a strange golden yellow, the warm brown eyes from breakfast just days ago gone.

If Pierse made it to the water, he would be gone forever. The cursed Adrialians would disappear beneath the waves, drawn down to be Trayon's playthings in the depths of the Great Sea.

Perhaps a life on shore would be different for those affected they saved, but at least here they would have a life.

That was the thought I clung to as Captain leapt forward, grabbing a stray line to Pierse's bindings and hauled back on it, steering the cursed man away from the water once more.

My throat ached at the dismay that flashed across Pierse's familiar face. I had considered us friends. Pierse was a good man who had served the kingdom loyally for most of his young life. I couldn't let him go without trying. Maybe, just maybe he was strong enough to hold on, to let us fight for his right to stay alive.

"Heads up. We have incoming," a masculine voice shouted down at Rhoe and me from the rigging above us.

As a unit, we moved back, preparing for what the Sea God had sent our way today. My hand gave one last tug on the thick heavy strips of leather hung over the sturdy beams nailed into place at the prow. A harness, designed for only one thing.

Rhoe's hands were warm on my shoulders, pushing me to the side with a hiss of frustration as I dug in my heels.

"I'm staying, Rhoe."

"You're trying my patience, Princess Mira."

I wrinkled my nose at him and gave into the pressure of his grip, stepping farther from the rail. It was his job to protect me, but that didn't mean I had to enjoy it.

Pierse was a big man. His heavy frame had been encased with muscles, but his face had always been kind, friendly. Always eager to learn. The man who was being escorted up the bow by his friends bore almost no resemblance to the man I had known. It tore away at my hope once more, and I saw it in all of the faces of the crew.

Pierse could barely walk now, his excitement evident in his every move. From his bare feet slipping across the boards of the deck to the sounds falling from his mouth. His voice was different now, his expression tortured as he tried to look over his shoulders at the water once more. The desire to rejoin his new master overwhelming all else.

For a long moment, I wished that I'd let Rhoe convince me to remain below deck for this.

Rhoe released me, moving a half step in front of me as the crew attempted to guide Pierse towards the harness. While Rhoe was more than capable of taking Perse in a brawl, I wouldn't want to see them mixed up together right now. Not when Pierse's mind was already so far gone.

"Easy, Pierse," I whispered, my voice tight in the warm morning air. "We're going to try to help you."

The man in front of me twitched all over, muscles bulging and rolling under his torn uniform as the soldiers finally pushed him up to the final steps. The harness I had set up was close, but not close enough, as evidenced by the swearing people still towing him along.

"You know me, right, Pierse? We're trying to help you."

Suddenly, Pierse stilled completely. He tilted his head into the breeze once more.

I stepped closer to him, joy warm in my veins for a moment. "Is he snapping out of it?" I moved around Rhoe, chest tight. "Pierse? My friend, do you know what's happening?"

The moment I looked into his yellow eyes, I knew I was wrong. They were a predator's eyes. Only the smallest glimmer of humanity shone back at me. I swallowed the disappointment.

"We are taking you there." I pointed at the sea in front of us. "You're going to feel better soon, I promise."

"You." Pierse's wild expression didn't change, but he swallowed hard, a flash of normalcy in his craze. "Take me."

"Yes, yes, Pierse, we're going to take you." My throat was rough as I reached forward to pat Pierse's shoulder over the dozens of ropes that we'd used to bind him within the harness. My touch must've been either unexpected, or broke his sanity once more, because Pierse reared back from the touch and began to thrash wildly once more.

I covered my mouth, something between a cry and a plea sitting on my tongue. Still I didn't look away. I would rule these people one day. It was only right that I should know their pain.

Rhoe was there in an instant, pressing me back with a hand on my arm. "Don't touch him, Your Highness."

"I'm sorry," I whispered as the trio of soldiers finally managed to hook Pierse into his harness.

The chains slipped to the ground, and I prayed to the Mother that this was the last time I would have to witness one of my friends in this state.

"I hope this works," one of the soldiers, a first timer, said to us, panting. "I'm not sure I'll be able to unhook him again."

Rhoe moved a bit closer to Pierse, tugging a strap a few notches tighter. "You won't have to. Either they will claim him, or Trayon will. It's the way of the curse."

I turned back to the sea, the beautiful, white-tipped waves cursing us as *The DeArtinan* cut its way into the deadliest part of the Adrial.

Our waters.

Chapter Two

I wished I understood what my ancestors were doing when they damned us to this existence. Every Adrialian man or woman was raised to fear the waters that surround our capital city of Port Sol. And it wasn't because the water was dangerous or storm-ridden, though it was for certain seasons. The Great Sea was cursed, our kingdom forced to carry the weight of a centuries-old curse so that we may never enter the waters here.

Not a touch, or else they risk the Sea God's wrath or being struck down with the curse like Pierse. At times it would mean that whoever risked it would slowly grow more and more ill. Others it would manifest like Pierse had, this growing wildness taking root into him until the people went absolutely wild and usually raced to their death in the waves.

I swallowed, my knees bending as the ship bounced through a rough patch leaving harbor. In my mother's case of the curse, the young queen had leapt into the Great Sea one night when I was only a few years old. No other symptoms, no signs until she began to scream to my father that she was being called home.

That the sea needed her.

And then she was gone.

I glanced over at Pierse, who had quieted again, his eyes desperately searching the waters as if looking for someone. Or, more likely, something.

I looked to Rhoe. He knew, like me, what awaited us the moment we stepped off the heavily guarded beaches of Port Sol and into Trayon's turbulent realm. Sometimes Trayon's subjects appeared as sea animals, massive sharks, unusually large whales, or even more ominous creatures that didn't belong on the surface, incredible long-armed squids. Whatever they were, they always had one thing in mind. To claim whoever was affected by the sea sickness.

They would attack anyone who came in between them and the cursed Adrialians. The captain had lost many sailors and soldiers in his attempts to save those he could from a life of being torn beneath the waves to their watery death. I knew that before the captain had developed this elite squad, most families would tie their family members to chairs, beds, even chain them to posts in an effort to keep them from diving back beneath the waves and fulfilling Trayon's curse.

Those were often the rare few who survived and returned back to a shell of their former selves. But over the years, the best solution was this, to place the affected at the prow of the ship and let their movements, their eyes guide us to wherever the creatures were waiting.

Once there, the crew could fight back. If we managed to turn Trayon's soldiers back, many times the cursed would be snapped from the illness, their bodies breaking out in sweat and many feeling as if a fever had been broken after a long bout of illness.

I knew without asking how much we all hoped that would be how today would go. That we would free our friend from this madness.

Rhoe had moved to stand beside Pierse. Watching as Pierse began to jerk at the harness, clearly wanting to change direction slightly. "Starboard, Lile."

The youngest in our crew nodded then altered our path ever so slightly from his position behind the wheel. Pierse stilled, obviously more content for a moment. My chest grew tight once more, winding ever more as the spiraling towers of my home in Port Sol became a gray speck along the horizon.

We were firmly in Trayon's territory now. And while the sickness held Pierse tight in its thrall, so did the powerful, cruel lord of the sea. My lips parted, a prayer sent to the Mother Moon and Father Sky. We would need all the help we could get. Perhaps the Mother would be feeling gracious.

A quick movement out of the corner of my eye caught my attention. Even while he seemed content, I could see Pierse's fingers racing over the harness holding his body in place. I'd never seen one of the cursed do this and resisted the urge to smack his hands away from the buckles. Usually when we took a cursed Adrialian out to sea, they were so beyond human recognition that all they did was throw themselves about the bow in their harness, guiding the ship this way and that as they did.

This was…different. A chill that had nothing to do with the biting spray of water below me grew in my veins. Something was wrong.

"Rhoe," I whispered, my voice hoarse and soft. But I didn't really need to say anything. My friend was already staring too, every line in his powerful body tense and tight as he watched.

"Pierse, my friend, we're going to free you." Rhoe reached to press a hand to our friend's back.

But instead of comfort, the touch again unleashed the untamable side of the man once more. Pierse roared into the clear blue sky until his throat grew dry and silent and then continued to hum, to plead silently with something just out of our sight.

Something that wasn't there. I knew that, but the sight of his mouth moving still sent waves of fear over my flesh.

Rhoe swallowed hard, his angular face turning from Pierse back to the sea. "We are almost there."

I wasn't sure who he was talking to. Pierse was blind to all of us now, his body tensing and relaxing as he lunged around in his harness, demonstrating to our coxswain where exactly our battle would lie.

As the sun burned down on us, Pierse suddenly sagged in his leathers, face slack and content for the first time since he'd arrived on board. He looked almost human. He looked pleased.

My stomach churned.

This was it.

"Swords at the ready. Load the cannons and harpoons," Captain Sheldon shouted from below. "And for Artio's sake, no one falls into the water. Because no one here is going after you." He caught sight of me and gave me an ugly smile. "Even you, Princess."

"I'll manage," I said to him, unsheathing my short sword and moving to stand next to Pierse and Rhoe once more. Rhoe was sitting against the rail, his long legs pushing his vantage far beyond mine, making his upper body dangle precariously over the edge. I grimaced, wishing I could order him to lean back. While he claimed to be afraid of the sea, uninterested in even the safety of our freshwater lakes and streams, he seemed calm now. Perhaps it was the incoming battle that had him settled, as it did with the other warriors.

Just as I opened my mouth to ask him to step back again, for my desperate heart's sake, Rhoe swiveled to me, a smirk pulling at his lips. "Are you going to be a good girl and listen to me?"

I bristled at the acquisition and tone. "Do you think talking to me like that will convince me to?"

"No, but neither would asking nicely."

I shrugged. "Maybe."

"You are the bane of my existence," he said dryly. He didn't mean it. He never did. This was part of our ritual, this banter, this verbal swordplay. It was better than stretching and more beneficial than prayers. At least for me.

The ship dipped through a large wave, and I stepped back as a small smattering of droplets marked the ship railing. Splashes like that wouldn't curse us, only true immersion, but still, I flinched back. "You would miss me. Face it."

"I would, so please attempt to keep your feet on the ship. And then immediately on land once we get home." Rhoe twirled his sword neatly then tossed it from his left to his right hand.

"Yeah, that's the plan, idiot."

I opened my mouth to serve him another tease, another joke, when a splitting scream had the words dying in my throat. The wood beneath *The DeArtinan* creaked, the water around us quieting as the wind went still.

Rhoe went to stand at the top of the stairs, looking down at the captain. Though he outranked every other individual on this ship, Rhoe didn't usually call attention to his station. It was obvious, though, in the way he moved and spoke. Every soul on board waited, eyes scanning the deck.

"What was that?" someone shouted from behind me.

Rhoe turned, his eyes finding mine.

"A battle cry," he whispered, but I heard. Adrenaline shot through me as far above, a scout shouted the alarm.

"Brace yourself. Whale ahead."

I reached out, bracing my free hand against the elaborately carved rail, and waited. Only a few moments later, a tremendous thunk sounded below as an enormous whale appeared, broadsiding us as men scrambled for the harpoon stations.

I'd long lost my pity for the animals who attacked us during Captain Sheldons's missions. They were unlike anything else we'd ever seen. They were larger, more intelligent, more dangerous. And not unlike the man who we'd harnessed to our ship, they were out of their own control. God-bound, we'd called it. A term from centuries ago, when the gods chose to roam among us, choosing champions and favorites and creating chaos in their wake. It had been their way to bind people's and creature's wills to their own.

It was obvious from the first moment I'd seen one of the God-bound creatures that it was far beyond my reach or reason. Animals who had no right knowing what they did, understanding what they could do. It was further proof that another was behind that creature's eyes, treating it like a puppet. It was a tragedy that they had been dragged into this war between land and sea, but I couldn't surrender to that pain now. Not when the God-bound whale was turning in the water, coming back for another attack.

Across the ship, I saw Lile and another man already behind the harpoon, aiming carefully as the water frothed up over the enormous dorsal fin.

"Free!" he screamed, releasing the harpoon from its hold. It sailed forward, true in aim, but at the last moment, the whale rolled over, bright-white belly showing as it dived deep again.

There was only a moment's pause before it rammed the bottom of the ship, sending the crew on board scattering to hold on to the lines. I saw Rhoe launch down the stairs and yank people back to their feet, his voice cutting through the chaos like a knife.

Captain Sheldon was shouting orders, and there was a flurry of activity as the whale again rammed into the ship, this time hard enough it tilted us precariously close to one side. My sword slipped from my hand as I lurched forward, my other hand desperately clinging on to Pierse's harness as I struggled to stay on the ship.

"Oh Gods," I said, my hands burning with the effort of holding myself on the dry side of the railing. The sea below swirled, and something slipped into my mind, a sort of chant. No, not a chant—a song, circling over and over as I stared down into those cerulean depths.

"Wraps on!" Captain yelled.

The crew ran for the other end of the ship, where the whale arched out of the water and slammed into the hull again.

I grimaced, forcing the words from my mind. My hands were still busy keeping me from pitching over into the water, so much so that I couldn't reach into the belt where my specially made soundproof headband was attached. I'd never been on a mission where I'd heard the songs before. Our Adrialian fisherman often discussed the songs that whispered across the waves on quiet nights in the Great Sea. The farther out to sea you were, the deeper and louder the songs became. I had never heard one, but I knew exactly what they could do to unsuspecting sailors.

They believed the words could control you. Most people who heard the songs and didn't manage to plug their ears or cover them quickly would be persuaded to walk straight into the cursed water. Or, in my case, let go and fall into the white-tipped waves just a few lengths below where Pierse and I were.

Free him.

I tilted my head, humming loudly, attempting to avoid thinking about the sweetness of the sound and how much I wanted to see what kind of creature made that sound.

The ship tilted again, precariously pushing me farther from Pierse as my boots slipped against the polished boards.

Free him now.

"No!" I shouted into the pounding fury of a whale's approach. I wrapped myself tightly around the closest rigging, begging the ship to stay true to its form. When I dared to look up again, Pierse's face was full of joy. His body shook in his holds as an immense wave swept towards us.

I opened my mouth to scream at the wrongness of that water, at the way the wave was growing, building, getting tall enough that I knew instantly it would soak the entire ship. My heart skipped a beat. Would it curse us all?

All around us, everywhere but this wave, the water was still, save the foaming fight that was still happening at the other end of the ship.

"Pierse! Look at me," I pleaded, fighting gravity and the cockeyed lean of the ship. Whether it was the adrenaline of the moment or the fact that he was about to finally achieve the goal of the sickness, Pierse responded, looking right into my eyes.

Dread curled in my gut.

"I'm safe now. You can let me go," Pierse said softly, his eyes still that unearthly yellow.

"No, Pierse." My voice was just a croaking sound now, fear and dread changing it and making it nearly impossible to get the words out.

The ship rocked again, throwing me even farther from Pierse. With a grunt, I slammed into the harsh edge of a barrel, my footing lost as the whale turned its attention to the other end of the ship. I heard it then, Rhoe's command to protect the other side of the ship.

I was slipping, the wood slick under my desperate fingers as I drew ever closer to the dreaded edge. I flung my arms wide, feeling around for anything to keep me from plummeting straight into Trayon's realm. The railing hit the small of my back, sending me flailing, ass over teakettle, as water and sky blurred.

Ropes were the first things my fingers found, and I latched on to them, the rough lines snapping tight and hurling me back against the ship's hull as I found myself dangling only a body's length above the ocean. The wave, in all its unworldly ease, had almost reached Pierse and me. The song continued on, filling my ears, making my mind foggy and slow as I stared out at the wave until it began to descend again, sinking back into the waters below.

Everything in my body was telling me that I was in danger, copious amounts of it. I opened my mouth to scream.

Then, just before me, a creature rose from the frothing water. My scream died in my throat as a humanlike torso rose from the water. Bright golden scales covered the torso, but the arms, the belly, even the pair of breasts were so much like a human woman that my thoughts stuttered to a halt.

But their face—her face—it was different. Sharp cheekbones highlighted by deeper gold scales glowed on her skin as she easily propelled herself out of the sea, seeming to balance there, her naval flexing and rolling as my eyes finally trailed low enough to see that just below the waves, another full human's body length of metallic-finned tail swished below her.

She was a Mer.

Chapter Three

My heart hammered as I watched her, finally realizing that she was the source of the song too, her impossible voice filling my mind as she planted a hand against the edge of the hull, tilted her chin back, and sang again, deeper this time, louder. I was close enough I could see the droplets of water on her cheeks, shimmering and dancing as they slid down her face.

Somewhere deep in my mind, another voice grew louder. I jerked my chin, ears throbbing with my blood as I watched the water. There were more? Panic should've been flooding my body now, but there was nothing below me. Nothing but that soft voice, its deep tones tugging at my subconscious as this mermaid balanced so carefully on her tail, singing at Pierse.

Then her fingers reached down, dancing across the water's surface as if inscribing some kind of secret writing there. The ocean rose again, swelling around her, letting the Mer get even closer to where Pierse strained down for her.

His eyes were wild, every muscle standing out in stark relief against the leathers. As soon as she was close enough, she swirled her fingers through the water once again and then raised her hand, which I noticed had translucent webbing between each finger, and sent a stream of water at Pierse.

Now I did scream, my entire body coming back to life as if snapped from a trance myself. "No! Pierse!"

The mermaid swung around, baring a mouth full of dagger-like teeth as she screeched at where I still held on to the outside of the ship.

"You stupid fish. Leave him alone." Desperation roared in my veins as I tugged on the ropes, my toes pushing against the wooden hull as I tried to climb back up. If I could just get to that ledge, then I could probably climb up. Then I could pull Pierse to safety.

But my toes slipped, my soft leather boots useless against empty air and a smooth hull. The Mer seemed satisfied I wasn't a threat and turned back to Pierse and sent another stream of water his way.

The minute the water broke over his skin, he arched his back, his mouth open as he screamed into the sky. I started, my blood cold in my veins as I watched the rivets of water drip from Pierse. We had been too late. Trayon and the curse had come to claim my friend, and we had lost.

I choked back another angry scream, my hands aching as I scrambled on the edge of the hull once again. That would be my end too. As soon as I slipped a few more feet, my body would break the surface, and either I'd be devoured by this Mer and her God-bound whale, or Gods help me, Trayon, himself might be waiting just beyond to curse me to a life of servitude. After all, that's what the Gods always did. I was a child of the land, a daughter of the sun. My family served Artio and the Mother.

But I was far, far from them now; nothing but a tiny pawn in their master plans. I didn't flatter myself by thinking I might be of interest to the Gods for my skills on the battlefield or my role in politics. But I was the sole heir of a powerful seaside kingdom, dangling above Trayon's kingdom with no chance of escape. Even I recognized how badly this might go.

"Artio, suns above, please, help me."

But Adrial's God must not be listening. Or perhaps I was so far out of the realm of land and sun that he was unavailable to me. Either way, I slipped another hand down the rope, my flesh tearing as I did.

Pierse bellowed again, and I looked up just in time to see him snap the leather of his harness, his body freeing itself in a show of strength that should've impressed me, but instead horrified me.

Because no mortal man would be able to snap those bonds.

I swallowed hard as the Mer let her wave drop low, level with the rest of the sea around us. Pierse's face was at peace as he dove over the edge of the ship. He hit the water with a small splash. He did not reappear.

"No!" I screamed, my body coiling around on the end of the rope, mind and body both losing control. The Mer looked at me, that beautiful, dangerous face so focused that, for a moment, I thought she would come for me next. But instead, she inclined her sharp, pointed head.

Princess. The voice hissed through my mind, as clear as if they'd spoken directly into my ear.

And then with a flash, she disappeared beneath the waves with a flip of a gold and green tail.

They were both gone. No evidence they even existed, if not for what I'd witnessed herself.

I had known the Mer and other of Trayon's creatures had come for the cursed in the past. But seeing it in person was an entirely different matter. And now, I was going to die, these last images of my friend being stolen to his death fresh in my mind. One final failure before I myself was cursed.

Fury gave me a short spurt of energy, and I was strong enough to make it a small way back up the rope, but I couldn't get far. Every muscle in my arms was quivering, my neck twisted and aching as I reached a toe out, attempting to hook another rope. Anything to take some of my own weight off my trembling upper body.

But it was useless. There was nothing but the cursed waters for me. With a whimper, I rolled my legs around the rope again, feeling the shake of my arm muscles as I hung there.

"Please, please, please, please," I chanted over and over again. Something slipped through my mind, a sort of cool caress, and I raised my head, thinking that the Mer must be coming back.

But instead there was nothing, just that sense, a cool hollowness that took hold of my chest. I glanced down, into the calming waves below, and saw a flash of silver beneath me.

"Oh Gods," I moaned, my heart hammering as adrenaline thumped back into my body. There was another. Because this creature, whatever it was, wasn't the long, delicate golden body. This was an ominous shadow, curling and twisting within my own, flashing silver and onyx as the sunlight streamed around us.

I couldn't see any features, but I knew now what this was. Another Mer. I had been correct about never leaving this ship. About a predator never leaving a fresh meal like me. A tear slipped from my eyes and dripped down and over one cheek as I stared down into the silvery shadow. It was unmoving, waiting, and even as my tears dripped down into the water. I felt my grip slackening as fatigue took its toll.

"Come and get me," I yelled at the sea. My biceps were shaking, and I knew the muscles there were tearing, ripping apart in their effort to hold my body above water. With a grimace, I released one hand and pulled a hidden dagger from the back of my breeches. I was a princess, raised as a warrior. If I was about to die, I would do it with honor.

My eyes blurred with tears as I stared down at the shadow of death below me.

"Why don't you come and get me?" I growled.

Slowly, the shadow moved, a slick of silver, and it began to clarify, becoming sharper but no less dark as it rose towards the surface. I gritted my teeth, chest aching as I waited for the end.

A hand broke from the waves to reach for me. I held my dagger high. They would be on me in a moment, the rope was sliding in my weak palms. The surface of the water inched higher.

And I surrendered to it, to that waiting hand, to the dark creature just below. The rope slipped as my body finally gave in. With something like relief, my muscles gave way, and my eyes fluttered shut as I breathed out.

But as the water rushed towards me, an incredible pain lanced across the middle, yanking my fall to a halt with a sick slide of rope on flesh. I turned, staring back at the source of the pain, a rope slung over my dagger hand and across to the edge of my neck. Following it, my body feeling disjointed and uncomfortable, my gaze found its way back up to the edge of the ship.

Rhoe was over the railing, a heavy rope around his middle. He was holding tight to the rope he must've thrown over me. I reached an arm up, winding it through the rope, the burn of the fibers making me cringe. He'd saved me.

My head lolled as sensation ebbed across my body. Pain. Euphoria. And disappointment, clear and deadly, warred with the rest. Groaning, I tried to pinpoint what was happening in my mind just as the captain began yelling once more.

More proof that I was indeed alive. Too bad my body hadn't realized that. My full weight sagged in their lasso.

"Hold on, Princess," Captain Sheldon yelled, and I stared blankly up at the ship again. There are a half dozen men involved in my rescue, and each of them took the rope from Rhoe and began to heave me up higher and higher, away from the water.

With a grunt, I looked back to the waves for a moment, neck aching. Nothing. Not even a glimpse of color beneath the waves. That shadow of death, the Mer who had waited for me. He was gone.

As soon as he could, Rhoe reached out and hauled me up against his body, taking the weight of the ropes held on me. I moaned in thanks, burrowing into his familiar chest as they dragged the pair of us back on board the ship.

Rhoe and I landed in a pile of limbs, my body slack from exhaustion, stress, and grief.

"You're crazy," I whispered to Rhoe.

"I took an oath to take care of you." Rhoe tried to smile but didn't quite execute the expression. "Glad you finally let me."

I chuckled but it hurt a little, so the sound trailed off to a soft groan. "I'll tell Father. You'll get a whole promotion. Maybe even a star named after you." Delirious over the joy that I wasn't dead and that I'd somehow managed to stay out of the cursed waters, I waved an arm at the men surrounding us. "All of you. You're brilliant, a thousand court honors for each of you."

Captain Sheldon moved forward, patting my shoulder with a heavy hand, which made me flinch again. "Did Pierse go in?"

My hysteria vanished in a moment, replaced by the dim awareness that we had failed. Our friend was gone. "Yes, she came for him, right out of the waves."

Captain Sheldon's eyes grew serious, and he looked over his shoulder at his men. A chin jerk, and they all were suddenly busy elsewhere. "She?"

Rhoe pulled himself into a sitting position then helped me do the same. "A Mer."

Captain Sheldon's jaw flexed under the greying shadow of a beard. "You saw one."

"Yeah, she was gold and scaley and did something weird with the waves." My tongue was thick and awkward in my mouth.

Rhoe stepped up, looping an arm around my shoulders to provide support.

Captain Sheldon took a huge breath, holding it in his chest. After a long moment, he released it. "Water movers, I call them. But I haven't seen one in a long time." He looked out at the sea thoughtfully. "They must've really wanted to take him."

"What will they do with him? The Mer, that is."

He looked back at me sharply. "No one knows, Your Highness. The Mer serve Trayon and only Trayon."

Rhoe planted a warm hand over mine, flipping it over to see my mangled palms. They were bright red, burned from the ropes. "We need to get her taken care of."

The captain nodded, but his eyes still stared out into the sea. "Thank you for trying, Highness. Pierse was a good man, but not many people would've done what you did. Even as stupid as it was."

Rhoe was guiding me away, shepherding me towards the private quarters.

"He would've done it for me," I said quietly.

"Even still, it's a special kind of royal who would hang off the side of the ship trying to help their soldier." The compliment was as painful for me to receive as it was for him to give. I knew that instantly and savored it for what it was. The truth was that my father would've never set foot on this ship, not even for a friend.

I was an anomaly, and while my morals might gain my favor on the seas, the risks I'd taken to be here today would go virtually unnoticed in the court. "He was a friend."

Captain Sheldon nodded, turning back to the sea. In a voice so quiet I barely heard him, he said, "There are no friends in this sea. May the Mother take pity on him."

I didn't bother responding. Because he was right. Out here, humans were the prey. The Mer? They were the predators, ones who served a vengeful master. And for a moment, I wondered what to do next, my thoughts consumed by the joyful, relieved expression on Pierse's face right before his body was swallowed into the sea.

"Let's go home, boys," Captain called out and then bowed at the waist to me, formal once more as our stations dictated. "Highness, you should see to your injuries."

I jerked my chin in acknowledgement, and then Rhoe, steady hand on my lower back, guided me away.

"I can't believe he's gone," I whispered to Rhoe as he pushed me along, straight to the captain's quarters. Shameful tears threatened at the backs of my eyes as we ducked into the small room. Inside, the dim lighting of the cabin greeted us, and there was no longer any excuse to hide the tears that slipped free.

Rhoe forced me down to a chair, and I stared up into his face, watching his jaw work, clenching and tightening. A clear sign he was trying to come with the right thing to say. In another world, on another day, I might have laughed at how he seemed to struggle so much with these words. Usually that was what came easy to him.

"You don't have to do that with me," I said with a sigh. "Just say what you're thinking. Not what will get you another year of being the King's Chosen."

Rhoe's ice-blue eye flickered up to mine. Even in the dim lighting, I could see the pain there. And so I clenched his hand tight for a moment, until my injuries began to hurt again.

"There are so many things I want to understand, but the pain and misery that this sickness brings, it plagues me constantly."

I nodded, letting him rub salve borrowed from the captain's shelves across my rope-burned palms. "We will find a way."

I looked up to find Rhoe staring at me so intensely that I felt my cheeks heat. A friend shouldn't look at another friend that way, especially not while they were holding their hand like this.

"Rhoe…." I trailed off, confused and a little flustered by his touch.

"You will find a way. I believe it." His hand rose, and for a moment, the back of his knuckles brushed at the tears that I'd forced to stay hidden for too long. His skin on mine was shocking but also familiar, and for a breath I let myself sink into the pleasure of this simple touch.

Every Adrialian in the kingdom flinched away at my touch. But not Rhoe. We'd tried our hardest to stay away from each other, but in the last few weeks, something had been shifting, pulling us together. And I wasn't interested in resisting today. Not when I had needed this so badly, when I ached for the smallest comfort.

I smiled with a soft exhale, the tension broken as he switched hands and began to doctor that palm. "Your confidence is very flattering." I poked at his leg with my boot. "Flattering, but probably not due."

His face was lowered, hidden, when he finally responded again. "I have never doubted you, Your Highness, and I never will."

Chapter Four

Every night, for as long as I could remember, I dreamed of water. Not in ponds, lakes, or oceans, but the liquid itself. It would curl and twine around my body languidly, up to my face, where it caressed me tenderly, as a mother's hands might have.

Surrounded by it, I would tip my head back, my thick, dark hair swirling around my face. Eyes closing, I would breathe deep and let the water fill my body. In the moments before I would wake up, I finally felt at ease; contentment would fill me slowly. As if the water itself brought the calm to my soul that I sought after so desperately while I was awake.

As my heart slowed, calmed, and relaxed, a silken voice would whisper in my ear, reverberating through my body like the underwater currents of the ocean.

You belong with me.

I always dreaded this part, this seductive, magnetic voice as familiar to me as my father's voice. It signaled the end of my dreams, the end of being suspended in the comfort of the water. As soon as those words were uttered, I would jerk awake in my bed, heart pounding, my nightclothes plastered to my skin with clammy sweat.

"Mira? Are you awake in there? Your father is going to be in court any moment." The thick, garbled voice belonged to Homer Larken, my father's most trusted advisor. I could picture him perfectly, his slender, crane-like body leaning against the heavy slab of oak that served as my door.

A mop of curling gray hair would be styled with pomade in the latest fashion that was sweeping the kingdom and the Adrialian courts. His long fingers would be habitually tugging at the edges, standing it on end in an effort to make himself seem even taller than he already was.

"The King's Advisor should be an example for the entire kingdom of Adrial," he had told me once when I had giggled at his flamboyant, brilliantly colored attire during dinner.

I smiled at the memory, sliding my legs from under the covers and stepping eagerly across the stone floor to throw the door open wide. Homer practically fell into my chambers, huffing at my state of undress before tossing a stack of pamphlets onto my unmade bed.

Groaning, I flopped back onto my bed, fanning my still-hot skin with the stack of agendas he had delivered. Running one finger down the list of my royal duties for the day, I felt less and less like getting my day started. Getting to the bottom of page one, I cast a desperate, pleading expression to where Homer lounged against my nightstand, looking purposefully bored.

"Homer, what is this nonsense?" I prodded the paper repeatedly with one short, bitten-down nail. Pierse's disappearance, coupled with my brush with the Mer yesterday, had driven me back to the nervous habit.

Homer focused very hard on the sleeve of his overcoat, unusually heavy for late summer, plucking at an invisible thread as he avoided my gaze. "What do you mean, Your Highness?"

"Don't play dumb. You know exactly what. If I've told you once, I've told you a hundred times. I am not being matched. Not even by you." I unfolded my legs once more, coming to stand in front of my father's dearest friend. Homer diligently avoided my gaze as I flapped the page in front of his eyes. "Homer. What is this?"

I knew him well enough that he would start talking any moment. The man couldn't keep a secret to save his life. Especially not one that he was so personally invested in. And matches, of the royal variety—those were his specialty.

Currently I was the only unsolved match in Homer's twenty years of courtside marital interference, and it miffed the man to no end. Regardless of his earlier failures, Homer vowed at least once a week that he had found the man who would complete my marriage as well as bow to my crown.

I was less convinced, but my father insisted that we continue anyway.

"I have no idea what you are talking about, Highness." One delicately plucked brow arched above his cool blue eyes as he denied my inquiry once again.

"So you're telling me that this, this right here"—I held up the agenda, pointing to the finely scripted text at the bottom—"this wasn't you? It looks a lot like your handwriting."

Homer rolled his eyes. "I won't lie. I saw the agenda, but for once, this is your father's doing. I've given up on interfering in your nonexistent love life."

I snorted, rolling my eyes, while something deep in my belly tugged in worry. "My father would never set me up with the count's son. He's obnoxious. Have you ever seen the man eat? Or tried to have a conversation with him. Painful. Homer, it is painful."

Homer hesitated, obviously thinking back over his tenure at the palace in Port Sol. I softened in an instant, shoving down the anxiety that had made my words sharp. This man had rescued my family when we had needed it the most. My mother had been cursed by the waters shortly after my fourth birthday. My father had done everything to help her, but every attempt left her more desperate than before to get back to the Great Sea. And finally, one night while my father slept, she leaped from the palace's balcony into Trayon's waters. Completing the curse and leaving my father and me in utter ruin.

Homer, an Adrialian Lord and my father's oldest friend since childhood, had arrived shortly after, dragging both man and kingdom out of their dark pool of depression. He had been there for every part of my life since. Homer was as constant as the waves upon the palace walls and twice as powerful in my mind.

Homer had what I had always craved above all else: my father, Henrich's ear, at all times. There was something there, deeply hidden in their friendship, that reminded me every day that when I was queen, my life would forever be different. No more hunting trips with the captain. No more training with Rhoe every day. Each relationship, each person in my life, would serve a purpose. Even those I called friends.

I was Mira Cyrus, the only child of Henrich, and while there were plenty of opportunities, the king had no interest in marrying again to produce a male heir. In fact, he had begun the process early on to make sure that I would inherit his throne and the respect of Adrial. First the laws had fallen, and then the people, who saw me as the spitting image of my beloved mother, Damona.

Based on the elegant paintings in the living quarters of this part of the palace, my mother and I shared pale, glowing skin, dusted by freckles and eyes blue enough that in some lights, they appeared nearly violet. That was where the similarities ended, however. She had fit in easily everywhere she went, from the courtiers to the foot soldiers, Damona had garnered love at all levels within Adrialian society. I was constantly compared to her, measured against my own mother in ways that no daughter ever wanted to be.

"No, Princess Mira, I haven't seen the man eat. And I don't see why that matters so much to you? It seems every possible candidate we have mentioned to you has some kind of fatal flaw."

Homer straightened over me, his lined eyes unblinking, forcing me to raise my chin to keep eye contact.

"My dear, how long must we do this dance? I'm getting bored."

I planted my feet, meeting his stare dead on. "As long as you insist that it is necessary. My father has proven a king doesn't need a queen. Why should it be any different the other way around?" I swallowed hard, the sound loud against the sullen silence of my chambers.

Homer rolled his eyes, shoulders dropping dramatically. "He knows you don't need a king, *minu*. He wants you to have a partner. Someone to help you when things get hard. Because they will. Especially for someone like you, who doesn't appear all that interested in being Adrial's queen." The last words were spoken with emphasis.

I turned from him, tossing the agenda aside. I jerkily pulled my hair from its position piled upon my head, releasing the dark waves down to brush my shoulders. I shot Homer a glare over my shoulder before ducking behind a partition and peeling my nightgown off.

"Fine. You win," I finally answered, yanking on a flowing purple top and tight navy pants. The purple shirt left my arms bare, the gilded thread spiraling across my breasts, my belly, to where it ended just above my pant line. On my feet I wore my favorite leather sandals, the straps warped and worn by my everyday use. Walking out fully dressed, I scowled at Homer's observation of my outfit choice. I'd left his selection where he'd placed it over the edge of the partition.

"You realize we are going to court, right?" Homer asked, emphasizing my exposed skin.

I smirked. "Yes, my lord. Why do you ask?"

Homer breathed deep and wordlessly marched from the room.

"Let's get a move on, then. Your father will want to hear from your mouth what is wrong with his latest choice for a bridegroom."

I hurried to catch up with his enormous strides. "Wonderful. I can make him a list."

"Please don't. Hurry up, Your Highness."

I was practically jogging by the time we made it through the royal suite and turned to descend into the main sections of the castle. Stopping, Homer turned to me to primp my already voluminous mane of hair, obviously displeased that I let the heavy locks fall naturally versus pinning them up in the elaborate hairstyles that the ladies of the Adrialian Court would be wearing.

I reached out to catch Homer's fingers as they tugged on the bottom of my shirt. "Homer, please, it's fine."

He gave me a small smile then dropped into a formal bow at the waist. He was back to being the King's Advisor. My father had made it explicitly clear that the royal family's living quarters were a separate, private part of the palace. No one, other than those personally invited, were allowed to be in the space. Even those servants who served the family were minimal, a chosen few, who I knew by name.

Homer waited, allowing me to lead the way. "You're beautiful, Your Highness."

Taking a deep breath, I stepped into my role. Nodding my gratitude, I turned and placed a hand on the thick, carved handrail leading into the main entry of the palace.

The first floor was the heart of the palace, bursting with people and energy. There we held public hearings, catered to foreign guests, hosted Adrialian celebrations. Here, I was Princess Mira, Heir to Adrial, Lady of Port Sol, and I was expected to act that way.

Each step I took, the sound of my sandals were drowned out by the chattering souls who moved through the vast entryway like waves against the sea walls. Most clamoring for their chance to see my father.

He met with his constituents every morning, as well as other valued members of the Adrialian Court. Then he would open the throne room up to any citizen of Adrial who had something they needed to speak to the king about.

Most of the time they were placated by just being in the presence of their leader, and in others, he was able to bestow helpful advice or enact services. It was in these moments I was most proud of my father. Proud and envious.

He would sit on the edge of his throne, a vast ivory centerpiece, elaborately arching whalebones that had been carved to create the king's favored altar. Under each arm, strong, weathered hands rested casually on rubies the size of a fists.

His crown was a complex creation, the delicately wrought gold bands twisting like the throned branches of the royal roses against his inky black hair. As each citizen stepped forward, he would look at them with his deep-brown eyes, kindness warming his voice as he spoke. The man was Adrial personified, and they adored him as such.

A young Adrialian woman stood before him now, flushed a bright pink as my father smiled down at her. As I watched, the girl, who clutched a prodigious, pregnant belly, attempted to kneel, as was custom. My father raised his hand, stopping her movements and taking the three steps down from his throne to greet her.

They spoke face to face, his face tilted down to the young mother as she spoke quickly in the common tongue, the rough slang making it clear she had traveled from the interior of Adrial, closer to the foot of the Crimson Mountains. It was a long journey, especially for someone in her condition.

I walked into the throne room slowly, slipping between courtiers to stand just to the side of the throne, my form in the shadows. Nodding along to the girl's words, my father stepped back wide, turning to the waiting crowd.

"A blessing, from myself and on behalf of our city's generous God Artio, onto this child. May they grow in safety and health for all of their days." His voice boomed out, echoing through the vaulted ceilings. My blood warmed in my veins as it did any time I watched my father with our people. He was magnificent, assured, and humble. They loved him. I could see it in the wide-eyed observers as they applauded, adding their own prayers to his own.

His dark beard was shaved neatly in stark, straight lines along his high cheekbones, emphasizing his natural good looks and honey-toned skin. The shoulder-length dark hair was combed back from his face, held in place by the gold of his crown.

His temples showed sparse signs of gray, but they only served to make him look more divine. For that was what they saw him as—no mortal man, but Artio's vessel among them. As he turned from the now bowing, blushing young mother, he caught sight of me.

A quick look over my outfit made Father's eyes crinkle, a half-smile curling his lips. Holding an arm out, he gestured for me to join him. I moved easily into the room, knowing that every eye in the room jumped from my father to me. Shoulders back, I strolled into his arms, letting my own sneak around his waist, feeling the scratch of his ruby tunic against my cheek.

"Papa, good morning," I murmured into the fabric, letting him guide me back towards the throne. I could hear the guards speaking to the crowd waiting at the back of the room. While I knew they couldn't hear us, I felt their eyes on my back. It made me hesitate, as always, before I shared anything personal with my father.

He didn't share that same hesitation and eagerly looked me over again. "Mira, how are you? I heard you had a rough night?" His voice was laced with worry.

I furrowed my brow, pulling back slightly. "My night? But how?" I looked into my father's face. Panic over what had happened on *The DeArtinan* yesterday slipped back over me. Pierse's face, the Mer's manipulation of the very water I nearly swam in. He already knew about what happened with Pierse? Rhoe would've told him the essentials, but how much more had he heard?

He scoffed at my question, nodding his head to the corner, where Rhoe stood sheepishly, bright-blond hair causing him to stand out from the crowd of courtiers. "I thought we agreed that you were allowed into the city, but no starting fights you can't win."

"Oh, uh…" I blinked rapidly, buying time. I looked from Rhoe's guilty face to my father's. Of course, he wasn't talking about the nightmarish day on the waters. Was it possible the king hadn't heard of Pierse's death yet? From what I was hearing, my father was talking about the fact that Rhoe and I had run into trouble at one of the local pubs the night before last.

"I mean…" I cut him my most devious grin. "We did win."

My father roared with laughter, the sound filling the throne room.

One of the dockside workers had recognized me, even under my hood, and had berated me for the recent trade issues, accusing the crown of betraying them all, forcing them into starvation. Rhoe had been with me, as usual, and while I was more than capable of protecting myself, he had stepped in. It saved us the conversation with my father or any courtiers crying out that their princess was a common street fighter.

It would've only taken me only a moment to deposit the angry man onto his back on the floor. Instead, I had stepped to the side, letting Rhoe silence him.

The owner of the establishment had apologized a dozen times, begging Rhoe and me to remain for another drink. The mood was gone, and I simply wanted to hurry home, where I could be left in peace.

Finally, Fatherf sobered, wiping a tear from his eye. "Mira, my love, you are missing the point."

I narrowed my eyes at my father's Chosen, where he still lurked to the side of the room. Rhoe looked away deliberately.

"I know, Papa. It was an unnecessary risk. And I'm sorry." I shifted on my sandaled feet, murmured voices reaching my ears even now. Heat flooded my face as irritation bloomed deep inside. My entire life was a public statement. I'd accepted that long ago.

But it didn't need to be a public interrogation. "Really, Papa, I mean it."

"I just want to keep you safe, Mira. Please do try to help me." He moved up the stairs to this throne once more, looking out at the crowd still waiting for attention at the back of the room. "You are all I have."

With a sigh, he swept one arm out, his muscular frame ushering people from the space. Everyone obeyed quickly, crowding against each other as they pushed to leave through the immense arched doorways. Rhoe moved with the crowd, making his escape as well. I still sent him a look that meant I'd be finding him as soon as I was dismissed. He had some explaining to do.

"Now that we are alone," my father began, stretching his legs out, slouching back for a moment into the ivory throne, the jeweled rings flashing as the monarch took a rare moment to relax, "we should talk about tonight."

I stared at him, surprised that the irritation in my body only spread, encompassing my entire chest as I stared down at him. My friend was dead, I was in trouble for getting into a fight over my father's policies, and yet he wanted to talk about some man-child who wanted to wed me, bed me, and then take over the power of my family's crown.

I leaned against the throne, ignoring the bite of the intricate carvings against my bare skin. "Honestly, I'd rather we didn't."

"Exactly why we must, Mira." His tone lost its kingly edge but took up a distinctively fatherly undercurrent as worry clouded his eyes. "It is important that you find a partner. Not because of the old laws, or even those stiff old men on the council, but because you deserve to have someone. I loved your mother very much, and—"

"Yes, and I want to love my husband too."

My father's jaw clenched, and he looked down for a long moment. "Perhaps it is better you didn't."

That wasn't what I was expecting. "What do you mean by that?"

"When I lost your mother, my entire world stopped. I was inconsolable, lost, unable to lead or even be led." Warm brown eyes found mine, and he searched my face earnestly. "Do you understand what I'm saying?"

"You're saying love hurts, loss hurts." I swallowed thickly. "But you always forget, I was there too. I know how much it can hurt, Father. I lost her too."

"You don't know." His voice sliced through the air, his body facing mine. "They all say that love is all powerful, but what they don't realize is that love can bring you to your knees." My father rose and stepped up to me, his fingers tight on my chin. "And you, my heir, bow to no one, especially a traitorous and riotous emotion such as love."

His grip on my face hurt, but I didn't dare look away. I didn't blink. My father's kind, friendly exterior had slipped for a moment, giving me a peek at the king behind the mask. "You want me to rule beside someone I can barely stand."

"No." My father searched my face again, his eyes softening. "I want you to rule. To be the first queen of Adrial, you will have to be better than them, better than everyone, Mira. You will know love, I'm sure of it. But I beg of you to do it in a way where you are never at its mercy."

He released me, moving down the steps to the main part of the throne room, where he began to pace. "Do you understand now why these matches are so important? The potential alliances could make or break your transition onto the throne. And Merclino, they are a powerful force in the trade with the rest of the continent. Valuable allies, Mira. Too valuable to lose."

Clearing my throat, I nodded. It was the best I could do with the ugly stickiness that coated my throat and made it impossible to breathe. My father wouldn't be swayed by complaints or emotions, but rather logic. That was what I must stick to. At least for now.

"Good. I'm glad we agree. You know, if you tried, then you could get to know the count's son. He might have some redeeming features." He looked up at me from under straight black brows, briefly pausing his pacing. I avoided his gaze. Get to know, not fall in love. That was apparently no longer a requirement for my marriage.

Which meant there was only so much standing between me and a wedding altar. I was running out of time.

"I would never want anyone, especially my own daughter, to have to do this job alone. Plus, is it so obvious that I must remind you that you will be the first Adrial queen in over two centuries? Your road will not be an easy one, Mira." His voice was somber, his face graying under his tan. I hated seeing him like this, worrying over me. He had enough on his plate without spending his days attempting to wed off his unruly princess to someone tolerant enough to deal with my quirks.

"Okay, I will try." I pushed a smile to my lips.

"Thank you." He brightened a bit. "Now get out of here so you can scold Rhoe for spilling your secrets. That man couldn't keep something to himself to save his own life."

"Don't worry. I won't be too hard on him." I turned and hurried through the empty throne room, turning at the floor-to-ceiling doors to look again at my father. He moved back to sit on his throne, alone, his strong body sagging into the seat, as if it and only it held him from the floor. His strength and bravado gone as he soaked in the temporary solitude. I knew at that moment that I would always do whatever I could to make his life easier, even if it meant putting up with the chewing habits of the count's son.

Closing the door behind me, I sought out my best friend. I had a few things I wanted to get off my chest.

Chapter Five

I knew where Rhoe would be hiding. It wasn't difficult,
considering while father was in court, Rhoe must remain close to
the king at all times. That, coupled with the man's lack of
innovation in his hiding technique, meant that it took only a few
minutes for me to home in on him.

When I left the throne room, heads bowed to me as I passed
quickly down the corridor to a bright, wide open dining space.
Across the marble-floored room, wide, round tables filled the space.

Adrial was blessed by the God of Land, Artio, with beautiful
warm weather most of the year. The short winter season was
marked only by the dauntless, cool gray rains that filled up Adrial's
canals and watered the crops growing across the fields.

As such, the castle was built to be open. With nary a
windowpane in sight, gauzy linen curtains blew into the rooms
with every breath of breeze, reaching out to me as if driven by
ghostly ambitions when I moved through the room.

The seating was mercifully nearly empty as the courtier and
castle staff moved on with their days. Those diners who remained
watched me warily. Should I come any closer, or look directly into
their eyes, they would drop to a knee, signifying their complete and
utter devotion to the crown princess of Adrial.

It never failed to make me anxious. I did not yet hold the power and authority that my father did. Every time I watched a citizen drop to their knees before me, I felt the sharp, prickling fear of failure spring up in my mind, filling it entirely until I was forced to retreat.

A princess who rather conquer a cursed ocean than face my own people. Some queen I would be.

Dropping my gaze quickly, lest they feel the need to worship me further, I breezed through the wide line of doorways and out into the heat of the shining sun. The tang of salt air filled my nose as I drew ever closer to the source of my hunt.

Sprawled out, Rhoe's long, lean body was balanced precariously along the smooth, sculpted balcony edge off of the main dining hall. He didn't seem to notice the sheer drop that lay only a hands with from his armored chest.

I propped my hands up on the curve of my hips, glaring at the king's Chosen. "Are you kidding me? You must've buckled the moment my father looked at you."

Rhoe responded by throwing an arm over his eyes and groaning. "Can you keep it down a little?"

"I will not. Perhaps if you had skipped that fourth round of ale, then you wouldn't be so uncomfortable," I said, quivering a brow at my closest friend. From under his forearm, I could see his wide lips mimic my words sarcastically. I swallowed my laugh, reinforcing the frown that crossed my face.

"Besides, how many times will you let yourself get conned by those city girls? They just want you for your pretty face." I jabbed at his shoulder, my fingers bouncing lightly off the wall of muscle under the loose blue fabric.

Rhoe lifted his arm slightly, and his bright cerulean eyes met mine, filled with laughter. "I know, I know. That's the best part. Pierse would've been proud." He stretched languidly, his long arms reaching above his head.

My smile slipped at the mention of our friend. "You're right he would've been." But that didn't matter now. Pierse and his kind smile were residing in the Dark now. I glanced out at the water, my palms twitching in pain as I clenched my hands on the stone wall.

I tipped my head back to soak in some of the morning sun then released a sign, looking back down into the swirling roads and alleys below us. My home was beautiful, I thought, dropping an elbow and musing down at the happenings below.

This balcony, one of several, overhung the Great Sea, far beyond the Adrial sea walls that outlined Port Sol. Here, if Rhoe were to roll off accidentally, there was nothing between him and the forbidden waters but thin, unforgiving air. I could hear the frothing of the waves far below, as if they hissed and groaned at me, warning me of its hunger.

"Stop that. You're scaring me." I said breathlessly.

Rhoe ignored me, yawning. Showing off a mouthful of white teeth, he sent a smirking smile in my direction. He often played this game to torture me, balancing gracefully as a jungle cat on the edge of the stone edges. Taunting fate with the possibility he might fall into the water below and become another victim of Trayon.

Every citizen of Adrial knew the laws, the warnings, that came with living along the coast of the Great Sea. On land, they were safe, protected by Artio, the gracious God of Land. But should they fall into the waters of the Great Sea, even for a moment, they could be claimed by the right of Trayon for his undersea kingdom of darkness, of death. I shivered.

While my people were traders, merchants, shipbuilders, they never dared to actually touch the immense ocean that surrounded them. There were stories of those who dangled limbs there, to taunt the water god, only to find themselves ripped from the arms of their fellow sailors.

Some would disappear in the dark of night, only to reappear later, confused, disorientated, insane. Forever screaming about the salt of the sea and of the nightmares that dwelled beneath its waves.

I had once heard a sailor weaving a tale about an entire crew that had disappeared just a breath away from the safety of the seawalls. The ship was found bobbing a short distance from the jagged edges of the palace walls, empty of all souls. The rest of the ship was perfectly intact, resting gently against the seawall as if jesting at the castle high above.

It was no wonder that the Adrial people feared the sea. Seeing him dangling his body without reservation for the hungry waters below made me angry. Glaring at him, I crossed my arms over my chest.

"Oh, don't worry, minnow. I will never fall." Rhoe smirked at me, using a version of my father's childhood nickname for me. I huffed. We'd had this argument a hundred times. He would tease me until I forgot while I was angry, and together we would move on.

"Don't call me that. I'm not little anymore," I said testily. Minu, in the ancient tongue, meant little, but as a child I had been obsessed with the water.

I had begged my father to let my play in the fountains, or in the extensive network of inland pools that Adrial was famous for. One of my last memories was of my mother and me swirling around the palace's private pool, my mother's flashing purple eyes filling my mind.

"I can see that." I barely heard Rhoe's soft response, the wind suddenly billowing around them, sending the long white drapes snapping in retaliation.

I leaned over the edge of the balcony, ignoring the strange pull in my belly as I had looked at Rhoe. Now I glanced discreetly behind us, wondering how many people watched the two of us.

I knew that most of the court believed we were together. Lovers. *Such a beautiful couple they would make.* I'd heard it whispered more than once.

But the problem remained simple. He was the king's Chosen. His pledge to the crown was to protect the royal family.

It was a pledge only freed by death. No marriage. No family. No future in Adrial other than stolen moments on balconies and a twitching desire that kept me up late into the night.

It was easier to not dwell on such things as beautiful friends. Not that he would ever have given me a moment's interest. I'd seen the women that he was drawn to. They were petite, delicate little wisps of flesh who giggled too much and couldn't hold their whiskey. He picked them up everywhere he went.

I had been raised to rule a kingdom. I was talented at many things, none of which included seduction. And as far as appearances went, I'd been told I was lovely. That my face was so like my mother's that it must be a compliment. After all, Damona had brought the king to his knees, their love inspiring a hundred ballads and nearly as many plays and performances.

I saw them often enough, the love story between my parents, that I had never bothered to ask what was real and what was fiction. Perhaps I didn't want to dwell on it because when I was married, it would be to secure the most powerful partner possible so that my bid to the crown would remain. It would not be a love story like my parents'.

The sharp edge of the stone pushed into my hip bones, freeing my mind from such distractions. Sighing, I settled across the rail, the warmth seeping into my body, chasing away the memories of the past.

"I'm not worried about you. I'm worried about what they would say about me. Pushing a king's guard, even one as obnoxious as you, off a cliff would be quite the spectacle." I grinned at my friend as he hopped down from the rail and came to stand beside me.

His broad shoulders bumped mine as he grinned down at me. "Your father would be sorely disappointed. Mine is not an easy role to fill. The royal family here is atrocious."

"Don't worry. I will help," I answered promptly, clicking my tongue at him.

Rhoe leaned back, rolling his eyes, their color almost iridescent in the bright sunlight. Against my better judgment, my gaze looked him over. I understood why all the girls followed him around, why the courtiers stared at him.

His smooth skin, so pale it was almost translucent in some places, was stretched over a body of pliant muscle. His face was beautiful, angelic, with wide, smiling lips and a straight nose. His eyelashes and brows were a shade darker than his bright hair on his head, the lashes impossibly thick and dark in comparison. It gave the illusion that he was wearing kohl lining his eyes, illuminating those strange, intriguing eyes even further.

And while I found herself watching him, admiring his skills with a blade and spear, the man showed little to no interest in me.

Treating me more like an errant sibling than the eligible daughter of a king. It was a relief and a torment to be his friend.

"What did you do last night? Really?" I questioned him. Although he wasn't above taking those girls from the pub back to his rooms at the palace, I doubted that he was as much of a rake as others claimed him to be.

Rhoe waggled his eyebrows at me suggestively. "I went for a swim." Laughing, he ran a hand through his short locks, dropping his eyes to the frothing water below.

I laughed, knowing he was avoiding my question entirely. Proof that I didn't want to know the answer. Leaning back, I fixed my stare onto his wrist watching as his veins shifted under his tattoos, the ink a series of silver vee-shaped marks across the skin.

"Will you at least help me drown my sorrows tonight? After I put up with the Count all through dinner?" I looked up at him, puckering a lip, hoping to invoke pity.

Rhoe didn't seem moved, his eyes still looked on the water far below. The muscles along his jaw and neck were taut and twitching under his skin.

"Rhoe, did you hear me?"

Rhoe suddenly snapped back, looking at me curiously. I blinked, fighting the desire to step backwards as those unnaturally blue irises looked at me. I knew that my own were a strange shade of violet. Some people found them unnerving.

It was part of the reason I had first found solstice in Rhoe's company. He was utterly unshakable. His only interest in me seemed to be in torturing me with endless training and making me laugh during serious court meetings.

"Sorry, *my lady*. I got distracted. Yes, let's go out tonight. Somewhere not so close to home, eh?" Rhoe slung an arm around my shoulder, turning me from the seaside views and ushering me into the shadowy depths of the palace.

"Deal." I ducked my head as the eyes all swiveled back at me.

"Now, I have a king to protect, and you have babies to kiss. Get." Rhoe waved one pale hand in the air, as if waving to adoring crowds. I pushed him off, shrugging the heavy weight of his muscular arm off my shoulders.

"Fine, but we have a deal. Don't forget," I shouted over my shoulder, walking through the tiled dining floor to find Homer and my list of duties. Rhoe stayed where I left him, his head turned, staring through the arched doorways and at the churning sea just beyond.

Chapter Six

While today's festivities would be concluding with a simple court dinner, there was an entire day of activities mapped out for me. And after my behavior lately, my father obviously felt I needed some additional tasks to complete my day. Beginning with playing tour guide to the visiting ambassador's daughter.

Homer fluttered around me for hours after I left court this morning. And just when I finally calmed down his multitude of concerns, my handmaids had taken over. One of them had left this dress out, draped across the edge of my bed after I got out of the bath. The fabric was the color of ripe mulberries, so fine that it felt like water rippling against my skin as I pulled it over my head.

The cut was conservative, and I resisted the urge to shimmy the fabric down my shoulders. While styled in a popular way, it felt entirely too constricting. I grimaced at my reflection, the beautiful fabric flowing over my slender form and pooling around my bare feet.

Even my wild waves had been tamed by my stylist, tied back in elaborate twists until my face was bare to everyone's gaze. My time in the sun meant a generous smattering of freckles graced my cheekbones. I felt exposed, unable to let my curls hide the myriad of expressions I knew flew across my face.

It was one of the reasons that Rhoe loved to play cards and games with me. I couldn't lie to save a life, even my own. My face gave me away every time.

After attending a variety of council meetings this morning, I had gone down to greet the Emen ambassadors who had arrived today. Emen was a small but proud island which currently acted as a safe harbor for when merchants had to approach Adrial from the southeast. While the curse didn't apply to their people, they were still nervous about angering the Sea God, and we routinely welcomed visitors to our shores in order to keep the peace between the two kingdoms.

The ambassadors today were a polished-looking couple, with warm olive skin and sharp dark features that brightened as they introduced the third in their party. Their daughter, Shanna, looked to be around my age. She was pretty, with soft hazel eyes and a nearly constant smile.

As I was told to, I offered to take her on a tour this afternoon. She accepted and eagerly bounced on her toes as an Adrialian guard delivered her to me outside of the main castle entry.

"Where would you like to go first?"

Shanna blinked quickly then gave a small smile. "If you don't mind, Highness, I'd love to see what you would be doing this time of day. If you weren't entertaining me."

My brows rose. "Are you sure?"

"Absolutely, Princess Mira. Your life here is so different than in Emen. I want to see what your life is like."

"Well, I guess we can do that. It's probably not what you're expecting though."

Shanna fell into step, our combined guards slipping back to shadow us from a distance. "No offense meant, Your Highness, but from what I can tell, you and your father commonly break many of the Adrialian stereotypes."

Humming, I considered her words, guiding her outside to the training yards that I often spent my afternoons in. "We both want to change the future for Adrial. To leave our kingdom a better, safer place than before."

"A worthy cause," Shanna said, beaming up at me.

"I spend many of my afternoons here, in the training yards. If I'm to be a queen of Adrial, I have to be known for my strength, not just my politics." The words were true. While I was convinced, I would not be capable of ruling with the gentle touch of my mother, I could bring something else to the table. My unwillingness to give up. Father called it stubbornness. Rhoe called it a pain in his ass.

But I called it devotion. Adrialians didn't need to love me for to love them.

I gestured around us, at the carefully controlled chaos of our soldiers' training. From the everyday foot soldier to my father's select guard, every member of our military spent time here.

Shanna made a surprised noise at my side, but when I looked at her, she had neatly covered up her surprise with a wide smile.

"Are they all…" She trailed off, swallowing as another soldier moved past us. "Do they all look like that?"

I glanced around, trying to see through a newcomers eyes. Most Adrialian citizens had descended from a desert people who had roamed the northern continent thousands of years ago. Those bloodlines, coupled with the foundation of ancient northern cities such as Preet, Thanyia and Whollan Rivers meant that Adrial was a showcase of various cultures. The shades of skin and hair varied from my own fair-skinned appearance to a deep mahogany skin-tone that spoke of shimmering dark nights. But to her question, I knew she was addressing the common features that all Adrialian soldier's shared.

"Most of our soldier's are happy to carry a sign of Artio on their person. Whether it be in jewelry," I nodded towards a slender soldier standing by the archery lanes who wore a gold earring in one ear, the sun god's trademark shape dangling from the lobe, "Or even in a more permanent fashion." Shanna's wide eyes took in a pair of sparing partners, one with the shape of the sun actually shaved into the side of his short, cropped hair. His opponent, whose chest was bare, was tattooed with brilliant gold ink, the sun symbol swirling across his chest.

"Is that gold?"

"A special concoction made by Artio's priests, saved only for those soldiers who are especially valiant in battle. Hence the gold most often denotes our most prized soldiers or officers."

Shanna nodded, but I wasn't sure how much she heard as she continued to stare at the soldiers. "They are all so…erm…distracting."

"Do you want to be distracted?" asked a suave voice from behind us.

I rolled my eyes skyward, begging Mother above for the patience to deal with this man. But Shanna leapt away with a squeak, obviously unprepared to be in Rhoe's shadow.

"I assure you, we train hard for our King and our God, but we also do it to show off, especially to visitors," he continued, "Honored Ambassador," Rhoe said, bowing deeply from the hips, his casual blue tunic gaping at the neck as he moved. "Welcome to Adrial."

Shanna's mouth dropped open, staring at the play of smooth muscle across his chest and stomach. Rhoe crossed his arms slowly, that wide smile still on his mouth. Had the situation been any more different, I would've burst out laughing. The man did know how to put on a show.

"Thank you, but I'm not really an ambassador. Only my parents are," Shanna finally mustered the words, a hot flush turning her olive skin rosy. "I recognize you from our arrival."

"This is my father's Chosen, Rhoe Karasea." Shanna remained frozen, so I carefully brushed her shoulder. "I believe your king has a champion back in the Emenian Isles?"

Shanna nodded, eyes still transfixed on Rhoe. Her unabashed interest made my skin itch. "A champion?"

"Adrialian kings prefer the term Chosen, as they are carefully selected for their experience on the battlefield as well as wit and political strategy." I jerked my thumb at the tall man beside us. "They serve until they are dismissed, untethered to anything else while in service to their King."

Shanna nodded, still silent as Rhoe preened in front of us.

"Come to think of it, I'm not sure how he got the job."

"My ability to laugh on cue," Rhoe said, sarcasm dripping.

Shanna giggled and leaned into me. "Your Highness, he's allowed to talk to you like that?"

I shrugged, glaring at Rhoe. "When I am queen and I select my Chosen, they will not."

"Until then, you have to put up with me." Rhoe gave me a quick bow.

Shanna's eyes flickered back to me but couldn't focus. I hid a smile. I couldn't blame the girl. Rhoe was a heavy dose of personality to take in all at once.

Dropping into a small curtsey, she said, "It is nice to meet you, King's Chosen."

The volley of swordplay and staff practice almost drowned out her words.

"We really should go. I can tell you more about the history of Adrial as we walk back," I said, watching Shanna flutter her long lashes rapidly then turn back towards the main entry to the yards.

Rhoe went to follow, but I turned, blocking him with a hand on his chest. I lowered my voice, desperately trying to ignore the way his muscles quivered under my fingertips. "We need some space, Rhoe. Why don't you finish training? Or at the very least, get a shirt on. You're upsetting the Emenian."

Rhoe looked after Shanna, who walked slowly from the field. An obnoxious smile lit his face. "Are you sure she's the one who is upset?" Under my fingers, his voice was a deep rumble. "Having trouble focusing, Princess Mira?"

My belly warmed as his voice purred over the honorific. Why did something people called me a hundred times a day sound so different from his mouth?

"Never." I pivoted on the spot, making a case to ignore the deep laughter that followed me from the training yards.

Chapter Seven

I strolled down the hall, past my father's rooms as well as the immense stone fireplace that dominated one wall of the common room that we shared. The Emenians were running late, and I had been pacing the hall for far too long. I glanced over the comfortable, warm living space filled with a variety of seating options and floor poufs that I knew from experience were perfect for napping.

I had grown up here, my father and I sharing midnight snacks, playing games, reading the thick books that lined the wall opposite the fireplace. Just below us, the palace life bustled on, distinct noises of music and conversation filtering into the rooms. The palace was many things, but this space, away from the desperate, prying eyes of the kingdom… It had been home.

Taking a deep breath, I reached my family's private dining quarters. For small, intimate dinners like the one tonight, with the Emen ambassadors, my father preferred to invite them upstairs for the meal. Footsteps sounded behind me, and my skin prickled at the presence of strangers in my sanctuary. My father had assured me that this was a sign of respect, or welcome, that Adrial needed to offer.

There was no room to disagree. Our dinner guests filtered down the halls, bowing and murmuring the myriad of compliments that I smiled through.

The Emen ambassadors and their daughter, Shanna, along with an eager Count Merclino and his eldest son, Grante, all found seats around the intimate table. A casual hand weighed against my hip, urging me to sit alongside my father. Glancing over my shoulder, I found a pair of sky-blue eyes smiling down at me. "Rhoe?"

My father's Chosen gave me a heady wink before disappearing back to the shadows along the dining room walls. He was in full dress armor, the gleam of gold across his chest matching the bright blond of his hair.

I was shocked but quickly smothered my next question with a polite nod and settled into my chair. While the king's guards were among the servants allowed to come and go from the royal family's quarters, Rhoe was often off duty during this time frame.

I shook my head, refocusing on the dinner in front of me. My father believed this was an important night. I needed to be on my best behavior. And that meant schooling my transparent expressions into something that resembled a smile.

I had met both Merclino and Grante several times before, and while I knew my father wanted this match, I was already dreading having to sit next to him all night. I could only hope that Grante had recently acquired a personality. Or that Shanna would prove a worthy distraction.

As it turned out, I was wrong on both accounts.

With my father on one side of me, Grante was seated directly beside me on the other . And beyond being a loud, ostentatious chewer, he was quite simply as dull as the stones that paved our streets. Having any type of conversation with him was painful. The only good thing to come out of the first course of the night was that my father appeared also frustrated by the Count's son's lack of manners.

I hid my smile behind my hand. Another potential match successfully undone. Thank Artio. And while I knew it wouldn't last long, that there'd be more matches coming, at least it wouldn't be this person.

His lips pulled back in a quick smile, and he nodded subtly towards Shanna, who was also finding her seat across from me. I rolled my eyes up to Rhoe, who waggled his eyebrows at me knowingly.

I silently mouthed, *"What are you doing here?"* to my friend. He ignored my question, resuming his place at my father's shoulder as servants began to file in with immense golden trays of food. They set them at the center of the wide table, and my father rose, his wineglass in his fist.

"To new friends and old, may Artio shine bright upon your path for many, many years to come."

All hands around the table rose. "To the sun."

My father held his glass to the ceiling. "To the sea." He moved towards the billowing open balcony off the dining space.

"To the sun and sea," we all echoed.

My father beamed down at us, his hand falling to my shoulder. "Please, let's enjoy good food and good company before either gets cold."

I couldn't stop the small smile that slipped out. From all that Adrial was a bright, warm city, it often got cool at night, and it nearly always surprised our visitors.

Tugging at the tight, confining fabric across my chest, I tried to settle into the political conversations bubbling around me. I asked questions, smiled my best smile, and ate in neat, even little bites. The Emen ambassadors were a warm, welcoming couple who clearly adored their daughter. And while Shanna and her mother quickly stuck up a conversation with Count Merclino about the disappearances along the merchant lines of the Great Sea, I was stuck talking to Grante.

Or attempting to.

"Are you enjoying your time in the city?"

Grante took a large drink of his wine then nodded. A single nod.

"I've heard your family's estate is on the mountainous edge of the kingdom. Is that true?"

Another nod.

I sighed, and I could've sworn I heard Rhoe laugh behind me. I tried something that required an actual, real answer. "What is your favorite food?"

"I eat just about anything, Your Highness."

"Lovely. Good to know."

A servant reached between us to place another tray of plated sauces and dips to go along with the tray of meats that was already within range. I carefully selected a soft pink shrimp and covered it in my favorite decadent sauce before popping it into my mouth. The food was spicy, sharp, with a tang of the salt water it had been caught from. I scooted the place towards Grante. "If you like spicy foods, you should try these."

Grante took a large shrimp, dragging it through the sauce before grinding it into his mouth with a noise that I knew my father heard. For a second, I watched, half in awe, half in horror, as Grante, who obviously liked the taste, began to turn his attention to clearing as much of the shrimp as possible. And as quickly as possible.

I could actually feel my father's horror, and as I watched, his head tilted up slowly to catch the eye of Homer, who was valiantly attempting to pay attention to Count Merclino, while his eyes were being drawn back to Grante's eating.

My father slowly blotted his mouth, the lips behind the napkin pulled back in a grin. But it did no good. I knew he was laughing with me. I had tried to warn Homer. Maybe next time I would get to have a little more insight into my matches.

"I'm glad you like it," was the last thing that I had to say to him. I was gloriously free to listen in to my father's conversations from there, or even the vivacious Count Merclino, who was leaning into Shanna's father's, Lord Vertia, conversation with great interest.

"How many did you say have gone missing?" Count Merclino asked.

"Over a dozen," my father answered, his voice lowering. "All along the Emenian routes."

Lord Vertia nodded. "We've sent out scouting ships, as many as we can offer, but we are a small island."

"They are all Adrialian merchant ships?" Count Merclino asked.

My father sighed. "All but two, but they had the unfortunate experience of being painted in Adrialian colors. They must've been originally built here in Port Sol."

"Someone is targeting Adrialian merchants," Count Merclino said. "But why? It's well known that the route to the Emenian Islands is a hard passing, but this seems larger than that."

"Is it the curse?" Shanna's voice was quiet in the room.

My brows rose at her direct question. "The Sea God's curse?" Every head in the room turned to Shanna.

"It would make sense," she said, her voice growing bolder. "The curse only target Adrialians, right?"

My father pushed his plate back, leveling his most charming smile at the Emenians. "Indeed it does."

"And that's because of what the ancient king did to his brother?" My shoulders tensed. My father didn't enjoy talking about this story. Not anymore.

"My daughter is a scholar and is fascinated by the Adrialian legends," Her father said. The sharp look he gave his daughter made me wonder if the young woman had planned on bringing this up against her family's wishes. "She finds our Emenian myths rather boring in comparison."

"Not boring, Father, but you have to admit that a major god cursing an entire kingdom… Can you imagine the power required to do that? And it's been so long since anyone has even seen the gods. Why is it still in place?"

"Your daughter is a curious mind, Ambassador." I heard the warning there, and my spine stiffened as my father considered the young woman across the table from him.

"There are so many out there, you can hardly tell which are true." Shanna calmly pinned my father with an unfaltering gaze.

"Ah, my dear, that is the nature of myths. They confuse history with legend." My father leaned back in his chair, his eyes unclouded by the wine from dinner. "Perhaps they were once founded in truth, but not necessarily true."

Shanna smiled, bowing her head in acknowledgement of his comment. "I understand that. Excuse my exuberance. It isn't often you get to hear a kingdom's myths from their leader."

My father hummed lightly, looking at Lady Vertia as she leaned over, refilling her own wineglass.

"I don't understand it myself. I cannot believe that entire kingdom lives on the edge of the Great Sea, but not a soul touches it." Lady Vertia laughed lightly, looking to her husband to reinforce the strangeness of this arrangement.

Slowly, he nodded, as did Shanna.

"That is a very long story," my father said. I pushed my plate away, noting that my father's mood was shifting. He was smiling indulgently at the Emenians, but I didn't miss the way his gaze leapt pointedly to Homer from his station by the door. Yet he continued, "But I'd be happy to tell you as much of it as I can."

Shanna beamed at me, and I couldn't help but return her smile. Our plates were cleared, and the servants moved silently around the table, refiling glasses, placing slender mugs of strong Emenian coffee at our fingertips.

I picked up mine, curling into my chair, ignoring the bite of the dress's seams against my skin. Shanna and her parents watched my father with rapt interest.

"Port Sol used to be much larger. In the days before my grandfather's grandfather, it was a thriving fortress was the very epicenter of culture, arts, and agriculture in the western continent. Sommerso, as it was called then, was ruled by two brothers, twins, born only minutes apart. Because they were both raised for the throne, they decided that when they turned eighteen, they would both rule. The elder would take the upper kingdom, the younger, the lower kingdom. For many years, they worked side by side, building Adrial into a powerful kingdom where the citizens adored their rulers."

He glanced around at his audience, who were all listening with rapt attention. "One day, a foreign princess arrived in Adrial. An island tribe, with its chief at the helm who meant to negotiate a marriage for his daughter. She was stunning, a walking vision of power and beauty. With a kindness that shone from her like rays of the run. The brothers, identical in appearance, were besotted by her in an instant. Over time, both brothers courted the princess. They were both wildly in love with her and begged for her to choose them, to put them out of their misery of not knowing who she wanted."

My father took a long swig of cider, his eyes darting around his guests' face, the silence of the room only broken by the soft sea breeze that sent goose bumps up my arms.

"The princess told them that she was in love with the younger and that they wanted to be married as soon as it could be arranged. The entire kingdom celebrated, and together the brothers planned the wedding of the century. On the day of the wedding, the elder brother was overcome with jealousy. He captured his brother, making sure he would never make it to his wedding. Then, acting as his brother, the eldest stood in and married the beautiful princess."

"What a monster," Shanna said, her voice hushed.

My father smiled, his fingers steepling on the table in front of him. The flash of his wedding band caught my eye, as it often did. "Love can make you do crazy things," he answered calmly, the room immediately refocused on him.

"Later that night, after celebrating their wedding, the elder confessed. He attempted to explain what he had done. And the depths of his love. But the princess couldn't be reconciled. Devastated to be married to the brother she didn't love, the princess pushed open the window and, with one last pledge of her undying love, jumped into the Great Sea below."

The table was silent. I watched my father closely. I had forgotten how close to his heart this story really was. Pressing a hand against my nervous stomach, I cleared my throat. My father broke from his trance, looking out at this captive audience. A half smile on his lips, he pushed onwards.

"The younger brother, freed by his associates, breached the tower's doors to find his lover falling into the ocean below. They say his scream blew the walls of the tower open, and in his desperation, he called to the deep, to the god under the waves."

"Trayon," Shanna's mother supplied.

"Yes, Trayon, the younger brother of Artio, the God of the Sun, was listening. The princess had been a powerful ally of his, and her loss would be a spear to the heart of his campaign against his brother."

"What was her magic?" Grante interrupted, surprising everyone at the table with his question.

My father waved his question aside with one hand. "They believe it was weather based, a rarity in her culture and a desperately needed one in Adrial. You see, this was back when magic was not only cultivated, but desired in the continent. Only certain families, certain bloodlines, seemed to have a proficiency for magic. But this princess and her tribe were unusually powerful."

I swirled my glass.

"Do you have magic?" Shanna asked me pointedly, her painted fingertips scraping against the table as she looked first at me, then to my father.

"No, it's mostly a lost ability here in Adrial, and you'll understand why in just a moment. Trayon, the God of the Sea, had seen the younger twin's torment. He rose from the depths to pull the younger brother into a bubble of safety, offering the man comfort in his grief, his fury. The God listened to his story, his anger at his brother, and saw a moment of opportunity. See, Artio, and

Trayon had waged war for as long as time existed, and the sea god saw a chance to take a swing at his brother."

My father was, as usual, a magnificent storyteller, and he had all of our guests enthralled.

"The younger brother pledged his undying service to the water god, binding him eternally to the god in exchange for Trayon saving his love and making him a king in his own right. Together, the god and his servant would send a message to his brother so significant that history could never forget it. The deal was signed in blood. Then the lower kingdom, the part of Adrial that used to be right out that window—" my father gestured out to the sea "—was pulled into the sea."

Count Merclino leaned into the table. "Impossible."

"Not for a god. The people, the shops, the ships, the buildings… All of it crashed in with heaving waves. The younger brother took a new name in honor of his new god master. He appeared only once more to his brother's court, to tell them that any Adrialian soul that touched the Great Sea would be considered tribute to Trayon and would be dragged down into the underwater world that he was now lord of."

The audience's intake of breath brought a smile to my father's face. He slowly slipped his now cooling coffee.

"And there are hundreds of cases over the generations, maybe thousands. Sometimes it's one or two people disappearing after swimming off the university docks. Others it is entire ships dipping into the ocean as if Trayon himself is pulling them down by their anchor. So we Adrialians, we stay out of the Great Sea, lest we awaken Trayon and his malice."

The curtains by the door snapped in the wind, making me jump lightly in my seat. In an instant, Rhoe's hand brushed the exposed skin of my back, and I shivered, this time for a whole new reason.

"That is quite the story," the Count said, his head bowing towards my father, who raised his mug towards the man in return. "I've been hearing more and more rumors of this curse taking Adrialians. Nasty business all along the coast here. It seems odd that nothing has been done in so many generations."

Lady Vertia's eyes snapped to attention. Deep in my chest, something thrummed in a soft warning. I glared at Grante, hoping he might step in for his father before my father was forced to act.

The Count's cheeks grew red, his obvious misstep enough to make even his tongue quiet for a moment.

I cleared my throat. "We have had very few cases in recent years. In fact, we've been able to set up a night guard to patrol the most common areas in the city where our citizens find themselves drawn to the water."

"Drawn to the water? What do you mean?" Lord Vertia looked uncomfortable.

"That's something else right? A sea sickness of sorts. It doesn't have the same aspects as the curse," Shanna said, ducking her chin slightly. My father nodded, but I could see the way his brows dipped. He was surprised how much she knew, and frankly, so was I. "It doesn't have a pattern necessarily, and not from exposure to the water. It just strikes randomly, making people long for the water. I read once that it was Trayon's curse's lure, tempting the people of Adrial closer to the deadly waters.

Lady Vertia spoke up. "Couldn't it be a siren's song? Even in the isles we have many similar tales."

"I can assure you, it is not a siren's song, as we've seen those many times during trading missions. They seem to be best combated by simply blocking the sound." I tapped on the edge of the table, smiling around at the solemn faces. "Simple solutions. The sickness, like you said, only affects certain people and most simply ignore it. The curse, of course, is much more serious."

I faced the ambassadors directly. "That said, you do not have any reason to be concerned with our trading routes. We will deal with the sea sickness and the curse. We grow closer every day to finding a way to stop them both entirely." My tongue burned at the exaggeration, but the topic was growing tired and I didn't want the Emenian's to think we weren't capable of handling our own affairs.

"Mira is correct. Someday this curse, this attack from Trayon will be nothing but the ending in a very long myth." My father smiled, but the look was far away. "For now, I'm proud of my daughter, who spends her nights keeping our people safe until a curse is secured."

"You?" Grante broke his silence now, observing me with far more interest than before. "You patrol the walls?"

I straightened my slender shoulders. "I do." There was no need to mention the sea-bound quests to cure the affected. That would only lead to more questions.

"A warrior princess. How…interesting." Lord Vertia words slowed as both Rhoe and my father seemed to grow in size.

The threat was clear, as was my intention when I fixed my gaze on the ambassadors once again. "Do you not have female warriors?"

Lord Vertia appeared more nervous than before. I wondered briefly what kind of expression was on Rhoe's face, but I didn't dare look back. Finally, he took a quick sip of his coffee and said, "We do, your highness, just not of royal blood."

I didn't blink. It was nothing new. "What a pity." I turned to address Shanna. "If you should choose to learn while you are here, you're welcome to join us in training each morning."

Shanna gave me a surprised look, her mouth making a tiny *O* for a long moment before she hid it with her napkin.

"I believe it's time for me to turn in. Night patrol tonight," I lied easily. The words rolled off my tongue with as much authority as I could manage.

"It's time for us to retire for the night as well," Shanna's father said. "Thank you, Your Majesty, for sharing your evening with us."

The Emen ambassadors rose gracefully from their seats to reach for my hand. Shanna stood alongside her parents, waiting her turn to kneel before my father then sending a wink to my way that I couldn't help but return.

As she bowed to me, I stepped up and ran a hand down Shanna's arm, subtly tucking a note into her fist before pulling back.

"It was lovely to meet you. I hope you enjoy your time in Port Sol," I said as her fingers wrapped more tightly around the note.

"The same to you. You must let me know if you are ever in Emen. I can return the courtesy," she responded then dropped into another deep bow. Her parents joined her this time, staying low as they murmured a myriad of nice things about the meal.

I hated this part. The reverence of the crowds, of the people was one thing, but having someone bow to me at the same table I choked down breakfast made my stomach clench. A quick look at my father, though, and I saw the relief, the pride that crossed his face as I held court over our guests.

Swallowing hard, I gestured for them to rise, putting my best smile on as they were escorted from the room.

My father stood by the window, his drink long forgotten. Behind him, I could hear the steady beat of the waves against the Adrial sea walls, Port Sol's heartbeat filled the room.

"Are you alright, Papa? I had forgotten how close to home that story really is." I kept my voice quiet, ignoring the way that Rhoe lurked in the hall, obviously waiting for me. But I couldn't leave my father yet, not until I knew he would not fall into one of his depressive nights.

His wide shoulders slumped. I could see the white of his knuckles against the column of the terrace. "I'll be fine, *minu*. Go enjoy your night."

"You aren't supposed to know about that," I said, coming to stand directly behind him. I raised a hand and gently pressed it to my father's drawn shoulders.

"I'm the king. I know everything." His voice rumbled with more of that humor that I loved so dearly.

"Not everything." I chewed at my lip. "That story, I know it reminds you of Mama…" I trailed off, leaving my hand on his shoulder, feeling the heat, the solidarity under my hand.

"It is nothing like your mother's story. It never will be."

I flinched, resisting the urge to snap my hand back.

"She was pushed, or tripped, or something. Damona would have never jumped. She was happy. She had you. She had me. She had everything. *We* had everything." His deep voice cracked.

My throat grew thick. The rumors, the stories that came out after my mother had fallen from the palace balcony, had nearly destroyed the kingdom. People had accused the king of abuse, or neglect, that he had driven the kingdom's beloved queen to suicide.

My father had practically crumbled. First under the loss of his wife, but then at the voices that called him the instigator, the murderer. It had been the end of a chapter and the beginning of another for him. Homer had arrived at Port Sol, shortly after, and slowly, very slowly, they had rebuilt this palace into the home I now loved.

"I know, Papa. I know," I whispered at his back. He didn't move, just staring out into the heavy, salt-ridden air.

"I love you, Papa. I will be back later." I didn't bother to kiss or hug him goodbye. When he was in one of his moods, it was safest to leave him be. While my father was a noble man, he had a temper as sharp as the business end of a spear. I had no desire to quarrel with him further.

Chapter Eight

Slipping into my room down the hall, I nearly jumped out of my skin at Rhoe. He was draped across my bed, throwing various pieces of body armor across my room with decisive grunts.

"I've been waiting forever. What did you have to talk to him about?" Rhoe chucked his heavy belt to the floor. He stretched like an overgrown feral cat, eyes narrowing as I moved into the room. I focused hard on appearing unmoved by the familiarity this man seemed to have with not just my room, but with my bed. I swallowed hard, forcing the words up a rough throat.

"I wonder if I need to call for Homer. Father's in one of his moods again." I looked at myself in the mirror, tugging on the purple gown with distaste.

Rhoe sat up quickly, his brilliant eyes scanned my face.

"Why don't I leave a message for him on my way out? He can check in on him tonight." Rhoe nudged a shin guard with the toe of his boot. "I need to throw this stuff back in the armory anyway."

"Thank you. I worry about him." I looked at him through the reflection in the mirror. He was half-kicking, half-picking up the various armor pieces he had just rid himself of. I wrinkled my nose at the curses that came slinging out of his wide mouth. Sometimes I wondered how he had come to be my father's Chosen. Sure, he came with excellent experience, and the way he moved in battle was something to behold. But he was so young, so frank with us, even when he was new to Adrial.

Rhoe turned in the door, catching me with a long, pensive stare. "It'll be okay, Mira. I'll make sure of it."

I grinned. There, that was why he was the Chosen. The man was as loyal as one could get, and his heart was the strongest part of him, which was saying something.

"Get out of here, Chosen. I need to change," I responded gently, heat rushing up my neck.

Rhoe pulled a face then slammed the heavy door shut between us.

Quickly peeling my way out of the deep-purple dress, I selected a loose-cut short top and a pair of tight-fitted pants, both a shade of blue so dark that they were almost black. Against my fair skin, the effect was dramatic. The simple design and plain fabric might even buy me additional time before people caught on that someone decidedly not common was in their midst.

Stretching my arms over my head, I threw open the door again, this time to find Rhoe waiting patiently, with Shanna blushing prettily at his side.

The Emenian girl was humming with barely contained energy. The moment I opened my door, Shanna launched herself at me, wrapping her arms around my bare midriff and squeezing. She must've suddenly remembered herself, because just as quickly, she pushed away, bowing low.

"I'm so honored you thought to invite me, your highness."

Subconsciously, I felt Shanna's eyes smooth over my attire. When the moment grew long, I started to feel embarrassed.

"Is there something wrong?"

"I love it," Shanna squealed, quickly giving my torso one last tug before I stepped back, eyes shining with adoration. "You look every inch a powerful warrior queen, Lady Mira."

"Thank you, Shanna. I think." I smiled, my lips feeling stiff, and Shanna grinned back.

"Ladies, we've got a short walk ahead. Shall we get going?" Rhoe's voice held notes of laughter, but he kept his handsome face straight and serious as he led the way back down the hall. The palace held a dozen escape tunnels. Some were still undiscovered or lost through the generations of building and changes that it had undergone since half of the castle and lower city sank into the Great Sea. The one we chose tonight was smooth, well-traveled, at the edge of the sea wall before curling through the center of the city.

"Do you sneak out often, highness?" Shannan asked her breath coming in little puffs as she hurried to keep up with Rhoe's and my longer steps. I slowed myself, waiting for the more petite woman to catch up as we passed through the Qualdrid, or the main square. A statue of Artio, Adrial's token God, rose from the center.

For the first time since we set off, I grew nervous. Shanna had opted to go without her cloak, and her pretty, dark features were lit with curiosity, the torchlight illuminating her plunging neckline.

Rhoe had dressed for the evening. During dinner he had been dressed from head to toe in the deep red and gold tones that my family had chosen decades ago. Now his fresh, white shirt was loose, the ties practically undone, exposing a wide section of his skin. His vivid, nearly white-blond hair seemed to glow in the dark, swinging loose and curling to his shoulders. When he met my pointed look, he raked one large hand through the locks, pushing them back from a pensive face.

"Shanna, make sure to stay close tonight, alright?" Rhoe smiled as he said the words, but he had stepped closer to the young woman, casting a protective shadow over her form. The girl practically swooned, staring up at Rhoe with adoration-filled eyes. He, however, was still looking at me.

Shanna blinked, glancing from Rhoe to me and back again.

"I must ask…Are the two of you…"

"Oh Gods," I gasped. "No."

"Don't say it like that, Princess Mira. You've mortally wounded my pride," Rhoe said, sarcasm dripping from his every word.

"Stop saying princess," I hissed at him pulling my hood closer around my face. To Shanna, I explained, "Rhoe and I are only friends."

A beat later, Rhoe spoke up. "Chosen are not allowed to have true relationships."

"Ever?" Shannan asked, voice rising.

Rhoe's eyes darkened as he dropped his chin. "We are allowed physical relationships, Lady Shanna, but as the relationship can never progress past a certain point, we are discouraged from sharing deeper emotions with anyone."

Shannan looked him up and down. "You aren't dressed like the Chosen tonight."

I burst out laughing. "He's not working for King and duty tonight. He's looking for the physical side of the relationship, not the emotional."

To my surprise, Rhoe's smile faltered for a moment, but as soon as I blinked, that devilish smirk that I adored so much had returned

"Rhoe has only been serving my father for a few years. And the first time we met, my father suspected I had snuck out after a particularly horrible day of princess training. I blatantly refused to leave the little pub I had found my way into. Fueled by too many glasses of sweet fruit wine, I challenged who I thought was a boring guard to a drinking contest. If I won, I got to stay out as long as I wanted. But if I lost, I had to go back home. I made a face to show my opinion of that.

"The bartender had set up the game, and much to Rhoe's horror and my immense pride, it turned out that my hand-to-eye coordination was nothing short of a miracle. I won easily, and we spent the entire night hustling other patrons with my skills."

I smiled at the memory of it, seeing a mirror of my expression on Rhoe's face over Shannan's head. "When we had staggered home just before dawn to face my father and Homer's disapproving looks, it had been as best friends."

Now it was a fairly regular thing. Not the hustling and the bets, but the excursions into the city. While I was sure my father didn't exactly approve of my need to see more of my kingdom, he didn't raise any questions about either of us.

"Are we getting close? While I don't mind a little walk, this dress isn't the best choice." Shanna leaned into Rhoe's arm, her steps bouncing.

"Yes. Very close now," I answered her. A salted breeze floated by us as we made our way down the stone stairs that led from the Qualdrid to the cluster of shops and pubs just beyond. I tasted the tang of the Great Sea as we grew closer, my skin growing tight and warm.

There was something about the Great Sea, the endless, vast water, that called to me. As a child I had begged to visit the docks with my father, standing so close to the dock's edge that eventually he had demanded I stay home, lest I fall in and under Trayon's curse. After my mother's death, neither Father nor I went down to the docks for years.

Even now, as the three of us made our way through the dark pathways, I found myself staring towards the Great Sea, catching glimpses of the dark water's restless waves between buildings and the man-high wall that my grandfather had ordered built a half a century ago. Rhoe was hurrying us along now, his keen eyes taking in the other Adrialians who were out for a late-night drink or rendezvous.

I trusted him completely but also knew that years as a guard had made him suspicious, even overly so. Every time anyone passed us by, Rhoe's face clenched, his jaw moving in a way that I always wondered about, as if he were muttering something that I could never hear.

Even with Rhoe's worry, we made it to our destination quickly, a squat, dingy-looking little place that didn't appear to have a name. Above the bar, it simply said, *Drinks*, in bold, sloppy lettering.

Shanna hesitated only a beat before following us eagerly into our place. The usual crowd didn't blink at our presence, and in a breath we were absorbed into the hubbub. The first drink went down easy, the second slower.

Shanna proved to be as sweet and energetic as earlier, making easy friends with the bartender. My lips pulled as I watched her eagerly engage with the patrons. I had been here dozens of times since I turned eighteen and possessed only a fraction of the relationship with the burly man that Shanna had cultivated in a single evening.

Rhoe sat a few chairs away, pretending to be deeply engrossed in a story a tipsy-looking young woman was telling him. Her hands were moving between them, her pretty dark eyes fluttering as they ghosted over Rhoe's muscular chest. His head tilted, and I knew he was looking for his exit, and while I enjoyed letting him reap as he had sowed, I was feeling generous this evening. Blame the liquor or the lively music that the band played, but I decided to intervene.

Sauntering over, I slid my hand up his shoulder blade, up and over the thick, tense muscle of his neck. Letting my fingers dangle across his collarbone, I leaned into his side with a coy smile. Pressing my lips close to his ear, I felt Rhoe grow still.

"What have you gotten yourself into now?" I whispered for his ears only.

Rhoe turned slowly, his face a breath from mine, our noses nearly brushing. While mine was covered in a teasing smile, his was strained, drawn as Rhoe's shining blue eyes met my violet.

For a moment, my heart skipped at the heat in my friend's expression. Then, as if it had never happened, Rhoe grinned at me. Reaching around to clasp my hip, Rhoe pulled me sideways, across his lap. I hid my intake of breath against his neck, watching the bob of his Adam's apple as his other hand curled around my knee, holding me cradled across his thighs. He was so hot against me, his fingers a fiery brand, even through my clothing.

"Ah, look at this one coming to check on me. Always jealous." Rhoe's voice was ragged. His new friend's glazed eyes took in every inch of me, including the parts now held flush against Rhoe's body. I met her bold look head on, letting my fingertips trail lazily along the skin of his jaw. It was so soft.

"This one is taken," I said smoothly, hating and loving the temper that flared under my skin when she sneered at us.

As if sensing the fire warming beneath my skin, Rhoe spoke again. "It was lovely to meet you. But it's time for you to go. I need to take care of my girl." Rhoe stood, and slowly I let my body slide along his until my feet brushed the ground. Had he always been that tall, I wondered, or was it because I was still plastered against him, looking up, that made him seem larger than usual?

Dark eyes burned into mine and made my breath come short, and I was viscerally aware of the fact that he was still holding me, his hands on my lower back. Warmth pooled there, spreading through my body with every breath. I could feel my skin tingle, my heart race thrumming lightly as my hand spread out over his belly. The muscles under contracted, hardened at my touch.

"You love this song," he said suddenly.

I blinked then listened carefully, recognizing the soft, lilting tones over the din of the crowd. "You're right. I do love this song."

"It would be a shame to waste it."

I grinned up at him. "It would, wouldn't it?"

Rhoe's chest was rising and falling so quickly against me, his jaw tight and clenched as we stood there, the crowded bar so unaware of the moment we were sharing. "Mira…"

I lurched away, a shock of fear filling my belly as I moved back a step, turning and grabbing his hand with mine as I dragged him towards the narrow dance floor at the back of the bar. I could see Shanna talking with another young woman, both smiling and sipping their cups of fruity wine. And as I tried to force the feeling of Rhoe out of my mind, he stood in front of me, guiding my hands into his once more.

"Rhoe, we can't." Even as I said the words, our fingers met and tangled.

"It's a dance, Mira. We can."

We began to sway. The steps were simple and habitual at this point. I followed his lead, looking everywhere but at him. We'd danced many times together, but this time, something felt different.

There was a change in the atmosphere, in the way his breath felt against my cheek or the heat of his skin as we touched.

And when he spun me out and finally back in, my steps weren't perfect, and I stumbled, falling into Rhoe's powerful grip with a soft noise.

"It's okay," he murmured, curling me closer to him. "I've got you."

I looked up into his face, so close to mine, and I couldn't help but look at his lips, at the soft line of them. Would they be soft, like they looked? What would he taste like? I would've bet my crown on knowing that Rhoe kissed like he did everything in life—with enthusiasm and passion.

"Rhoe," I whispered, pushing up on my toes. My nose brushed his, and I felt a shudder go through his body.

"Hey, golden boy, where's your girl?"

I startled, and Rhoe blinked slowly, the moment growing cool between us as I remembered that we were in the middle of a dance floor, in a public place. And I was the future queen of Adrial, wrapped up in my father's guard.

I struggled away, swallowing and straightening my top as we turned to face the bartender.

Rhoe gestured at me. "This is my girl."

My heart leaped at that casual comment.

But the bartender was already shaking his head. "No, lover boy. The other one. The one with the pretty little accent."

"Shanna," I said, panic making my voice tight as I stepped into the room. "Where is she?"

"I was going to ask the same thing. She was buying another round of these, but she didn't pay or come back."

I stared down at her drinks then turned to the crowd. As one, I and Rhoe scanned the rest of the dining space. Shanna would've stood out like a shrimp among sharks. She was nowhere to be seen. Dread uncurled in my gut, and all thoughts and worries about what I'd felt on Rhoe's lap were slashed away as it took hold.

"My father is going to kill me," I breathed. It seemed like this kept coming up.

"He will execute me first. Promise me you won't watch," Rhoe spoke beside me, his voice resolute.

Shock must have been making me light-headed. I reached out and gripped his arm. "We've got to find her."

Rhoe nodded hard.

We strode from the bar, Rhoe tossing some coins on the bar to cover our beverages. We knew that Shanna had been interested in the water legends, and here we were, only steps from the largest unguarded access point to the Adrialian port. She would be there, I knew it.

"The docks."

Rhoe nodded, tucking into my side as we set off. The cool summer air was choking me, and my mind was racing. Rhoe sprang into action, all flexed muscle and fury, his body rolling across the path as the two of us went to the most logical destination. My blood hummed, my strides lengthened as the two of us prowled past the darkened streets. Darkened buildings with shuttered windows seemed to loom over us, reminding me of exactly how far we were from the palace.

We dropped silently down onto the road directly above the wide mouth of the sea walls. I flinched as my thin-soled sandals failed to absorb the shock of landing on the cobbled road. Rising slowly, gingerly, I listened for any hint of Shanna. Now that we were out from under the imposing, decrepit buildings that lined the docks, the moonlight painted a vivid picture spread out below us.

A variety of fishing, shipping, and passenger vessels were tethered to the piers. Gentle waves caressed their hulls, and the only sound was my heart pounding in my chest. Looking farther, just outside of the sea walls, a three-mast ship sat quiet, bobbing in the water like a lurking monster silently stalking its prey. It didn't belong there. Any vessel that size should be tied down in the evening. A quick look told me its anchor hadn't been dropped either.

Rhoe had dropped to a crouch, his eyes scanning our surroundings. I felt the adrenaline receding. Perhaps I was wrong. Had Shanna simply left us to return home to the palace? Maybe she'd gotten lost along the way. I watched as a cloud passed sulkily in front of the full moon, throwing us into darkness. Rhoe breathed quietly beside me, both of us waiting for a sign.

When the moonlight lit the harbor again, my body physically recoiled. There was now a small group traveling quickly along the docks. At their center, covered in a dark cloak, was a squirming, fighting human. The hood slipped just a fraction, a flash of pink fabric against the black.

"Shanna," I shuttered out, unable to keep quiet. My feet were moving before my brain could catch up. Iron-banded fingers grabbed my shoulders, lurching me backwards so quickly that I almost tumbled to the street.

"No, no, no. Mira, you have to stay here." Rhoe's growl stunned me into obeying. He held up his hand, where a single Adrialian charm dangled on his wrist. He pressed it between two fingers, and I watched as the metal glowed red, as if freshly poured to its cast.

My mouth dropped open, shocked at his open use of magic. I knew that the throne held bits and pieces of magical runes and remnants aside for personal use. As my father's Chosen, it seemed that Rhoe had been given one.

Rhoe clamped his hand over my mouth. Against my lips, his hand was calloused, rough. "I just called in help from the Royal Guard. They will be here soon, but I've got to get the jump on them, or else we will lose her."

I nodded against his hand.

"You stay here. This is a good cover."

I started to resist, yanking at his grip on my face.

Rhoe's expression hardened. "You. Will. Stay. Here. I mean it, Mira. Right here."

"I can help," I insisted, wrenching free. My heart raced as I watched the small group drag Shanna farther down the pier.

"I cannot do my job unless I know you are safe. Please, Mira, this is how you help Shanna."

I bit into my lip, hard enough I knew that I would leave a mark. Nodding, I dropped down in a crouch similar to Rhoe's. The sloping hill behind me would keep me hidden from sight.

As soon as I was safely in position, Rhoe slipped into the night. Settling back on my heels, I tried my best to stay absolutely still. My ears strained, listening for Rhoe's movements or, better yet, the sound of approaching help from the palace. Yet, there was nothing but the distant lapping of water against stone that had always been my nightly lullaby. But tonight, instead of soothing, the Great Sea's song did nothing but stroke the fear that threatened to choke me.

The sharp sounds of engagement drew my gaze back to the docks. Rhoe had reached the group, and it seemed that any sign of conversation or negotiation had been declined quickly. From this distance, I could see nothing but the brightness of Rhoe's gleaming blonde hair in the moonlight. He moved through the group, sending a bevy of punches, kicks into the shadowy figures that held Shanna.

As soon as the group faltered, Rhoe shoved Shanna towards land, urging her to flee to safety. Dropping the cloak the kidnappers had thrown over her, Shanna yanked her dress up to her knees and sprinted towards safety. I rose slightly, waiting to signal Shanna over to me. The girl was moving quickly, her thick dark hair loose her shoulders.

I saw the lookout man before Shanna ever did. He must've been tasked with scouting out the harbor area and looked to foil Shanna's escape. He rose out of the darkness, tackling Shanna to the ground. Together, they skidded across the docks to the edge.

"Someone, please help me! Princess Mira!" Shanna was screaming. Before I knew what happened, I had leaped down the slope, my sandals flying off as I sprinted down the docks. Every step, my blood screamed in rage, fueling my speed. Without breaking stride, I dove into the tumbling pair, latching my fingers into the heavy jacket that Shanna's attacker wore. Using my momentum, I hurled my weight into his body, throwing him easily over my shoulder. Shanna scrambled to her feet.

"Go!" I screamed at the girl, my eyes still trained on her opponent. He stood slowly, wiping his jaw with a long, exaggerated movement.

"I'll be just a moment, love. You wait there." The man spoke to Shanna with an unusual accent. He was not from Adrial. I wrinkled my nose in distaste. Adrial had had issues with slave traders many years ago, but nothing of late. This man reeked of blood money, and I hated him for it.

"You're disgusting," I said softly, my voice deadly low.

My opponent shrugged, taking a few steps back from me. I narrowed my eyes. What was his play? Distantly, I could still hear Rhoe taking care of the rest of the traders. Closer there were Shanna's frantic steps against the wooden slats of the dock. I focused harder, trying to clear my mind.

There. Just the smallest whisper in the back of my mind. The steady beat of oars against water. I spun to warn Shanna. It was too late. Off to the side, I could see the narrow rowboat that was slicing through the quiet waves. From the bow of the boat flew a heavy length of rope. I watched as it streaked through the night towards Shanna.

His aim was excellent, and it landed neatly around one of the girl's upturned feet. With a jerk, the knot was set, and Shanna went hurtling to the dock. I scrambled towards the girl, picturing exactly what was about to happen. The worst thing that could happen for an Adrialian citizen. The fate that awaited her in that boat was a nightmare at best. And then there was the small matter of what would happen if they dragged her through the cursed water of the Great Sea. Perhaps drowning would be a blessing from Artio.

I yelled something, waving my arms as I sprinted back towards Shanna. The traders on the rowboat began to tighten their hold, dragging Shanna to the edge of the wooden walkway. Even from here, I could see the girl's fingers digging into the worn wood, looking desperately for a handhold.

Heart pounding, I recognized that I would never reach her in time. Turning my head a fraction, I saw Rhoe was running towards us too, but he was even farther. One more glance told me that Shanna's legs were now dangling from the edge, the heavily braided rope tight around one ankle.

Shanna's eyes found mine, wild, terrified. They stole my breath as she finally lost her grip on the dock and went plunging into the shallow waters.

98

Chapter Nine

"No!" I screamed, watching as the boat continued to reel in their catch, dragging the young woman through the dark waters. Shanna's dark head bobbing above the surface, her arms flailing as she was repeatedly dragged under the waves. The decision was easy, and I didn't hesitate. Adjusting my stride. I turned to the forbidden body of water, my body arching up as I leaped from the dock in a deep, exaggerated dive.

The first taste of the salty brine filled my mind with shock. I half expected to immediately be yanked down to the depths by Trayon himself, but to my surprise, nothing but water touched me. No demons sent from the deep, no deadly currents, no Mer. Just the softly lapping waves pushing my tumbling body skyward. I broke from the water gasping. The salt water stung, but I forced my eyes open to find my new friend.

Shanna was fighting for all she was worth, splashing up a storm just a length or two in front of me. Diving back under, I kicked hard, drawing even with her. At my first touch, the girl screeched, kicking out and yelling.

"It's me, Shanna. It's me!" I didn't wait for her answer. The small boat would be on us in moments. Ducking under, I followed the line for the girl's leg all the way down to the taut noose that held her prisoner. Sliding my fingers inside the knot, I yanked hard. Nothing happened, except for the painful pinch of the fiber against my still-healing skin. The salt burned my angry flesh as I pulled again. It was just too tight.

My lungs pleaded for me to find air, but I pushed on, digging stiff fingers into the knotted length. I prayed. I screamed in my mind. *Please, please help!*

Suddenly, the knot loosened, the tension on the rope giving way. I slipped the length from Shanna's narrow ankle and gave the girl's body a massive push. Finally breaking the surface, I found Shanna flailing atop the water. Rolling her to her back, I gripped the girl across her collarbones, holding her tightly to my body.

"It's okay. I've got you," I murmured, tilting my chin back and away from the spray of the ocean water. Shanna didn't answer but went slack against me, a slight moan coming from her lips.

I couldn't see much from behind Shanna's head, but I knew enough to see that a squad of my father's men stood on the beach, bows drawn. They must've struck down the traders in the rowboat. Gratitude bloomed in my chest for a moment before it was quickly extinguished.

They weren't moving.

Each of these men, carefully chosen, trained, and interviewed for a role protecting the royal family, stood like ancient statues at the very edge of the Great Sea, afraid to come a step farther.

A wave lapped at my jawline, and I growled in frustration, body shaking with the effort of keeping both Shanna and myself afloat. Kicking and pulling with my one free arm, I made it farther into the shallows, when a loud commotion broke through my consciousness. Someone was angry, yelling.

I was almost there. Just a few more strokes, and I would be able to walk. My body quivered as I hauled us towards the shore.

I rolled over, letting my toes find purchase against the sandy bottoms. Shanna moved easily with me but was shorter and couldn't touch yet. And that was even if the girl was capable of walking after her ordeal. I wasn't so sure. When I looked to the shore, my entire body warmed at the sight of Rhoe elbowing his way through the line of archers. It was his voice that ordered the bows to be put down.

Without hesitation, Rhoe, his hair glowing in the moonlight, raced into the water. Wordlessly, I shoved Shanna to him, begging him to take the weight of the exhausted young woman. Rhoe said nothing. He was muttering a long string of curses that I couldn't understand.

Casting a worried look at me, Rhoe scooped up Shanna and ran back through the water to deposit her along the beach. The squad actually flinched back from the splash of saltwater, afraid to get too close to any of us.

My body burned, every muscle tight and spasming. Even my skin seemed wrong, too tight and as if small needles prickled across every surface. I made it to thigh-deep before I collapsed, dark, painful stars erupting across my vision. I screamed as I fell back into the water.

As the warmth engulfed my body, the pain receded to sweet, silent bliss. In an instinct I couldn't understand, I opened unseeing eyes to the salty darkness. My heart pounded loudly in my ears as a massive vibration shook my world.

It reminded me of the feeling right before lightning struck, as if every fiber in my being was suddenly drawn tightly together then strummed on like an overdrawn lyrical instrument. Power rippled out from my body as I took a long, deep breath in. Instead of drowning, though, the brine filled me with strength, with healing. I could feel my aching, straining muscles relax as the water washed through my being.

Sighing, giving into the rushing pleasure of the power, I let myself go. This must be what Pierse felt when he finally made it into the water he'd craved so deeply.

Trayon could have me, as long as I could continue feeling this way. I took another breath in, the pressure in my chest easing until two strong, masculine hands gripped my arms. I flinched away from them, displeasure filling my mind.

"No, Mira, not now. You can't go. I need you here. Mira!" Rhoe's deep voice startled me. He was hauling me up, out of the Great Sea, and across his chest. I knew that people were staring, but I couldn't bear to meet their eyes. Breathing hard through my nose, I kept my eyes trained on my friend's jaw, the smooth skin just below. Had it been so long ago that I'd been able to touch that skin with my fingers, that I'd pressed my face just there?

It seemed like an age ago now.

He carried me through the crowd, his body almost hot against my cool skin, threatening to burn me up. No one stopped him as he marched to the first available carriage and deposited me gently inside. My wet clothes instantly soaked the cushions, and awkwardly I curled in on myself, trying to lessen the damage. I was deeply unsuccessful.

"Rhoe?"

"Take her back now. I'll take care of the Emenian."

"Yes Chosen." More deep voices filled my mind. I struggled to sit up, my muscles lethargic and unfamiliar. I could still taste the salt on my tongue. I grabbed for Rhoe's forearm, catching his wet sleeve in my hand.

"What happened?" I asked, my voice cracking.

"Don't worry. You got her out." Rhoe's voice was gentle, softer than I'd ever heard it. His body was drenched and his clothes were plastered to the smooth, muscular panes. Those brilliant blue eyes stared at me with an unreadable emotion. Silently, he leaned forwards until his forehead gently bumped into my own.

Only a breath apart, I let myself sag into his strength.

"Go home, Mira. It's going to be okay."

I nodded, biting my lip and turning to the driver.

With a curt word from Rhoe, the man slapped the lines against a pair of dark horses. Moments later, we were leaving the lower kingdom and I was on my way back to the palace. Curling up where I sat, I let my heavy eyes rest.

I didn't dream that night. My rest was a thick, heavy shroud around my shoulders, and when I finally woke up, I felt like my body actually resisted the action. Finally forcing my eyes open, I could tell that it was late in the morning.

The brightness of the sun shining in my window made me wince. I tried raising the cover over my face for a moment, but he quilt wouldn't go that far. Looking down, I felt my body flush with guilt. Father lay across the base of my bed, his face pinched and pale, even in sleep. He still wore his dressing gown, and the usually clean-cut decorative line of his beard was muddled by stubble.

Blinking rapidly and ignoring a pounding headache, I reached forward to brush fingers lightly along Father's extended hand.

"Papa," I said quietly. "Papa, wake up."

His shoulders twitched, and his lips pulled down in a frown. Then, opening his warm brown eyes, my father looked at me with sadness. "Mira! You're awake. Gods, I was so worried. How are you? Do you feel alright?" His voice was rough, tired.

"I'm fine, I think. Just a little groggy." I watched as my father sat up, stretching one arm, then the other over his head. His usual presence was diminished by the waves of anxiety and worry that rolled off him.

"What happened to Shanna?" My voice was strangled as I fought against my bedding. I needed to know if she was okay. I wanted to know what had happened.

Father moved quickly, pushing my shoulders back into the plush bed with a steady, heavy hand.

"Easy, now. Your friend is safe. Thank Artio." He took a deep breath, shaking his dark head. "Mira, what were you thinking, jumping into the water?"

I brushed his hands off, propping myself up on my elbows. I couldn't identify a part of me that didn't creak a little as I fought against his grip. My headache was forgotten by the lurking anger in my belly. I glared at my father; his usually kind eyes mirrored my anger. "What was I thinking? I was thinking that an innocent girl was being dragged through the harbor like a fish on the line. I had to do something."

His jaw clenched. "You jumped into the Great Sea, Mira. That's practically suicide. She is Emenian. You are Adrialian—"

"And it still wouldn't have kept her from drowning. Papa, I'm an excellent swimmer," I said stubbornly, jutting my chin out even more.

"You and I both know that there is far more to fear from those waters than the risk of drowning. And you risked it all to save an Emenian girl who got in over her head. The laws of Trayon's curse do not pertain to her. But they do to us. To you."

I felt myself shrink away from my father. His words were calloused, uncaring—both things I had never witnessed him being. Swallowing hard, I wanted to explain so he would understand, so he would care.

"It was my responsibility to protect her. I had to," I said weakly. "But I am sorry, Papa. I'm sure I scared you."

"Not just me. Everybody. You should've seen Rhoe on his rampage earlier. You jumped willingly into the damned water, the Great Sea itself." He stopped himself, dropping his gaze to his hands on the sheets.

"I know. I'm sorry. I don't know how many times I need to say it, but if you tell me, I'll keep working on it." I gave my father my best smile.

"Don't you smile at me like that. Even if you did manage to avoid the curse, you are still in plenty of trouble, daughter," he warned, his deep voice quiet.

I dropped the smile, save a small curl on one side of my lips.

My father patted my arm. "Get up, get dressed. Homer will be in shortly with your agenda." He walked through the door, one hand on his lower back as if he was sore.

I watched him go before dragging my body out from under my bedding. Planting my feet against the stone floor, I walked stiffly across my chambers. My body was sore, especially my chest. It felt tight, almost constricting as I peeled my nightclothes off.

Looking down, I let my fingers graze down my body, the skin twitching under my touch. Something felt different, but I couldn't see what. Even looking into my mirror as a maid helped me dress. I looked the same.

Yet at the same time, I knew I was different. Something lurked under my skin, whispering across my body just ahead of my eyes. A knock on the door thrust me from my thoughts. I snatched the first thing I found and threw it over my body. My maid opened the door and disappeared as heavy footfalls announced a new arrival.

"How are you?" A warm, familiar voice washed over me, bringing an easy smile to my face.

I turned to Rhoe, cocking my head at the concerned look he gave me. His usually dancing blue eyes were solemn, almost sad as he watched me.

"Aw. Were you worried about me?" I teased, sticking the tip of my tongue out at him, expecting him to joust with me. Instead, he leaned against the wall beside me.

"Rhoe…" I reached out and put my hand on his arm. His flesh, separated by a lightweight tunic, was warm beneath my hand. I remembered what he'd done last night. The risk he'd taken, as well as the way he'd felt against me as he carried me out the ocean. "I'm fine. Really. No interest in leaping into the Great Sea anytime soon."

I grinneded at him.

He continued to frown, lines growing between his light-colored brows. "Excuse me if I'm not ready to start joking about the fact that last night I thought I was going to lose someone I care about very deeply."

My traitorous heart leaped in my chest. I opened my mouth again to comfort him, when a memory flashed bright to my mind. I stared at him, combing over his form with critical eyes. "You went into the Great Sea too. You were the only one."

He looked away, his eyes distant and strained. "I couldn't let you drown."

"I wouldn't drown. You know my mother taught me well."

To my surprise, Rhoe jerked his arm away.

Worry grew heavy in my stomach.

Rhoe straightened, expression stormy as he looked over. "There are things in the Great Sea, things bigger than you or me. Do me a favor and stay out of the water, Mira. I mean it."

He sulked away before I could answer him, and I was left staring after him. My stomach rolled. His words had not only surprised me but brought another unwelcome wave of shame over my person. I had acted to save another. I was neither suicidal nor interested in becoming a hero. It had been instinct. So why was now strangely embarrassed by it?

I trudged back to sofa, my feet and head heavy with emotions I didn't want to acknowledge or deal with. Perhaps my father had been right. Last night must've taken more out of me than I thought. Dammit.

Rhoe had barely closed the door to my chambers when a tiny, leaping missile flew to me, wrapping impressively strong arms around my middle. I flinched, my hands flying wide as I made sure that neither of us went crashing to the floor.

"Princess Mira!" came the muffled cry. I glanced down to see Shanna hugging my torso with all her might, features marred by trails of tears.

"Shanna, Gods, are you okay?" My heart jumped again. Had something else befallen the girl? Or perhaps there really was something about the water and Emenians and it was changing her already. A million terrifying options raced through my mind as I struggled to loosen the girl's grip on me.

Succeeding only slightly, I finally gripped the girl's cheeks, quieting her as soothingly as I could.

"Calm down, Shanna. What's wrong?" I spoke quietly, channeling my father's soothing voice.

The girl took a deep, rattling breath, attempting to steady herself, the small, quivering hands tight on my arms.

"I was so worried about you." Shanna's eyes flickered over the room, as if someone may surprise us at any moment. "You're Adrialian, and you went into the cursed water. After what your father said, I wasn't sure what to think." She sniffled hard.

"I'm alright, Shanna. Really, I'm fine." I grinned at the girl, quickly wiping tears from her face. While the ambassador's daughter was a bit wild and a little hysterical, there was still something so charming about her. I had no regrets about risking the curse to make sure she was safe.

With a gut-wrenching sigh, I realized that I'd never really had a friend before. I wasn't sure Rhoe counted since he was technically paid to pay attention to me but… I didn't want to dwell on that right now. This feeling in my chest was foreign but oh so welcome.

Finally, I managed to extricate myself, and Shanna sat with me. For just a moment, I forgot my worries, letting the other woman's overexcited voice soothe my ragged soul.

Shanna didn't need much guidance from me and chattered without much input from me. Discussing her family's impending trip back home to Emen, her excitement at seeing her pets again, and even swooned over how Rhoe had carried me out of the water. "He came charging out. You were hanging on to his neck while he shouted orders. And Your Highness, the hand placement, it was everything." She covered her eyes with the back of her hand, and I grinned. I didn't remember that part and found it more enjoyable to remember through her memories than my own. Especially the part where my father's men had recoiled away from us…from me. Their future queen.

I'd seen the look in their eyes, and I saw it still, lurking behind the placid expressions of the men around me. They were worried. And unlike Shanna, I knew they weren't worried for me, but rather about me.

My mind wandered, soothed by Shanna's words, filled with the sounds of the ocean waves crashing into the sea walls below. Odd, since my room faced the city side of the palace, not the ocean. But nonetheless, the crashing, the deep churning was suddenly all I could hear. My mind was filled with thoughts of the foaming water, the smooth currents. The smell of salt flooded my nose, and my fingers tightened on the sofa as I pictured how easily I could cut through the water, my body smooth, fast, aerodynamic. It was both completely familiar and painfully alien. Power flew through my veins, hot and throbbing.

"Mira? Mira, wait, where are you going?" Shanna's voice broke through my thoughts.

The feel, the smell of the ocean suddenly vanished, replaced by a startling awareness that I now stood in my doorway, staring out into the hall. An on-duty king's guard watched me from a few paces away, his helmeted face shadowed.

I gave him a quick nod, trying not to sway on the spot, hoping my body wouldn't betray me enough to let me fall to the ground with him watching. I willed this into truth, forcing my knees to straighten and hold.

I'd heard of sleepwalking. Was that what had I just done? Had I dozed off during Shanna's conversation? The girl looked at me, obviously confused. I put on a shaky smile. There was no reason to confuse her, especially when I myself didn't know what happened. Guilt crowded into my mind as she bit her lip.

I'd just assured her I was fine, only to pull whatever this was.

"I'm sorry, Shanna. I just got distracted when I thought I heard someone in the other room." I tried my best to look apologetic. My heart was pounding in my ears. I hoped my lie would be good enough to cover it up.

Shanna bought the lie, grinning broadly at me. "I completely understand, your highness." She joined me by the door, reaching out to clasp my hand between hers, "I know that we are leaving today, but I'd love it if you'd write. Perhaps I can come back for another visit. You know that I'd love to see Rora or another of the northern cities."

My chest warmed as I gave the girl a small, quick hug, "That sounds perfect. Perhaps I can come to Emen someday and visit." My throat tightened at the joy and excitement that filled Shanna's face, followed quickly by another hug and a hundred goodbyes.

By the time Shanna left the private royal suites, I really was exhausted. I hesitated by my door again, looking around. When I drifted off in my thoughts, where had I been going?

My eye was caught by the billowing drapes at the very end of the hall, a wide arched balcony, white and black marble intertwined to form the structure, and it was inlaid with smooth dark sea stones. A commodity because of the risk it took to retrieve them from the bottom of the Great Sea. Just beyond the balcony lay a wide-open view of the crystal blue sky, and below, the Great Sea, its waves quiet and peaceful in the late-summer afternoon.

My heart pounded. Ignoring the flush that went through my body, I moved into my room, slamming the door shut. "I just haven't woken up yet. That's it," I chanted softly to myself as I toed on my sandals. As I smoothed my hands over the rich silks across my bed, I found myself watching the door once again.

My heart seemed to beat with each crash of the waves against the beaches below, the sound reverberating through my skull.

Blowing hard through my nose, I pushed up and dashed across the room, throwing the heavy lock across my door. Effectively sealed inside, I walked back to my bed, refusing to let my eyes or my mind stray again.

Chapter Ten

"What are you doing here?" I planted my hands my hips as I glared at Rhoe's tall figure in my doorway. I was ridiculously glad to see him, but I couldn't let him know that. He'd never let me hear the end of it.

He dropped a shoulder against the doorframe, handsome face twisting into his trademark smirk. "Now, now. Is that any way to greet your friend?" He tutted at me before shoving past into my room. "No wonder you're so well liked, Your Highness." Sarcasm laced every word.

Happiness raced in my blood, joy at the way that he'd obviously moved through his earlier anger at me. Thank the Gods, because my father was asking me to stay in these Gods-damned rooms for another three days now. I wasn't sure if it was because his advisors, including Homer, were still concerned I might be cursed or if they just weren't sure how to address the fact I hadn't been.

They knew that some people were more impacted by the cursed water and Trayon's call. But how to explain away the fact that a princess, a sole heir to the kingdom, hadn't been taken? They couldn't decide. I felt as if I were back on *The DeArtinan* dancing above the open water, an easy meal for the hungry gossip mill.

"I'm still not sick," I told Rhoe as he brushed by. "Aren't you impressed?"

He was in full armor today, most likely on his way to retrieve my father for court needs.

He cast an incredulous look. "You won't get sick, Mira."

"And how do you know that?"

"Because." Rhoe leaned over my lunch tray and picked at my leftovers. "I know everything."

I rolled my eyes, plopping down on a small settee by the window. "My father always says that."

"About me? Well, good. He's correct, then."

"Arrogance doesn't look good on you."

"Nor ignorance on you." His words were gentle, but the truth cut deeply. "Tell me what happened in the water."

I stared at him dumbly. "What do you mean?"

"You were almost ashore. You could've practically leapt onto the sand from where you were. Yet you went back to your knees. You chose to fall back into it."

I sputtered at the dangerous hiss in his voice as he spoke the last words. "Where is this coming from?"

"I'm saying something happened to you. Before I could get to you." Rhoe's throat worked, and a thread of worry wound its way around my heart. There was no way he had felt that bolt of power, had he? He couldn't have. I had imagined that.

"It was nothing."

"Nothing?" The word was a whisper from my lips. Rhoe was in my space now, leaning over me, his bright hair curtaining his face as those stunning blue eyes found mine. My breathing accelerated. It was real. My heart rate doubled, making my fingertips throb as I twisted them together.

"What really happened when you hit those waves?" he asked. "I know something did. I felt it."

"You felt it too?"

His sharp intake of breath made me realize that I'd stepped into him, my hands on his waist, my body against his. "Mira."

"I thought I was crazy. I thought that I had dreamed it."

"Mira, please. I need to know everything. All of it. Even what doesn't seem important."

"Rhoe, it felt like… I can't even describe it." My eyes fluttered shut, and this time the images were bright and vivid. Deep-blue waves, sparkling scales. The feeling of thick curls tangled in my fingers. Someone calling my name, deep and rumbling against my throat. I gasped, my eyes snapping open once again.

Rhoe was holding my hands away from his body, staring down at me with something akin to shock.

"What?"

"You…" Rhoe swallowed loudly. "You're right. You must've dreamed it. All I felt was fear."

I stared at my friend, feeling the tightness in his grip, seeing the way the pulse at his throat fluttered. He was lying to me. I couldn't remember another time in all of our friendship that he had lied to me. I was too worried to be upset. Something had to be very, very wrong.

Pushing down the anxiety that rose in my chest, I stepped back, rolling my eyes. A nervous laugh forced its way up my chest.

"You're right. I was covered in salt water. You throw in a little air deprivation, and I was feeling all kinds of things." I forced another laugh. "You're lucky you weren't in there with me. I probably would've accidentally drowned you."

The air around us calmed slightly, and Rhoe scoffed loudly before sauntering across the room.

"Nope, you're stuck with me, sunshine." Flopping onto the chair Shanna had been in earlier, Rhoe crossed one leg over his knee then began unloosening his boot laces. "And I mean that. I'm going to be here all night long."

I snorted, crossing my arms. "Don't you find it a little odd that my father assigns you, an unwed man, very capable of ruining or compromising his royal daughter, to sleep in the same bedroom as her?"

Silence fell around the room, and I choked back my need to retract the words. The statement hadn't sounded so brash in my mind. Rhoe had slept in the royal suites many times. Anytime there was a threat to either Father or me, he was here. But things were changing. *We* were changing.

Dropping his second boot, Rhoe approached me slowly, his face unreadable. He got so close that it took everything in my entire body to not step back, to not let my gaze falter as he looked down at me, those bright, unnerving eyes sparkling. Excruciatingly slow, Rhoe dropped to his knees in front of me.

I concentrated very hard on keeping my legs from shaking as he held himself a breath away from me. When he spoke again, his voice low and soft, it sent sparks across my skin.

"Perhaps it is because he knows that I would never do anything in this world or another that would put you in harm's way, even if that means protecting you from myself."

His head bowed, "I am yours, Princess Mira."

I couldn't breathe. The heat from his body throbbed around us.

After a breathless moment, he stood slowly. Raising two fingers to my chin, Rhoe gripped it firmly. "Always."

The moment drew before us, tight and begging. But I couldn't handle it or the intensity of his stare. I broke his gaze, stepping out of his grip.

Rhoe smirked, and instantly we were back to normal, "Or perhaps it is because he knows that I prefer my lovers to be less cursed, less trouble, and decidedly better dancers."

My jaw dropped with a mock gasp, and Rhoe only had a moment before my hand swiped for his face, barely missing. Growling, I shook free of his spell and jabbed a finger into the muscles of his chest.

"Take it back."

He was laughing, his brows raised as he shuffled back a few paces. "Which part?"

"All of it." I said, striking out with a quick jab, my fist landing playfully on his shoulder.

He swung to his feet, danced away, his feet light on the floor. Mocking me with every movement.

I followed, a grin on my face, even while a certain level of mortification remained in my brain.

Rhoe stopped, holding up a hand to his temple in the king's guard salute. "Princess Mira, I swore an oath to your father. And that oath included honesty."

He shot me a wide grin as I advanced upon him, taking advantage of his showboating. One quick swipe of my leg and a jerk of his wide shoulders, and I sent him tumbling to the floor.

Crowing with victory, I straddled him easily, like we had done so many other times in our training.

"Yield!" I shouted, hips and thighs pinning him to the floor. He cackled until I let my knees press into the soft muscle along his ribs.

I swept my arms wide, pumping them towards Artio in victory. Rolling his eyes, Rhoe patted my thigh twice. "Fine, fine, I yield. But you're still a horrible dancer."

I became more and more aware of the way his belly lifted and moved me with every breath. A sharp heat stung the edges of my mind. It was as if we were combined now, our bodies so comfortably moving together. Much like we would if I were…oh Suns. I had to stop this now, before I lost all matter of control.

I stuck my tongue out at him, desperate to lighten the mood. Yet Rhoe's eyes remained dark, boring into mine. I looked away, focusing on the reality that I'd temporarily forgotten all about the curse and even the pitiful sorrow that had been cascading through my veins since Pierse's death.

"I'm sorry…I can't do this right now." I relaxed my thighs, rising to my knees to put more distance between myself and the plane of his body. A hot blush crept up my neck. It didn't matter how many times I'd been in that same position during training. There was something different about it tonight. Something more primal and forbidden.

The feeling only increased as Rhoe gently reached up and held my hips. His flesh was burning, even through my clothing. My breath caught.

Rhoe tightened his hold, unbothered by my flurry of emotions. His white teeth flashed as he levered himself up. Our faces were suddenly closer than ever.

For a moment, insanity took over, and I considered throwing caution to the wind, dropping my hips, and letting myself sink into the delightful heat that was Rhoe. How many times had I thought of him like this? Imagining what he'd feel like against me?

"Princess," Rhoe said, his voice rough.

"Chosen," I answered, swallowing back those lurking desires. I was a princess, a future queen and ruler. There was no world in which I could indulge in anything even close to this. And Rhoe knew it.

Distance. We needed distance. Moving so quickly I almost stumbled, I thrust myself back and up, standing over Rhoe with what I hoped was a cool expression. Before he was even on his feet, I'd moved back to my bed, sitting on the edge and picking up one of Homer's agendas to mindlessly stare at. Anything to cool the embarrassment and shame at my own needs.

I was a future queen.

Queens did not spar unsupervised with handsome soldiers. My chin came up. I wouldn't disappoint my father in this way.

Rhoe was either an excellent actor or was unaware of the tumultuous feelings I battled down into my belly. He remained on the floor, stretching now with the jaunty confidence of a spoiled house cat as he reached for the small table alongside my sofa. "Now, what do you have around here in the way of cards? I've heard you're an atrocious gambler as well, and I mean to pad my wallet this week."

I almost hugged him with relief at the comfortable return to normalcy but then realized it would get us back right where we'd just barely gotten out of. So with a laugh, I snagged a stack of playing cards from my nightstand, and after tossing it at Rhoe, I led my friend to the common room. My heart may have been a little confused, but somehow as he sat down across from me, it still felt lighter than it had in days.

***

"Mira," a deep voice boomed loud in my ears.

I sat up with a grunt of pain. The ground under me was hard, nothing like the soft silks of my bed. Where in the Dark Realm was I? Groaning, I parted my eyes and stared blankly up into Rhoe's face. He and several king's guard stood over me, their expressions grim and pale.

I tried for humor, even as a wave of nauseating dread unfurled in my belly. "Just because I didn't let you win last night, you don't need to wake me up like this."

"Easy, *minu*," another voice spoke, drawing my attention to another member of my welcoming party. Homer was there, his clothes rumbled in a way that was decidedly not him. Since when had it gotten so bright in my room?

I reached up, my hand spreading wide to block out the offensive morning sunlight. "Homer? What's going on?"

Homer spoke again, but I couldn't see past the glare of the sun off the guards' golden armor. His voice was rushed and anxious. "Get her back to her room. Now, Chosen. We will meet you there as soon as we can."

The harsh ground was gone in an instant as the familiar scent of Rhoe settled over my nose. For the first time I could remember, he smelled…different. I couldn't decide if I hated the scent or loved it, but either way, I allowed him to loop his arms around my body, carrying me bridal style.

"This is a little embarrassing," I whispered to him. "Did I fall asleep on the couch?" The light was so bright around us. I clenched my eyes shut hard, trying to remember what had happened after Rhoe had won his handful of coins in our game of poker.

"You did," Rhoe spoke, his voice sharp and laced with nerves. "And then I took you to your bed."

I huffed in the smell of him, his neck salty from the warm morning air. It was still appealing, but I found myself wanting something else too. My skin itched, and I curled farther into myself. Everything felt wrong.

"Wait. Did you say you took me back to my bed?"

"The back way. Open it up now." Rhoe wasn't speaking to me anymore, but his voice hadn't lost any of that sharpness. I tried to look around him but saw only flashes of stone and polished walkways. We were traveling up one of the back ways to the royal quarters. Every time I tried to focus, my head would ache and throb, and so finally, I gave up, sagging into the security and warmth of Rhoe's arms once again.

"Rhoe, my body, it aches. What happened to me?"

Rhoe hitched me higher. "Not another word until we get you to your rooms."

I nodded, overcome by the tiredness that tugged at my muscles. My eyes slowly fluttered shut as the familiar rocking motion of Rhoe's gait pulled me into another dark, dreamless sleep.

A cool, damp cloth woke me from this sleep again, but the fog cleared from my mind quickly.

I jerked up in bed, the familiar room dim and quiet around me. "Rhoe?"

"He'll be back in a bit. I'm here, love," my father spoke, his voice gentle.

I smiled, relieved that my father's presence helped pry me from the last vestiges of my sleep. Ever so slowly, I was able to force one eye open then the other. My father was there, his usually warm face drawn tight with stress. He was staring at me hard enough that I nearly recoiled away when my vision cleared enough to read his features. I'd never seen him look like this, except maybe when he told me what happened to Mama.

His thumbs stroked the backs of my hands as I took a deep breath. Fear was a living thing, racing through my mind, my veins, my belly. "Father. What happened? No one would tell me before."

There was silence then, long enough that I pushed up on my hands, needing to see what had silenced him. Heart pounding, I asked again, "What happened?"

Father shook his head, dark hair looking ever more silver as he glanced over his shoulder. His personal guards, Astran and Loucas, stood at either side of my closed doors. Their faces were stoic as always, but there was something different today.

They were armed.

I cocked my head, staring at those long broadswords. There were no weapons in the royal suites. Maybe a small dagger or two, a ceremonial blade. But not like what they wore today. Those were battle gear. Deadly and at the ready.

"Papa…" My voice broke over the word. Something was very, very wrong. My hand reached for his on the sheets, only to find I could only move my limbs a small distance before something pinched at my wrist.

I glanced down, surprised. There were manacles on my wrists, the metal cold and heavy against my skin. I blinked rapidly, wondering if I was still in some kind of dream. Raising one wrist, I turned it this way and that, unable to process what was happening.

"Father, what is this?"

"You're sick, *minu*. Very sick."

"I feel fine. This isn't necessary. My mind is intact." I tugged hard at the cuffs, staring at where they'd been attached to the wall with fist-sized bolts. When my knees jerked, fear making me want to curl into a fetal position, the same tugging motion made me realize that my legs were cuffed as well, the chains falling to the floor, where they were bolted against the pillar closest to the door.

I had been jailed.

In a matter of moments, I'd gone from being the second-highest-ranking Adrialian citizen to nothing but a prisoner. The thought sent frosty panic down my bloodstream, and I couldn't stop staring down at those chains. The ones on my wrist were smaller, easier to move, and so I did, shifting my body so that I could look at my father as I picked up one wrist and then the other.

"You've chained me? Why?"

His jaw flexed. "It's for your own safety, daughter."

"For my own safety," I said quietly, still processing, trying to remember. Everything was so fuzzy after I'd stretched out on the sofa. The last thing I remembered was being carried. Hysteria rose in my chest as I looked down at my hands once more. "My safety, or yours?"

Astran, the more nervous of my father's personal guard, shifted by the door. My gaze flew to them. "And you let him do this? I am the future queen of Adrial!"

Fury made my words shake, but neither guard moved again.

My father's hands cupped my face, forcing my eyes from the guard. "Mira, listen to me. You can do this. You can beat this. I know it. I've already spoken with Captain Shelden. We're going to keep you here for a few days and see if you come out of it on your own. Otherwise I will send all my best, and Captain will lead us to fight whatever it is that compels you so."

"Compels me?"

My father's eyes closed.

"Father, what do you mean by compels?"

For a second, I didn't think he would answer. But then he spoke, the words stiff and unyielding. "You were found climbing the wall."

"The wall," I repeated, my voice strange even to my own ears. "The sea wall?"

He nodded. "Rhoe was able to reach you before you climbed over, but it was close." His eyes dropped to my wrists. "Too close. I won't let this curse take you."

"So now you've chained me up," I said again, still staring down at my hands.

"I had no choice."

Every part of my body was suddenly filled with white-hot strength and power, so strong and powerful that when I lurched forward, fury giving me power, my father fell backwards, flinching away from me as I snapped the words at him. "There's always a choice."

"No," he said, grunting as Loucas helped him to his feet. "There is not. I love you, *minu*. You will be safe here. We just have to get through the first few days. I have the entire Court working on a solution. We can fight this!"

"No, no, no…" I had stepped off the bed, my feet awkward and heavy as the chains milled around my ankles. "Please don't leave me. I don't want to be alone."

"You will be safe here," he repeated again, his voice dull and sad.

I stumbled forward, suddenly desperate for him to stay, for someone to explain why this was happening to me, for someone to tell me what to do.

"Please, please," I shouted, running towards my father, blind and desperate as the shackles on my ankles drew tight and caught me off balance, forcing me to my knees as Astran and Loucas surged forward, thrusting my father behind them and towards the door.

They were acting like I was a monster. As if I might really hurt my father. The thought made bile bubble up in my chest. "Please," I whispered one last time, meeting Astran's wide eyes as he forced Loucas out after my father.

With one sweep of his arm, they were gone, out of my line of sight. The next moment, Astran was gone too, leaving me completely alone, trapped not only in my room, but in a flurry of thoughts more dangerous than any sickness I'd ever felt.

***

"Mira? Hello, Mira, wake up."

I bolted upright, my body aching with the impossibility of the position I'd fallen asleep in, draped over the edge of my bed, my body contorted as I had tried to sleep with the chains and still be as close to the door and my father as possible.

"Rhoe?" My voice was rough, and I cleared my throat before trying again. "Rhoe, are you here?"

A match was struck, lighting a candle, and I jerked sideways, groaning at the pain in my muscles as I found Rhoe in the mostly dark. He was stripped of his armor and weapons, standing in front of me in loose, long pants, a haphazard tunic, and bare feet.

My eyes grew round. "How did you get in here? Astran and Loucas—"

"Still report to me," Rhoe said, shrugging, the candle throwing off flickers of light over his body. "At least in theory. Besides, those two would never guess I'd go over the railing."

"Why would you go over the railing?"

Rhoe didn't answer, and maybe that was because he was staring wildly at me. "Chains? They put you in chains?"

Something in his voice, the choked-out words, broke me, and I crumbled towards the ground, only to have a strong pair of arms sweep me up and hold me against a warm chest. The candle was moved somewhere to the floor and cast a strange eerie orange glow over the pair of us.

"Shhh," Rhoe murmured into my hair, his breath hot on my skin. So hot that I shivered as he clutched me closer, moving across the room so that he could sit on the edge of my bed. My body straddled his, drenched in the salty scent of him.

"I'm so sorry," Rhoe said again, not releasing me. "I didn't mean for this to happen. I didn't think that it would be like this."

"You're still not sick," I said after a long moment, nuzzling into the soft skin of his neck. "I'm so glad."

Rhoe was quiet, rocking me back and forth in the dark. "We're going to find a way."

"There is no way. I'm cursed, Rhoe. Unless you strap me to the front of *The DeArtinan* and fight Trayon himself, I'm doomed."

Silence fell again, but it was tense, just like Rhoe's arms around my waist. I'd never been held like this, and while the panic from the day wasn't gone, there was a pleasant ache forming, a heat that seemed to bloom across every part of my skin.

"There's another way," Rhoe said quietly.

"What other way?" I pushed away, my body bowing away from his hold. "What do you mean, Rhoe?"

"You could go."

"Go where?"

Rhoe was completely and utterly still. "To the water."

"The water? Why? Trayon will…"

"Yes, he will send his best and worst. Especially for you. Daughter of the sun…" Rhoe's throat bobbed, and for the first time since he entered the room, suspicion began to wind through my mind.

"I don't understand." I pushed him away, stumbling off his lap. "You don't want me to survive?"

"You're the princess of Adrial. There's a very good chance that Trayon will want more from you than food for his fish. Do you understand that?"

My chest heaved, and again I wished for the room to be better lit. That way I could see for myself if my dearest friend—was telling the truth.

"How do you know all of this?"

Rhoe stood, shifting me to the bed I could hear the sound of his bare feet slapping along the marble. "I…"

"No more lies, Rhoe. I want to know."

I moved away from him, into the moonlight streaming in from my window. In the back of my mind, I could hear the crashing of the sea. "Now, Rhoe."

Rhoe had moved so that the brilliant summer night outlined his tall, muscular form. He was running his hands through his hair, his features desperate, even in the near-dark. I felt fear for the first time since he'd arrived.

Time passed. Too much time.

"You know what? Leave, Rhoe. Leave if you won't tell me."

"Mira—"

"Leave!" I shouted, but this time my voice echoed off the walls, the ceiling, making the sound bounce and sting my own eardrums. I clapped my hands over them, cringing at the sound of my own voice. What was happening, I wondered, angry tears gathering in my eyes.

Curling up on the floor, my back to the balcony that Rhoe had climbed in on, I promised myself over and over again that I would beat this, that I would be better than this. And on that promise, I once again gave in to sleep and let it take me away.

Chapter Eleven

I couldn't say how long I'd been stuck in my rooms. After the first day, I started to lose track of time. There was only the darkness that lurked at the back of my vision and the ever-present crashing of waves against the sea walls.

I wanted to see them. At first I begged.

Rhoe was the first. I remember his face as a blur. I screamed at him. Furious. Or I thought I had. I was honestly not sure. I had lost all control. There had been only me and the chains keeping me attached to this land.

In my thoughts and dreams, I'd seen Artio, the tall, dark-skinned male who rose above me, shaking his head, his lips curled in fury as he yelled at a figure just beyond me. In other dreams, I held my father's crown at the beaches of Trayon's sea. But when I stumbled and dropped the gilded crown into the water, it dissolved.

I thought of my father, begging at my bedside, dragging Artio's priests in. Another day, I thought perhaps Captain Shelden was there, his deep, gruff tones so at odds with my father's smooth comments.

In the end, they all left.

Everyone left.

It was just me and my chains and the crashing of waves.

I wondered if Pierse was at peace now. And if I would join him. I wondered if Rhoe's strange words about the sea god needing me might hold more weight than I'd imagined.

And in my dreams, I saw someone. A dark male. Instinct told me he was dangerous, but it didn't matter anymore.

He was important. That much was clear. But as days passed, he blurred into desperation and madness.

The solution to my madness came to me simply.

I would go to the God of the Sea, and I would make him remove the curse. I just had to find the right moment, when my chains were off, and then I would jump into the water.

My balcony wouldn't work. But the answer came to me as I remembered the origin story of this curse.

How the bride of Adrial had leaped into the ocean from her wedding balcony. The palace in Port Sol had been built around and onto from the original castle here. And there were balconies that hung over the ocean.

The plan was simple. Remove the chains. Leap into the water. And when Trayon came for me, strike a bargain to save not just me, but all of my people. Turning catastrophe into opportunity. My father would be proud once I secured the curse's demise and our people's future.

These thoughts were the only things that kept my sane while I waited for my moment. It arrived on a sunny, hot morning days after Father first chained me. A young guard, nervous as could be, arrived to deliver my breakfast.

I sat on my sofa, waiting, watching as he fumbled his way through the room to put down my breakfast tray. Once he did, he straightened, and I saw the nervous sweat dotting his forehead.

"Hello," I murmured, keeping my voice quiet.

He moved forward, as I had hoped, saluting me briefly before gesturing to the food. "I brought you breakfast, Your Highness."

"Thank you." I stood slowly, watching as his gaze followed the lines of my body. "I have a small request for you, if you have the time."

"Of course, Your Highness. What can I do to help?"

"My new jewelry…" I held up my wrists. "They're rubbing. My father sent over some medication to put underneath. Would you mind releasing them so I could treat them?"

"I can't do that, Your Highness."

I pouted. "He told me it was alright. He sent it himself. You can check."

The guard hesitated then walked to the container that I had pointed out. The note beside it was indeed from my father and explained what the healer recommended.

The guard read it quickly then scanned my body once more. "Everything does seem in order."

I held out my wrist and waited. The chink of metal on metal confirmed exactly what I had hoped. I was free. The moment the metal fell from my wrist, I twisted it around to grip the guard's arm. His startled face was the last thing I saw before I flipped him around, pressing my still-chained arm around his neck and slowly, carefully rendering him unconscious.

As he slumped to the ground, I grabbed the pair of keys that I knew unlocked all of my remaining locks. Nothing had felt so good in my entire life as when the metal chains slithered to the floor.

Free. Finally.

I walked resolutely through the quarters, my eyes fixed on the balcony at the end of the hall. At the spiraling white and black marble there. It took only a moment—or perhaps it was an entire year—and then I was standing there, at the edge, leaning over the rail.

Behind me was my old life, ahead of me a new one. The curse thrummed in my veins, calling out for me.

"I'll be back, Father," I said into the summer breeze, and then with every intention I could gather, I plunged myself into my next quest.

I hit the water, my mouth wide open in a scream. Every part of my cried out at the wrongness, the danger of the liquid all around me, but my body seemed to rejoice. I cursed the sea sickness as I flailed underwater, the fall plunging my body deep into the dark waters of the Great Sea.

There was a current around my legs, tangling them and confusing my sense of direction. As I reached desperately out into the cold water, my fingers found nothing. No sense of up or down, no movement or pressure to fight with.

Nothing.

My lungs ached, desperately hanging on to the last vestiges of my earlier breath as I kicked and failed, legs awkward as I tried to find my way back to air. My eyes were slowly getting used to the briny water, and I looked around, vision blurry as I searched for safety, for life.

But instead, it was there. My shadow, the silvery dark cloud that I'd seen when Pierse was taken. I knew it then, felt it more strongly than I felt the life being pulled from my body. He'd come for me, for my death, this shadow of power.

I arched away from the shadowy black hands that reached for me. The last of my air bubbled out of my lips as my eyes cleared, and I found myself staring at another Mer. This one was not the delicate beauty of the golden one who took Pierse. This… This was a warrior, a bringer of bloodshed and pain.

His skin was a smooth cream, silver scales framing his forehead, his cheekbones. His body was powerful, big, marked with inked lines that swirled and snaked across his torso and down across a muscular belly. The rest of him darkened into a pair of shining black fins that swirled and contracted behind him.

He was beautiful, dazzling in his deadliness. For a moment, I almost wished for him to act, to do something, because I could no longer stand to linger here, between him and the ocean's grasp.

But still, he just watched, obsidian eyes on my face. His hair swirled around his face in the current's pull, and for an instant I almost grew angry. Was he just going to sit there, watching me die?

My anger must've been visible, as suddenly he snarled at me, a deadly smile showing off the sharp incisors. Then, quick as lightning, he struck.

His hand gripped my ankle first, yanking me deeper as thick arms wrapped around my body. I slapped at his grip, desperate even as my eyes began to blur again. I was out of time. I was out of air.

It was time for death's decision.

Distantly, I felt the pressure of his thumbs on my jaw, claws scratching as he tilted my head away from him. And then pain, sharp and clarifying, as the dark Mer bit into the side of my neck.

Ah, I thought. This made sense. Out of everything that had happened, this made sense.

It was the end.

Pure, simple. Dark. I welcomed it, my hands moving to cup the back of the Mer's head, where his dark hair swirled across my fingertips. I could feel his pulse somehow, or perhaps that was my own desperate beat pounding in my ears.

Pain throbbed through my entire body, the water rushing past my lips, into my throat, flooding my body from the inside out, even as those razor-sharp teeth held. My hands gave up on holding him. I was powerless against him, a small inconvenience to his attacking form.

I felt the vibrations of his body against my neck. He was growling? Or perhaps I was simply dying. I hadn't expected it to be pain free. But I also hadn't expected to feel so weightless and relaxed.

I gave over to it completely, letting the Mer take what he wanted.

The ocean had claimed me, and I had nothing left in me to fight.

Chapter Twelve

My consciousness tugged at me, a surge of heat making me gasp. I recoiled, arching away from hands that brushed across my skin. Their grip was hard, warm, and unmovable.

I was trapped. I dragged more air into my aching lungs, trying to get my eyes to open. They were sluggish, my hands weak as I fought the hands still holding me.

"Please," I shouted, but only a grunted whisper came out. And then we were moving, quick jolting steps that made me realize that I wasn't caged. I was being held. And suddenly my memories were slamming back into my system. My desperate jump, the strangling water filling my lungs, and the shadow waiting for me in the cursed water.

And his bite.

I struggled harder, lashing out. There was a muffled curse and then more noises, more footsteps. Someone must've found me, must've saved me. The shadow hadn't won after all.

I coughed, and my belly and chest spasmed uncontrollably as air slid into my throat. My body rejected the air even as it craved it, and I knew my fingernails were tearing apart whomever had managed to find me. Desperate, I wanted it to stop. I wanted to quiet my body, but I couldn't. Everything instinct was begging me to move, to fight, to breathe.

A soft rumble under my cheek briefly quieted me. But still, panic rose in my chest.

Hot breath warmed my forehead as more footsteps surrounded us, and a flurry of words were thrown around. They seemed familiar, but I couldn't decipher the meaning, my brain still trapped in its panic.

"Easy, Princess. Easy. I've got you," a deep voice said, so close I knew it had to have come from whomever carried me. I was lifted then, even higher as more hands pressed over me. For a moment, I couldn't breathe at all, and then energy seemed to pulse into me, filling my body in a moment and making me accurately aware of every inch of my skin, as if the skin itself, or perhaps my body itself, was stretching, changing, adjusting itself over the skeleton I'd had my entire life.

It was horrible.

I writhed on the ground, grateful for the fresh air in my lungs but horrified at the pressure of the hard floor at my back. I wanted my father. I wanted Rhoe. Hell, I would even take Homer. Anyone I could get that would take my pain away. To make my body feel less like it was a stranger, like it was attempting to crawl away from my very soul.

The energy slowly subsided, and while I no longer felt the pulsing power flooding my body, the sense of discontent still lurked below the surface. Something was wrong, something deep, deep in my chest.

As I slowly became more aware, my eyes focused. The sky above me was unfocused, but there were faces all around. A swirl of bright eyes and colorful clothing. I tried to smile but began to cough again instead. A large man pressed a hand against my shoulder, gently easing me back flat to the marble. My muscles quivered and shook in his hold, and I focused on the inked lines that climbed up his neck.

"Rest now. You will need it." His voice was relaxing, but not the same one as before. Another man, his bright-red hair gleaming, leaned over the one who had first spoken to whisper in his ear.

"She's coming. The General went for her."

I licked my lips, desperate to communicate with them. They should know who I was. How badly I needed to get home. My father would be completely distraught. I needed to tell him I was alright. That I was so sorry, what a stupid idea this had all been.

"My father…" I tried to say, but again the words came out garbled and unintelligible. I swallowed, my throat feeling more raw than I could ever remember it. "I need…" Frustration bloomed as all I managed to do was squeak out a few sounds before collapsing back onto the floor.

One of the women, still a blur in my eyes, kneeled by where my hand lay limply against the hard floor. I felt her fingers in mine, intertwining them as she murmured soft, senseless things. A song of sweetness that sliced through my worries like a blade through silk.

Comfort seeped into my person, not enough to completely combat the panic coursing through my body, but enough to draw my attention briefly. I closed my eyes, trying to focus on my body, my limbs. I wondered briefly why my neck didn't hurt after that bite, but I couldn't focus long enough to dwell on it.

There was the sound of running now, a group of people from what I could tell. "Please, where am I? I think I fell…" To my relief, my mouth formed the words now. My voice was soft, but every head snapped to me. The pounding footsteps joined us, and I took the opportunity to try to sit up one last time. I made it to my elbow, my eyes focusing on a newcomer who the group parted to allow through.

Something about her struck me deep in my chest.

Her hair was dark as night, but something about it made it seem to glow with color, dark blues and purples swirling in as she fell to her knees at my side. Eyes like sapphires stared at me, glossy and wide as her cool hands found the sides of my face. A spark of something raced from her fingers to my skin.

"My name is…" I coughed once more then wetted my lips.

But she was already smiling, a tear slipping free to race down her cheeks. "We know exactly who you are," the woman said, her voice hushed and full of awe. A gentle hand pressed my hair away from my face.

My chest heaved, and I couldn't look away. She smiled at me again, but the gesture was broken by a quiet sob. The big man behind me shifted, leveraging his knees under my shoulders so that I could sit up a bit more and face the woman now holding me. I was stuck again by her beauty, the creamy smooth skin, the way she was staring at me.

The singing stopped, and suddenly a pit grew in my stomach. I could feel my nerves as they skittered down my body, making goose bumps race along my skin.

Not because of this woman, but because of what I saw directly behind her. Her head shifted again, but no pretty play of colors on dark hair could distract me now.

Because I was staring into the water. Not just any water. I was staring directly into an ocean, a school of small yellow fishing swimming by as I watched. A breath later, a long, angular silver fish darted through the lapis-colored water.

My heart pounded in my ears. Mere steps from where I lay across a smooth stone walkway, sea creatures were going about their usual underwater activities. The hauntingly beautiful blue tones of the ocean were deep and dark in some places, and as I tilted my head back, I watched as the rippling waters lightened as they grew more and more shallow.

My eyes abandoned the waves, refocusing on the wall of water that loomed over us. It curled away from the platform, arcing up and away from us. And directly in front of me, a circle of stones, twice as tall as any man I'd met, stood looking for all the world like an enormous entryway. Here, the water suspended in a flowing stasis and glittered like a reflecting pool tilted on its end.

I was quite literally staring into the bottom of the Great Sea. My heart was hammering, my body tight and panicked, but I couldn't move. I moved my hand to the side, dragging my legs under my body as I leaned towards the water, drawn to the impossibility of it all.

My fingers spread across the smooth ground. I realized for the first time that I was sprawled across a platform of some kind, various walkways curling away into a plethora of buildings and structures. No, not just buildings. There was organization to them, in the neat way they were laid out.

A city. And not one in ruin. Even from here I could hear the soft chattering noises that always accompanied city life.

"Where am I?" I asked, surprising myself with the volume of it, how it echoed off the strange wall of liquid in front of me. I sounded different, and for a moment, I rationalized that I must be dead and in the Dark Realm.

The woman who had held my face so lovingly moved back to my side, picking up my hand. Her lips were cool against my palm as she cradled my still weak limb. "You are home, Miraceti. Home."

Darkness took me once again.

The next time I opened my eyes, I was staring up into a smooth stone ceiling. The light from the window filling the room with a warm glow that brought a soft smile to my face. I'd been dreaming of an underwater city. It had only been a dream. That made sense now.

I stretched a little, wondering how late I'd slept and if I could still catch my father at court. Swinging my legs over the edge of the bed, I stared briefly down at my legs. I was wearing a sort of thin, tight pants that ended mid-calf. Touching it, something uncurled in my chest. Because I'd never seen this kind of clothing before. But it was silky and soft and stretched over my skin as I stood, wobbling a little as I moved to the end of the bed.

I took a step forward and froze. Because no matter how much I wanted to rationalize the new clothes, the strange feelings... I remembered why my father had put me in this room. I had been a danger, a threat.

But my steps were light. The heavy chains that had been on my ankles for so many days were gone. Yet, where I'd expected joy, there was only dread.

Awareness slammed into me, making my breath come short in my lungs. I wasn't home with my father. I wasn't even locked up in that fucking tower.

I was under the Great Sea and in some kind of—I looked around—stone building. The furniture around me appeared similar to what we had in Port Sol, maybe more sparse, with none of the massive rugs that covered the floors at home. But still, familiar enough. Swallowing hard, I moved across the room towards the window that glowed back at me. But that couldn't be right. There was no way the sun could reach here.

When the glowing exterior came into view, I couldn't stop the gasp that fell from my lips. It wasn't the sun lighting up the room around me. Instead, it appeared the building itself was glowing slightly, or really, not the stones, but the sporadic and beautiful corals that had grown over innumerable areas of it. The coral, which I'd never seen so close, was a hundred different colors and shapes. The beautiful, chaotically placed corals put off light, not unlike a flickering candle, the illumination shifting, moving, a living thing against the harshness of the stone.

My eyes darted out to see what lay outside my window and the bright coral scattered there. I pressed against the open window, one finger gently inching towards a twisted coral in pale blue that spiraled up the side of the accented wall. The coral glowed brighter the moment my skin brushed it, and I snapped my hand back with a squeal of shock.

As soon as I recoiled, the coral resumed its normal warm light, and I tore my gaze from the fascinating lighting to look down over the edge of my balcony's wall. My breath left in a swift whoosh, and I gripped the wall to settle myself.

A city lay before me, an entire kingdom, mapped out in mostly neat lines. Buildings of varying heights and styles sprung up from all sides. I caught a glimpse of a centered oval, rising above the buildings near to it. And even in the back, a thin ribbon of smoke cut through the air. There were even people on the streets, going about their business as if today were any other day of their life. It was painfully ordinary, which made it all the more shocking to me.

And entire world existed under the very waves I was raised to fear.

Shaking, I turned, craning my neck to first look down over the wall, then to look up above my balcony. Below me there were more levels, more tiers to this immense building.

My stomach clenched nervously as I saw not only other tiers and windows above me, but beyond that also a vast open space, seemingly full of air, before more of that glittering wall of water separating the unfathomable mass of water from all of us.

It reminded me of the large bubbles that the dishwashers would occasionally create while they scrubbed in the castle's kitchen. A sheen danced across it, vibrant and colorful. As I watched, I could see the flickering colors of fish and other sea creatures that continued their travels through the water above us. My jaw loosened in a mixture of shock and awe.

"My lady…" A shocked voice came from behind me, followed by the dropping of what sounded like metal plates. Spinning, I found myself face-to-face with a woman around my age, her face pale with shock. Hastily, she had dropped to her knees, gathering the plates up with quick, efficient moves. When she rose again, I recognized her.

I pointed at her, pieces of my memory filtering back through. "You… You were the one who was singing to me. When I woke up."

She gave a short bow, the fitted black dress that fell to her knees moving with her, the heavy gold threading catching my eye, "My name's Mehri, my lady. I am here to assist you in whatever you may need."

I didn't know the proper custom, so I remained very still, focusing on battling the anxiety that ebbed and flowed in my chest.

When the silence felt too thick, I finally cleared my throat and forced my tongue to move.

"Lady Mehri, where am I?"

She straightened, the delicate lines of her face solemn as she looked me up and down. "It is just Mehri, Your Highness. I know you have questions, my lady, and I've been instructed to answer them all. But first, let's get something for you to eat. You were asleep for some time."

I wanted to protest, but Mehri was already moving, gathering the final platter that she'd dropped. Tossing her deep-auburn hair over her shoulder, she disappeared briefly through a tall double-door entryway, reappearing before I had a chance to wonder where she was going. This platter remained intact as she brought it to me on the bed.

"There's a little bit of everything here, Your Highness. I wasn't sure what you liked best."

I stared down at the finely crafted tray, which was covered in a variety of colorful foods, none of which I had seen before, as well as a group of leafy greens and a charbroiled fish, head still intact. It all appeared to be normal, yet my stomach was still protesting the idea of putting anything else in my belly right now.

"Thank you, but I can't. My stomach… I can't imagine eating anything right now."

"You must, Your Highness. It's so important for the newcomers to Ceanus. You need to eat." Mehri set the tray on the edge of my bed and backed away. Her spine was rigid and straight, but the hand that reached over to brush my wrist was gentle.

I licked my lips, feeling how dry they were against my tongue as I scooted towards the other woman. "Ceanus." The word was foreign on my tongue but rolled smoothly off. Mehri gave me a small smile even as she pressed the tray closer. "How is…. How is all of this possible? I don't understand. I mean, this is an entire city, under the ocean. I—we—have no idea this place exists."

"Ceanus was a gift from the God Trayon, a place for us to gather and be safe," Mehri said, practiced and smooth. I noticed she slid farther from me once again.

"Mehri please. I need to ask you this." I watched her get up and begin to smooth the covers I'd tossed aside when I woke up. "Are we really in a bubble at the bottom of the Great Sea?"

Her throat worked, hands still busy with the blankets, and then she gave a short nod. "You are in Ceanus, my lady, in the palace to be more exact. The queen's gift and the arc keep us healthy, and Trayon's blessing keeps us safe."

"Trayon…" A shiver went down my spine. The same God who had cursed my people to a lifetime of madness had blessed these people with an entire underwater kingdom. "The God of the Sea? He made this place?"

Mehri nodded, and Father's wild tale about the Adrialian brothers who had split the city of Adrial raced across my mind. It couldn't be true.

"I've heard a story about a city that was taken into the ocean. But I just… I thought it was a story." Picking up a bit of fish with my fingers, I dropped it onto my tongue, needing to be doing something as my brain scrambled to process this new reality.

Mehri grinned at me, obviously pleased I was eating. "Don't worry, Your Highness. We are safe here." Behind my curtain of messy hair, I closed my eyes tight. I prayed to Artio, to the Mother, to Father in the dark, and even to the tricky God of the Sea.

Please, whatever this is… Make it be real.

When I opened my eyes, everything around me remained intact. The warmly lit room, the handmaiden looking at me quizzically. Even the soft noises of the city below rose up through my windows and filled my ears.

I took a rattling breath in.

I really was in Ceanus, the cursed kingdom at the bottom of the Great Sea. Which, until I'd woken up, I would've sworn was the punchline in a fairy tale meant to make sure children didn't venture into the ocean.

But it was real.

And I wasn't alone. There were more people—hundreds, maybe thousands from what I'd seen, and I'd only seen a fraction I was sure. My mind raced, my pulse rapidly quickening as Mehri suddenly pressed a hand against my shoulder, her slender fingers cupping my bare skin. A moment later, she began to hum again, the sound soft in the chaos of my thoughts.

Before I could pull away, my nerves settled and focused. I breathed deep, my shoulders shaking as I slowly got a grip on the gravity of the situation.

"I thought…" I swallowed, my dry throat aching. "We all thought that Ceanus was a story. I had no idea. I didn't understand any of this. How is this possible?"

Mehri released me but didn't go far. "From what we've learned over the years, aspects of the myth Adrialians are so fond of are true. Others are not."

"Which ones?"

Her lips quivered, and there was a break in her humming melody. She looked meaningfully at the remaining fish. I took another small bite as she watched approvingly. "There is more to Ceanus than you can ever imagine. The story does not do it justice."

I leaned back, took another long breath in then released it. "Alright, Mehri, tell me everything."

Her humming stopped a moment as a soft laugh slipped out of her mouth. "Everything, Your Highness? You should know we are a very old kingdom."

My lips curled and I relaxed a bit. "As much as you can tell me before we are interrupted."

Mehri blinked, her teeth working her bottom lip before she made a quick decision and plopped down on the bed beside me.

"Ceanus was created when the Adrialian King, Janus stole his brother's bride. She was a powerful mage, beloved by Trayon, and he took the trickery rather personally. He was determined to have her continue to serve him, but if she became queen of Adrial, he worried that she would fall under the spell of the God of the Sun."

I nodded. This part I knew.

"When the betrayed brother, Mikel returned to his brother's castle, from which this very palace was carved, he cursed the young king, and using Trayon's trident, he channeled the Sea God's power into the ground, shattering the castle and all of the nearby city. It fell into the ocean, where Trayon was waiting. It was Trayon who built the arc, allowing us to stay safely under the water and under his protection."

A sharp knock at the door made both of our heads turn. A moment later, a man entered. Tall and dark, with thick wavy locks that arched back from his furrowed brow, he strode into my room like he owned it.

My fists curled in surprise. And in preparation. Every instinct I'd ever felt screamed at me to be prepared around this man.

Immediately, his gaze was locked with mine, the deep-brown color of his eyes nearly black as he gave a short bow to both Mehri

and me. Mehri hurried to curtsy back, but I remained still and tall I
watched him.

"General Kairos, to what do we owe this pleasure?" Mehri's
voice was soft, hushed.

A soft huff told me that he heard her question, but his stare
remained on me. It burned, this dark gaze. There was something in
that look… Was it hatred? Fury? It sure as hell wasn't happiness.

I approached him, my spine stiff. His gaze raked down my form
quickly, a sneer coming to his mouth as I returned his bow with one
of my own.

"You don't bow to me, Princess."

My brows rose before I could stop them, both at the tone in his
voice and the savagery of being called out so readily. "Excuse my
mistake, General. I am new here. What exactly do I do in this
situation?"

Mehri pressed against my side, a warm, nervous presence there.
"Your Highness, the proper Ceanian greeting from your status
would be a nod with your hand over your heart."

I blew through my nose, pushing a smile to my lips. "Thank you,
Mehri." I turned my attention to the General once more, noting the
lines of black ink that I could see on his skin through the loose black
shirt that he wore. There, between the lines of his pectorals, a gold
charm hung on a leather necklace. Glowing against the warm tan of
his skin. Something about it drew my attention. A warm buzz rang
in my mind until the General wrapped his hand around the charm.
He took a half step back, frown deepening the lines on his face as he
did.

My mind cleared. Very slowly, I nodded to the General then
pressed my hand over my chest.

He grunted a response, clearly unimpressed, and bowed again. "Now that we have completed these worthless court exchanges, I have come to tell you, Your Highness, that you will be meeting with the queen shortly."

"The queen?" Relief washed over me.

"Yes, the queen. I thought you might want a chance to clean up first." His dark eyes crawled up my body, his forehead wrinkling in disapproval.

Heat flooded my cheeks. This man was insufferable. But he was also right, Artio damn him, even if his delivery was severely flawed. "Of course. I am thrilled to be received."

Mehri disappeared from my side, and I immediately wished she would come back. Something about this man set me on edge, from the tips of his slightly pointed ears to the sandals that wrapped around his feet, his presence here rattled me down to my core.

Mehri must've read my mind, because a moment later, she calmly announced, "My lady needs to prepare, General, if you don't mind."

Kairos nodded, his face relaxing as he gave another short bow to both Mehri and me. "Your escorts will be here shortly, Your Highness."

"Thank you, General," I said immediately, locking my knees so that I wasn't tempted to either bow or curtsy. These foreign mannerisms were going to take some getting used to. As if aware of my struggle, an annoying smirk pulled at Kairos's lips once again.

He turned sharply, his loose gray pants moving around his legs as he strode back to the door and marched through it, not bothering to close it. Before he could do anything, I had reached through and, gripping the handle, closed it for him.

I turned to Mehri. She stood a few strides away, her hands on her cheeks as she stared wide-eyed at the door. I pointed my finger at her. "Forget what I said earlier. Let's start with that one. I want to know everything." I jabbed a finger at the door the general had just left from.

Mehri twittered for a moment, guiding me towards a small antechamber, where I was able to take care of any personal needs, followed by her yanking me back into another small chair, where she could hover over my hair. A carved-handled comb appeared in her hand, picking through the dark waves on my head.

"You mean General Kairos. Your—I mean our General… He's the head of the military and a member of the queen's court and council. Many people believe he is her right hand."

"He seems too young to be a General," I mumbled, cringing as Mehri worked a snarl.

Mehri giggled. "He has quite the reputation in Ceanus."

"What kind of reputation?"

"Well, he's a brutal fighter. He won his way up the rankings through both battles, but also in accolades off the battlefield." She paused the comb. "He's supposedly very brave and has saved many of us from…"

"From who?"

Mehri shrugged, and I glanced over my shoulder to see the handmaiden's face. Her delicate features were tight, her gaze slowly meeting mine. There was fear there, lurking in her eyes, so light blue they were nearly silver.

"We are not free from danger simply because we are at the bottom of the sea, my lady."

I shivered then turned back around, and Mehri began combing once again. "Well, he's very….coarse."

Mehri's soft laugh made me smile. "Perhaps a little. But did you see his jawbone? Now I see why all the females get so worked up over him."

"You think he's handsome?" I practically spat out the word.

Mehri's noise of agreement made my cheeks hot again. "You don't?"

"Maybe, but I couldn't see past the ego."

"Of course, my lady. Excuse my candor."

I shook my head a little, dismissing her apology. She had every right to lust after the pompous General. "Tell me more. Please."

"About the General?"

I snorted. "No, that's enough about him for now. About everything else."

"Well…" Mehri took a deep breath and began.

By the time I exited my room, Mehri had filled my head to the brim with a variety of Ceanian facts that I was still trying to digest.

Ceanus was a full-functioning kingdom at the bottom of the Great Sea. And while Mehri was only around twenty years old, her parents, grandparents, and great-grandparents had all lived here in Trayon's drowned city. The kingdom itself was divided into four Houses, which functioned like clans within the arc, each with a variety of features that remained at the forefront of that House's individual personality.

From what Mehri said, House Leviathan consisted mostly of soldiers. That included the warriors employed by the crown to patrol the arc, as well as the military. Ceanians who pledged House Leviathan were known to be bold, maybe a little brash, but deeply loyal. They were considered the protectors of the city.

House Kraken were Ceanus's craftspeople, the merchants, the builders, the farmers. Deeply loyal and hardworking, they provided for the thousands of Ceanian citizens that made the arc their home.

Then there was House Cirein-Croin; they were the record keepers, the educators, and often the keepers of Ceanian law. They maintained powerful alliances with the other Houses and were known to be kind and clever.

And finally, House Cetus. Something about the way she said the name got my attention. I leaned down to listen to the smaller woman as we wound our way through the castle halls. Unlike the palace at Port Sol, this building was a mass of twisting hallways and staircases.

"They are the politicians, the leaders, often called to pass judgment in disputes. The queen is House Cetus, as was her father, the king before her."

I wanted to ask more but realized I hadn't asked something very important. "Mehri, what house do you serve?"

Mehri's lips quivered and her head pulled high. "I am House Kraken, Your Highness."

I grinned at the obvious pride in her voice. After glancing around the nearly deserted hallway, Mehri reached up and pulled down the neckline of her simple blue dress. A silver necklace hung there, the charm so low it nearly pressed between her breasts. She pulled it up and freed it so she could show me. The silver charm shone in the coral light, the metallic outline of a hammer at the center of the round shape.

"Our symbol," Mehri whispered before dropping the necklace down her shirt once again.

A thought occurred to me. "And everyone is born into the Houses they serve?"

"No, not necessarily. Many change Houses once they reach adulthood. There is a ceremony each season, on the darkest night of the month. It is then you can petition Trayon and the House Wardens to change your pledge."

My mind whirled. Trayon came here, it seemed, and on a regular basis. My heart thumped in my chest. "And that's well received? Changing your pledge?"

"It depends. The house you are moving to must accept you as well, and you can only move if you are following a mate or if you choose to leave your family's house when you turn eighteen. It's not an easy process, Your Highness. The Houses do not want to take on less-desirable citizens, but you must sever the ties to your previous house before you can bid for a new one. And if you aren't accepted?" Mehri hummed softly, "To be unclaimed is a fate that no Ceanus citizen wants to share in."

I nodded, dread rising in my stomach as we entered a massive entryway space, where a set of five soldiers stood, all dressed in tight black shirts, similar to the bottoms I still wore, and matching black pants. Each of them wore a matching leather-looking harness across their chest, to which a multitude of weapons were strapped to.

As we approached, the soldiers all bowed, dropping even lower than Kairos had.

Mehri dropped back, walking a few steps behind me as we passed through a door that two soldiers held.

My jaw nearly dropped as we moved into what appeared to be a throne room. It wasn't as large as the one at home, but that didn't matter. It was beautiful, unusual, the walls and floors a muted glow from the softly glowing corals. The effect meant that it looked polished and forgotten all at the same time. I stepped around a brightly lit blue coral, feeling the soft warmth that it seemed to exude as I continued into the room.

Arched columns lined the slender room, leaving the sides open so that I could see straight out into the kingdom's center, where the voices of castle-goers slowly filtered up and into the room. They echoed softly from the gilded walls. Where sconces may have been in Adrial, there were only beautiful, unique coral features spiraling this way and that.

Farther away through the arches, I could see the shimmering walls that kept the Great Sea water at bay. The arc of Ceanus, Mehri had called it.

Deep in my chest, recognition bloomed as I noticed that behind the throne, which itself looked like it was built from coral and gilded with gold and silver bits, was a wall of stone. But not the smooth polished stones that were used in the walls of the rest of the building. This looked like rocks that were fresh from the ground or as if the castle here was pressed directly against an underwater cliffside. The rough edges reached into the rooms, wild and irregular.

As we reached the end of the aisle, Mehri broke away to kneel to one side, her eyes fast on the door at the side, nearly hidden in the walls. My heart thumped hard, bare feet slapping against the marbled floors as I halted and waited.

The door opened, revealing a pair of broad, armor-covered shoulders then a now familiar form as General Kairos stepped into the room. His steps stuttered as he caught sight of me, standing before the wild rock wall. My belly tightened as his obsidian eyes swept over me, his mouth twisting as he straightened.

I couldn't help but wonder for a moment if he was noting the tight black pants that Mehri had put me into, or the soft, short white top that cupped my breasts, while sheer sleeves fluttered around my shoulders with every breath.

Was there a flash of approval there? Or had I imagined that? Because now he was ducking his head, turning and bowing respectfully as another followed him in. A woman, nowhere near as tall as I was, stepped in. Every movement she made was full of grace and dignity. Her hair, which at first was dark, shone with a handful of other deep colors—rich magenta, dark navys. It gave her a nearly opalesque sheen as she moved forward, the room glowing brighter as wide blue eyes found mine.

I knew her in an instant.

I'd seen her thousands of times.

Even in my wildest dreams, in my more desperate prayers, I never thought I would see her again.

My throat clenched and stuck as I moved forward a step.

"Mother?"

My voice was a harsh crack, my entire being poised on the edge of destruction as I awaited her answer.

The queen smiled at me, her arms opening wide. "Come here, baby."

Chapter Thirteen

Her arms felt like home, wrapping me up tight as she swayed slightly. I knew I was crying, but there was no sobs, just a silent stream of tears that slipped down my cheeks and onto her skin.

Damona of Adrial, the cursed queen, stroked my hair, gentle soothing noises spilling from her throat as I clutched her closer.

"How? How?"

She hummed softly, her hand cupping the back of my head. "I'm here now, and I'm so sorry." Mother—my mother—let me hold her like this for what seemed like hours, until I finally recovered enough to pull back from her embrace,

"But how is this possible? Father saw you fall..." My words trailed off as her face tightened. My throat felt rough as I swallowed a prickling of unease. "You didn't fall, did you?"

"I can explain."

"You jumped." The words were strange, driving an ice-like dagger through the warmth of her hold. I stepped back farther, and her hands fell from my body. I missed them immediately, and I wrapped my own hands around my elbows in a mockery of the embrace I'd waited nearly my entire life to feel.

I turned from her, not wanting to see the truth that looked back at me. Swiping at my face, I noticed that General Kairos and Mehri had both disappeared from the room. "I'm so confused. Father thinks you are dead. He mourned. The entire kingdom did. We had a funeral! We..."

My mother held out her hand to mine. A black inked symbol wrapped around her fingers and spiraled up her arms, fading in darkness as it did. That was new. She hadn't had any tattoos in the portraits. It was oddly comforting, this blatant difference between the woman I'd longed for and the woman standing in front of me.

I wanted some fucking answers. I wanted Trayon to answer for his curse. But most of all, I wanted to understand why she was here. Why *I* was here. I sniffled and slid my palm over hers. I could see the relief in her face as she drew me down to the stair that rose directly in front of her throne. "It is a very long story, *minu*. A horrible story, but one that I know I owe you."

Her face was sad now, pale against the beautiful dark locks that tumbled down her back. "All these years, I fell asleep thinking about what I'd do if I could tell you. All the parts I would include in some pitiful attempt to explain what I had done to you. But now that you're here, I can't seem to find any of the words."

I stayed silent, watching her throat work.

"Because there are no words for what I did. No forgiveness. Not above or below that can explain what I did to you. A mother should not leave her child, no matter what the excuse was."

"Damona... Mother..." The word was awkward in my mouth, yet it hung between us like a strung bow, the arrow awaiting release.

"Oh, my dear..." Her eyes shone with unshed tears. "I've decided I don't want to be forgiven. At least not yet." She gave a quick smile, though her lips quivered. "Forgiveness should be earned."

I nodded, but whispered words slipped past. "You left us."

"I know, *minu,* and I promise that I will try to tell you everything. Not because I want your forgiveness, but because you deserve it." She pressed her free hand against my wrist. "You have no idea what it means to have you here. We have been waiting, but I never thought…"

I blinked, surprised, but she was already continuing, her hand moving to subconsciously brush against the crown settled in her dark hair. "It must be Trayon's doing. A blessing. You'll see."

I *didn't* see. I wasn't sure how my jumping into the ocean after an almost-kidnapped ambassador was important to the God of the Sea. But she was allowed to believe what she wanted. For the first time, my eyes left her face to stare at the delicate silver crown that sat on her hair. It was so different from our crowns in Adrial a fine-boned piece of art with diamond-encrusted seashells woven through silver and pearls.

"Oh Gods. You're the queen. Of Ceanus." My words were halting, even to my own ears. Under my feet, the ground moved, and I wondered briefly if I was going to faint. I braced my legs wider, begging my body to adjust to this newest bout of news.

She was already nodding, blue eyes examining my every breath. "Yes, I am, Mira. Which means that you, my daughter, are not only a princess of Adrial."

I closed my eyes, the news settling over me like a net, capturing and pulling me until I was not sure if I was floating or standing, saved or surrendered.

"Mira? Mira, are you alright?"

I dragged breath into my lungs. "I'm a princess of Ceanus." I blinked slowly, savoring the sweet darkness on every one. "Oh my Gods, do I have siblings? Or more family here?"

My mother laughed, the sound warm, like honey against my tongue. "No, I'm sorry, no siblings."

That laugh, it loosened something again between us. "I always wanted a little brother or something to spoil."

"Sorry," my mother said with a worried smile. "You are my one and only."

"And that means that…"

"Yes, Mira. You are heir to this throne as much as you are heir to Henrich's throne. A princess of two kingdoms."

"Two kingdoms…" I glanced behind us at the craggy wall. "Until this morning, I believed this place was something from a fairy tale."

My mother considered me closely. "It's true that Ceanus was built on the part of the city of Adrial that sank into the ocean. But this is no fairy tale, Mira. There are things here that you must learn, parts of the story that no other knows." Her fingers found mine. "And I want to share them with you. There's so much I've been wanting to tell you. I didn't think my prayers would be answered."

"I don't understand. Did you expect me to show up here?"

"No," she admitted. "We did not. At least not yet. My plan had always been to let you grow up, find your way, and then show you that there was more to your family than expected. I never wanted to force Ceanus on you. It should've been your choice."

"Then why am I here?" Her hesitation tempted my temper. "You say you want forgiveness, but honesty is where that begins."

Mother's sharp intake of breath forced me to take a moment.

Confusion and exhaustion pricked the backs of my eyes as I looked around the room. "I'm twenty-three, Your Majesty. That's nineteen years of life without you. Without the truth about who you are, so excuse me, this is taking me a moment to catch up."

I bent at the waist, taking a deep breath in. "Gods, who I am? Until this past week the biggest concern I had other than assuming Adrial's throne years down the line was whether I was going to be forced to endure another of Homer's potential love matches."

My mother rolled her eyes, surprising me. "Homer has horrible taste in men."

"I know—wait, you know Homer?"

"He's been your father's best friend and shadow since long before me," she said. "Truthfully, he was not the biggest fan of Henrich marrying me. And Mira, I know this is a lot to take in. I should've come to you years ago. But recently it has become more and more difficult for me to leave the arc. I prayed to Trayon to bring you to me when you were needed the most. I trusted him. And now, here you are."

"Here I am," I sighed. "Why didn't you and Homer get along?"

The smile that curved her lips was wry and a little sad. "I wasn't supposed to stay in Adrial. I was having a rebellious moment and ran away. But that day, standing on the beach, I saw your father, and everything changed."

I had only ever heard my father's side of the story. Her voice drew me in, and I moved closer to her. "I couldn't leave him. He was…everything to me. Henrich was my first love, my only love. And when I got pregnant…" Her dark hair slipped forward over part of her face. "I was ready to give it all up."

My mother sighed, breaking my gaze and standing. She offered me a hand and then tugged me to a standing position before we moved together to the arched balconies off of the throne room. Leaning on one wall, she breathed into the air then turned back to me.

"My father passed to the Dark Realm. You were only a few years old. I thought we would have more time. He was young, healthy, and powerful. But the kingdom below must always have a ruler, and our bloodline is the most powerful, as we are descended from the originals."

"You couldn't rule from Adrial?"

"Ruling Ceanus doesn't mean the same thing there as it does here." Her voice was serious. "Here, the ruler, whomever wears this crown, sits on this throne, makes the pledge that I did. We alone are responsible for maintaining the relationship with Trayon; that is what keeps this kingdom alive. Without us, the city dies."

"How can a kingdom die?"

A smile flickered across her face. "We are not just figureheads and politicians. We are light." She reached out, pressing a finger against the coral that snaked up the side of the wall. It glowed vibrantly, making me blink at the brightness. "We are life." She released the coral as I stared at her, my jaw slack. It dimmed immediately back to the soft warmth it had begun with.

"I did that earlier," I said finally, pointing at the coral, "but I thought…maybe that it was normal for you here."

"No, absolutely not. Only a few of us can power Ceanus." Her face darkened. "And by the time I heard my father had passed, the kingdom was already in dire straits. There was no chance to tell anyone, to do anything. I had to come home quickly, and even then, the city had begun to fall apart."

"So you came home to save the kingdom." I shook my head. "Father thought you had been cursed. It nearly killed him to lose you. He was so lost for such a long time. He missed you that much. He still misses you." I swallowed back my own confession, remembering the child I had been, staring at her portrait in our suites and crying for her to come back to us.

But she never had.

She had been ruling a kingdom here, steps from where I sat crying. My throat ached again. The Gods were cruel sometimes.

"I *was* cursed, Mira. Not in the way he thought, but since I took the crown and this throne, I can no longer leave Ceanus. To do so would be to tempt Trayon himself. And so I have been trapped here, recovering in the city, while you and Henrich continued your life above sea." She reached for my hand, and I gripped it hard. "It was torture, knowing you but never knowing you in the way that I wanted."

"Mama…" The endearment slipped out before I could stop it.

My mother didn't look at me, but I could feel the tremor in her grip. Heat flooded my cheeks, and I felt a strange sort of embarrassment at my obvious need for this woman's love.

"I know this is all wild, but I need you to know how much I love you, how much I hated that I wasn't there."

My heart ached. So many things I didn't understand. So much I needed to know. But in my chest, I could feel that it was possible. I could forgive her.

I reached for her, her slim body pressing against mine. I pressed my nose against her dark hair, breathing her in, the recesses of my brain screaming in joy while my chest ached with the thought of reliving the pain of her leaving all over again.

"What happens now?"

I could feel her body sag a little.

"I'm afraid it is shaping up to be a little complicated," Mother said as she pulled back, her eyes searching my face as she spoke. "Ceanus is not some fantastical paradise. It is a kingdom with all the issues that Adrial has, just with the added complication that, well…"

"You mean that tiny detail about existing at the bottom of the sea?"

She nodded. "Yes, but that's only the beginning." She took my arm and began to walk me back to the doors. "I've assigned Mehri to you. She will act as both a handmaiden and as a consultant on all things Ceanus." Pausing by the door, she continued, "And while I know that it might not seem like it, there are dangers here, just as dark and precarious as above."

"Alright, I understand."

"No, I'm not sure you do." She moved away a few paces, her hand straying to her crown once again. "I won't ask you to stay within the confines of your room or even the castle, but you will have a guard at all times. And not just the ones that are spread throughout the castle." She knocked on the heavy doors, and they opened to reveal a new man on the other side, a heavy broadsword that was nearly half of his massive body strapped to his back. His hair was a close-cropped warm brown, paired with a pair of pale-blue eyes that swept around the room quickly before he dropped to a low bow in front of her.

I flexed my knees, stamping out the habit of returning the bow as my mother quickly nodded to the man.

"At ease, Lieutenant. Mira, this is Akram. He is a captain in the second wave here in Ceanus."

"The second wave?" I looked him over. He was only an inch or two taller than me, but he might as well have been two of me wide. He was thickly built, heavy muscles clinging to a bone structure that said even more about his prowess on the battlefield than the easy confidence that he faced us down with.

"They are an advanced arm of the military here in Ceanus. We have three of them—first wave, second wave, third wave—each with their own specialties. Lieutenant Akram has agreed to take a short hiatus from his duties elsewhere to support you during your transition."

"Nice to meet you, Lieutenant."

"Likewise, Your Highness." Akram bowed low once more, and when he straightened, I could see a faint scar across his lower lip.

"Akram will be assigned to rooms closer to your suite, and when not stationed outside of your doors, he will be your first line of defense."

I coughed. "Your Majesty, I'm not completely useless. If you wanted to tell me a little more, I'm sure I can get by with the palace guards without affecting the Lieutenant's life so drastically."

My mother tilted her head at me, pensive, as Akram's chin ducked, a small smile on his lips. "You may not be helpless, *minu*, but it is also not appropriate for a princess to be slaughtering people in my halls."

My brows rose. "But he can?"

She smiled. "Now you are catching on. And as for who might be attacking, it is more a level of intimidation that I don't want you subjected to."

She and Akram shared a quick look. "There are those here who will be very disappointed that my heir has finally come to save Ceanus."

"To save Ceanus? Does it need saving?"

"Well, we don't know that for sure. But why else would the ocean claim you in such a way?"

"I thought this was because I touched the water. I know it's cursed."

Mother let out a soft sigh. "There's so much you don't know yet. But you will. And then you will realize what we all have. You were brought here because you are needed."

My mind was briefly stuck on her statement, but I pushed that aside to think about later. "I need to talk to Trayon, Your Majesty, to find out why the curse remains on Adrial. My people, *your* people, are going mad by the dozen, and the deaths… They are horrific."

Silence followed, and I could feel the disappointment that filled the space around us. After a long moment, Akram cleared his throat. My mother blinked, as if drawn back to the moment, and offered me a quick, tight smile. "Of course, Mira. I'm sure he would be happy to hear your concerns. Perhaps we can take them to Trayon when he arrives at pledging."

The way she spoke didn't comfort me at all. I had passed some kind of boundary that I was unaware of. Vividly aware of how wrong this conversation was going, I turned to Akram.

"That's wonderful news. Perhaps while we wait on Trayon's arrival, we can brush up on my swordplay. It has been months since I last had a worthy opponent."

The spell lifted a little, and my mother's face relaxed.

Akram bowed slightly, first to me, then to my mother. "Anytime, Your Highness. Your Majesty, permission to wait outside?"

"You're dismissed, Lieutenant. Continue seeing about your rooms tonight. I want you stationed outside of Mira's door as soon as you can."

Akram marched back out of the room, and tension returned to the air as my mother knitted her fingers together.

I swallowed, the sound obscenely noisy in the quiet. "How much more is there that I don't know?"

"Plenty," my mother said, tone serious. "I have dreamed about this day every night since I had to leave Adrial. But having you here, it suddenly seems so overwhelming. How do you teach someone about an entire culture in a matter of moments?"

"I don't know. How long did it take you to acclimate to Adrial and Port Sol?"

My mother's face was grim. "Longer than I believed it would."

"What is most important, then? So far having a hulking guard and a handmaiden is nothing new for me. Even if the setting is." I gestured to the globe of water waiting to drown me, a smile softening the words.

"I guess I'll start with the most important. Since you were brought here by the curse, you have to remain in Ceanus for at least a month while your body heals and adjusts to Trayon's magic. It is not necessarily the magic that makes the Adrialians suffer. It is the inability to complete the spell that he placed on the waters."

"A month?"

She nodded. "If you would like to have a word with Trayon, then the best time would be his visits during Pledging."

That word – she had said it twice now. "Pledging?"

Mother nodded. "Each of the cursed who make it to Ceanus are put through a program to introduce them to Ceanus as well as each of the Houses. At the end of the month, they pledge to the house they desire to join, and if their bid is accepted, then they will be considered claimed and a true citizen of both their chosen House and Ceanus."

"Do I need to do that?" Some part of me desperately wanted to confess that I didn't want to pledge a house, since there was no way I was going to stay.

Mother walked back across the room, settling herself on her throne. "No, I don't think so. Call me selfish, but I'd rather you spend the time with me."

Her words warmed my skin, and I ducked my chin. "Of course. I'd love that."

"I have a few things I must attend to today, but I've arranged for Mehri to send over the best books about Ceanus for you to look at."

"Thank you."

Mother's face turned, and I could see her grip the throne's arms with long, elegant fingers. I was being dismissed, but there was still one more thing, and I couldn't leave without asking it.

"Father and…everyone, they will believe I'm dead. That's what we always believed of the people who went into the ocean." *That's what they believed about you* was what I wanted to say, but the words didn't emerge. "I can't let them suffer or wonder what happened to me."

Something changed in her face, tightening and straining. "I understand that you're frustrated, Mira."

I heard the doors behind me open again and assumed Akram had returned for me. My next words fell out fast and desperate. "I just wanted to know if I could send him a message or a note. I don't want him to hurt like he did when…when you disappeared."

General Kairos brushed by me. He gave a bow to my mother before climbing the stairs and assuming a casual pose at her side. His eyes were pure black now, a void of emotion shining back at me as a frown pulled his lips.

"Your Majesty, we cannot possibly allow this."

"What? Why not?" An edge slipped into my words, but I didn't explain it away. I didn't understand at all why this man was so against everything I said. "It's just a note."

My mother sighed, and I could see General Kairos's head move ever so slightly. I took a step forward, feeling left out of my own conversation. I didn't get far before my mother's sapphire gaze found mine. The apology shone out of them and I knew her answer before her lips ever moved.

"I'm sorry, Miraceti. We cannot allow Adrial to know about Ceanus. Not yet."

Swallowing back my disappointment, I shot General Kairos a sharp look then bowed to my mother. "Of course."

"I'll be in touch soon so we can talk more."

I nodded, afraid if I spoke now that the General would know how badly his words and her agreement with them had wounded me. I had thought I was finding a common space with my mother. All it took was a few words and a look from him, and I was back in that water, drowning and lost.

"We can have our healers look you over again since you're awake now. They may be able to speed up the healing process for you."

"Thank you." I stood, her voice telling me that I was being dismissed. As I moved towards the door and the heavily armored guard who opened the door for me, she spoke one more time.

"Miraceti," she called.

I turned.

"Can I teach you? About Ceanus? It is a part of you, whether or not you decide to stay any longer."

Hope burned in my chest as I nodded. "I would love that."

I bowed, twisting my face away from the throne as I hurried to the door. Akram waited there, now dressed in the same black uniform that the rest of the castle guard wore. But his arms were bared, the ink that twisted across his skin visible.

"Can we go?"

Akram nodded, ushering me out into the hallway.

Chapter Fourteen

My mother didn't ease me into anything after that. The following nights, I spent as much time as possible reading volumes and scrolls by the armload that Mehri delivered. Details about the creation of Ceanus blended with beautifully illustrated maps of Ceanus as it had evolved over the years.

Even Akram had gotten interested in them and changed positions from the wall by my door to the wall closest to my desk where Mehri and I were thumbing through the documentation. But today when I had reached for a smaller, new stack of leather-bound tomes, Mehri had scooped them up, tucking them closer to her slender body.

"Not those, Your Highness," she whispered, embarrassed.

"Why not?"

"They contain sensitive information, and I can't let you read about it until after Her Majesty grants me leave."

"Oh." I closed the book I was currently reading. "How long do I have to wait?"

"I'm not sure. That is up to the queen."

"Can I at least get a hint? You are holding those awfully tight."

"No, Your Highness," Mehri said, but her shoulder relaxed. "I'll just put them in my room for now."

I laughed, watching her dart across to her room carrying the large stack. A moment later, Akram appeared there, his big body moving faster than I'd seen it as he carefully opened Mehri's door for her. When the female moved through the door, I felt like Mehri lingered just a little longer than necessary under the arch of his arms.

"Thank you," Mehri murmured to the Leviathan guard.

Akram grunted but then as if changing his mind, cleared his throat and said roughly, "Of course. Do you need me to carry them?"

"No," Mehri said, a little smile on her lips. "I can handle it." The door closed softly behind her, and when Akram turned back to face me, I couldn't help but raise my brows at him.

Seemed a lot like my silent bodyguard may have some feelings for Mehri. I grinned as he grunted again and moved back to his usual space by the door.

"Do you like her?"

Silence.

"Akram, you are no fun."

Akram's expression didn't change, but I would swear on the Mother goddess that there was a little smile on his face. I spent the rest of the afternoon alternating between tiny pacing sprints around my room, worrying about spending the night with my mother, and poring over more Ceanian history.

When Mehri reappeared and told me it was time to get ready, I was filled with relief. Anything to break this torture of waiting. What did my mother want to talk about? Would we just talk about Ceanus? Could I share about my life in Adrial without upsetting her? Where the fuck were the boundaries between a long-lost mother who happened to be a mermaid queen?

I sure as Hell didn't know.

I guessed it was time to find out. By the time Mehri and I arrived at my mother's throne room, I was practically vibrating with nervous energy. So much that I knew that Mehri was secretly wishing she could use her gift on me. Every so often, she'd begin to hum, realize what she was doing, and then stop again.

"I'm fine, Mehri," I said finally, turning to face her. "It's fine."

"Why do I feel like you're trying to convince yourself as well as me, Your Highness?"

I huffed and then, with a decisive twist, spoke to my mother's guard. "I'm ready to be announced."

The guard, who had stood patiently during all of this, pushed the door wide. "Princess Mira, Your Majesty."

I strode in, leaving Mehri and the guard in the hallway. Looking around the long room, I was surprised to realize that we were completely alone.

Just my mother and me.

My mother hurried across the room, her hands reaching for mine. I took them, noticing the soft, nearly skin-toned tattoos there. Our skin hummed at the contact, and my anxiety lessened immediately.

"Can you come with me, *minu*? Unless you are starving, I'd like to show you something very important before we do anything else." She wound her fingers through mine and guided me to the small, closed door that I'd entered through yesterday. Behind there was a smaller room, comfortable and warmly lit. But we didn't stop there, continuing through another door, then another, until I was standing at an extended balcony nearby, double the size of my own suite.

No, I realized, not a balcony. It was a bridge that arched and wound over the first level of the palace. The end of it flared out to where it pressed against the shimmering globe that kept the water at bay. There was a low railing along the edges, and as I stole closer, I could see that the paths and the streets of the city below wound under us in a bevy of bright-white pathways. My mother tugged my hand, returning my attention to the globe wall ahead of us.

"When the land split and Ceanus was created, there were certain conditions that Trayon gifted us with in order to make it livable for us here."

"That makes sense."

"We were able to maintain the powers that so many of us already had. I'm sure you've noticed that people here look quite a bit different than Adrialians."

I smiled. "So you're saying the hair color is all-natural? Even the bright colors, like Mehri's?"

"I am. Since the oldest of our bloodlines are mostly developed from a mage-centric island nation who was pulled into Trayon's spell, we were blessed enough to not only inherit some additional coloring shades, her hand moved to her hair but also our gifts."

"Gifts? As in magical powers? Father always told me that most magic-wielders in Adrial had died out generations ago."

"That is their own doing. The Adrialians were scared of the abilities, the Gods' gift. And therefore anyone with any abilities were hunted and destroyed. There were a lucky few who we were able to bring to Ceanus. But many, many more were killed."

I had heard the stories. But seeing my mother's pain, hearing the soft pain in her voice, I felt these stories resonate in my chest. "I'm sorry."

She shook her head. "You shouldn't be, Miraceti. You were not there. You are not responsible for the doings of your ancestors. But the magics lost..." She sighed. "They were devastating."

We looked out at the waters. "Why do you call me that? Miraceti. Is it a term of endearment?" My cheeks heated. "I mean, it sounds like a pet name."

Blinking rapidly, my mother pressed a hand to her chest. "I can't believe I didn't tell you, but Mira, that is your Ceanian name, the one that even your father agreed to, even if he didn't understand what he was agreeing to."

"Miraceti?"

"Yes, named after my Houses' monster, the mighty Cetus." She cleared her throat. "I imagine you've seen the constellation Cetus, although I don't believe you call it that."

"I'm named after a star…" I shot her a tremulous smile. Another thing I hadn't known about myself, but still, now that I knew the truth, it fit against my skin like a comfortable caress. I shook my head, my dark waves brushing my cheeks as I looked away. "Sorry. You can continue on, Your Majesty. I got distracted."

"I'm glad you did. I want you to be able to ask me these questions, and maybe I can explain a little more about who we are." She tucked her arm through mine, towing me forward once again. As if she could feel my resistance to the strange magic that undulated and moved like a living thing, her fingers tightened on me. "The gifts were a blessing, this world a fresh start for all of us. But there was more. Trayon wanted to make sure his people were superior, not trapped here, but could thrive here and create a new world, just for ourselves."

We stopped in front of a small rock archway that was constructed at the end of the pathway where it touched the magical wall. "The wall? Your Highness?"

She turned me to face her. "No, not just the wall. But what is beyond it. We are designed to rule the sea, *minu*. And in order to do that, we became a part of it."

"I don't understand."

My mother raised her hand, and together we stepped up to the undulating wall of water that shimmered back at me. Lifting her hand, she pressed her fingers against the barrier. Her long digits slipped through, as if nothing were there. Awe flooded my heart and made my heart race.

Something in me knew to mimic my mother's movement, and a moment later, the cool water washed over my fingers, dripping down my wrists and off my elbow. The barrier, whatever magical aspects it held, was not thick. It wasn't hard. It was simply a boundary between air and water, magic and wild, dry and wet.

My lips pulled back in a smile as I watched my fingers wiggle in the ocean water, experiencing the strangest feelings of being in two worlds at once. Something moved beyond my hand, and my eyes refocused, leaving my fingers alone and looking instead at the variety of figures that were gathering just on the other side of the barrier.

Mer.

Chapter Fifteen

There were so many. I yanked my hand back, moving to stand in front of my mother, arms spread wide to protect her as I stared open mouthed at the myriad of Mer. They were close now, so close that I could see the relaxed expressions on their faces. Some carried weapons; others volleyed amongst themselves. Their tails were a plethora of colors, from the inky black tone for one, all the way to the shimmer of a ruby red on the far end.

Beautiful.

Terrifying.

And I had no idea what to do. Putting all my faith in that barrier, I braced myself wide, my feet firmly against the ground as I prepared to protect my mother.

But instead, she gently placed her hands on my hips, urging me to step to the side. A soft word, in a language my mind couldn't place, fell from the queen's mouth. And then the Mer were pushing closer to the arch of stones, the thick, flexing tails drawing them upright as they touched the shimmering pool of water just before them.

Then with a zip of light, the first of the Mer broke the surface of the interior of the arc of Ceanus and stepped forward, not flopping forward onto their tails as I might have thought, but rather stepping in, the flashing red scales that had just been so visible appearing to sink into warm brown skin that formed over human-looking toes, feet, ankles, feet, all taking form right in front of us.

Trayon's magic. It had to be. My mind scrambled to keep up.

The Mer stopped a few steps into the arc's smooth platform, his face friendly as he bowed to my mother and me. I wondered if he was able to hear my heartbeat as it roared in my ears.

"Your Majesty," he said, his deep voice pleasant and kind.

Even so, I considered grabbing my mother and racing for her rooms. Akram would be there, maybe even General Kairos. While the man seemed like a massive asshole, I bet he would keep us safe.

And yet, as my mind began to clear, realization encompassed me as more came through the barrier.

They were Mer. That's how they lived down here. The Mer and creatures that we'd only glimpsed from the surface were a thing of normalcy here. At least, that's what I could assume based on the casual way each Mer now bowed to my mother.

The once red-tailed, red-haired male cast a glance over his shoulder as one after the other, the rest of the Mer began to filter into the interior arc's air, each of them trading their tails for a pair of legs, all encased in that same black fabric that I also wore. My throat moved as I finally caught sight of the final Mer traveling through the arc portal.

His scales were as black as the starless night, peeling up his legs as the scales sank into flesh and fins slipped away to corded muscles and a bone structure that would've had even Homer fanning himself.

He was beautiful. My eyes were helpless to turn away as his scales bled away into black pants, up to a torso that was covered in a variety of black-inked tattoos. Some mimicked the lines of a shirt, beginning at his wrist, crawling up his shoulders with lines and scaled patterns, until they crested across his collarbones and met in a sharp point.

Right where a golden charm winked back at me. And then there were his eyes, black and soulless as could be. Yet, I was arrested by them, consumed and besotted in a moment. They were a predator's eyes, yet I couldn't fault them for their beauty and danger. My breath hitched, something deep in my belly unfurling at his presence. And his power.

Fuck. Mother above, lend me strength.

I crossed my arms demurely, willing my body to calm down as he approached.

"General Kairos," Mother said pleasantly. "How are your recruits fairing? This class looks smaller than the last."

The General bowed to both of us then ran a strong hand through his shoulder-length hair, shaking the water from the dark strands. The droplets landed in a frustrating pattern across his chest and belly and drew my eyes for a moment before I snapped them back up to meet his smugly knowing gaze.

Was that humor I detected there in those dark depths? I blew out a loud breath and put my hands on my hips.

Kairos finally spoke. "They are doing well. A few Cirein-Croin who are still grappling with reality outside of the classroom. What they lack in numbers, they make up for in eagerness. Bayrah and I will have them whipped into shape before the end of season."

"Good news, General," Mother said, as who I assumed were the recruits based on the anxious expressions they continued to throw at my mother and me, moved past us, towards the castle. "I'm glad to hear it. We may need it."

"Understood, Your Majesty," Kairos said seriously, still not acknowledging me.

"Your Highness, if I may ask, how was your first day? I know that many of our newcomers find the city a little unsettling at first." The formerly ruby red Mer now stood in front of me, a wide smile on his face.

I stared at him, his face's wide grin so at odds with the thunderous expression that Kairos wore. I licked dry lips, knowing whatever I said here would have an implication on not only my mother and our relationship, but also on how this culture thought of me.

"Uh…it has been astonishing, in all honesty." I placed my hand over my heart for a moment, trying out the custom that Mehri had shown me. "I can't wait to see more of Ceanus. Did he say your name is Bayrah?"

"It is, but I prefer Baye to be honest, highnes. Lieutenant Baye, House Leviathan," he said, his own hand going to his chest. Baye had inked designs across his chest as well, and right over his chest, there was a shield-shaped design tattooed into the golden skin there.

Of course, I realized, remembering Akram's shield as well. "Your house symbol."

"Yes." Baye's smile broadened, if that were possible. He shifted to throw a look at Kairos, who continued to brood at his side. "I may not have been born into House Levithan, but it is the house of my heart, and I am happy to serve Ceanus."

"They are lucky to have you," my mother said, speaking quickly over the question that waited on my lips. "If you don't mind, we are going to continue back to the castle now. I fear my daughter may have had enough shock for the day."

The house of his heart? What did any of that mean? I took a deep breath in, trying to steady my heartrate. When my eyes lifted, they met Kairos's dark gaze once more. And while I knew that Baye continued on, unaware of my anxiety, something in Kairos's eyes made me think he knew exactly how much I was struggling to absorb all of this.

Which only drove my anxiety higher.

Baye gave another short bow our direction. "Our recruits have abandoned us for their meals. Please, Your Majesty, allow us to escort you back."

Kairos's expression grew darker. I almost laughed at his dislike of the idea, but then, he couldn't say anything. Baye ushered my mother forward, dropping a step behind her elegant stroll out of respect, which left Kairos and me briefly standing together.

"After you," he said, his bright-white teeth gritted.

I tilted my head, and he loomed closer. "You are the Mer who saved me when I jumped in. Aren't you?" My hand moved to my neck before I could stop it. Kairos's eyes darted to my mother and Baye, walking ahead, and then back to me.

"You bit me, General. Why didn't you say anything before?"

Kairos gave a deep sigh and then began to follow the other pair. I huffed at his attitude but followed. I nearly had to jog to catch up with his long, smooth steps. Baye and my mother were deep in conversation, heads and hands moving through the air as they spoke. I kept my gaze glued to my mother as we moved along, ignoring the male at my side.

To my surprise, his voice broke our silence. "Yes, it was me."

"Why would you do that? I don't understand."

"Would you have preferred to drown, princess?"

"No, of course not," I hissed.

Kairos's stupidly handsome face was smug again, and irrationally I wanted to reach up and touch it. To wipe the smugness off his face, I added quickly to myself. Shaking myself free of my thoughts, I leveled my best glare at him.

"I'm sorry, but you're going to have to start explaining, because I'm really, really confused about how I ended up here. My mother seems to think your Sea God brought me here, but all I remember is you." I swiveled to face him. "You know something, and you're not saying anything. Otherwise, you wouldn't have such a problem with me being here. So please, tell me."

His broad features were tight. "As I'm sure your mother has said, we do not commonly let Adrialians drown in our waters. And regarding the bite, our venom renders our prey nearly comatose. I was attempting to keep you alive until I could reach the interior of our arc. Unlike the rest of us, your body did not shift when you hit the water." He said it all as if I were an idiot for not knowing.

"Oh." I stared at him, my feet slowing as I registered his gruff words. I didn't realize I was supposed to have shifted. I'd have to ask Mehri about that tonight. "Did you know who I was?"

"Not at first." General Kairos attempted to move past me, but I side-stepped into his path, my hands against his chest. His jaw flexed, drawing my eyes for a moment. "But yes, after I got close enough, I knew you were the princess. Our princess."

He said the word as if it disgusted him.

My brow furrowed. "What did you say about all the cursed people trying to make it to the waters? In Adrial, we believed they drowned. But that's not right, is it?"

Kairos's lips pulled in a smirk that made me feel like I was purposefully being dense. "What do you think happens, Princess?"

I blinked, suddenly looking around me. We had ended up in a small rotund room off the pathway, where others were milling about. I tried not to stare at the males and females moving around, wondering if they were Mer or not and realizing that they probably all were.

People bowed and pressed hands over their heart as they moved out of our way. The reverence was not reserved only for my mother.

They openly stared at me from faces that appeared to be Adrialian in nature, but their hair was as vibrant and colorful as an Adrialian sunset. Blue, green, purple, all paired with blue, hazel, green, and yes…brown eyes. I didn't see any as dark and bottomless as Kairos's but wasn't stupid enough to ask him about that.

A girl who looked to be in her teens bowed low to me, holding a stack of empty plates, her deep-green hair bound back in a plaited. When she rose, flashing gold eyes caught mine and widened. "Princess Miraceti," she whispered, my name a prayer on her lips.

I knew I was staring back at all of them, but at the same time I couldn't stop myself. They were beautiful. So unusual and interesting that I knew I would need to find a way to acquaint myself with these people sooner rather than later. Because suddenly, my dark hair, which had always lended itself towards the deep purple and red undertones, looked positively boring.

"You're staring," General Kairos said blandly, still at my shoulder.

I huffed, moving away from him.

"Sorry, General. I got distracted." I turned back to him. "You were about to tell me what happens to all the cursed Adrialians when they enter the sea."

His brow quivered. I remembered Pierse, the desperate way he'd pulled towards the water, the Mer as she rose from the waves to capture him.

"Oh my Gods, are these…" I gestured around us at the plethora of vividly colored citizens. "Are these all cursed Adrialians?"

Mother turned now, her face serious. "Not in the way that you would think, Mira, but yes, there are many Ceanian who were originally from Adrial."

"You…" I gulped, lowering my voice when a guard cast a glance my way. "Are you the ones who enact this curse for Trayon?"

Suddenly, Kairos's hand was on my wrist, moving me fast into a staircase. Behind me, I could see my mother filling in, her guards side by side behind as we moved back up the hallway. I recognized my doorway now, as well as the guard outside of it. Mine. At least for now.

My mother gave a polite salute to Akram's deep bow then turned to me. "I'm afraid that I've shown you too much at once. I didn't want to overwhelm you, I promise that."

Silence fell until I cleared my throat. "I'm fine, Your Majesty. Really. I still have plenty of questions though, and I…"

"And I will be happy to answer in the very near future. But for tonight, I was hoping to invite you to something very special." She smiled at me, her eyes warm.

"What is it?"

"It is—" she seemed to consider her words closely "—a sort of welcome party."

"Oh Gods, for me? Please, we don't need to do that."

"Oh don't worry," said General Kairos, my mother's shadow. "We didn't."

"What General Kairos means to say is that this party is for all of those going through the pledging ceremony this month. It is a celebration of our Houses and our culture. I think you would enjoy it very much."

"Oh." I swallowed. "I'd love to attend."

"Good," my mother said, her cheeks rosy. "I will have Akram bring you down when it is time. And Mehri will have all the appropriate clothing for you."

"Oh, thank you."

"I'm so glad you're here, Mira." Mother gripped me in a quick, tight hug before stepping back. Her hands immediately moved to her crown, straightening it before looking at a still-present Baye.

"I believe it is time to get ready for a party, Lieutenant. You are dismissed."

The Mer disappeared, and a moment later, another male took his place, this time wearing more of the crown's all-black uniform.

"I will see you tonight, Miraceti." My mother's face softened as she looked at me. "There are so many things that I need to tell you, Mira. But right now, I have an urgent meeting to attend. I'm sure that Mehri can answer some of your questions. And then tonight, we will sit together at the Welcome and discuss whatever you'd like."

My chest was rising and falling, Kairos's hand still tight on my wrist. I wondered briefly if he knew he was still braced as if to throw me away from my mother.

"I understand," I told her finally, "I look forward to it, Your Majesty. While I appreciate everything today, I still don't see the reason a mother, my mother, would leave their family behind. So until you want to talk about that, then I suggest you place me elsewhere for the event."

I wasn't sure where the heat that flooded my veins came from or the way that my temper was wavering, shaking under my chest. Today had been good. I knew that she was trying to offer me information. But I was no stranger to this tactic. She gave me information that she chose, that she wanted to wow me with, yet retained the information I wanted the most.

And it only added to the hurt that thickened my throat.

She flinched—actually flinched. I could see the minute motion flicker across her body before she pulled a fresh smile to her mouth and nodded just once. "Of course, Mira. Anything I can give you to make you feel more at home."

And then she was gone, moving down the hallway and out of my view a few moments later. Baye clapped a heavy hand down on Kairos's shoulders and then also departed, taking another spiraling staircase out of my vision, leaving General Kairos, Akram, and me.

Raising my brow, I turned to General Kairos. "What aren't you telling me?"

Kairos's voice was a low growl. "What do you mean?"

"I've been here one day, and you've shown me an entire city that exists underwater because of an ancient love triangle. And yet..." I tapped my chin. "Something seems off, and I know you feel it too."

I stepped up to him, secretly triumphant as General Kairos took a step back.

"You have no idea what is going on here. You can't just accuse your mother of things like that out in the open. She isn't hiding things from you, Princess. She's preparing you for the future."

"The future?"

His teeth flash in a snarl. "Yes, Princess. Some of us have to consider that."

"That's enough, General Kairos." The order fell from my lips easily, and to my surprise, Kairos stopped speaking, placing a hand over his heart before turning. Once he straightened again, his attention was held by only one other.

"Akram, report."

Akram stepped forward, still wearing that immense sword.

Kairos released me to stand, arms crossed over his chest as he observed the guard. "You've been briefed on Her Highness's needs."

Akram nodded, dropping a half bow.

"What needs?" I said, breaking into their conversation.

Kairos gave me a lazy once-over before addressing Akram once more. "Until dinner tonight, she is to stay here, warded and safe. After that, we will have to readdress."

"You're locking me up?"

Kairos ignored me, walking around Akram and to the doors. When he got closer, he turned, one long-fingered hand slipping over the door, where it gripped the handle.

"I'm keeping you safe. There's a difference."

A hint of panic entered my voice. "Not to me." This was all too much. Ceanus, the arc, the people changing shape, the Mer, the cursed. The core of me shook with the knowledge that threatened to overwhelm every one of my senses.

I ducked my chin, desperate to hide the welling of tears in my eyes. To my surprise, a warm finger immediately slipped under my chin and tilted it up. Unbidden, one tear escaped and ran down my cheek.

Kairos had the oddest expression on his face, his mouth twisted in words unsaid as he stared down at me. After a few loud breaths, his thumb swept over my jaw. "I'm sorry, Your Highness. The moment I know what we are dealing with is the moment I set you free."

"The danger," I repeated, attempting to retch my chin free.

His fingers only gripped me harder, and his eyes widened a fraction, as if surprised I'd heard him. "There are more things at play in Ceanus than just your arrival. It is House Leviathan's duty to keep Ceanus safe."

My eyes dropped to the shield tattoo still visible through his shirt's open front. Unable to stop myself, I asked, "What about me? Am I part of Ceanus?"

His hand jerked away. "My loyalty lies with the crown, which I serve completely." He stepped back, dropping into a bow as he pressed his hand over his heart in a salute. The air between us was cold and strange as I nodded and stepped back into my room once again.

He reached for the handle and disappeared into the hall, closing us within my rooms. Frustrated, I turned to face Akram, who had taken up a casual stance against the wall by my bed.

"Is he like that with everybody?" I gestured at the door.

"General Kairos is entrusted by the crown to care for the royal family on top of his other tasks." The guard didn't so much as blink as he spoke. The perfect emotionless statue.

My eyes narrowed. "So, is that a yes or a no? Trying to decide if he's a special brand of awful for just me or whether it's the same for everyone."

Akram didn't answer.

Sighing, I padded barefoot to my bed before perching on the edge of it facing him. I drummed my fingers against my leg.

My head felt like it weighed a hundred pounds, but I couldn't risk falling asleep. Not when there was so much more information to consider and whatever event that I was needed at tonight. I could tell it was important that I participate. I glanced around my room, my attention catching on the elaborately painted mural along one wall.

Trayon, the God of the Sea, was depicted there as a larger-than-life human male with pale-blue skin and deep-navy hair that flowed down his chest. He was cradling a globe—no, not a globe. It was Ceanus in his palms. And he was smiling down at it, a creation of his own making.

Did he mean for all of this to happen, I wondered. When he had cursed the waves of the Great Sea and dragged half of his brother's favorite city under the surface, had he intended for all of this? And the most important question in my mind, constantly circling and pressing at my lips.

Would he ever release Adrial from his curse? Something deep in my chest turned with worry. Because there was no reason for him to do so. From his perspective, everything was going very well for the Sea God.

But my father had raised me to be a queen. I knew how the world worked. There was always something the other person wanted.

I just needed to find out what Trayon wanted.

"Mehri will be here shortly with beverages and something for you to eat."

"How do you know that?"

A muscle in his jaw twitched. "She told me."

I looked around. My room's balcony was open to the arc's interior, but there wasn't another soul in sight. "She told you? When?"

Akram's head, just his head, turned to look at me. "Before she left, Your Highness."

Heat flushed my cheeks as I realized that I was thinking they had some kind of telekinetic connection. When they really had just communicated like any other time.

"Oh." I fiddled with the blankets on my bed. Why was I so disappointed? "Can I ask you a few questions, then?"

There was a soft noise, as if Akram was mentally bracing himself, and then he gave the tiniest of nods.

I scooted closer. "Are you a Mer too?"

He nodded silently, and my jaw dropped. "You are! How many of you are there?"

"The majority of Ceanus is Mer, Your Highness. We would have to consult the census if you need exact numbers."

I scoffed at the underlying sass in his words while my mind raced. An entire kingdom of Mer. And not just Mer, but Mer with special gifts. A thought occurred to me. "Did you ever live in Adrial?"

"No, I'm finfolk, born to two Mer. Not a sandwalker like those who join us later."

"Sandwalker? Is that what you call us?"

Akram gave another one of those small nods. "An old term."

I got off the bed and approached. Other than the muscle leaping in his jaw, he made no movement until I was right next to him. "You said earlier you were House Leviathan, like the General."

No nod this time, but I could see his eyes looking at me curiously.

I continued on. "Are you related to him or anything? Are the Leviathans a family?"

Akram's brows rose, and he shook his head. "No, Your Highness."

"You're sure?"

"I am." Akram's lips barely moved. "The Houses are not based on blood, but you can rest assured that the General and I are not related in any way." Something about the way he said it, as if I should be relieved he wasn't related to Kairos, gained my interest.

"Is he one of the cursed who turned?"

Akram shook his head again. "No, we are not sure where the General is from. He arrived at Ceanus as a child, with no guardians or family to speak of. He chose to serve the queen and later Leviathan. Your mother was smart enough to recognize the power in him, and he quickly rose through the ranks to where he now stands."

I watched Akram's face, curious how far I could push him. "And why does he hate me so much?"

Akram was silent for two long beats. "He doesn't hate you, Your Highness."

"Don't lie to me, Akram. I can tell."

More silence.

I narrowed my eyes. "Fine. I guess I'm going to have to find it out on my own, aren't I?" I strolled closer, pushing into Akram's personal space with a bold push of my heels.

The warrior's jaw tensed, but his lips remained sealed.

"Nothing to say, Akram?"

Akram's eyes jumped around the room, and I could almost picture the thoughts of his mind, the way he was thinking it over. But then, there was a soft knock at the door and the petite pink form that was Mehri interrupted our conversation.

"Hello, Mehri," I said, tone a little dejected as I stepped away from Akram.

"Hello, Your Highness." Mehri hurried to the center of the room and paused, setting down the meal. "Did I miss something?"

Akram and I grunted in unison.

Mehri pressed hands to her cheeks. "Oh my. Akram, what have you told her?"

Chapter Sixteen

I was no stranger to parties or events or luxury, but there was something about the Wecloming that set my nerves on edge.

It was beautiful. The whirling fabrics and decorations that hung all along the ballroom of the castle were enough to impress even Homer. He would've wanted more, of course, but not because they weren't stunning as they were. Just because he was Homer.

Mehri had brought me a gown to wear tonight, the soft, nearly silver fabric covering my breasts, my belly before plummeting to the ground to brush against my freshly painted and jeweled toes. The sandals she'd selected for me were dark leather, spiraling up my calves. Nearly my entire back was revealed, and while Adrial was not shy about showing off our skin, there was something in the air tonight that made me wish I could've skipped out on the beautifully braided straps and instead worn shining armor like that of Akram as we walked down to the castle's ballroom.

Mehri walked directly behind me, whispering a never-ending conversation of customs and information about what would be happening tonight. I reminded myself to put one foot after the other as I let her words flood my mind.

The Welcoming was a seasonal event, meant to celebrate those who had joined Ceanus from Adrial in the past weeks as well as the

Ceanians who had turned of age and were beginning their training to become a functioning member of the society. Each of the Houses would wear their token colors, and it was a time for leadership within all of the Houses to gather and celebrate their individuality.

A tray of steaming vegetables passed by on a servant's shoulder, the scent wafting over me, and I jealously watched a Mer close to me reach out and select a bite. I had been told to stay away from any food or drinks until Mehri specifically picked them out for me. And while I had no interest in accidentally upsetting my already nerve-wrecked belly, it still smelled divine.

"Do you think someone could be trying to poison me? Maybe just a little bite? I'm starving."

Mehri huffed. "I don't think that's a good idea. I can't imagine the resulting reaction to some of these foods is the first impression you'd like to make on your mother's council members."

"Good point, but I've been eating everything just fine so far."

Mehri was quiet, and I snuck a look back at her, noticing the guilty smile tugging at her lips. "Oh Mehri! You've been taking out the less familiar foods, haven't you?"

"Maybe."

I groaned. "Please stop babying me. I'm trying to acclimate to how things work down here."

"As you wish, Your Highness." Mehri fell in step once more as we wound our way to the final steps of the castle.

The ballroom before us was brightly lit, and there were crowds already filtering in. Happy chatter and conversation bloomed around me, bouncing off the walls and filling my belly with even more nerves. Mehri had been right to avoid food.

I had never been very good at this part. I preferred to meet with my constituents one on one or in controlled groups. Parties like this were a nightmare even on a good day.

And as for this one, I didn't even know who to find or where to begin. Everywhere I looked, Ceanians were chatting, their vibrant hair colors a splash of brightness against the pale white marble walls and floor of the ballroom.

An empty throne sat on one side, a long, elevated table at the center, where five large goblets were situated, with the largest at the center of the others. I could feel the gaze of many of the people, curious and warm as I stood at the arched entry.

I didn't know anyone, I realized, other than the Mer at my shoulder and the handmaiden at my back. I was a stranger in my mother's house, and it left my chest feeling tight and aching as I took a deep breath in.

Just then, a server swept past me, a tray that smelled very strongly of raw fish balanced on their shoulder. My eyes watered, and I coughed a little.

"Mehri," I choked out.

"Yes, Your Highness."

"I'll start acclimating myself tomorrow."

"Very good, Your Highness."

I straightened my spine, pushing a strand of hair behind my ear, and then faced the crowd once more. Picking up my skirts with one hand, I balanced the other on my bodyguard's thick forearm. "Akram, lead the way."

And we dove into the fray.

Or rather, it came to me. The moment I stepped into the ballroom, I was greeted by a stoic-looking Mer who had a mane of brilliant white hair, his hazel eyes assessing as he bowed before me.

"Your Highness, if I may, we met briefly the other day."

My brows rose, my memories trying to reconstruct who this might be. But he continued on. "You were freshly moved into the arc. I'm not sure you will remember. I'm Timor of House Cetus."

"Oh, of course." I pressed a hand over my heart, nodding quickly. "Nice to meet you, again." Internally, I grimaced at my words, but Timor didn't seem to mind my strange wording at all.

"I'm not sure how much you've been informed of yet, but I serve as Warden of House Cetus."

"Warden?"

"Yes, Warden. A sort of figurehead and guide for the House's decisions within Ceanus. I sit on the council with your mother and the other House Wardens. It is our job to guide and develop Ceanus to be the best it can be for its citizens. It is my honor to serve our new princess."

I nodded, knowing immediately that this was a subtle power play. And while I didn't realize he was the Warden, Mehri had already informed me of the situation with the House leaders in the case that I would've been dragged into a council meeting before I'd had a chance to meet any of them.

She had wanted me to be ready.

And I was.

I smiled at him. "And I'm sure that both your House and my mother, Her Majesty, are grateful for your time and effort. Now excuse me if I'm incorrect, but I believe I was told that it takes all four Houses to vote to oppose a royal decree?"

Timor's smile dipped for a breath then widened.

"Or am I incorrect? I'm sitting in on the council meeting later this week and want to be sure that I get it right."

"It is, Your Highness. It is one of the beauties of our society's setup. We make decisions as a unit, ruling in the mighty Trayon's name."

"Oh good. Glad to see my reading has been helping." I accepted a full glass of ruby-colored liquid and brought it to my lips. "Everything is so new here. I'm just trying to keep up."

"I'm sure, Your Highness, no one expects you to attend any of the council meetings if you do not feel ready. After all, as her daughter, your opinion will no doubt sway the queen's opinion. For better or for worse."

The liquid was sweet and bright on my tongue. I took my time taking another sip before I answered him. "I never speak on things that I don't understand."

Timor's silver brows rose, and something in the back of my mind pressed forward, demanding. He was familiar. He was…someone I should have known. Or perhaps I already did.

I swallowed the drink, the pleasant sweetness making my tongue tingle.

"Then it sounds like we can look forward to hearing your opinion, as well as your mother's, soon."

There was no time for me to respond, or even consider that I was starting a fight much bigger than myself, before Timor bowed low to the ground.

"Your Highness, enjoy your night."

I saluted him back then watched as the powerful-looking man strolled away, his hands folded at his back. Blowing through my teeth, I turned to Mehri. "I didn't handle that very well, did I?"

Mehri blinked rapidly. "There is always room for improvement, Your Highness."

I couldn't help it. A short laugh escaped. "I don't deserve you."

That made Mehri grin, her head tilting as she moved in closer. "Let's try someone else, then. Perhaps starting with your mother's past lover was a bad idea."

I groaned, my fingers curling as I followed Mehri back into the throng of people. "I did not need to know that."

"You do, though. Everyone else does." Stopping a passing tray of food, Mehri handed me a me a small ball of some food I didn't recognize.

"Try this. You will like it."

I popped it into my mouth, rewarded by a salty and savory bite that soothed my stomach as we made our way across the room. "That was delicious." I looked around for more. "What was it?"

"It is better that you don't know, Your Highness."

"Noted."

Mehri was moving quickly now, her petite body curling though the crowd like a pale-pink ribbon, Akram and me following blindly behind. Eyes still followed, hands occasionally still brushed my sides as the Ceanians cleared the way for me.

Or maybe they were just moving because Akram had his scary face on again. Either way, I was relieved when Mehri stopped in front of a pair of Mer. One, a tiny, crooked woman, gray hair slicked back from her face, offered Mehri a small smile as we stopped. The other, a fit-looking male, observed me closely, his dark-blond locks wrapped in a bun atop his head.

Mehri gestured to me. "Honorable Warden Nidian, may I present Miraceti of Adrial."

Nidian's face split into a warm smile, dimples flashing as the delicate lines around his eyes deepened. "Your Highness, welcome to Ceanus."

"Thank you, Warden." I saluted his bow, turning to the other woman as she bowed as well.

"And this is Ionia of House Cirein-Croin," Mehri continued.

I watched as the female also bowed to me, gnarled fingers curled tight over her heart.

"The pleasure is mine," I said, watching her straighten as much as she could. She was a tiny creature, not even reaching my collarbone, but something in the way she looked up at me told me that she was as powerful as any other Mer in the room. And that she was used to people knowing that. And respecting it. I nodded deeper to her.

"Ionia and I were just discussing the month's latest batch of trainees," Warden Nidian said, his tone light. "There are often more this time of year due to the storms along the isles."

I froze, and I could feel Akram breath in. "Is that so? How interesting."

"This training class will be among the largest we've had in several months," Ionia said, her eyes still coolly assessing me.

I clamped down on my temper and the need to turn to Nidian and demand he tell me everything he knew about more Adrialians being pulled below.

"But they are good souls," Ionia continued. "I believe they will all be valued citizens after a few more weeks."

"When do they begin?"

"Tomorrow," Nidian stated. "They will have the rest of the moon's journey to train and learn about Ceanus and our Houses before they are asked to make their choice."

"Their choice?"

Ionia and Nidian exchanged glances. "Why yes," Ionia said. "At the conclusion of training, they can bid for their preferred House. Should that House accept them, they are brought into the House for life."

"And if the House doesn't accept?"

Nidian's face was tight, and I could see that I'd made them uncomfortable. Even Akram behind me continued to give out waves of stress. I wondered briefly if Mehri was already hard at work calming the situation.

Swallowing, I broke the silence. "It seems this is a sore subject and clearly not a party conversation. You'll have to excuse my bluntness. There's just so much that I don't know. I feel like I'm working on borrowed time, trying to learn it all before I leave."

Ionia tilted her head, as if needing to hear me more clearly. "Before you leave?"

"Yes. While I understand the curse brought me to Ceanus, I can't stay here forever. My father needs me in Adrial."

"Ah, yes. Of course," Nidian said, his eyes straying to Ionia, where a message flew between them before I could read it. A beat later, the conversation moved on. "Tell me about your home, Mira. We in Cirein-Croin are endlessly curious, and I want to know everything about life above the waters."

That made me smile. "Where do you want me to start, Warden?"

Nidian's eyes shone greedily. "We often have cursed who can provide us a tangible look at life in the city. But you… You have such a unique perspective. You are royalty. You live with the king of one of the oldest kingdoms on the continent. It's not often we have a chance to learn like this."

I could practically feel the excitement rolling off the male. "Of course. Um, alright, something that an Adrialian may not know. I…uh… I guess I could share that we have recently sealed new trade negotiations with the Emenians."

That seemed safe enough to confess. The Mer should have no interest with the Emenians and their island nation.

"Emenians…" Nidian's voice rose with enthusiasm. "Wonderful sailors. They have crafted some of the finest boats this part of the world has ever seen."

I blinked. "Yes, they have. Fastest we've seen as well. I attempted to barter with some craftsman who would stay in Adrial to work on building us a small fleet for fast-moving merchants. But it didn't work out."

I left out the part that it didn't work because the Emenians had to explain that many of their craftsmen were avid swimmers and sailors, and they believed that by residing in Adrial, they may become susceptible to the curse as well. Therefore ending their career and lifestyle of sand and sun and sea.

I didn't blame them.

Ionia shook her head. "I assumed that Adrialians would stop putting themselves out on the Great Sea and move farther into the continent. It is too risky."

"We don't have another choice right now. There is too much chaos with the northern kingdoms, and we are first and foremost a trading outlet."

"When I lived there, it was a thriving city, but the king at the time, your grandfather, was young and hungry. He spent most of his time devising ways to acquire more land through blood and war."

"You lived in Adrial?"

Ionia grinned, showing off a shining gold tooth. "Am I the first cursed that you have met, Your Highness?"

"I believe so. There don't seem to be very many."

"Once there were far more. But over time, the arc and its God have demanded less and less." Ionia spread her hands around the room. "Fewer young born every year. Fewer curses that find us. The arc is telling us something."

A deep, jovial voice broke into the conversation. "The arc is telling you things? Ionia, please, I told you not too much wine before the ceremony."

Ionia swatted at the newcomer, who I recognized in an instant as General Kairos's second-in-command, Baye. "You hush, boy. When you've lived as long as I have, you remember that the ocean only takes what it needs."

Baye's laughing eyes found mine, and I couldn't help but smile at him. "Can you tell it, then, Grandmother, that what we really need is the female of my heart, plucked straight from my dreams and put straight through the portal so that I may whisk her way for a lifetime of love and adoration?"

"And what have you done for the ocean, Lieutenant, that makes you think it would ever be so giving?" Ionia swatted the male with her hand. "You should trying giving before taking, youngling."

Baye rolled his eyes but pulled away from Ionia to offer a deep bow to me. "In all seriousness, Your Highness, I was sent over to bring you to your mother. The ceremony is about to begin."

"Ceremony?" I quickly looked down, straightening the folds of my dress.

"Don't worry. Nothing to do on your part," Nidian said, amusement filling his words. "I do hope we can talk more, Princess Miraceti, once you are able to settle in. There are so many things I'd love to learn." That hungry look stole across his features once more.

I nodded, offering a small smile as I took Baye's hand.

"Where's the General?" Ionia said, looking suspiciously at Baye.

"Temporarily held up. He sent me in his stead."

Ionia nodded, but I could see her looking away as if expecting the General to come barreling in at any moment.

I nodded to her and then Nidian. "Thank you for making me feel welcome."

"Anytime, Princess," Ionia said.

Baye tugged me away, his face tilting down to mine. While he wasn't as tall as General Kairos or Akram, he was still taller than me, his bulk a comforting presence as he steered me through the crowd. Mehri vanished, while Akram appeared to back off as the lieutenant guided me towards the long table I'd seen earlier.

"I hope I am an acceptable replacement for the General," Baye said, running a hand over his fiery curls.

"More than acceptable. I'm sure if General Kairos was here, then he would have already growled and grunted at me a half dozen times."

"Growled and grunted, Your Highness?"

"I believe it is his second language." I leaned closer, dropping my voice. "I believe rampant disapproval is the General's native tongue."

Baye laughed from deep in his belly, making me grin. "He is a disapproving male, isn't he? I promise it is all a front for the most devoted and generous-hearted Mer in all of Ceanus."

I stared at him, checking for sarcasm. He kept his expression stony and serious for all of two breaths then burst into laughter again. Grinning, I let him tow me the rest of the way to the table. Before I could open my mouth to ask what we were going to be doing, my mother was at my side, flanked by guards in armor similar to Akram's.

Her face was painted, a dusting of scales the color of rubies showing along her cheekbones. The silver crown on her dark hair gleamed as she gripped my wrists, her palms nearly hot against my skin.

"Miraceti, you look stunning," she said, her scales showing off her high cheekbones, gleaming in the coral light.

I swallowed twice. "You do too, Your Majesty. Your…" I didn't know what to call them, so I made an assumption. "Your scales are so pretty."

Her eyes crinkled as she smiled widely at me. "Thank you. I recently returned from a swim and thought I would leave them for the Welcoming." Realizing that Baye had also stepped back into the masses, I saw that it was just Akram and me standing alongside the queen and table.

I cleared my throat as quietly as possible, leaning closer to my mother. "What happens now?"

"We open with a drink. You don't have to do anything, just stand by my side if you will."

I nodded, moving aside as she stepped to the table, her hand reached for the goblet in the center, the largest of all of them. The moment her fingers touched the goblet the pottery began to glow, a deep blue, the lines and wave etching illuminating the contours of my mother's face. Talking around us dimmed, and the crowd turned to face my mother.

Effortlessly, Mother raised the goblet above her head. "We are Ceanus, gifted and blessed by the God, Trayon. It is with his power that we remain safe within the arc." Her free hand gestured to the crowd. "House Kraken, House Cirein-Croin, House Leviathan, House Cetus, step forward."

My eyes jumped to the first who stepped forward. Nidian of House Cirein-Croin stepped to the table, standing in front of an empty goblet.

"House Cirein-Croin is here to honor Ceanus."

Another flurry of clothing, and then a tall, waiflike female who could only be in her early teens, stepped forward. "House Leviathan is here to honor Ceanus."

Timor was next, stepping up to his goblet. "House Cetus is here to honor Ceanus."

And finally, a newcomer, powerful body wrapped in a pale-blue robe, his matching blue hair contrasting beautifully with his deeply tanned skin. "House Kraken is here to honor Ceanus."

My mother leaned over the table, pouring the wine into the center goblet, where it split into four, the wine running down the spigots into each of the house's goblets. "May Trayon's blessing break across us, always."

The Wardens each lifted their drinks high. "For Ceanus."

And they each drank, tipping their glasses up to the coral lights, I could see that each goblet depicted an etched silver brand.

A shield on House Leviathan. A crossed spear on Cetus. A wrapped scroll on Cirein-Croin. A hammer on House Kraken.

As they drank, the lights brightened, making me blink as I watched. Mother stepped back, her arms spreading wide.

"We are Ceanus." Her voice echoed across the room, filling my chest with a burst of warmth and joy so intense I nearly pressed a hand there.

The crowd answered her eagerly, many raising their own glasses, others holding a fist above their head and then pressing it over their heart. They stared at her with wide-eyed adoration, and I could understand why.

As soon as she broke contact with the pitcher, it ceased glowing. The spell around us was broken, and the crowd began to mingle once more, more attendees moving through the room with food and small plates.

"How did you do that?" I whispered to my mother when she stood before me once again.

"My gift is fed by Ceanus, and Ceanus feeds my gift," she said, a smile tugging at the corners of her lips.

My brows lowered. "I have no idea what that means."

"You know what? I'm not sure I do either. My father used to tell me that all the time though, and I felt like I had to confuse you just as much as I was always confused."

I huffed. "Hereditary confusion. Lovely."

Mother laughed, linking her arm through mine. "Come with me. I'll try to explain more." Her guards cleared a path for us, and together we wound our way over to the throne.

"Many of the Adrialians who went into the sea that legendary night were already mages. Some powerful, some less so. But all of them were aware of the magic, even if some feared it. But our time here in the arc has only served to show us more and more abilities. It is as if by being inside of Trayon's magic and inside of the spell he cast on Adrial, we are exposed to magic at all times."

"Does that mean you are becoming more powerful?"

"Some of us, yes. My great-grandfather would be shocked and maybe a little fearful of some of the gifts that have recently become more possible." My mother leaned her head closer to mine. "Do you see the House Warden for Leviathan?"

I found the young-looking Mer standing beside a short, burly looking male. "I do."

"You should know she is one of the most powerful fighters we've ever seen."

I stared. The Mer was delicately built, her soft, youthful expression one of boredom and disinterest as the male, who could only be her bodyguard, scowled at anyone who got close. "Her? You're sure."

"Absolutely. While our gifts are sometimes private to us, I have permission to share hers, so I will tell you this. Atlana, the Warden, can turn any part of her body to stone."

I reeled back. "What?"

"Imagine fighting with her, and when she hits you, it is not a Mer or human fist that impacts you but something that feels akin to being smashed with a stone."

I eyed the girl with renewed interest. "She just wills her body to change?"

Mother nodded. "It is similar to how our bodies know to shift and change in the water."

"That's amazing. I will definitely avoid picking a fight with her."

Mother smiled crookedly. "Please do. House Leviathan is always looking for a way to assert their authority, and while she's young, she knows what she is doing."

A companionable silence fell between us as we watched the leadership of Ceanus mill around the trainees After tonight, they were trainees, and they stood out far more than I'd expected. Perhaps it was because of their hair. The Ceanian-born Mer had brightly colored hair like the elders, while the cursed had a variety of what I used to call normal hair tones. I briefly pictured Mehri's bright locks strolling down the streets of Port Sol and realize they would cause quite the stir among all the burnettes and blondes of Adrial.

Yet now, those plain colors were a dead giveaway of who was born and who had been cursed. Subconsciously, I touched my own hair. "Was your hair always that color? I have a hard time imaging someone didn't notice."

Mother leaned back in her throne. "I dyed it—quite often, to be honest. For many of us, our hair tones change during our shifts. For those who pledge and stay, they also tend to change as well. Again, we aren't sure whether it is the proximity to the power here or whether that's just part of being Mer."

"Will mine change?"

That made her look up at me. "Oh, I don't know, *minu*. I think it is beautiful the way it is."

"Thank you." The compliment settled in my chest, warming me. "Will I… Will I learn to shift?"

"I'm not sure, Mira. Most of the cursed Adrialians shift after they get closer to the arc. You did not. We aren't sure whether that was a direct result of General Kairos's venom or something else." She looked me over critically. "We will take you outside the arc soon to see. I didn't want to rush you."

She was right. This was all very overwhelming, but there was a large part of me that wished I could go now. I wanted to feel the Great Sea against my skin again and know that it wouldn't hurt me. "I'd like that—going outside the arc, that is. I want to see what color my scales would be."

My mother's expression lightened, her fingers twisting together lazily as she considered me. "We will go tomorrow, as soon as we can."

"Really?"

"Yes, absolutely. And if I'm not able to get away, then I will make sure the very best Ceanus has will take you."

I was going to see the sea from a completely new angle. I was going to experience this world as it was meant to be. "That sounds great. Thank you, Mother."

My attention was pulled from her as loud voices suddenly broke across the room. A uniformed Mer ran in, dodging between people, moving expertly up to Timor. The Warden's eyes flashed up to the throne, finding first me before they settled on my mother. His lips moved, and then the messenger was moving again, bowing low as he hurtled to his knees before the throne.

I had the overwhelming urge to move closer, any chance of hearing the messenger was drowned by the distance and noise between us. Disappointed tugged at me as the moment he had spoken his piece, the messenger fell forward to brace himself against the stairs. My mother stood quickly, her guards moving together as she disappeared through a door at the back of the room.

Akram's hands were on my shoulders now, guiding me away, a snarl deep in his throat as more guards closed in on the party. "What's this? What is going on?"

"We have to move, Highness," Akram grunted, moving me towards the exit, where I could see others were filtering through. There was no panic, but a certain level of urgency hummed in the air.

"Akram?"

I turned, but he was a step behind, Baye's hand tight around his bicep. The two men were conversing in voices too low for me to understand, but based on the frown on the usually jovial Mer's face, it was serious.

Another male Mer bumped into me, unaware. But before I could say anything to them, I heard what they were saying to their companion.

"He's in rough shape, they said. I bet that's where the queen is going. To question him."

"I bet she has plenty of questions for this one."

"They said he was the royal guard in Adrial, but he just showed up here tonight, completely unplanned. I can't imagine they'll be happy to see him."

I gripped the male's shoulder, turning him to face me. "Who do they have?"

The male's eyes widened, gold irises growing as he moved to bow and salute.

I brushed him off, stepping closer. "Who do they have?"

He licked his lips, eyes flashing to his companion and then back to me. "They're saying it's your guard, Your Highness."

I jerked my head back. "Akram?" I had just seen him. He was just behind me.

"No, Your Highness. The one from Adrial."

My heart plummeted to my belly.

Rhoe.

Rhoe was here. Did that mean the curse had gotten him as well? Or did my mother's people attack him? Fear chilled my skin as I stepped away from the pair. Had he come down here to save me?

"Your Highness." The other Mer stepped up, worry in their gaze. "Are you alright?"

"Where?" I licked painfully dry lips. "Where are they keeping him?"

"The throne room, Your Highness," he said simply, hand gesturing to the door.

I was running before the final word left his lips.

I raced through the palace, my focus centered on one person, one being. The pounding of my heart was nothing compared to the overwhelming need to get to him. Rhoe. They had him.

He was sprawled on the floor of the throne room, my mother's ominous form hovering a few feet away. That enormous General of hers was nearby, another dark-haired, armored soldier kneeling beside him. Beside Rhoe.

Rhoe.

Rhoe.

Rhoe.

I chanted his name in my head as my bare feet slapped against the marble. I'd torn off my beautiful sandals the moment I'd left the ballroom. Anything to get here faster. But now, I may still be too late. My mother raised a delicate, long-nailed hand to Rhoe's forehead. Her gift, this strange ability... She could use it on him. Would she use it on him?

I didn't know how he managed to get down here to try to save me. And I didn't know what my mother was doing. But the collective gasp in the room wasn't my arrival. It was the spark of her gift that made my mother's hand glow.

For the first time, I recognized it not for the beauty, but for the danger. I couldn't let her hurt him.

"No! You can't," I screamed, shoving through the royal guards who stood around Rhoe's prone body. I knelt over him, pressing my body into his back and wrapping my arms around him. Somewhere, a sword was unsheathed. I snarled and held on tighter.

"He's mine. You are not allowed to touch him. And by Artio or Trayon, if you hurt him, I will never forgive you." Silence only broken by the ragged breathing from my chest filled the space. Then I said it again, for emphasis. "Never."

My mother stared at me, shocked.

"Mira," a soft voice echoed.

For a long moment, I looked around the circle of watchers for who might have that voice.

"Mira," it said again, deep and low.

Shock radiated through me as I slowly, deliberately removed my body from atop Rhoe's. He kept his face averted, his oh-so-familiar frame unfolding from the position on the floor. When he was about halfway up, Kairos stepped closer to Rhoe, offering a hand to him. Rhoe hesitated, and a trickling awareness flew down my spine.

My mouth opened, prepared to shout him down from touching my friend. But then something happened that I couldn't have pictured if I'd had a hundred years to dream it up.

Rhoe didn't panic. He was calmly looking up at the *creature* who had bitten into my neck like the predator that he was, but not with fear. Not with disgust. With something that I could barely recognize in this situation. The truth was so impossible, my mind couldn't register it.

Pieces of memories and bits of recognition began to filter into my mind, like the sunlight shining under the surface of the water.

It couldn't be.

He couldn't be.

"Rhoe?" I whispered, my lips frozen in shock.

Rhoe's big body gave one last shudder as he clasped the other male at the elbow and allowed Kairos to pull him to his feet. Kairos released him a breath later, moving to stand with arms crossed at my side. My stomach roiled dangerously as I stared at them both.

Rhoe cursed, running a hand through his hair in that trademark move, the one that always made him look so boyishly charming. I caught sight of something on his arm. A line of shimmering blue and teal shapes going down the backside of his arm.

No, not shapes.

Scales.

"Oh Gods," I whispered again. I clamped a hand over my mouth, pushing myself back and standing shakily. "It can't be."

My body curled in on itself, my eyes unable to look away from his dear face. I had been so wrong about so much. How was it possible to be this wrong?

Rhoe opened his eyes, training them on me as my entire body wavered on the spot. But even now, I was hypnotized by him, just as I'd been the first day I'd met him in my father's court years ago. But now, I knew him for what he was. Even if I couldn't say it. Not yet.

His gaze burned into mine, his irises glowing teal blue. For a moment, all I could absorb was the pure beauty that radiated from those unreal, shocking eyes. Then something twisted deep inside my chest, making my lungs fail and my vision grow fuzzy.

They were Mer eyes. Inhuman and unreal, glowing back at me with a power that belonged to so few remaining humans.

Rhoe had not come for me.

He had simply come home.

Chapter Seventeen

"Mira," Rhoe said, stepping towards me.

I gasped, throwing out an arm to block him. "No. No. It can't be."

"Mira, please, I can explain."

Why did everyone keep saying that to me? And worse, not a single one of them actually explained anything.

"You lied to my father. You lied to me, Rhoe." I covered my mouth again. "Is that even your name?" I knew he could understand me, even behind the muffle of my fingers.

Rhoe's eyes begged me to listen, the glow softening. "This was the only lie, Mira. I promise. I was sent to protect you, and when your father took a shine to me, I saw it as an opportunity."

"An opportunity? This is my life, Rhoe, and you were a part of it. We were friends. We did everything together. Oh Gods, I thought you cared about me."

"I do," Rhoe said.

The softest rumble echoed from Kairos, who now stepped closer.

"That doesn't matter now, does it? How am I supposed to believe anything you tell me?"

The other Mer in the chamber eased closer, curious eyes and bold whispers racing around me.

"I can show you. You just have to believe me."

The crowd was louder now, the noise ringing in my ears as I looked up into the face of my best friend, the man I thought I'd been falling for. The one I'd been prepared to risk it all for. I couldn't be here any longer. "I don't believe you. Not anymore."

I had to go. I had to leave. My dress swirled around my legs as I spun, looking for an exit.

Rhoe reached out, his hand sealing around my wrist. In my desperation to leave, I was caught off balance and found myself tumbling to the ground. My knees hit, then my elbow, my eyes watering at the impact. A moment later, in a flash of black, my wrist was dropped. When I opened my eyes, I saw my former best friend hovering above the platform, his legs dangling as the caped form of General Kairos held him by his throat.

Snarls filled the air as I rolled to my back and stared up at the two men.

"How dare you touch her!"

Rhoe grunted, his hands now on General Kairos's wrists as the larger male held him aloft, captured. "Kairos..."

Another snarl slipped from the General's mouth, and suddenly there was a gentle hand on my shoulder.

Akram was there, his eyes on the two males as he guided me away. "This is not the place," Akram said.

My mother stepped backward to her throne, sitting slowly, her gaze hot on my face. I had stopped her from touching him, but there was no way that she didn't know about Rhoe being my father's Chosen. She had known. Had she sent him?

I wanted to not care. I wanted to run. But now my body was sluggish, weaving on the spot as Rhoe continued to sputter curses at General Kairos.

"You have been gone too long, son of Cetus. But in case you were looking for a reminder, in Ceanus, we bow before our queen. And her heir."

General Kairos released Rhoe, whose bare feet stumbled on the platform for a moment before he rebalanced himself. He was breathing hard, staring between General Kairos and me with wide eyes.

"Mira, please."

"Do it," the General commanded.

The crowd went completely silent. Rhoe's brows lowered. Akram stood at my back, Kairos at my side.

General Kairos took a step towards Rhoe, closing the gap between them. "Do it!" he shouted, his voice echoing through the chamber.

Rhoe bristled, stepping towards me, and finally met my eyes again. They were no longer apologetic but filled with hurt. I felt nothing at all as he bowed at the waist, his hand pressed against his chest.

"Your Highness."

General Kairos moved to stand behind him, his black gaze intent on the bowing male. "On your knees," he murmured, "Apologize to your princess."

Rhoe's shoulders dropped, and with a rattling sigh, he bent his knee and dropped farther to kneel before me. His blond hair swept forward, cutting off my view of his face as he bowed over his knee.

"My deepest apologies, Your Highness. It will not happen again."

I swallowed, feeling the stares of all of those still gathered around us. Yet, out of everyone, it was General Kairos who captured my attention. His face was still twisted in a half snarl, his hands curled to fists.

But for the first time, I recognized that all the fury and menace he constantly exuded may not be *at* me, but rather *about* me. Heat engulfed my spine as those black eyes found mine.

"Stand up, Rhoe."

Rhoe's head snapped up, and for a second, I thought maybe he was going to grin at me, maybe brush my hair out of my face. But there was nothing now, his face a careful, beautiful mask. The same one he'd worn so much in the presence of the courtiers of Adrial, he now donned it for me.

Hurt throbbed in my chest as I nodded. "Akram, I want to go to my rooms." I turned to my mother, bowing without raising my face. I didn't want her to see my expression, at the rapidly cracking exterior that threatened to give way, spilling out my devastation and frustration, at any moment.

Rhoe pushed to his feet but stayed still.

I stepped away from all of them. "Now, Akram. I want to go home now." And by home, I meant to my comfortable room in Adrial, where my father grieved for me. That's where I belonged. Not in this city of secrets. Not with these people who told half-truths and false promises. I could never belong here.

"Of course, Your Highness." Akram's hand brushed my shoulder. "This way."

My tears blurred the path to my room, and I knew without a doubt that I would be just as lost tomorrow as I was tonight.

And I didn't just mean about the winding pathways of Ceanus.

***

"Your Highness, you must get up."

I rolled over, away from Mehri's urgent voice. I had no interest in getting out of this bed anytime soon. Rhoe's betrayal was not just the latest in the sequence of secrets that had been revealed to me but apparently the last that I'd been able to weather.

I was done with secrets. I had once been laid up with an infection for nearly a month. I could tell my mother that I was sick and couldn't meet with her today. I wasn't capable of talking about what had happened last night after the Welcoming. I was going to just stay here until I could talk to Trayon, and then I was going home.

I swiped at my face. There were no more tears. They had come after Akram dropped me off to my rooms. Slipping silently down my face as Mehri tucked me into my bed. And stopping somewhere after the nightmares of being held under the water, a swirling black presence dragging me down, down, down until I had woken up this morning still exhausted.

"I'm not going anywhere today, Mehri." I tugged the softness of the blankets back up over my burning eyes.

Mehri grabbed the foot of the blankets and yanked, tearing my shield from the world away in one sharp movement. "Oh yes, you are, Your Highness. You have to."

"Excuse me?" I blinked up at her.

"There was a council meeting called after last night. I heard from your mother's handmaiden that they believe it is because of the situation with Rhoe and General Kairos."

I bolted upright in bed. "What? Why?"

"There are concerns. Some Ceanians are claiming that you are purposefully stirring up a fight between Cetus and Leviathan."

"I didn't even know Rhoe was House Cetus last night. How would I have done that?"

"Rhoe is the heir apparent for his father. He will be Warden someday."

I blinked, letting her drag my sleepshirt over my head. "He's Timor's son? I also didn't know that. Wonderful. Just wonderful." And yet, the announcement made sense. I had recognized something in Timor's features during our very tense conversation at the party. "But even then, why does that matter? General Kairos works for the crown, and he was offended for me. It wasn't some kind of House-declared rumble in the streets."

Mehri made a sound and then hurried across the room, selecting a dress from my wardrobe and returning to my side. Her voice was low, rushed. "Because, Highness, you are also House Cetus."

"I am? That's news to me. I didn't think I had pledged anything. I thought that's why all those people last night were, I don't know, recruiting me."

Mehri yanked the dress over my head. It was soft and clingy, wrapping around my body and dropping to below my knees, the light-green color making my skin seem even more pale than usual. "They might have been trying, but House Cetus has always had ruling power. It's even in your name, Princess Miraceti. Ceti for Cetus."

She handed me earrings, which I took as I gave her a dubious look. "I did catch on to that part. I thought it was just because of my mother or something."

"To a certain degree, maybe, but I believe it was your mother's way to make sure that House Cetus remained the ruling House. To make it easier if you were ever to show up here and people wondered who you were."

The earrings tugged at my lobes, but I shoved them through, grimacing at the pinch as Mehri slid a gold bracelet over my wrist. "But why is it such a big deal about Rhoe?" My throat got tight, and I pressed a hand to my stomach to quell the nausea that lurked each time I thought about his betrayal.

"Didn't you hear me, Highness?" Mehri stepped back. "He will be the Warden of Cetus someday. You have met the Wardens, right? You understand that they believe whatever house wears the crown controls Ceanus."

"Yes."

"Wouldn't it be interesting if one of their unmarried sons, a certain blond soldier, married the newly recovered princess of Ceanus? Then House Cetus would be all but guaranteed the power of the throne. Before you showed up, there was a plan to reassess succession in Ceanus. But now, with both you and Rhoe here..." Mehri clicked her tongue. "Seems like Cetus is making sure they have the only option well within grasp."

"They think I'm supposed to marry Rhoe?"

Mehri shrugged. "That's why I thought you needed to wake up."

I gaped at her. "But I can't marr—"

To my surprise, my handmaiden put her hand over my lips then pointed at the open door. Akram stood there, silent and enormous. "It's better you go now, find out what the problem is, Your Highness."

"You can't come with me?"

"My ears are better served down in the service rooms with the other royal staff. I will report back on what I find out. Akram will take you."

I nodded, watching her dash past Akram, giving the stone-faced warrior a pat on the shoulder as she passed. The room was quiet again as I approached Akram. I hadn't spoken to him last night, not even when the tears had started.

"Akram…"

"Your Highness." He bowed.

"About last night…"

"I'm glad I could provide some directions and assistance to Her Highness," Akram said, his voice calm.

I stared down at the top of his bowed head, his golden sword hilt shining back at me. He was offering me this little solstice. The chance to pretend.

I took it.

"Of course. Thank you, Akram." I gestured to the door. "Shall we go?"

Chapter Eighteen

My eyes felt gritty with the echo of my earlier tears and tumultuous sleep as I walked beside Akram down one of the castle's endless hallways, lit by soft coral light. We curled down around the base of the castle to a wide dais, where seven chairs were already positioned in a circle.

Mehri's intel was very good. We were not the first to arrive. Timor of House Cetus, Rhoe's father, was already standing at the center of the dais speaking in hushed tones to the Warden of Kraken, Arthic. Arthic, who I had only glimpsed the night before, perched within a sea of Krakens at the Welcoming. Both men went silent as soon as Akram's broad figure stepped onto the tile floor. They bowed in my direction, but I did notice that Arthic's was slower, more pronounced.

"Good morning, Your Highness," Timor said, straightening and gesturing to the circle of seating. "It is typical for House heirs to stand behind their Warden's chair during council meetings. You will stand behind your mother at the helm."

"Thank you, Warden," I said, giving him a soft nod with my chin like I'd seen my mother do. I glanced around the circle, seeing the chair with an additional flourish on the arm rests and a curling crown along the spine. Clearly my mother's.

Without waiting for more information, I moved to stand beside it, drawing my finger down the smooth carved lines. A tiny spark raced from my finger down the carefully inlaid coral, and to my surprise, the coral lit up, the delicate stones displaying an array of bright colors that made the dark-colored chair glow.

I gasped, surprised as the chair returned the spark, making my finger tingle.

"Your Highness," a voice choked out, and I released the chair quickly, turning to watch as Nidian made his way into the room. He was in a bold purple wrap, his eyes painted as they were the night before. He bowed to me, taking the chair directly to the right of my mother's.

"Good morning," I murmured.

Nidian's eyes crinkled. "Is it?"

I snorted then turned to the door as my mother walked in, flanked by her usual guard. "I guess we'll find out together."

Mother moved quickly through the room, her presence the catalyst for the other Mer in the room to assume their positions. The Wardens all took their chairs, their heirs at their back. General Kairos as well as Ionia stepped into the room. Ionia took a seat, but Kairos stood, a looming shadow at the back of the room.

"Let us begin," my mother said. While her face remained relaxed, I could feel the atmosphere crackle with energy.

Looking around, I wished I knew what abilities everyone else possessed.

Timor stood slowly, and for the first time since last night, I forced myself to take in the appearance of his heir, formerly my best friend. Rhoe stood tall and still behind his father. I didn't let myself linger on him. I still don't trust my raw-feeling heart to behave itself. "House Cetus has concerns about Her Highness, Princess Miraceti."

"Concerns?" My mother remained at ease, even as my heartrate went wild.

"Indeed, your majesty. After last night, what would've been a minor miscommunication was turned into something that can only be described as a demonstration from House Leviathan."

General Kairos took two steps forward, standing nearly at my side now. My mother raised one hand, and Kairos stilled.

"And you think that this demonstration was Princess Mira's fault?" She shifted in her chair, eyeing the Warden. "I had heard, Timor, that your son put his hands on my daughter."

Chatter broke out around us, and again Damona raised her hand. "While I understand that this was not an ideal situation by any stretch of the imagination, my daughter acted to the best of her abilities, knowing what little she did of the situation. And that is not her fault. Not knowing is actually my fault since I had not told her the truth about Rhoe." She cocked her head at Timor. "So perhaps it is me who is at fault."

Timor shook his head. "Your Majesty, I meant no disrespect."

"And yet, here you stand, calling my council together in order to lay down half-truths about my General, who happens to be of a different House, doing the job he was trained to do."

"He didn't need to handle it that way," Timor said, a growl entering his voice.

Rhoe's head dropped, even as his father kept going.

"It was an insult to the honor that is House Cetus. And they both us an apology."

"An apology?" Kairos remained still, but I could see the line of his jaw tense and shake. "She owes you nothing."

My chest tightened at his words.

"Timor is correct, though. Princes Mira doesn't know our ways. Nor how a proper challenge would've occurred."

I opened my mouth, but Ionia caught my eye around Kairos and shook her head quickly. I snapped my jaw shut and forced myself into silence.

"What would you expect of someone who arrived in Ceanus days ago?" my mother spoke again.

"Your Majesty, she is not like the other newcomers. We both know that." Timor stepped back and seated himself back in his chair. "She is our princess, Your Majesty. She should act like it."

I grimaced at those words. Not just because they were painful, but because they were true.

With more clarity than I had felt for days, the solution to my current issues slowly came to light. I cleared my throat, and with narrowed eyes, Timor stopped speaking, looking over at me with barely contained irritation. "May I have the floor, Warden?"

"Yes, of course, Your Highness," he said, the words dripping with sarcasm.

I ignored him, turning in my chair so that I could stare at each of the House Warden's faces. I wanted them to all see how sure I was about this.

"I would like to join them."

"You want to join who?" Mother echoed from beside me.

I cast her a quick glance but addressed everyone once again. "I want to join the cursed, the trainees."

That got their attention, eyes casting sideways. Someone to my left made a hushed noise under their breath. I kept my face completely blank, a comfortable smile on my lips.

Rhoe surprised me by speaking first, over the shoulder of his father. His voice was forceful, angry. "She shouldn't have to do this. This is insane."

Timor's eyes were burning into mine, and I met them easily then continued to look around the room. "I want to."

"Mira," my mother began, reaching around the back of her chair to brush my arm. Her loose hold on my hand was unfamiliar, her concern even more so. "You don't have to do this."

"I want to be a member of Ceanus in the way that every other citizen is. If this is what they have to do, then it is what I have to do too."

My mother shifted, looking over her shoulder at Kairos and then back at me. The dark male remained still and silent, his solemn gaze leveled across the room at the House Wardens. Quickly and almost indiscernible, he nodded.

My mother's hand tightened on my wrist, and her voice was low under the hushed speaking around the room. "Mira, this is too dangerous. I cannot let you put yourself at risk."

"The people of Ceanus will never accept me otherwise. This is what I need to do."

The twist of her mouth told me that she hated my response, but I knew she wouldn't contest me. Not here, not when she knew that I was right.

Nidian's voice broke the silence. "Does that mean that the princess will declare for a House at the conclusion of her training?"

I blinked at him. I'd forgotten that part. "I...uh... I'm..."

Atlana spoke now, the young Mer leaning forward in her chair to study me. "And for that matter, who will sponsor her? No mate has come forward, nor does she have a family who can participate in the training."

"I will sponsor her," Rhoe said in a breath.

My breath hitched. Anyone but him, I begged Artio. Please, Gods.

"No," Kairos said from behind us. "I will."

Fuck. I was mistaken. Anyone but him too, I begged the silent Gods. I swallowed back my outcry and met those obsidian eyes.

"You'll do what, General?"

Kairos's mouth opened to respond, but Rhoe wasn't ready to back down. His shoulders straightened. "I am the better choice to support Princess Mira in her training. General, you have duties to attend to."

"Those duties, by the way, that also include training of our newly joined citizens." Kairos didn't so much as glance down at me. "Besides, you have been out of arc for years, Rhoe. Your House needs you."

"And as for the declaration, Princess Mira was born of House Cetus, and as such she will remain unless she wishes to sever those ties in lieu of a new house." Nidian looked around the room. "Does that satisfy everyone? Perhaps then we can get back to real business."

I hid a smile and looked at my mother expectantly. A breath later, she nodded.

"It is settled. Mira will participate in the training with General Kairos as her sponsor. Any opposition?"

My belly pulled tight, but other than casting me multiple worried looks, Rhoe stayed quiet this time.

My mother pressed her hand against her heart, and the matter was settled. Something deep inside my chest warmed and swelled. For the first time in some time, I felt that maybe I'd done something right.

Chapter Nineteen

Mehri poured me a drink, the scent rising from the elaborately painted cup reminding me of tea. She drank first, nodding for me to join her. When I did, the taste was only a little fishy and very herbal. I choked a little then managed to keep the second mouthful down.

Hurriedly putting it back on the floor, I watched as my handmaid giggled at me then mimicked my movements. "I've heard that many do not like the kelp tea at first."

"Kelp?"

"The tea. It's made of a particular type of kelp that grows here near Ceanus."

I made a face then quickly hit it with a placid smile. Mehri clearly enjoyed it and was only doing what I had asked her to do. "It's fine, just maybe not my favorite thing."

Mehri laughed again. "Pardon me, Highness, but you may have to get used to it. It's rather common around here. The kelp is easy to maintain and provides us with many of the vitamins that we are lacking due to the distance we are from the sun."

I hadn't thought of that yet. How different their bodies must be from mine in order to survive here. "Do you still need the sun? Like we do?"

Mehri looked thoughtful. "Not need, specifically, but some days we long for it. As if our skin is craving the feel for the warmth on it. During certain seasons, the Leviathan arranges escorted trips to the surface so that we can sun ourselves." She spread her arms wide, face tilted up to the ceiling, mimicking what had to be a sunbathing pose.

"Are you always…" I gestured to the slender legs that she had tucked under herself. "Like this? Or do you shift like the Mer?"

Mehri dropped her arms, "I was wondering how much the queen was able to tell you. I'm quite able to transition, like most Ceanians, but I chose to only get into the water when absolutely necessary."

"Necessary? It's a rule or…"

"No, no rules, but most Ceanian citizens will die if we are kept from water for too long. It is why the queen made the rules about walking in the land above. We can only be on the ground for a few hours before we will begin to wither away. Those who attempt to stay ashore longer than that will suffer a fate worse than death."

"What's that?"

Mehri leaned in, conspiratorial. "We will forfeit our rights to Trayon's wish, giving up our fins forever."

I hadn't heard this yet. But it made sense. Otherwise, there would be Ceanians and other sea creatures like the sirens walking around Port Sol all the time. But since they had to return to the water, Trayon still remained in control. "And if you stay ashore too long, you'll just be…what? A human like me?"

Suddenly, Mehri looked nervous, bending down to pick up her teacup. "Yes, but there are effects on those in the kingdom below."

"For you turning into a human?"

She nodded, delicate fingers curling around her cup. "Our families are affected as well. And if they do not also make it to the surface, to the land in time, they drown. Just like a sandwalker would." Mehri shook her head. "It is a horrible thing."

She was saying that if one person betrayed my mother, Ceanus, or Trayon and remained on the shore too long, then the entire family would drown as well. What kind of magic was that? My stomach quivered. No wonder the Houses were so strict within their organization. If one person went rogue, that could mean the death of an entire tree. And from what I was learning here, that wasn't something Ceanus could survive for long.

And how would the person, now doomed to their new two-legged existence, survive knowing that they abandoned their entire family to death.

"That is awful. Does that happen a lot?"

Wide eyes snapped to mine. "Oh no, Highness, never. We are taught early on to never betray Ceanus or our Houses."

Without thinking I took another sip of the kelp tea and then grimaced. The taste was slightly better now, or perhaps I was getting used to it. I took another sip. "When we are alone like this, would you please call me Mira? You are the one who is helping me. I can't keep listening to you call me by honorifics. It doesn't feel right."

Mehri stood so quickly, her own tea sloshed in the cup, and she began to shuffle around the room. Confused, I looked to Akram, who may as well have been a Mer-sized statue standing in his usual spot along the front wall of my room.

"Mehri, you're fluttering. Did I say something wrong?"

"No." And yet she fluttered around some more.

I lunged for her, cupping her elbow in my hand. Her face turned to mine, pale with fear. I released her in an instant.

"Highness, please, you have to understand. Things here are not as simple as life in Adrial. Not for me. Not for…" The delicate line of her throat worked, and I saw her eyes flicker around the room.

"Alright, alright, I take it back. I meant no harm. Please call me Princess or Your Highness or whatever you need to feel better. It was meant as an extension of friendship. When I was home…" My words trailed off, and I cleared my throat to try again. "When I was in Adrial, I allowed those very closest to me to call me by my first name. My father was the same way. He said it was bond stronger than any title could give, the exchange of their real name."

My eyes ached for a moment. I ducked my chin, biting down hard on my bottom lip to quell the tears that seemed to come so easily to me here. During this past week of change and chaos, I'd nearly forgotten my father. How he was so close and yet so unreachable. And that he was mourning a daughter who still lived. I prayed to Artio that he would still accept me when I returned. That he might forgive all the pain that this had brought to him.

I drew in a shaking breath. If I could talk to Trayon, I could remove the curse. If I could talk to Trayon, I could save my people. I ran it over and over in my mind like a mantra until a small hand appeared on my forearm.

"Your Highness? Are you alright?"

I shook myself free of my thoughts, focusing again on the woman in front of me. Her pale-pink hair swung at her jawline as she regarded me closely, worry in every line of her face. "I'm sorry. I'm fine. Really."

Mehri nodded, removing her hand and tucking it behind her back.

I rubbed a finger across my sore bottom lip. "Could you at least tell me why calling me by my name upset you so much?"

Mehri blinked at me. "I'm sure that you've noticed that I'm a little different than the others?"

"You're half-siren, right?"

She nodded, but I didn't miss the sadness that darkened her eyes. "I am merely a half-blooded Ceanian, Your Highness, not worthy to be calling you by your first name. You are the heir to the throne, and I am lucky to be accepted to any of the Houses. We cannot be that familiar. It is just not right."

Interested, I leaned forward, my elbows on my knees. "Being half-siren means you aren't as…what, important as the others in your House?"

After a long moment, she nodded. Until now, I hadn't seen many clues on how the hierarchy worked within the kingdom. From what I could tell, my mother, her council, as well as the Wardens were the top of the pile. But after that, it got more and more confusing. Except for in House Leviathan, since they had adopted nearly militant titles to distinguish authority and status.

I was filled with curiosity on learning more about the siren half of her bloodline, but it didn't take a genius to notice that Mehri was obviously uncomfortable speaking about it. Especially to me.

"Does your blood matter that much to you? Or just to everyone else?"

Her head tilted slowly. "I'm not sure I understand the question. I am half-siren, practically feral, and should be grateful for both my House and this chance to work under the throne."

I held up my hands. "I'm sorry. I didn't mean to upset you. I'm just trying to decipher everything here. This is all new to me."

I glanced back down at my hands, trying to relax her. "The other half of you is siren, right?"

"Yes, Your Highness," Mehri said, voice hushed.

Akram shifted against the wall but didn't say anything.

"My mother was a siren."

"Are there a lot of you who are half-sirens?"

She shook her head aggressively. "No, not at all. We are quite rare."

"And that's…bad?"

Mehri's eyes were low, "Bloodlines, pledges, alliances are all very important here in Ceanus. My father fell in love with a siren. He brought her here, under special permission from the queen's council. But she couldn't stay. She was miserable here, even in the outskirts, closest to the ocean. I haven't seen her since I was a small child."

My heart ached for her. "I'm so sorry."

"I wondered at first, when I took the job working for Her Majesty, if she might come back. My, uh—" Mehri swallowed hard "—capabilities, even as a half-siren, are well known in Ceanus. My mother was quite powerful, and I always wondered if she was curious how much my ability had grown over the years. My father had been deeply in love with her, and I believe she loved him too. But now he can't even talk her anyone about her, save me. Not without everyone theorizing that she had been spelling him through their entire relationship. It would've been easy for her, you know. To use her gift to make him merely a servant to her every whim. She could've even forced him to feel something he didn't really feel."

I stared at her. The only legends I knew of sirens were about beautiful creatures who seduced sailors and men, drawing them into dangerous waters or pushing them to their deaths in order to steal from them.

"I'm sure that's not true."

Mehri raised a slender shoulder. "Even if I were to find out now, I would never tell him. He is waiting, always hoping that she might come back. He never found another mate. He just said that when the time was right, she would return to him. Knowing I had questioned the validity of their love would devastate him more than the truth would."

"And so you inherited your gift from her? Does that mean you can coerce feelings? Or emotions?"

"I did. My father is only minorly gifted. He can shift and partake in House activities, but that is his limit. I know my power comes from her, but siren magic is more primal than the usual gift. Your mother had remembered my mother and her power from the short time she lived in the arc with us. When Her Majesty came to me, she offered training and an honorable job. I couldn't say no."

That made my lips curl. "She has a knack for remembering people, that's for sure."

Mehri offered a return smile, and I couldn't stop the next question as it tumbled free. "Can you sing like sirens do? I swore to Artio that you sang to me, that first night by the portal, when I was panicking on the path."

Mehri nodded but looked worried. "I did."

A smile pulled at my lips. "Thank you. You have no idea how much better that made me feel."

"I'm glad you feel that way, Your Highness, because that's why people are hesitant. Changing someone's emotions…" Mehri let out a sigh. "It is deeply personal, and I know that many times people can feel that it is an invasion."

"An invasion?"

"I can make you feel happy, Your Highness, on your worst day. I could make you weep in despair during your wedding. People who have had their emotions managed by sirens over a long period of time become changed. Sometimes they cannot handle their own emotions any longer and choose to meet the Dark God rather than try."

I'd never thought of that before. The power to not just change the emotion of the people you are around, but to affect them long term. She could be a deadly weapon in the wrong hands.

"Would you do that? I've heard the stories from the docks of sirens singing people into the ocean."

Mehri recoiled. "No, the sirens have a strict code against manipulating others against their will."

"A strict code? Wait… How many of them are you?"

"I'm not sure of the exact number, Your Highness. I'm not welcome in that world."

"If you were to guess?"

"The number of sirens living near Ceanus?" Her pink head tilted. "I would say there are around a little over a hundred living around the arc."

"And elsewhere?"

"We were some of Trayon's first creations, Your Highness. I suspect we have very high numbers in places we are welcome." Her mouth snapped shut on that last word, eyes wide as she regarded me.

"You are not welcome here, then."

Mehri shook her head. "You should ask someone within House Cirein-Croin. There is an expert in siren culture there."

"I want to ask you."

"My House speaks about a time before our grandparents, when the arc was much larger and not just Mer lived within the arc, but creatures of all types. But as the magic faded, the Houses made a choice to move many of the more aquatic creatures outside of the arc. Sirens were among the first to volunteer. Unlike the Mer, they don't feel the need to shift back and forth as frequently."

"Do they ever come in? To visit or shop or anything?"

Mehri looked guarded. "They are feral now, Your Highness, not capable of coming in and obeying our rules. It is best that they stay where they are comfortable and we stay where we are comfortable."

"Do you really believe that?"

"I do."

A companionable silence fell between us. "Can I ask another question?"

"I knew you would have many more, Your Highness." The half-siren grinned at me. "I'll be happy to answer any I can."

I leaned in. "The part about sirens being irresistible… Is that a real thing too?"

Mehri's eyes were wide as saucers. "Your Highness, I cannot…"

I laughed, pushing up and moving across the room to lean against the window. "I'm sorry Mehri. My curiosity went too far. Please don't answer."

"Of course, Highness." The relief was evident in every syllable. Cheeks pink, Mehri ducked into the adjoining room.

I stared out at the bustling market just below me. The brightly colored heads of the Mer and their people moving around the sidewalks, just going about their business as usual. An entire civilization I'd never imagined. And one with just as many idiosyncrasies and dramas as Adrial. It was beautiful, unique, and yet so much like home in some ways that I could nearly forget if I closed my eyes. If I just listened.

"How did we not know about you? About all of you?"

No one answered.

Part Two

Chapter Twenty

It was less than a day after I announced my intention to be trained to the Council of Ceanus, and already the regret was palatable.

"It's all in water? Does it have to be?"

Mehri squeaked a little as she pushed me to the side of the archway that opened the arc up to the open ocean. The very same one I'd first witnessed Baye and Kairos come through as Mer. "My lady, you have to be quiet with your questions. Or at the least have better questions."

It was the closest she'd come in the past days of scolding me, and something about it tickled my humor, and I grinned down at her.

"Good point. Guessing that they don't want to hear me having a meltdown about the water."

Mehri looked around, nodding at a few individuals who had approached and were lining up at the edge of the arc, obviously waiting for the start of training too. "You are the princess of an underwater kingdom. You are not supposed to be afraid of the water."

"I'm not afraid of water, Mehri. I love the water. I'm afraid of drowning, and before you get fired up, you would be too if you didn't magically grow gills and swim around like a fish every time you touched it." I held up the necklace Akram had delivered to my door this morning with an unhappy grunt. A single claw dangled on the delicate silver chain. "Remember, if my mother's magical necklace here fails, I go, quite literally, belly up." I eyed the other side of the arc anxiously.

Mehri sighed. "It is not your mother's necklace." Her voice was low, filled with scandal. "That is the Claw of Cetus at your throat, Your Highness. It was given to King Durneh by the monster herself, a gift to unite the House monsters and the rulers of Ceanus. It hasn't been worn in two generations." One of the first scrolls that Mehri had brought to my room had gone in depth about the original creations that each of the houses were named after. Each created by Trayon, they were rumored to be larger than life and after the arc was settled they had each taken turns guarding the kingdom, pledging their loyalty to Ceanus.

Generations ago, before my grandfather had ever ruled Ceanus, they had apparently warred with Trayon over something and been captured and hidden in the deep. The God of the Sea relished in this victory and believed that having the house monsters still represented his power to not only create, but to destroy. Hence they remained marked in the history and culture all around Ceanus.

"You're right, I'm sorry." I swallowed hard then closed my fist around the shining silver claw, the still sharp edge pricking my palm. "I'm awkward when I'm nervous."

Akram snorted.

Mehri's face softened. "I just think you should keep your concerns to yourself, Your Highness. At least until the council has gotten more comfortable with you here and without your powers."

Her words struck fear through my heart. The idea that I might never manifest the same abilities that my mother had or that most of my family had was something that was wearing on me daily. But hearing it from someone else's lips made it all the more apparent that I was a very real disappointment.

I nodded jerkily. "Thank you, Mehri."

"I'll be back to walk you home after training," she responded quietly.

"You don't have to do that."

"I do, actually," Mehri said decisively. "Now smile, don't drown, and I will see you this afternoon." Then with a gentle push towards the arc wall, she was gone, her lithe form disappearing from view as she made her way out of the platform.

Ignoring the pang of fear from the unknown, I turned and joined the others who were gathering there.

There were three Ceanians waiting so far. Trainees, they preferred to be called, as Mehri had informed me on our walk here. One, the smallest, her delicate build reminding me of the tiny acrobats who attended court every season to entertain and amaze actually bobbed with excitement. Her eyes glued to the portal with such reverence that it made goosebumps rise along my forearms. As soon as I approached, she turned, her pixie-like face confused for only a moment.

"Your Highness." She bowed, smile bright on her face, slender hand curled over her heart. "Are you joining us for training as well?"

I hesitated a half step, tempted to look over my shoulder to see if she was talking to someone else. But her face remained happy and eager to see me as I blinked rapidly then stepped closer.

"I am."

"I'm Delta," the woman said happily. She was maybe a few years older than me, with sparkling gray eyes and a wide smile. Best of all, she didn't seem to care who I was—which, after the past few days, was a welcome relief. "Isn't this all so exciting?"

My brows flew up. Exciting? "Which part?"

Delta turned, her voice dropping out a dramatic and therefore not hushed whisper. "We're in Ceanus, the home of the Sea God, and we are going to train to become proper Mer!"

"Oh." The word came out strained. "Um, yes, of course it is."

Delta's shining face dimmed a little. "You aren't excited, Your Highness?" She looked at me inquisitively, as if she couldn't imagine a world in which I didn't want to become a Mer.

"I'm just nervous, I guess."

Delta swatted at the air. "Don't be. I'm the only cursed who came through lately without a mate bond to anchor me. If anyone should be nervous, it should be me."

"Wait, what? I'm not mated either."

Delta's brows drew together and she looked over my shoulder. "I'm sorry. I guess I just thought… Ionia told us you were being sponsored by, um…." Her words trailed off as a dark presence skittered down my spine and settled somewhere beneath the hollow of my belly.

"Spreading rumors, Princess?"

My lips pulled back in a smirk as I swung around to face Kairos. "Not in the least. In fact, I was clarifying." I turned back to Delta. "This is General Kairos, and he's here because he's convinced that I can't hold my own against you all and will undoubtedly embarrass my mother and the crown."

Delta's eyes were wide. "The crown?"

Kairos sighed loudly. "Your Highness…"

"Yes, the crown." And then I turned to her with a falsely bright smile. "I believe that you have as good of a chance as me of securing a House and a future here. Don't you think, General? Especially seeing as my partner is someone who definitely wants me gone."

Delta didn't look like she wanted to be in this conversation very much anymore, and I could see her subtly moving backward. My mouth opened to seal the deal and completely ruin any chance I had of making friends here, but then I spotted him.

My heart swelled in my chest, making my throat ache for a long moment.

"Pierse?" I side-stepped Delta. "Is that you?"

Pierse's head whipped around when he heard his name, and a moment later, there were powerful, familiar arms wrapped around me.

"What are you doing there? I mean…" I tried again. "I know why you're here, but why are you here in this spot? I thought you were dead. I don't understand…"

Pierse squeezed me harder then set me back on my feet and looked me up and down. "Princess Mira, you are looking hale and hearty in your new Ceanian get up. But I must admit… You're about the last person I expected to be down here. That is, until I heard what happened after the Welcoming…"

I waited, confused, until Pierse ducked his head. "Rhoe showed back up at House Cetus. His family works with my mate frequently, and I heard some things." His eyes burned into mine. "I heard you're the heir, Princess Mira. And not just to your father's throne in Adrial."

Shrugging, I stepped away from his touch, suddenly less comfortable with the way he looked at me. "Queen Damona is offering me the chance to know more about my family here and what it means for who I will be as queen of Adrial. I couldn't very well turn it down."

He slowly licked his lips, and my entire body tensed, waiting for what my old friend might say. "What are you doing here, Princess? Really?"

"Here? Well, I'm going to train to be Housed. Just like everyone else." I held out a hand towards the gathering group around us.

"But why?" Pierse's frown deepened. "I know why I'm here. The mate bond called me here. But they're saying…"

I crossed my arms. "They're saying what?"

"That your mother and the crown called you here after you touched the water."

"What if she did?"

Pierse shook his head. "Because if she called for her heir, something more than just a reunion was in mind."

"You don't know that."

"Don't play stupid, Your Highness." Pierse's features softened. "It was never your best look."

I huffed and looked away, his words ringing around my head. My mother had said that the ocean had called for me. Had that been her subtle way of saying that she'd called for me? And if she had, then why all the mystery and confusion since I arrived? My thoughts curled around each other, tangled and confusing. But the group around us was shifting towards the archway. I didn't have time to worry about this yet.

Soon.

But first, I had to be sure I wasn't going to drown.

"Well, playing conspiracy theories was never your best look either," I shot back, a small smile pulling at my mouth. "But here you are."

Pierse shrugged one shoulder, wearing a similar all-black, body-fitting garb that nearly every Ceanian wore into the water, "I've been waiting for training to start. Not much else to do besides listen to the idle gossip."

"You've been waiting?"

"They only have the training every so often. Until now, I've been staying in a Kraken house with Jahya. I'm unpledged, but my mate bond keeps me safe for the time being."

"Was she the mermaid? From that day?"

Pierse's grin was roguish, but I could see the way his cheeks darkened. Now he looked more like the playful, kind Pierse I'd known so much better up on the surface. "My mate. She is incredible."

"Wow." I smiled widely at him, feeling strange tears prickling at the backs of my eyes. "I guess congratulations are in order, then?"

Pierse laughed good-naturedly, and more of my worry eased. Pierse was still who I thought he'd been. And I could still be who I had been.

"I need to be Housed before we can make it official in the eyes of Ceanus, but as for everything else…" Pierse's eyes lingered to the slender beauty who walked towards us. "It's a done deal."

Jahya gave me a short bow, pressing her hand over her heart before looking at me. "Pierse told me that you served alongside him in Adrial, Your Highness."

"I did." I gave her a slow nod. "He is a fine warrior and an even better friend."

Jahya's eyes were sharp as blades. "It is not a usual custom to have a princess serving aboard a battleship, is it?"

"I'm not exactly usual. I never have been." I spread my arms wide. "Although I have to admit even I didn't think I would be this unusual."

Jahya's features relaxed into a small smile. "I'm sure."

"You know, I remember you, from the day that Pierse was taken." As soon as the words left my mouth, I hated them. I cleared my throat quickly. "The day Pierse left."

Jahya nodded at me, the skin of her cheekbones shimmering as the coral lights above us brightened and softened periodically. "The General wanted me to stay behind—I'm not a member of the squalls—but I couldn't stay. The bond was so strong, even at that point, I knew I couldn't wait. I needed to be there when he was brought below."

"The general? General Kairos?"

"Yes. And finally, he allowed me to go and came as well to make sure everything went smoothly."

The dark shape under the waters. The one who had reached for me, made my heartbeat double as I hung there above the waves. Had that been him? Goose bumps raced across my skin. Something told me it had been. What that meant, I still didn't know.

Jahya continued, "He's a great male, our General. I'm very lucky he allowed me to come." Her head tilted, making her seem more like a predator than before. "I heard he is sponsoring you."

Looking around, I noticed that Kairos had abandoned conversations and instead was stalking around the archway, casting meaningful looks at the guards as they stood stiffly at each side. The tension that male radiated could be felt for sure.

I nodded. "He is. Against his preferences, I'm sure."

Jahya seemed to consider something, but her thin lips remained sealed. Pierse's arm snaked around her slender waist, and he

dragged her closer. "Princess Mira has a way of worming her way
into people's good graces. I'm sure he'll change his tune soon
enough."

My brows went up. "I highly doubt that, Pierse, but I do
appreciate the vote of confidence."

Just as I finished speaking, the subject of our conversation
stalked onto the dais. Unlike the other day when he'd been bare
chested wearing only the swimming pants Ceanians favored, today
Kairos was in full armor, the plated gold so polished that I blinked
as he reflected the coral light back at me.

The small crowd shifted as he approached. All except me, which
meant the General could waltz up and stand directly in front of me.
I tried not to tilt my chin too much as he moved into my space. I
didn't want him to think I was intimidated by him or his size.

Even if the proximity to him did leave me oddly breathless.

"Are you ready?"

"Good morning to you too," I crooned. When he only continued
glare at me, I popped a hip and relaxed purposefully. "I'll be fine,
General. Mother and I went over the necklace's abilities last night."

We had, but I hadn't had a chance to test the final element,
which was, sadly, the most important. But Kairos didn't need to
know that.

It had been House Cirein-Croin's idea, a magical artifact that had
been in residence at the archives for generations. A gift from the
monster of House Cetus to the first Warden. The necklace would
allow even a sandwalker to breathe in the water, and while it
wouldn't give me fins like the Mer, when my own gift emerged, it
also wouldn't prevent them.

Along with my mother's gift, the necklace had glowed and
hummed against my skin as Mehri had put it on me this morning. I

would wear it continuously or until we were able to subtly test more about my rather slow-to-show gift.

Kairos held my gaze for a long beat then stepped back. Instantly the breath whooshed back into my chest. "Very good, Your Highness. Then perhaps you should lead the squall into the water?"

My smile vanished. Kairos knew very well that the last time I'd been outside of the arc, I'd nearly drowned. Apparently his faith in the necklace was even higher than mine. Or he was secretly hoping I would drown and he wouldn't be on babysitting duty for the next few weeks of training.

I would bet my life it was the second one. I gritted my teeth, forcing my chin high as I stepped up to him. Only a breath between our chests, I leaned forward, watching in fascination as his onyx gaze flickered, darkening before I heard the smallest intake of breath.

In response, my belly tightened. "Of course, General. It's like you read my mind."

Flipping my hair back, I brushed past him, ignoring the jolt of pleasure that contact with him brought, even in such a casual, frustrating way. As I moved towards the circular entry into the sea, the water just beyond rippled and fluctuated at the precipice of falling into the arc.

Yet it did not. The magic remained, holding the wild freedom of the ocean at bay.

Unbidden, my hand crawled to my throat, pressing a finger against the claw charm at the center of the necklace.

Please work, I chanted desperately in my mind.

I cast one last glance over my shoulder to see Kairos looming only a few steps away. His forearms flexed from where he had them crossed, but otherwise he didn't move. None of them did, I noticed.

Even Delta, who had been so talkative and engaging earlier, was as still as a statue at the corner of the group.

They were all waiting. Watching.

Judging.

Gods damn it.

I steeled myself, breathing hard through my nose as I picked one foot up. Praying to Trayon that he didn't send me straight to his brother in the Dark Realm, I stepped through the portal and into the Great Sea once more.

Chapter Twenty-One

The water thrummed around me, feeling different than it had ever felt before. It was like being in the high towers of Adrial during a lightning storm. Sparks raced through my body, making my muscles quiver, my heart pause. For a moment, I stilled in the cool water, my body hovering in transition, and then I felt it, the shiver that raced down my spine, spreading heat as it moved. And then, miraculously, I breathed in.

Instead of the brine-filled water racing into my chest as before, there was only sweet, blissful air that channeled into my anxious lungs, making me buoyant as my momentum from the platform pushed me the rest of the way into the ocean water.

It felt wonderful. Laughter bubbled in my throat, relief and joy warring together in my chest until I released it in a soft smile, one just for myself.

Using my arms, I pushed the water around so I could face the others who were waiting. Kairos stood by the portal, closer than he had been before. I sent him a wide, triumphant smile. Just for a moment, I thought he might return it, but instead he turned to speak to the group. My stomach twisted since I couldn't hear what he was saying.

I could guess, though, since the other trainees immediately began to step through, joining me in the water. Each trainee, cursed or legacy, was followed by their assigned sponsor.

Unlike me, however, they all shifted, their legs and feet molding together in a shimmering of improbable sparks of magic, as well as the delicate ruffles of gills that lifted from the curve of their throats.

Mer. They really all were Mer.

I was… I was something else. I swallowed down the disappointment that lurked high in my chest as I watched them swirl around me, colorful and bright, completely at ease in the deep waters.

My feet, still very human, were at least capable of movement in the gentle current, and I propelled myself a little farther into the water. At the very back of the group was Kairos, followed by a stern-looking older Mer, whose tail was a slightly dull purple tone. Her scales were tiny and gave her an almost snake-like appearance as she moved into the water alongside us. One by one she approached us, pressing her fingers against our skin, dangerous nails flashing in the coral light wand that she held in one hand.

I recognized her from the Welcoming. Ionia of House Cirein-Croin, the older Mer who had watched me with such interest.

I was confused at first but kept my mouth shut as everyone, including Kairos, willingly offered her their bodies to maim. One by one, she moved around the group, the sharp edge of her nails pricking each trainee and drawing blood. I flinched as she pricked Pierse, who now sported a stunning bronze-colored tail that gleamed alongside Jahya's silvery blue.

When Ionia finally turned to me, the childish part of me wanted to swat her away. Perhaps seeing that desire in my face, the old mermaid merely grinned at me, teeth sharp and white against her craggy skin.

My hesitation and study of her face gave her just the right amount of time to slice a tiny cut across the top of my shoulder. I gaped at her, covering the tiny wound, the blood winding into the water like a ribbon as she swam by.

Kairos was suddenly close, his thick opal-toned tail propelling him to hover in front of me. *It's a blood bond, Princess, so that she can speak to you in your.*

Carefully, I schooled my face not to react as his words filtered into my mind, as sarcastic and drawling as if he'd spoken them aloud. Slowly, I put together my own response.

Oh, now I feel stupid. That doesn't just happen?

No, Princess, it does not.

His ability to convey disdain and sarcasm through mental communication was impressive. Even if it did piss me off.

I can only hear you because of the bite.

Kairos appeared solemn for a moment before, to my surprise, he answered me. *In many cases of families, it's as simple as an awareness of each other. A child can call for his mother from nearly anywhere in Ceanus, and she could answer. But between two...* his lips wrinkled, *companions, the bond must be reinstated every few weeks if there's no other tie between them. It fades over time and with less exposure.*

I watched Pierse and Jahya twirl around each other in the water, his tail flashing brilliantly, and I tried not to let a soft string of jealousy burn in my chest watching them. This time the jealousy wasn't over his beautiful tail or the smattering of scales that graced the edges of his cheekbones or ran up the backs of his arms.

It was the way he stared at Jahya as she danced around him, joy and love in every movement as they experienced this together. To think I had thought he'd been dragged to his death. And now he was here, dancing around in the water with his Gods-damned mate.

I blew out a breath, surprised when a wealth of tiny bubbles left on my lips.

Don't worry, Princess. You'll find some male to torture someday too.

I jerked. I'd completely forgotten how close the General was. Still unsure of my speaking abilities like this, I forced my other thoughts to the back of my mind.

I'm only jealous of his tail.

Uh-huh, I'm sure. Flashing a wide, placating smile, Kairos flipped his tail my way and sped off towards Ionia. She had apparently completed her task of slicing her way into our minds and was now treading water at the head of the group, her purple tail barely moving. Her scales were different than most of the rest of our group. They were small, dulled, almost a matte version of the color, even in the filtered sun from above. I wondered briefly if that was a sign of age, or perhaps it was simply a coloring.

Something told me Ionia wouldn't welcome that line of questioning.

I kicked my way over to the group, treading water beside Delta as the other female quaked with excitement. A moment later, a bold probe pressed against my mind. I breathed in sharply, as Ionia nodded, looking around at us.

You are all here to learn how to become valued citizens of Ceanus. Each day, we will focus on another cultural norm here, meant to capitalize and grow on each of your unique gifts. My name is Ionia of House Cirein-Croin, and I will be your lead.

Her voice in my mind was so different from Kairos's deep rumble, similar to her speaking voice, but as my mind absorbed her words, I actually pictured Ionia's face. Shock, then awe, coursed through me. These bonds were so unlike anything I had ever experienced and I was instantly aware of what a vital asset this must be for the Ceanians. A world where communication was as simple as thought.

It was beautiful.

We all remained silent, the softest echo from the waves above the only sound.

As each of you have noticed, I`ve created a temporary blood bond between each of you and myself so that we may speak as a squall might to each other. Ionia's voice echoed through my mind as I looked around our group.

Overeager hands flew up, and Delta's tail, which was a creamy white, flicked hard in excitement.

Ionia looked at the female—the mermaid, nodding once. *Yes, Delta?*

How long will it last? And would it overlap with any other bonds already in place?

Ionia's tail snapped. *It will last the duration of the training. On the day of the House selection, you will pledge your House and share blood with them. All bonds, other than the mating bond and your House bond, will fade over time.* Ionia gave her a sharp look. *Which I believe you already knew.*

Delta, looking properly scolded, sank a little in the water. *I just wanted to check.*

Ionia sighed, pushing off to swim back and forth across the front of our group. *Each of you has brought a sponsor. These people are here to not only provide the mental support that it requires, but physical as well. The Great Sea is a dangerous place.*

I cast a sidelong glance at Kairos, who had his arms crossed over his chest, appearing disinterested and glum as Ionia continued. At least he'd stayed with me. I could give him that much. He was taking this little assignment seriously.

I hope you can trust your sponsors and that each of you are prepared for what you will face together. Today we will focus primarily on a swimming tour around the arc. Tomorrow... Her sharp teeth flashed once again. *Tomorrow, the real fun begins.*

I didn't stop the shudder that went through my body. In Adrial, I might've thought that I trained just as hard as the others, but I had also had privilege on my side. Here, I had nothing but an angry general who appeared to hate the water I swam in.

If it came down to me surviving or me getting eaten by some deep sea monster, I had a distinct feeling Kairos would serve me on a platter for the monster and ask if he wanted seconds.

As the rest of the group began to swim off, I kicked my legs, swimming hard after them. For a short distance, I kept pace easily, my legs and arms cutting through the gentle current as we reapproached the arc. Ionia's voice spoke into my mind once again.

The arc of Ceanus was one of the first queen's most impressive endeavors. Although it was her husband who cast the spell with Trayon's help, it was the queen who sustained the magic for her entire life. Much like Queen Damona, we know that Divina was a uniquely powerful woman who laid down the foundation for everything Ceanus would someday become.

My lungs ached a little as my arms tired, and I found myself distracted as I focused on my strokes, slowly dropping back in our party as their tails pushed them in front of me.

Princess. Kairos' voice rumbled into my mind again, distracting me further.

I'm fine.

Hmm, yes, of course you are. Kairos swam in front of me, his arms still crossed over his chest, forcing the muscles to jump. *Are you planning on catching the rest of Ionia's speech when they come back around to this side and lap you?*

I growled at him then slapped a hand over my mouth. I didn't growl. Princesses don't growl. But the asshole merely smiled at me.

I'm fine, General.

You're not, and you know it. Kairos unfolded his arms, swooping lower and forcing me to stop swimming, as I would've run right into him. *Let me help.*

I don't want your help.

And I don't want to have to explain to your mother why a shark ate you because you can't keep up with the group.

A shark? Fuck! There are sharks down here?

Kairos rolled his eyes, and I barely resisted the urge to slap him. Then again, he was right, and I wasn't about to become fish food because of my pride.

Fine.

Say it, Your Highness. His beautiful face lifted in a smirk once more.

General Kairos…

I swam closer to him, my toes accidentally brushing against the smooth, dark scales of his tail. His throat moved, and I savored that little human-like gesture.

Yes, Princess?

Dearest and most loyal of all the Ceanus people.

You have my attention, Princess.

Please, can you pull your head out of your ass long enough to help me keep up with the training group?

Black eyes narrowed. *I don't like that last part as much, but the first part was definitely an improvement.*

General, for Gods' sake.

Calm down, Princess. We're fine. And then he dove behind me, curling around until his chest pressed against my back. I gasped as his arms slipped around my ribs, gently caging me in for a moment before his tail swished and drove us forward through the water. He was so warm, his skin burning mine even through our matching black training clothing. It felt amazing.

While the water brushed over my face, Kairos propelled us both forward towards the group. I had never been more aware of how much larger the Mer general was than me. The way his hands wrapped around my entire waist, the spread of his fingers meaning that his fingertips brushed both hip bones and high on my ribcage all at once.

My belly quivered. As if he felt it, Kairos shifted a little, moving his hands lower again, his fingers nearly a caress as they did. Suddenly aware that we were both too quiet, I fumbled for something to say.

Nothing came to mind, at least nothing but a mumbled, *Thank you.*

Anytime, Princess.

Since they were moving at a more casual pace, we were on them in only a few moments, and I found myself disappointed as he slowed his pace. The distance between our bodies suddenly increased, and I shivered as the water ran between us, reminding me just how close I'd been to him a breath before.

I should not be harboring any of those feelings about my mother's right-hand soldier, but looking at him, it wasn't hard to imagine how he might feel towards me. And now I knew.

Curling my lips together, I focused on Ionia's age-rough voice as she swam along, pointing out a series of low-slung buildings and dilapidated structures.

These are parts of old town, where the arc has inevitably shifted over time and given the city back to the deep.

My brows furrowed, looking down at the remnants of the city, noting that it must've only been surrendered to the ocean a short time, since the coral and sea life hadn't taken over all of it yet. As I watched, a dark shadow moved, the flash of silver scales and dark hair between the buildings.

Who was that?

I must've said it loud enough for the whole group because Ionia slowed her pace. *There are many who choose to inhabit the abandoned parts of the city instead of complying with the laws of Ceanus.*

I nodded, suddenly feeling self-conscious that everyone was staring at me again, and this time I was being essentially held in place by my grumpy sponsor.

Pierse spoke up, saving me from more stares. *Are they Mer?*

Yes. Mer mostly, an occasional siren.

Thank you, Ionia. I apologize for interrupting.

Her brows lifted as the ghost of a smile stretched her cheeks. *And we must continue. Come along.*

We had made it around half of the arc, Kairos acting as my power source, propelling me forward with the group. Each stop was more fascinating than before, but the last place we stopped made my chest constrict all together.

What are they?

Awe filled my chest as I stared up at the sloping edge of the sea in this area. There, along with the kelp and plants, were the strangest and most beautiful creatures I'd ever seen.

The group paused, but Kairos gpt us closer to the animals, who appeared to be in a small herd, swimming amongst the foliage and grazing on it as they did. They were something out of a fever dream, a combination of sea horses and the four-legged equines of Adrial.

They had a long, rideable back, but instead of hooves, each of their front legs ended in a powerful-looking fin. The back legs were replaced all together with a thick, powerful tail. Their faces were delicate in appearance, but even from here I could see the plated scales that seemed to cover the creatures, making them appear both shimmering and strong at the same time.

Several, including the powerful-looking green-scaled one who was facing us, had a variety of sharp horns that lined the front of the skull, clearly meant for defense. Another one, lilac in color, swam up alongside the green and butted its companion with its nose.

What are they?

Hippocampus, Kairos said. *Stunning, aren't they?*

I twisted to see his face, sure that he would be patronizing or even making fun of my awe, but instead I found him smiling at the creatures as well.

They are beautiful. Do they always live here?

They like the kelp, or so we've been told, Ionia said, swimming up beside me. *They don't like us to get very close though. The Cirein-Croin claim that each school has a head mare. They are incredibly protective and keep their schools safe.*

A female in charge… I grinned at Ionia. *I like them even more.*

Ionia chuckled just once but pointed a short, thick finger my way. A warning. *Make sure to keep your distance though, Your*

Highness. There's venom in those horns, and I don't know of a Mer anywhere who has managed to survive the strike from a hippocampus.

I blinked as Ionia swam back to the rest of the group.

They don't seem so dangerous, I thought out loud. The green-scaled beauty eyed me with interest, its head turning this way and that as it hovered in the water.

Appearances can be deceiving, isn't that right?

That surprised a short laugh out of me. I craned my neck to look at the General, nearly forgetting he would be able to hear me. *Yes, generally, they can be.*

I allowed him then to tow me away, but my eyes went back not once but twice to watch the shimmering coats of the hippocampus until I couldn't see them anymore.

Kairos released me close to the arc doorway we had come in through, choosing to drift back in the current to speak with Ionia. My arms were shaky, but having Kairos do so much of the swimming today had replenished my muscles enough that I could pull and kick my way to the doorway. Pushing my weight down to my feet, I passed through the magical barrier. I felt the air slip over me and managed to only take two stumbling steps on the other side of the arc instead of flat out falling forward. Improvement, perhaps, but still embarrassing.

Two sturdy hands gripped my shoulders as I moved forward, halting the momentum. I looked up into Akram's serious face.

"Oh," I croaked, surprised by how strange it felt to talk with my tongue again. "Thank you, Akram."

He nodded, stepping back and resuming his usual protective stance. Mehri, who must've been somewhere in the Mer's broad shadow, moved around him, her delicate features alit with joy.

"It worked, Princess?" Her hands pressed together at her chest, her glee at our success warming me from the inside out.

I nodded, unable to stop the smile that bloomed on my lips. "Very well." I glanced down at my feet, wiggling my toes against the smooth pathway. "Well, I still didn't get my tail, but at least I didn't drown."

Mehri beamed.

"At least," a now familiar voice drawled from behind me. Mehri and Akram each gave a small bow to the General as he joined our little group. "I'm off to attend to the rest of my duties, Princess. I will meet you here tomorrow, after a morning meal."

Kairos seemed frustrated, his olive-toned cheeks flushed dark. Glancing back, I saw Ionia standing at the edge of our squall, eyes on Kairos. Clearly something had been said. I blinked, turning back to the General. "Of course."

The big male made to leave the platform, but I couldn't stop myself from raising my voice after him. "Thank you, General Kairos."

His steps faltered ever so slightly, and I preened internally at being able to throw the self-confident male off his game a little. But he didn't turn around, nor did he acknowledge me. I knew he had heard, and that was all that mattered for me.

Mehri's hand brushed my elbow, and her whispered words made me crane my head down. "Your Highness, I spoke with my uncle and was able to procure some of the books that you asked for."

Interest surged through my mind, washing away my wondering about the departing General. "Really? Can we go now?"

"Your mother was hoping you could drop by her suite and tell her how your training was first."

A nervous bubble rose in my belly, but I forced it down. It was good to have someone checking up on me. I just wasn't used to it. Maybe she just wanted to hear about my training from someone other than General Kairos or Ionia. I frowned. I should consider this a blessing. No telling what Kairos would tell her, should he give his report of my activities first.

"Perfect." I opened my mouth to ask her to lead the way when I noticed that Delta, the stoic-looking House Cetus male who had been her sponsor, as well as Ionia were all watching us.

There are eyes on you all the time, the queen had said. I raised my chin, giving them a short nod and a smile as I dragged my memory for any idea of which of the sidewalks that I needed to take to get back to my rooms.

Hoping that my mind would clear, I stepped off, Akram and Mehri falling in step behind me. The first branch was easy, one clearly driving down to the lower rungs of the city buildings, but as I approached a three-way split in the roads, I faltered a half step.

Knowing I was still in clear view of everyone from training, I decided that no matter what path this took, I was going to pretend that it was exactly where I was going to go. And pray to Artio that no one had heard where Mehri said we were going.

I headed for the middle fork, my head held high. But then, only a second later, Akram shifted his heavy broadsword, a soft grunting noise slipping from his mouth. It surprised me, and I nearly stopped to ask if he'd hurt himself, when I realized what his grunt had sounded a lot like.

Oh fuck… I veered left, taking the left sidewalk that, after rising a little more, pulled off to deliver me to the immense entryway of the castle. I didn't dare look back. But that didn't mean that I couldn't quietly whisper.

"Thank you."

Akram only let out another grunt. I was smiling when the doors of my mother's suite swung wide.

261

Chapter Twenty-Two

My mother sat on a pillowed bench along the wall of her room. With her dark hair pinned up over her head and a quill in her hand, she looked more relaxed than I'd ever seen her. I immediately relaxed as well, coming to a stop a few strides from where she sat. Her guards closed the door, and I offered a bow and a salute to her.

She waved them both away, patting the seat next to her. "Mira, come sit. I want to hear all about it."

The pillows looked divinely soft and instantly sparked my interest. "How do you get all these soft goods down here?"

She chuckled. "I wondered when you might ask. You're going to think of us as awful, but some of the merchant ships that are robbed are the results of us being especially desperate for certain goods."

"You robbed all those ships?"

"No, not all. When I became queen, it was one of the first things my father discussed with me. As it turns out, to everyone except for the terrified Adrialians, we are just another stop on the trading route. Not for just anyone, of course, but we've established a hearty list of merchants who are willing to meet up and sell things with all the discretion that we require. Some merchants are related to Mer living below. Others are just more open-minded with hungry pockets."

"Are all the rumors about Mer attacking merchant ships lies?"

My mother laughed. "Maybe in the past there could've been a rogue Mer or two. But *minu*, even if we did not have these trading situations set up, we wouldn't need to steal. That's what we use the sandwalkers for."

I moved closer, intrigued.

"It is quite simple to send one of our gifted citizens to Adrial, or even to the Emen Isles, to bring back as many goods as we like."

"I thought there were rules about leaving Ceanus. And how long you can stay out of the ocean."

"There are—strict ones, too. There are many of us who, like you, can survive on Artio's land. But the longer we are there, the more we risk losing our gifts or the ability to shift. We would be trapped in that form forever. But as you'll find, there are plenty of us below who have spent time up on the land and have been able to return to the arc. Maybe not as long as I did, but there are accounts of this happening through the generations. I believe it might have been part of their gift."

"Does that mean that is my gift, then?" I couldn't stop the disappointed pang in my voice. I had seen the many gifts of Ceanus. Most Mer possessed small magics, or gifts, and they used them in everyday life. To heat their homes, to light coral and illuminate the streets. Others, like the powerful judges and bankers in Cetus, would be able to sense lies and serve their Houses. But so far, every Ceanian I'd met had been able to shift into what they considered their true form. Except for me. Being able to walk around on the land, like I already had for my twenty years, seemed like a rather significant disappointment in my opinion.

My mother smiled. "I don't believe so. Many of the cursed who come to live in Ceanus are sandwalkers. At least to some extent. I'm sure that your gift will be beautiful and special, whenever it decides to emerge."

It made sense that the cursed would be more viable sandwalkers. My mother had lived in Port Sol for years, and yet she'd been able to come right home. "How did you maintain your abilities? You know, when you left Ceanus? You were queen of Adrial for years."

"I snuck out as much as I could, and honestly it was luck and the glory of Trayon that allowed me to maintain my gift. I'm still shocked every day that this is how my life went."

I released the pillow, offering a smile to her sadness. "I'm sorry. You asked me a question, and I got you sidetracked about pillows."

"It's fine. I love how curious you are. But now I'm the curious one. I'm so interested to hear how Ionia was and about the first full day of training."

"Ionia? She seems…." I searched for the right word. "On task."

My mother laughed, her head flopping back and filling the room with her humor. "She is that." Conspiratorially, she urged me to lean in. "She was my private tutor for a short time when I was a child, and I was petrified of her. Her personality is striking enough, but then add in her gift, and I practically wilted the first time she looked my way. Yet, I'm glad to hear you're getting the same experience."

I laughed a little, still entranced by her easy joy. How long had it been since I'd seen my father this way? "So, she's always been a teacher?"

"Yes, House Cirein-Croin takes great pride in their portion of training the new Ceanians," she said, nodding. "Her family could've been Warden, their line is so old, but they deferred to another since Ionia and her mate wanted to remain on the education side."

"Interesting choice. She must truly love teaching." I wasn't sure who I was trying to convince with that statement. I believed the only thing Ionia loved was hearing herself talk. I would happily tell her that myself and believed she would agree with me wholeheartedly.

"When I was a child, I never understood it. Ionia chose to live what I had thought seemed like such a basic life instead of having the power of an entire House behind her. But then I grew up and realized that she probably made the best choice out of all of us. And honestly, the female has more power than all of us combined. She's trained half of Ceanus by this point. If anything happens just about anywhere, she knows. Not to mention, she's an incredibly gifted bondsman, which is why she's so comfortable juggling so many communication bonds while out training."

"Bondsman?"

Damona nodded, "Ionia's gift is quite rare. She's able to detect, establish, and even manage the bonds that are set out by the Gods. That includes both our powers, our mates, even our House bonds. It's a powerful thing, and we are blessed she has not had to utilize it much in Ceanus."

"When was the last time she did use it?"

Damona's expression grew stony. "A little over a year ago, I banished someone from Ceanus. Ionia stripped him of his House bond and any remaining ties to his squall."

"I see." I thought a moment and then said, "Your gift is so tied up in the kingdom. Do you ever wish that you had a more, I don't know, aggressive gift? Something like Ionia's?"

"Perhaps at times. I don't fear the more powerful Mer here. Although there are many here who wish to sit upon this throne, to hold the crown of Ceanus. But our power, the one that runs in our bloodstream, was designed to rule Trayon's kingdom. It is our touch that can gather the gifts of others and use it to power the city."

"What if I can't do it?" I didn't clarify to her whether I meant logistically because I meant to return to Adrial, or if I meant that my blood had been diluted by not enough magic on Father's side and I wasn't capable.

My mother sighed then got up to pace a short distance away before returning, her bare feet making almost no noise against the stone floors as she moved. After a moment, she spoke. "I was betrothed to a Cirein-Croin male when I was young. He would've been king at my side if I hadn't run away to Adrial. I would've healed age-old frustrations between Cirein-Croin and Cetus and set Ceanus on a path where continuous peace between the Houses would be possible."

"Ohhh…"

"There is bad blood between the Houses, not just because of that betrothal but because of that male. They are struggling to find a hold once again. After Ionia's refusal to be Warden, Nidian stepped in, the brother of my former betrothed, Gruen. Nidian has no heir, and when he passes to the Deep, the House will again change hands and be in the care of new Wardens. Three families in as many generations is not a stable source of power. But many blame me for the fact that it should've been Gruen who took the head of the House position and not Nidian, who is his younger brother."

"What happened to the male, then—this Gruen guy—when you disappeared to Adrial?"

"He went feral."

I guffawed, one hand flying to my mouth, until I realized that my mother had stopped, looking at me with renewed surprise. I swallowed my laughter, only to find her staring at me, confusion evident in every line of her face.

"Why are you looking at me like that?"

"It's not often someone laughs at what our people fear more than the surface."

"Going feral? That's a real occurrence?"

Her expression relaxed a little. "I thought that Mehri would've told you."

"No, nothing." My cheeks heated. "I'm sorry. I didn't mean to laugh at something so serious."

"No, it's not your fault. I've been doing a poor job of sharing information with you." She eyed me. "Perhaps we need to make our meetings a more regular thing."

I held myself very still, trying to tell my overeager heart to calm down. "That would be good. You know, I feel like every day, Mehri tells me something new, but I still don't know very much about how the council works or your role. Let alone the gift side. I'm completely in the dark on that."

My mother nodded. "You're right. How about dinner? We can plan it every other night. On evenings that I'm pulled away, I will simply send word to Mehri or Akram and we can reschedule."

I smiled. "That sounds great." We grinned at each other, and I held her stare for a long time, my chest dangerously warm and content.

She broke the moment first, ducking her chin. "I'll start tonight with the feral Mer."

I raised an eyebrow, pausing before I spoke again. "Right, okay. When we say creatures go feral in Adrial, the animal is just simply too wild to deal with anymore."

"It isn't so dissimilar," my mother said, "but you must add in the factors that our gifts make us both more powerful and more volatile. Can you imagine having a feral dog, for example, who can also lift vast amounts of weight? Or someone who can mimic voices?"

I flinched. "That bad?"

One delicate hand swept back the lock of dark hair that had fallen into her face. "That bad. Although we've not had many issues lately with the feral Mer, we are constantly aware of them."

"Why wouldn't they just move to another area? Are they drawn to the city?"

"In a way, I believe, yes. Mer that go feral are typically those whose gift overwhelms them, but in many cases…"

"What?"

"I know from my time in Adrial that the cursed were often chained and kept somewhere until the urges dissipated. Or went away."

"I've seen it."

"Well, for those that the mate bond is triggered with, the torment is just as real and just as desperate."

My jaw dropped. "You're saying the mate bond is that fast. And it's that…"

"Dangerous? Absolutely. Mate bonds are rare these days, fewer and fewer, perhaps due to Trayon's disinterest with working with his family in recent years. But regardless of that, the bond is an immediate need to find that other person. There may not be immediate love or even passion, but there is a need to find them. It is impossible to deny."

"But now we chain them up and the Mer never get to find them?"

Mother nodded. "Many have run to the surface to try to find them, but we only have so long on the shore before other consequences begin to take effect."

She frowned. "And therefore most of the tortured Mer simply give up, they let their instincts take over. Their gift, their entire personality, shifts to that of a feral mer. They live outside of the arc with the other creatures of the deep."

"That's awful. They either find love or they go insane."

"Not quite insane. They are very capable of functioning and behaving like us. But they have no interest anymore."

"I've heard some love stories in my time, but even that seems extreme."

"Love is beautiful, but it can also be dangerous, and have a deadly effect. There have been more wars fought for love than all other reasons combined. It shouldn't surprise us, and yet, it always does."

"Was my father… Was he your mate?"

Mother's dark hair slid forward, hiding her face. "No, not like that. He was my chosen mate, not something fate determined."

"Did you love him?"

"So, so much."

"He loved you too. He still does. He hung portraits of you everywhere, and I know that he's lonely, but he told Homer that he has no interest in remarrying ever." An idea occurred to me. "Oh my gosh! You're not dead."

Damona's voice deepened with humor. "Clearly not, Miraceti."

"So you're technically still married."

Her face changed then. I could see that she was catching on to where my thought pattern had gone. When she spoke now, there was a steely glint in her blue eyes. One I chose to ignore. "I am," she said cooly.

"You're still queen of Adrial."

My mind was racing, my entire body nearly vibrating with the possibilities. If nothing else, if Trayon denied me my request, then I could still have a shot of solving so many of our issues. My father could have his wife back. I would have a mother, and our people would rejoin at their beloved queen being back. Maybe with the help of the Mer, we could protect our trading lanes and reopen parts of the port that were too dangerous for Adrialians.

"You're correct."

"Do you know what this could mean? You could come home. You could help Father. You could reset the entire system. Can you imagine providing a unified kingdom between Adrial and Ceanus? There would be no bounds to what we could do."

"No, Mira."

My chest heaved as I stared at her. "What? To which part?"

"All of it."

I blinked, trying to calm my racing heart. I knew that I should be offended that she wouldn't want to ally with Adrial. But my silly little heart was trapped on the rejection. "Why not? Don't you want to come home?"

"Adrial was never my home, Mira. And while your father is and was everything I wanted in a partner, our time has passed. I'm needed here."

"With these people who are constantly trying to dethrone you," I said drily.

"Mira, there is more to it than that."

"I'm tired of not understanding. I'm tired of not knowing everything."

"I know you are, sweetheart."

I bristled at the placating way her voice sounded. "I'll see you at dinner, Your Majesty." I bowed my head to her, awaiting her dismissal.

A long moment drew out between us, and then two cool fingers touched under my chin, raising my head until I was forced to look her right in the eyes.

"You do not bow, Miraceti. No matter what and no matter who stands before you."

"You are my queen."

"And you will be a better queen and a better leader than I have ever been." She searched my eyes, looking for something in their depths. "You're dismissed, daughter."

I stepped back and locked my knees, forcing myself to stay straight and tall as I retreated to the hallway.

When I looked back, my mother was slumped, her slender shoulders rounded and low as she stared across the room at the throne there.

***

"There has to be a better way," I panted as I stepped through the opening and back into the air-filled arc. Every muscle in my body quivered in exhaustion. "I just can't keep up."

Kairos followed me through, his tail transforming in a soft swirl of magic and water until he was standing before me, glaring down with the ferocity that even I was impressed with.

Dragging more air into tired lungs, I stared up at him, briefly distracted by the trail of water that slipped down his neck. "You can't possibly enjoy dragging me around every morning."

His jaw flexed in his handsome face. "I do not."

"Then let's find another way. Maybe there's someone with a gift who would make me shift temporarily."

Kairos raised one arched dark brow. "We have gifts, abilities, but we cannot work miracles." He jabbed a finger at the claw. "You're wearing a Cetus claw. There are very few things in this world more powerful. And yet it still doesn't work."

The *it* he was referring to being my shift. I was days into training now and still needed the Claw of Cetus to remain alive and breathing during our training session. With no signs of my tail or any of my family's legacy of power and gifts, I was quickly becoming frustrated.

Not just because I was tired of being last and slowest in training. But also if I didn't make it to Pledging, then I may not have a chance to speak to Trayon directly. From what I'd gleaned from dinners with my mother was that Trayon himself congratulated each of the pledges as they joined the House who had accepted their bidding.

After that, Trayon may very well disappear for another month or more. I didn't have another month.

I needed answers for my people. My, well, other people.

Heat filled my cheeks, and against my will, tears sprung up in my eyes. "I cannot force myself to be something that I am not. I was just…" My hands fisted. "I need to be able to keep up."

Kairos eyed me, but his arms slowly uncrossed, and he shifted, his stiff posture finally relaxing marginally. "We'll find a way, Your Highness."

Surprised, I glanced up into his face, waiting for the sarcasm to appear. But nothing but stoic resolution remained as onyx eyes watch the other trainees make their way back into the arc.

I nodded. "Alright." I backed away, my cheeks still hot.

Mehri came charging up to me, her hands busy. "You're needed right now, my lady." She was running her hands over my hair, as if to frantically fix the waves that swirled around my jaw.

"What? Where?"

"You too, General."

Kairos's eyes were sharp. "What is it?"

Mehri looked nervously around us then back to me. Her fingertips brushed my shoulders. "I should've bought you more clothes. The council will be sensitive to your state of dress."

I looked down at myself. My still-wet black training shirt and pants were plastered to my flesh like a second skin. "I've been in training. They will have to deal with it."

Kairos was suddenly at my side, his large hand resting at the small of my back. While he'd spent hours this morning guiding my body around in the water, there was an intimacy that hit me deep in my belly. His fingers curled, a calming caress as I swallowed loudly.

"What happened, Mehri?"

"There was an incident last night, a large one. House Kraken is challenging House Leviathan over it."

Kairos's jaw clenched. "Publicly?"

"Of course, General. At the Heart. The queen is already en route."

Chapter Twenty-Three

Kairos cursed, turning to take his clothes from another servant who had appeared from somewhere. I hated the immediate disappointment that panged through me at the loss of his touch. "What do we do?"

Instead of answering me, Kairos slipped on the provided armor and then turned, dropping something heavy and warm over my shoulders.

"A cloak?" My fingers ran over the finely made garment.

"It's the best we can do for the time being," Kairos said sternly, taking my elbow. "It's warded with some basic protection spells. It'll keep you from getting stabbed but won't defer an Adrialian arrow. Does that make sense?"

I drew the edges of the cloak closed around my shoulders. It was warm, soft, and smelled wonderful. I barely resisted pressing my nose against the fabric as I nodded up at Kairos. "Completely."

Kairos breathed out hard, eyes scanning my form one more time. My cheeks heated as his gaze lingered. A moment later, he shook himself, blinking as he gestured towards the pathway. "I guess it's time you met your people, Your Highness, up close and personal."

And with that, we set off. I took extra care to not step in the hemline of the cloak, which was obviously made for the much taller male. But I was still glad for it. Not because I cared that much what the council thought of my bare skin, but because if Kairos was worried about potential dangers or assassinations, then I needed to be aware as well.

I was brave, but I wasn't stupid.

Mehri fell into step, her quiet humming surrounding us with a gentle melody as we made our way through the castle. My anxious heart eased a little, the combination of the heavy sweet-scented cloak and her gift offering me some solace.

Kairos stepped sideways, and a breath later, Akram leaped down from one of the above pathways, landing lightly on his toes in a crouch. I barely resisted looking down at the space that he landed in, wondering if he might have crushed a bit of that stone walkway when he landed. But before I could do anything, he turned, scanning me in a similar fashion to what Kairos had done but with none of the throbbing warmth in my belly.

The big warrior was good-looking, but he didn't leave me breathless and confused every time we interacted. It seemed my body preferred to lust over the arrogant, smirking General.

"I'm fine," I assured him, and then I addressed both of them. "What happens when we get there? You said it was a public challenge?"

Akram checked the sheath of his sword and then resettled the leather armor over his chest and the mark of Leviathan on his pectoral. "If they believe there is a grievance between two Houses, then they are allowed to publicly challenge one another. They can treat it as a trial, or they can turn to battle. With Kraken and Leviathan, it's sure to be a duel of some kind. The craftsmen may not often serve in the military or in our squalls, but they are the builders of all of our weaponry. No doubt they are quite familiar with the tools of their trade. You cannot underestimate them at any time."

I blinked at Akram. It was more than I'd ever heard him say in the entire time I'd known him. "Who would represent House Kraken?"

"In the case of a duel, it'd be Aden. Or in a verbal trial…" Akram shrugged. "Probably the Warden's oldest, Sultaran."

I nodded, stumbling a little on the bottom step as we climbed steadily towards what I could only describe as crowd noise. Until now, I'd only heard the soft rumble of shops or of people eating meals together at the markets that surrounded the castle. But this… This sounded aggressive. The jaunts and cheers and singing made the hair on my arms rise as we climbed to the top of an arena. It was small, overcrowded, with Mer crammed into every available space, each leaning over the level below them. Most were shouting at the two Ceanians who walked to the center of the arena floor.

Rising from the middle of a wave was a statue of Trayon, his trident in hand. The two males approached the statue, bowing low before unfolding two very different black flags and casting them over the top of their respective posts.

The one on my left was black, the fabric embossed with heavy gold décor, illustrating the legendary kraken monster, its coiling tentacles askew. Above the monster's detail was the emblem of a hammer.

The second male had also unrolled his banner, draping it over the second post. This monster was powerful, heavy bodied, with a set of snarling teeth. A leviathan. Above the House monster, a shield was carefully drawn into the dark fabric.

As soon as the males stepped away, the noise level dropped, leaving me standing on the top tier, Akram at my front, Mehri at my side, and a snarling Kairos had moved to stand at my back. I could practically feel the tension leaching from his body as we watched the proceedings unfold below us.

The House Kraken male bowed to Trayon's statue then to a dais about a quarter of the way around the arena. If I stood on my tiptoes, I could see the slightest outline of my mother standing there.

My mother's voice rang out, sharp and clear and beautiful. "Before Trayon and Her Majesty the crown, House Kraken would like to challenge House Leviathan to a duel. Do you accept?"

The Leviathan speaker stepped forward to bow to Trayon and then to the queen as well. "House Leviathan accepts the challenge, Your Majesty."

"What is the source of the disagreement?" the queen asked.

"House Leviathan has failed to patrol parts of House Kraken on purpose. This puts our citizens at risk and illuminates the disgusting favoritism on which Ceanus now stands."

A jeering cry from House Kraken caught my attention. Each House seemed to contain themselves to a certain area of the arena. And while I was close to where my mother's balcony stood, I could hear the Leviathans on my right.

Their shouted words shocked me.

"Fucking Krakens. Can't take care of themselves so they want us to do it for them."

"At least they pull their weight, unlike the Cirein-Croin. Never leave their fancy little apartments."

"These people forget who the real power is here."

I looked at Akram and then Kairos, wondering if they were listening. Something in their stiff postures told me they were.

Mer continued to filter in all around me, and I was shocked by how close they were getting. But then, only a few people had even learned who I was. They wouldn't recognize me. Especially not in Kairos's cloak. And while he loomed over many of the onlookers, they stayed still and resolute as he ushered us all forward towards a small dais set to the side of the circular space.

"They don't move for him?" I hissed at Mehri, shocked.

"At our hearts, we are all the same. No House, no title, nor bloodline can divide us here."

"What?"

Mehri pointed at the inscription that twined around the top of the circular bowl that people were still climbing down into, claiming seating and shouting across at each other. "Trayon's rule. Here, we are all equal. You are the same as me. He—" she pointed at Kairos "—is just another member of Ceanus. Not a general. At least while he is in the arena."

"That's fucking convenient," I snorted.

"It was Trayon's temple before the divide. And since then it has been a sort of meeting place for the Houses when there are issues between them. A neutral zone of sorts," Kairos said, his hand on my lower back as he pressed me forward.

Akram grunted and folded in at my back as we made our way around the middle tier of the arena. At the center, my mother stood on an overhanging balcony, her crown gleaming against her pale face as she stared down at the roiling masses below her. The atmosphere left me feeling jittery, and when I reached my mother's side, she actually gripped my elbow, her fingers clammy as she continued to stare down at her people.

"What's happening?" I asked, half-shouting over the din of it all.

"They've elected for a duel instead of a trial."

I swallowed, dread thickening my throat as I could practically feel the emotions in the room continue to rise. I suddenly wished Mehri was here, singing or humming or working some of her magic to calm this crowd.

But she didn't move from her space down the steps. Instead, her eyes were blown wide, her lips slightly parted and slack as she stared across the bowl to the other side. I followed her gaze, wondering how she could make out anyone in this wildness. But when I did, it was very clear who she was looking at, because holding the flag of the Kraken people and standing directly opposite of Mehri, was a tall, gray-haired male, far younger in the face than his hair would ever appear. His facial features may have been attractive had they not been pulled back in a snarl that I could practically feel from here.

I racked my brain, trying to remember what I knew about the Warden of Kraken's family. Nothing came to mind, at least until I watched the sharp-eyed male reach down and carefully lift the Warden of Cirein-Croin up to stand beside him.

Recognition bloomed, and I looked to my mother. Timor stood at her back now, one powerful arm resting against his sword as he stared down into the mix of people.

"Call it to order," the queen said, her words only a whisper. "Now."

Nodding, Timor stepped in front of my mother and pressed a hand over his chest in salute then raised a shell to his lips. When he blew through it, the sound reverberated around us, replacing the din of the crowd below with silence as every citizen turned to stare.

"House Kraken has challenged House Leviathan and chosen to forgo a trial, moving straight to a duel."

Someone behind me snorted. "Typical."

Another soft grunt, and they were silent once again.

"House Leviathan, do you accept this challenge?"

Warden Lark stepped forward. "We do, High Lord Timor."

"House Kraken, your challenge has been accepted. As the challenging house, you reveal the nature of the battle and your representative first."

"We choose hand to hand." A roaring cry echoed his words, falling short when the warden raised his hand once again. "And Kraken House will be represented by Aden."

The shadow that was Kairos over me straightened further. At my back, Akram drew closer. Below us, a clearing began to form, the crowd slowly stepping back until a circle of tiles showed on the floor of the bowl. It was a small space, perhaps only the distance of two horses back to front. And with Trayon overlooking it, the crowd began to slowly stomp, separating only for a moment to produce a brunette male, with long dark hair that was braided down his back. He wore a simple white shirt, but it was clear that he was covered in tattoos, the winding black curling over the back of his hands and up his neck.

He moved to the center of the circle then raised his fists high. The cheers immediately broke out one again, and he spun in place, jaunting and cheering alongside his House.

"He doesn't seem so bad," I commented dryly. Plenty of fighters got amped up before a show. He didn't seem to be malicious, just eager.

Akram cursed. "Just wait for it."

"And who does House Kraken choose to challenge House Leviathan."

The warden stepped forward, but Aden was faster, his hand over his chest as he curled his lips back, small dark eyes finding us above the crowd. "We challenge General Kairos of House Leviathan."

Shock made my heart skip a beat. "He can't do that, can he?" I whispered to Akram, who was closer than ever. "The General isn't even involved in this. Is he?"

Kairos was back at my side, Mehri joining us immediately after. "I'm not."

After his words, Kairos leaned over and started talking animatedly to his lieutenant—Baye—and then my mother. Mehri moved closer, her slender body quaking as it reached mine. I folded my fingers through hers.

"It doesn't matter if the General is involved or not. House Kraken takes this deeply personally, and Aden is after his position in the squall."

"I thought House Kraken didn't join the military."

"Not usually, but there are several who have, especially most recently. Aden was one of them."

I looked down at Aden with renewed interest. "If he defeats Kairos now, will he win the role as General as well as the dispute?"

"No, but he would cause doubt in the General. Which could mean that a challenge for that position is coming."

"I thought my mother elected Kairos… She told me that he was her choice."

"She selected him, but he had to compete to be a part of the selection group."

Realization dawned. "And let me guess… Aden was the second choice."

"Kairos destroyed him in the final match, or so I heard. I was out of the city then, but I heard it was a brutal fight."

"And so this will be as well?"

"I'm not sure." Mehri's nose wrinkled. "Something feels different."

"Like what?"

Mehri shook her head. "I can't quite figure it out. I just know."

"Can they use their gift on each other?"

"No, only hand-to-hand is allowed here. To use your gift would be to forfeit and immediately lose."

I nodded, but the anchor lodged in my throat didn't move. Finally, I got the words out. "Can Kairos reject the nomination to be Leviathan's representative?"

"He could…but he won't."

As if he could hear our conversation, Kairos turned, his neck jerking first to one side and then the other, as he made his way lower into the arena. Cheers from all sides erupted at the sight of their General accepting the challenge. Kairos bore them all with a twisted smirk, his cold black eyes already fixed on Aden.

"I figured," I whispered under my breath as Kairos reached the floor of the theater and walked straight to where Aden stood, feet braced and wide. The two males appraised each other for a long moment before Kairos reached across and placed his hand on Aden's opposite shoulder. Slowly, with his mouth moving in words that I couldn't hear, Aden mimicked the movement.

Timor nodded, his voice sounding above the din once more. "The challenge has been accepted. Should House Kraken win, then Leviathan will have to give land retribution to House Kraken for their infringements upon Ceanus's citizen protection laws."

I blinked, turning incredulously to Mehri. "They pay with property."

Mehri didn't seem to understand my nonchalance. "Yes, my lady. Gold may be our currency like yours in Adrial, but land, space, buildings are the real source of wealth in Ceanus."

"Which district is the largest?"

Mehri considered the question. "Until recently, they were quite even, but I do feel like in the last arc shift, House Kraken lost more than the other Houses. Perhaps that's why they are even more upset today. Their district now borders ruins, which attracts feral Mer and other creatures."

House Kraken was upset that their home wasn't being patrolled by the Levithan, and they were concerned about their land being taken. No wonder they were so pissed off. "Did you say arc shift?"

"Someone has been poorly educating you," a gravelly voice said at my side, and I looked down to find Ionia at my elbow. Even more petite now that she was without her fins, my training leader leveled me with a knowing stare before fixing her eyes on Kairos. I could see the way a faint smile graced her lips as she looked at the General.

"Don't worry, Princess Mira. Your General won't have any issues dispatching the Kraken heir. Although I'm guessing his honor will probably ruin any chance of him just killing the welp and doing us all a favor."

I was surprised. "That's…um…a little aggressive."

"We are Mer, Princess. The first warriors of a powerful sea God. Aggression comes with the territory."

My gaze flickered back to the two males below us. My fingers curled in Kairos's cloak as the audience came back to life. Bets were being made, and shouts of encouragement and fury filled the air once again. "And you're sure he'll win?"

Ionia's forehead wrinkled. "Of course I am, girl. I trained him myself."

Akram grunted at my back at her casual phrasing. But I couldn't hold it against the cheeky elderly Mer and gave her a quick smile before following her gaze back down to the two males. Kairos pulled his shirt off, seemingly casual. Folding the shirt, he then handed it off to an eager-faced female who dodged back into the crowd as soon as she could, raising her fist with the shirt in it to a bright array of cheers.

Something pulled in my gut, and for a second I wanted to roll my eyes at the insanity of her reaction, but at the same I was irritated that she'd been the one he'd given that too.

"You're wearing his cloak, my lady," Mehri whispered, a note of humor in her voice.

"What?" How much had I said of that out loud, I wondered, shrugging. "He just didn't want the council pissed at us because of my training clothes."

Mehri's face was deliberately blank as she turned to the fight. "Yes, Yes, I know, of course."

I crossed my arms over my chest under the cloak, rolling my eyes. But not before I noticed my mother take in the cloak and my face with quick, decisive movements. I kept my face forward, unsure of how to meet her eyes without spelling out just how confused I was by my own actions.

Aden handed off his shirt as well, to a petite female whose golden waves nearly reached the top of her buttocks. As he handed the shirt off, he reached low, scooping her up against him and planting a loud, expressive kiss on her lips.

"Mates," Ionia said at my side. "Completely ridiculous."

My lips curled, but I couldn't stop watching as Aden began to circle Kairos. "Are they all like that?"

The older Mer huffed. "Every one, it seems. The true mates and chosen alike. Renders them completely useless at times."

"I think it's romantic," Mehri said softly at my side.

I reached out and gave her elbow a soft squeeze. But before I could find the right response to that, Timor slapped his hands loudly. Silence fell again. Aden and Kairos stared at each other, their House flags hanging behind them in a dark flash of gold.

My mother stood, moving to stand beside Timor at the front of the dais. Every Mer in the arena stared as she raised her hands. The tension in the arena drew taut, and the hair on the back of my neck rose.

"Begin."

Chapter Twenty-Four

Both Kairos and Aden were larger than life, their skin covered with a variety of tattoos, ending with the pronounced House tattoo, which each wore proudly. Kairos's shield was emblazoned across his chest, coupled with a scattering of sharp lines and decorated swirling ink across his forearms and chest. Aden's tattoos climbed from his spine, over a strong shoulder, across to his front, as if lining the muscle-linked ribcage of the male.

"What does Aden do within House Kraken?"

Mehri leaned in, her pink hair brushing my shoulder. "You mean other than training to be the Warden?"

"Yes."

"He and his brother, Sultaran, are Gifted blacksmiths. Perhaps the best Ceanus has ever seen. They are coveted. Not just because their line traces back to the first members of House Kraken but because the swords and armor that come out of their smith are imbued with their powers and are naturally protective and powerful."

My mother's eyes flickered over to me, as if she could hear what Mehri was whispering to me. "I believe that Kairos and Aden were good friends when they were young. Kairos grew up in the castle, and Aden's father was always in and out of the castle with his brother, the Warden. Naturally they became friends. But when they chose Kairos as General…things changed."

"They won't let things go too far, will they?" I found myself asking, surprised when neither Mehri nor Akram answered me. I bumped Akram's shoulder with my own. "Akram, tell me."

"There has not been a death during a challenge in many years, Your Highness."

That didn't make me feel better at all. "But they have in the past?"

Mehri spoke this time, her voice barely a whisper. "In order to save their representative, the House must admit fault and go back on their claim." Her throat worked. "In many cases, the shame is worse than death."

My head jerked to the circling males. Aden was snarling as Kairos displayed a cool indifference as he allowed his former friend to come closer and closer to him.

I cast a worried glance over at Timor, who stood at my mother's side. The intensity in his expression made my stomach churn. From my limited time here, I knew that House Leviathan would never change its opinions to save Kairos. While I didn't understand the angst there between the male below and his House, I could feel it. Maybe everyone did. That's why the arena was nearly silent as the two continued to circle each other.

Kairos had to win. Frustration and fear wrapped around my heart, squeezing as I leaned against the dais wall and stared down at them. The General had done nothing but scold me, tease me, and make my life more difficult. But at this moment, I could see no one else. I *wanted* to see no one else.

My mind was racing, considering my options if Aden was to take down Kairos. There surely were rules against another fighter coming into the arena. But could I weather those? Perhaps I could plead ignorance, after I made sure that Aden couldn't hurt him.

"Mira, it's going to be alright." My mother's hand found mine, her fingers cool and calming as she gripped me. "Kairos won't let it go that far."

I didn't ask why she knew where my thoughts were or why my body relaxed against her hold. I was still too consumed by the males below. In a flash of fists and a rough cry of anger, Kairos struck first. His movement was as quick as lightning, a heavy fist driving into Aden's cheekbone as the smaller male recoiled and turned under the power of the hit. Kairos didn't let up, immediately following with a knee to the belly that sent Aden sprawling to the ground.

Unlike the display with Rhoe the night of the Welcoming, Kairos kept himself tightly in control. In between strikes, he slipped away, dancing between Aden's thick fists with a lightness that I hadn't thought such a large male capable of.

Aden was obviously well trained though. And while Kairos might have sheer size, the other male wasn't backing down. He slunk low, his leg striking out and catching Kairos in his thigh, even as he blocked a second hook from the House Kraken fighter.

If it hurt, you couldn't tell. Kairos's face was shuttered—only his black eyes shone with that dangerous gleam as he forced Aden back with a volley of punches. Aden blocked the first, the second, but the third landed with a crack that I could practically feel in my chest.

Aden faltered, his legs spreading as he attempted to regain his equilibrium. Kairos must've sensed his impending victory and swept closer. Aden attempted another hit, this one batted down as Kairos stepped into him and sealed his hand around Aden's throat.

The cheering slowed, noise plummeting as Kairos stood there, one fist drawn back, the other splayed across Aden's throat.

Both of their chests rose and fell quickly.

"Do it," Aden snarled.

I jerked, looking at my mother. She stood completely still, blue eyes blazing down at the pair.

"Do it!" Aden screamed.

Kairos's fist slowly lowered.

"Does House Kraken submit?" This voice cut through the space—not my mother's, but rather Atlana, the willowy female standing in the front row of the arena. But before Kraken's Warden could speak, Aden snarled and broke free of Kairos's hold.

"I'm not finished with you." Aden circled, powerful body tense as he eyed Kairos, looking for a weak spot that I wasn't sure existed. Even now, my heart pounded. I pressed a hand to it, forcing a long, slow breath to try to calm its pace. When I looked up, I found Timor staring at me from around my mother. His eyes were cold, dark, and I flinched before I could stop myself. His lip lifted, just the smallest increment. A snarl, not unlike the ones the males below were throwing at each other.

A clear threat.

A warning.

I met his gaze head on, ignoring the way my instincts were screaming for me to run.

A moment later, Timor broke our stare to turn back to the fight, and I was back to trying to figure out if what I'd seen was real. Sure, I may have been furious at Timor's son, but I had never expected my issues with Rhoe to spark such a powerful reaction in his father.

"Your Highness?" Akram's hand was rough, coarse against the skin of my shoulder.

I jumped and then smiled guiltily at the Mer, dismissing his obvious concern. Turning my attention back to the arena floor, I watched as Kairos seemed to relax. Aden, on the other hand, only grew more agitated.

"You think you're so much better than us now," Aden growled, loud enough even I could hear. "All because of her."

"Aden, calm yourself," Kairos said, his patient voice irritating even to me. For a moment, I understood exactly why Aden took a huge leap forward, jabbing and swinging. The General had an unparalleled ability to rile people up.

"Just face it. She already owns you," Aden said. His mouth opened a moment later, to deliver what was probably another scalding remake, when Kairos swept in, his fists snapping in a catastrophic one-two hit that sent Aden stumbling back. Kairos followed, his hands sealing around Aden's throat once more.

This time, he simply picked the man up from the sandy floor and looked over at the now silent House Kraken crowd.

"House Kraken, do you submit?"

The Warden stood, eyes full of fire. "House Kraken accepts their defeat."

Kairos immediately released Aden. The other man slipped to the ground, his hands moving to his neck as his mate hurdled the low wall of the arena and ran to stand over him.

"House Leviathan is victorious!" The booming voice from above echoes around us.

I moved closer to the wall, Kairos's cloak warm on my shoulders as I looked down to him. Behind me, my mother rattled off ramifications of this fight followed by what seemed like a prayer to Trayon.

I barely noticed, because even though there were hundreds of Mer between us, Kairos was staring directly at me. As I watched, his hips flexed and folded, the massive form bowing. I know that to anyone else in the arena, they might have assumed that he was bowing to my mother. But I knew differently.

This victory was for me. I didn't know why, but I felt it in the depths of my soul.

Meeting his eyes, I slowly nodded. Aden's words filled my mind.

"She already owns you."

I wanted to believe that Aden had meant my mother.

But something—in my head or heart, I wasn't sure—told me it was a hint at something else altogether.

Chapter Twenty-Five

My routine over the next few days did stabilize. I grew used to the coral light that signified days and nights here in Ceanus. And while I still struggled in training, I showed up every day with the rest of the trainees.

Ionia didn't take it easy on me, even though I was still unable to shift or produce a single spark of a gift. Others had begun to show off their new abilities. Several I knew were attracting attention from the Wardens. Those were the trainees that I knew would be taken first during their House bids. And while I knew that I had a legacy bid for House Cetus, there was a large part of me that wished I had something else other than my bloodline to offer.

I had tried telling Kairos one day as he swam me from one end of the arc to the other, Ionia rattling on about the history of the arc, her gnarled fingers pointing at the ruinous buildings and walls that used to be included inside of the arc.

Kairos, of course, only grunted, shifting his hold on my waist and telling me to pay better attention to Ionia. After that moment in the arena, my relationship with the General had continued to be more confusing. Some days I felt like he hated every moment of training. Others, I would look up from a council meeting to find those onyx eyes staring into mine with a heat that I couldn't understand.

Whatever it was, I knew this for certain… I was deeply, deeply in debt to the General. With him acting as the muscle during the swimming portion of our training, I learned about Ceanian battle strategy. The way that they used their gifts to elevate life in the city for everyone. I paid particular attention to the day that Ionia finally explained the shift in the arc. The way that Ceanus and its surrounding ruins were like rings on a tree stump. Each layer of the ruins aged differently as the ocean claimed back the city from Trayon and my mother's magic.

Ionia said that most believed it was because the city itself molded and adapted to how many souls it contained.

What do you believe, I had asked Ionia. She had cast a wide, gap-toothed smile. I had gotten attached to the older Mer these past two weeks.

I believe that we are built to survive. Like the waves that beat upon the shore, we are constant and powerful. And whether the city is as large as it was in Queen Divina days or as small as a coin, we will survive.

I grinned at her. The Mer was a tricky one. And I knew that while that may be her opinion, she'd carefully avoided answering my question. I would have to seek her out later in the Cirein-Croin district and see if she would tell me in a different setting. The claw floated a little in the water as we listened to her discuss protocol for visiting the surface. But once again, my mind kept wandering.

Maybe it was Kairos's hands, which were still drifting against my sides. The currents were strong here, and while I was capable of bobbing in the water with the rest of the group, it appeared that Kairos wasn't taking any chances.

Or was it that he—like me—had grown used to touching whenever he wanted to?

Biting my lip, I watched as Ionia wrapped up her conversation and proceeded to tell us all that we were expected in the arc soon. The bells that organized time rang out of Trayon's new Ceanian temple, which was adjacent to the palace, guiding all Ceanians through their days.

In short, I needed to return to my rooms soon. I didn't have dinner with my mother this evening, so I would take all the time I could to prepare.

If General Kairos suspected anything, he was quiet about it as I hurried from the platform, no longer needing Mehri to get myself back to my rooms.

There, I cleaned up, ate a quick meal, and studied the history of Ceanus scrolls that Nidian had sent over until the corals throughout Ceanus dimmed and the bells tolled the late hour.

Thank Gods that Mehri preferred an earlier bedtime. By the time she slipped into her adjoining room, my nerves were raw with anticipation.

I knew for a fact that as much as I adored Mehri, I couldn't ask for her help in this area. If I got in trouble, I might be able to get out of it. But the half-siren? I'd seen the way others in the castle looked at her. Mehri always smiled and said they were just jealous of her unique colors. But I could see what she was hiding, the whispers that followed us around the castle. The fear that darkened others' eyes when she spoke to them.

I'd once asked her if she would be happier living with the sirens, but Mehri had shaken her head. *"Perhaps the Mer here whisper about me or worry over my voice, but here, I know who my enemy is. I have a*

House to protect me. A princess to take care of," she'd joked, prodding my side. *"And maybe a future here, once you are queen."*

My throat had ached at that last statement. Regardless of how many times I had told her, Mehri was deeply convinced that I was going to stay. When I asked her how she was so sure, when I was so sure I was leaving, she would just grin at me silently.

Her confidence in me was endearing, if misplaced. Yet another reason I couldn't risk her safety with my ideas.

Truthfully, I was hoping I didn't need anyone's help. I knew by now that Akram really only took one break from me a day. It was the hour between the midnight toll and the one that directly followed. I suppose this was his chance to go about his usual business before returning to the small bedroom that he occupied directly off of my own. And while the nosy part of my personality was dying to know what he was doing with that hour, today I could only be grateful he took the time at all.

I needed to get out of the castle.

Not just the castle, but also the arc.

Which was why I needed someone with rank and power to help me get in and out of the arc without the guards there immediately alerting my mother. Or worse, Timor.

Unfortunately for me, that left only one person I could trust to help me with this entire venture—the one person who may want me to fail. I groaned, cursing for the hundredth time my useless hands and feet.

In Adrial, I'd considered myself athletic and fit. Here, I was a useless human at the bottom of an ocean. What good was being able to breathe underwater if I couldn't keep up with my squall? Or prove to Trayon that I deserved his time at Pledging?

Everything hinged on me being able to keep up. To keep up meant my people had a chance to be safe once more.

If I couldn't keep up in training, if I couldn't understand what it meant to be a Mer…then why had I come here at all? What had brought me to this moment? Other than a cruel twist of fate that my bloodline dictated I endure…

There had to be a reason for all of this. I had to believe that there was some way I could save my people. A rational way to explain why I had been pulled into this world so different than my own.

But I couldn't ask those questions. Or any of the others, because as of now, I was virtually useless to Ceanus. In order to speak to Trayon, I had to make it through training. And not just by using Kairos's strength.

The tolling of the hour made me lift my head. I only had a few minutes. Hurrying to my door, I pressed my head against it, listening to the quiet conversation between Akram and another of the castle guards who always stood in for him. They chatted for just a moment before Akram's deeper tones softened and finally disappeared. He was gone.

I gulped, adrenaline flooding my system. I had one hour, Moon Mother guide me.

Moving quickly, I tiptoed to the door and cracked it open. The guard, a stocky female with bright-blue eyes, blinked at me in surprise before bowing low, saluting me. "Your Highness."

I cleared my throat, hoping to hide the tightness. "Did Akram just leave?"

"Yes, Your Highness," she said, head still bowed. "Would you like me to get him for you?"

"No, no." I played at being worried, dancing back and forth at the doorway and biting my lip. "Actually, I think I'll just run and catch him."

Without waiting for permission, I raced down the stairs. The guard, just as I predicted, jogged after me, her face grim. "Hold on, Highness. I have to stay with you."

I halted fast, turning to face her. "No, you can't. Please, my maid… She's asleep in my room. You can't leave her unguarded either."

"What?"

I took a gamble. "How do you think Akram would react if he found out you left her unguarded?"

The Mer blinked, her head turning slightly to the hall. She was torn. I just needed one more final push. "I know exactly where he's going. I can be there in just a moment."

The guard hesitated.

"I'm sure you know I can take care of myself. But that means you also know how some people treat the sirens here. I would hate it if something happened to Mehri while our rooms were unguarded. And my Mother—oh, she would be furious."

That settled it. I could see the moment I'd won as the guard's eyes hardened. "You are right, Highness. I will return to your rooms. The Temple of the Deep will be deserted tonight. You can catch Akram if you go now."

The Temple of the Deep? That's where Akram went each night? Turning, I made it as if I was running to the lower stairs, as the guard disappeared back in the direction of my rooms. At the last moment, I redirected my feet and climbed back higher. I wasn't sure exactly where Kairos's rooms were, but I had seen him on his balcony before, seeing the way he could leap from his balcony edge directly through the arc.

I wasn't sure how I knew it was his, but there was no way it couldn't be. Unguarded, with a simple door… I pressed a palm against it. Without hesitation, the door swung wide, revealing an immense suite, one side built to host people. A round set of chairs around a nearly perfect replica of Ceanus situated on a heavy wooden table dominated the room. At the other end, there was a gossamer curtain that separated the seating area from a bed built large enough for three males and several sets of dressers and wardrobes, one of which was wide open, showing the armor that I'd seen him wear only once.

"Kairos?" I hissed into the low-lit room. A bit of coral on the wall closest to me glowed warmly when I approached. I pressed a hand against the coral sconce, and without thought, it brightened even more, which made me smile. But still, I didn't see the male anywhere.

Moving farther in, I couldn't stop myself from walking closer to the replica of the city, each tiny archway and stone wall nearly perfect in its recreation. My finger gently brushed against the dueling grounds that we'd stood in just this morning, when I heard a noise.

I clapped a hand over my mouth, spotting a door that I hadn't noticed before opening. And at its center, in a brightly lit room, was Kairos, dressed only in a thick-looking towel. And a woman kneeling in front of him, her hands on either side of his hips.

I had tried to keep quiet, but something shifted, and suddenly Kairos's dark eyes were boring into mine, his handsome face twisted in surprise. But he didn't move. In fact, one of his hands moved down to the shoulder of the woman, his fingers gripping her shoulder.

"Nula, later."

The woman—Nula—looked up at Kairos first then over to me. Her cheeks were pink, the tone contrasting with her stunning short-cropped auburn hair. She was beautiful, delicate as a flower, and just as graceful as she rose from the ground, her hands leaving Kairos with a casualty that I could never have mustered.

Heat bloomed in my belly, filling my blood with something I couldn't understand. The woman left quickly with a hushed word for Kairos and a bow for me before she slipped quickly out the door.

I swallowed, bringing my fingers to up my face and glancing down at the nails I'd bitten down this afternoon worrying over my plans. "Entertaining, General?"

"Looking for entertainment, Princess?" Kairos picked up another towel, beginning to dry his still-damp hair as he sauntered across the room towards me.

Suddenly, fury bubbled under my flesh, making me want to tackle him, to rake my nails down his chest and back, to make him ache the way my chest did now.

Biting down on my lip, I shook my head, taking a small step back. "You're a pig."

Kairos slowed, leaning against the doorway to his suite, the bright coral light of the other room throwing his entire body into contrast. And it didn't matter that I saw him in his uniform nearly every day. He was still beautiful enough to take my breath away. I dragged in air, desperate to remain unbothered, even as his belly flexed and illuminated even more ink-lined muscle.

"And yet the question remains… Looking for entertainment, Princess?"

I snarled, "I am not one of your playthings." I nodded after Nula, my fingernails digging into my palms.

Something flashed in his eyes as I shifted, my heartrate drumming in my heart. "Then why, exactly, have you come here, in the middle of the night, sneaking into my room?"

Kairos moved now, coasting across the room to sit on the small couch a few strides from me. With slow precision, he crossed one leg over the other, smirking when my eyes dropped to his legs, half terrified he was bearing all, half wishing he was…and immediately being frustrated at myself for that.

I growled, forcing my eyes to look at the smooth plastered ceiling that arched over his room. "I need your help."

"That much is clear." I could hear the smirk in his voice, feel the rasp of it against my skin.

I crossed my arms over my chest, clenching hard to keep myself from reaching out and wrapping my hands around that thick neck of his and squeezing. "I need your help *tonight*."

Thinking it was safe, I looked back over at him. I regretted it instantly, as my belly curled with delight at the sight of the General's relaxed body still on display.

"Hmmm." Kairos leaned forward, his eyes glued to me, my skin heating as he swept his gaze over me once, twice, before asking, "Doing what exactly, Princess?"

"I need to get out of the arc."

Black eyes blinked slowly. "Absolutely not."

"You haven't even heard why."

"I don't need to." Kairos pushed out of the chair, moving to a small cabinet, where he poured himself a thick-looking brown drink

and immediately threw it back down his throat. I watched the bob
of his throat as he swallowed it, my skin still pinpricked with heat.

I had to convince him.

"You do, though. It's important, and not just for me."

He didn't even turn to look at me. "Leave, Mira."

I shivered at the sound of my name on his lips, my real name.
"Please, you and I both know that I'm not going to make it through
the training without more help. I can't have you hauling me across
the ocean every time I need to do something. And if the claw
doesn't work, then there's nothing else my mother can do. I might
just be…too human."

His shoulders were tense, the thick plates of muscles spread
there tight under the back ink that crawled from his shoulders
down. He wasn't happy, but he might just be listening.

"Listen, I have an idea. Something that I read when I first arrive.
In an old Ceanus historical parchment Mehri brought me. Did you
know that before the God of the Sea helped the original Adrialians
adapt, they often rode the hippocampus?"

His head tilted, dark eyes studying me. I had his attention, so I
rushed on. "They were able to bond with them, like Mer do with
their true mates. Obviously in a different way, but the hippocampus
are very intelligent, and I think if I could only get to them, maybe I
could see if I could bond with one, or perhaps just train one, to
accept me."

"That is truly insane," Kairos remarked, his voice low.

I could hear the interest in his deep tones. "It is a chance, Kairos,
and I need a chance."

"What happens if they attack you? Every hippocampus I've ever
experienced around the arc or even farther has been
rather…offended by any attempt to get close to them."

I snorted. "Well, I guess I won't be your problem or my mother's anymore, then." Silence fell, only the soft sound of his breathing between us as time slowly moved by. "I will find a way with or without your help."

"No, you won't," Kairos growled. "You won't make it out of my room if you keep talking like that, Princess."

I cocked my hip. "Don't be dramatic. I'll be fine."

He said nothing, so I pushed on, the words tumbling out in a rush. "I want my mother's people to love me. Not for my blood, but because I'm worthy to be loved."

"Your mother's people are *your* people."

I shrugged. "I want them to be. But they will never accept someone who can't even get through training. Let alone a princess from the shore who can't shift."

His head fell back, slightly curling strands of hair moving down his back as his hands rose and plastered themselves at the back of his skull. Hope bloomed in my chest.

"Kairos—"

"One chance."

"What?"

"One chance. If you cannot make contact with a hippocampus in one night, then we give up this insane notion." Kairos turned to me, face intense. "I know you think that you need to prove something to your mother, but she is more concerned with keeping you alive than making you powerful."

"That is maybe where Mother and I differ. In my world, power is safety."

Kairos approached, all long, graceful steps. "So you agree, one night."

"If I fail to make contact with a hippocampus tonight, then you will not bring me back another night."

His gaze narrowed. "Fine."

"Fine." I tried to play it off, but the word came out a soft squeal as I bounced on my toes.

Chapter Twenty-Six

Kairos rolled his eyes, but I felt like the usual venom he held for me wasn't there. "Let's get going, Princess."

"Aren't you going to get changed?" I gestured to his towel and then flushed when he raised one dark brow.

"While you are still here? I thought I should wait, but if you're in that big of a hurry…" His hand was at the top of the towel, freeing the knot, as I squawked and turned around, marching for the hall once again.

"You are foul."

His laughter followed, making my face all the hotter. A few moments later, Kairos jerked his door open wide. Redressed in a pair of training pants with his hair still tumbled around his shoulders, he gave me a quick glare before disappearing down the hallway.

"Wait, where are you going?"

"Let's get this over with."

I rolled my eyes, catching up to him and walking double speed to keep up with his long strides as we expertly made our way out of the castle and onto the myriad of pathways. Taking the same one that we'd used for training each morning, I was surprised when

Kairos reached out, gripping my upper arm as we arrived at the portal.

"What?"

"You're going to need this."

I raised my brow as he pressed a slender dagger into my palm. "For what? They are enormous. I don't think this little thing will do anything if they decide to charge or something."

Kairos sighed like I had completely worn him out. "You know how our magic works right, that we can imbue our gift into objects?"

"Yeah, I've heard that. House Kraken does it to all of their weaponry, right?"

My mother imbued her power into keeping the arc around Ceanus, she powered the lights, and kept the time. That was one of the few things about their magical gifts that did make sense. They were like fingerprints, scattered wherever the mage went.

"This one—" Kairos closed my fingers around the blade, his fingers warm and sure against mine "—is powered by mine."

"Your power is imbued in the blade?" I looked at the dagger with renewed interest. "Can you do that for just anyone?"

"To a degree, yes. The Krakens are best at it, but I picked up some helpful bits during my own training."

I remembered Mehri's pride in the training garments that she'd procured for me. She had said they were made with gifts that allowed them to flex and move with the Mer people's shifting forms. "What does the dagger do? I mean, I don't know much about your gift."

Kairos drew back. "No one has told you?"

I shook my head.

"I'm a healer, Princess."

I stared down at the dagger, even more confused now. "Does that mean that the dagger heals too?"

"There is much more to my healing gift than you would imagine. All you will have to do is to use it like any other dagger. But the cut of this blade will change the tide in any fight. Trust me."

"Thank you." I looked at the dagger with renewed interest. When I unsheathed it, the silver flashed brightly in the low coral light.

"Don't thank me yet. It still won't cut down a fully grown hippocampus." Kairos jerked his chin at the dagger. "Put that somewhere safe. You'll know when to use it."

I groaned, tucking the dagger into my waistband as he watched. "This whole kingdom is one giant secret. It's utter madness."

"It's survival, sweetheart." Kairos waited until I had tucked the blade in safely against my body before moving to stand behind me. "Ready? We will need to move fast."

I nodded, and as he followed me, I stepped through the clear barrier and through the portal, letting the cool water enclose me. The necklace at my throat hummed softly with its gift, and I could feel my lungs stretch and expand as I breathed easily in the water.

Kairos's warm hands found my sides, and I knew without turning that his tail had reappeared, replacing the legs that I'd almost seen too much of tonight.

With a swish of his powerful form, we were off, cutting across the darkened seabed towards the shallow end where the kelp forest grew. The necklace's gift granted me better vision in the water than I could've ever hoped for, and as Kairos propelled us through the water, I searched the area for any sign of the hippocampus herd I'd glimpsed the other day.

Do you think they are called a herd or a school? I sent my question down to the ever-present bond that still thrummed between us.

Kairos snorted into the connection then reset his hands lower on my waist so that he could bank to the right and push us up closer to the edge of the dark-green foliage.

I glanced up, my hair swirling around my face as I did. The moon must've been huge tonight, and I could actually see its light filtering down into the water as we hovered there. Good. Maybe the Mother was looking down on us. I clamped my eyes shut, muttering a quick and fervent prayer to the moon goddess, Mother of Artio and Trayon.

Please, Mother Moon, I need to find what I'm looking for.

Kairos pushed us farther into the kelp, the moonlight slowly disappearing from my skin. My heart suddenly ached with the loss, the need to feel the air on my skin, to see the stars above me.

Can you let go for a moment?

Why?

I looked up again. *I just have to see it.*

Highness, you cannot go up there.

Why not?

What if someone sees you?

Who is going to see me. It's the middle of the night, and there's no one here. I gestured around us both at the silent ocean. Gritting my teeth, I continued. *Please, Kairos. Just for a moment. It's been weeks already.*

Kairos looked both ways, frustration clear in his voice as he finally agreed. *Fine. Just for a moment.*

With a flick of that dark tail, we were moving, quickly making the last few lengths up through the strengthening waves. My heart raced, my entire body tingling as my head broke the surface, emerging into the moonlit night with a gasp of air. It was cool against my tongue and my chest as I arched in Kairos's hold, desperate to have as much of my skin touched by the moonlight as possible.

I took in a ragged breath, the air sharp and hot in my lungs, then another. And another. The smell of the sea nearly assaulted me now. How ironic that I didn't notice it at all in Ceanus or even at training. I pushed a shaking hand through my hair, wiping the droplets of water from my eyes.

A second later, Kairos's head broke the surface beside mine. He glanced around, on guard in an instant.

"Isn't it beautiful?" I said, joy filling me so full that it threatened to explode. I twirled in the water, my legs kicking against the current. A quick look at the stars told me which way to Adrial and I eagerly stared across the night towards the port. "Gods above, I've missed this."

"Are you satisfied, Your Highness?"

"Satisfied?" A strange emotion gripped me. My throat felt tight and stuck around the words that formed in my mind. I took in another breath of that sharp, salted air. "Do you think that it's been easy giving up my entire world? Two weeks ago, I knew exactly who I was and what I was going to do with my life. And now everything has changed. So, if you might excuse me for needing a moment to grieve the loss of, well, everything I knew before Ceanus."

Kairos treaded water, and then there was the softest shiver of pleasure that coasted over my mind as our eyes met and held. He stared at me like he was trying to see straight to my soul. I held his gaze, unblinking, unwilling to give on this one thing. Then Kairos swam backwards for a moment, giving me space as the dark waves crashed against our necks and shoulders.

"We are on borrowed time already, Princess," he said, words soft in the crashing melody of the waves around us.

I opened my mouth to protest again, my temper as raw as my eyes felt, when he suddenly sank beneath the waves. When he didn't immediately snatch my legs and drag me under with him, I blinked and looked around me. A moment later, a dark onyx tail flicked at the surface a few strokes away.

Breath. Space. He was giving me both. Relief flooding me, I turned my head up, letting the droplets from the waves leak down the sides of my face. I had once stared up at the stars from my balcony in Adrial, convinced that some nights, like tonight, when the moon was bright and the sky clear, they were close enough to touch.

Now, I felt even farther than them. Farther from everything. Hot pressure threaded through my veins, making my eyes water as I stared at them, the soft, friendly glow of the stars. Their presence was a powerful reminder that while I was worrying over trivial things in Ceanus, my people were still going mad. They were still suffering.

And now, now I knew that in many cases, their mates in Ceanus were suffering too.

I could change that. I could change everything. I just had to keep pushing. I needed to forget this grief and the pain that lurked under my skin each day. Because it was doing me no good. Not in Ceanus. Not when I returned to Adrial, a hero to my people.

Taking a deep breath in, I sealed my hand around the claw at my neck and ducked back beneath the surface.

And found myself staring right into the bright jade-green eyes of a hippocampus.

For the first time, I could confirm that they did have teeth. And they were very, very sharp.

Fuck.

Chapter Twenty-Seven

Miraceti!

The scream that Kairos gave echoed in my head, my chest, my very being—filled with fury and anger as he came throttling through the dark waters towards us.

But there was something else.

Oh, God… *Someone* else.

Her little mate thinks he can save her from us. The voice was soft, low-pitched. It ran over my mind like thunder, making me shudder at the otherworldly nature of it. But still, even in the condescending tone, there was something there. Something a lot like humor.

I prayed to all the Gods listening that I was making the right call. I held up a hand to Kairos, my fingers spread wide as the hippocampus curled through the water, cutting off Kairos's approach. *Stop. Don't come any closer.*

Kairos ignored me. He was only a few strokes away when I jerked my hand up again. *Kairos please, listen to me.*

Ah yes, you added please. Maybe now he'll listen. The condescension was back in her voice. Yes, *her* voice. She was clearly a female. But this time, a knowing tilt of her head caught my attention as her eyes, each as big as my fist, closed and opened slowly. Stunned by either my declaration or by the creature itself, Kairos stopped, one hand up as if preparing to throw something towards us.

The hippocampus swished her green and blue tail his direction, spinning both of us with the change of current. In a flurry of silver-tipped green and blue scales, she completely surrounded me. Her eyes were sharp and intelligent, and I could still see the sharp edge of her teeth as tiny bubbles followed her massive body movements. Easily as large in body as a warhorse, her long, elegant fins propelled her through the water with an ease that I envied immediately. As if noticing what I was watching, she stretched her long, muscular neck up, scales catching the sunlight that filtered through the shallow water.

Beautiful. She was the most beautiful creature I'd ever seen. My hands itched to reach forward, to touch her, but something else told me that this occurrence might be too good to be true.

And those teeth were still very, very sharp.

Why are you talking to me? Gambling, I attempted to speak to her just as I did with my training squall. I knew in an instant that it worked.

The hippocampus sighed into my mind, the noise a rustle there. Then with a smooth, coy voice, she said, *Perhaps I always talk to my dinner.*

I gulped, my legs jerking a little as my instincts screamed for me to run. *I think you're lying.*

And I think you are not supposed to be here, Artio's daughter.

What did you call me?

Her head jerked up, clearly offended, given the way she swam a small circle around me. *I can call you whatever I want, sandwalker. When you are as old as I am, then you have earned that right.*

I couldn't stop the soft laugh that spilled from my mind.

I was right, Kairos, I chanted down the connection to him, noting that he still hovered a few strokes away, his face thunderous as he watched the hippocampus circle me. His hands were extended as if he meant to lunge at the creature.

What should I call you? I asked her.

Her cackle filled my mind. *You may not call me anything, sandwalker. Most of your kind would be screaming by now. Just as you should be.*

I'm not like the rest of my kind. My belly twisted at the confession. I'd never fit in on land, and here I was struggling to keep up.

Clearly. The hippocampus slowed, her mass slowly coming to float in front of me, her eyes glittering as she tilted her head, somehow managing to look down on me, even as the waves gently moved around us.

Why did you come here, sandwalker?

There was real interest in her words now, in the shimmering scales that roiled over heavy muscles.

*I need help. I read that once—*I swallowed, choosing my next words with great care*—a long time ago, the hippocampus and Mer were partners, and they fought together to protect Ceanus.*

Her tail moved rhythmically through the water. *And who do you fight against now? Is Ceanus in danger?*

Heat crept into my face. *No. Not necessarily. I just…*

Perhaps in the old days, we allowed Mer to ride on our backs, to place armor on our bodies, because we knew that Trayon built Ceanus to help protect the oceans. But now, sandwalker, your people are changing. The arc is changing. Trayon has abandoned us, and my herds grow smaller and smaller. I have no reason to trust you or the God who hides in his forgotten kingdom.

Well shit. She wasn't going to make this easy on me. I kicked at the water, pushing myself closer to her. The hippocampus's body tensed, but she too held her ground. *If I can survive training and prove to my mother's council that I deserve a say in how Ceanus is governed, we can work together. We can be partners once more. I'm sure my mother would understand.*

Your mother?

The queen.

Her great long tail flicked. *You promise a great deal, sandwalker. About things you know nothing about.*

I don't have any other option. I'm risking everything, but I must save my people. And all of it hinges on me being able to survive here. I know what it's like to watch your kind suffer and not be able to do anything about it. I won't stop until I can talk to Trayon.

She tilted her head again, the pale-green ears flickering, the fins at the tip billowing slightly with the movement. *You will fail.*

What?

We need an ally that is strong and sure, not a finless Mer who doesn't understand the world she seeks to rule. She tossed her head, nostrils expanding silently. *I would have better luck with your angry mate over here.*

He's not my mate, just an unfortunate but necessary evil in my world right now.

Hmmm. The hippocampus raised her head, eyes focused on something over my shoulder. *There are far worse evils in your world than you can imagine.*

I studied her, unsure of what to say back to that. *I know I don't know everything* was what I finally got out, letting the words hang in the water between us. *But I refuse to fail my people.*

Her snort was accompanied with a new rush of bubbles. *You don't even know who your people are.*

And then she dove forward. I thought for a moment she was going to strike, but a breath from my skin, her twisted, elegant body arcing around the side of mine, fins flexing and moving as she swam into the darkness below us in a rush of cool water.

Wait! I—

But she was gone, nothing but a whirling of water between the darkening kelp forest and me. My chest ached, frustration rising up in my belly until I nearly screamed with it.

I take it she said no.

I startled, treading the water as I looked back at where Kairos still waited, his hands now lowered to his sides. *Could you hear any of that?*

No, nothing.

Well, you didn't miss much, I guess. I just insulted that beautiful creature, and she rightfully turned me down.

Kairos's face only hardened. *I thought that beautiful creature, as you called her, was going to kill you.*

I sighed, looking down again at the darkness she'd disappeared into. *I did too.*

Kairos snarled, his tail propelling him against me. His hands found mine in the cool water. I gasped, my chin jerking up to look into his face as he dragged my hands forward and pressed them into my chest. His grip was hot and firm. *Then why, Princess, did you not pull the weapon that I gave you for exactly this situation?*

I stared at him dumbly as he craned his neck over my shoulder, one hand leaving where he pressed my wrists to my chest, and he snatched the dagger out of the back of my waistband.

I…uh… I tried to formulate another response, but I was too distracted by how close his face was to mine. Close enough to see the darkness of his eyes and the way his nostrils flared wide.

Princess, you are trying my patience. At this point, it would've been easier if she did bite you, he growled. *Less stress and the council would actually allow your mother to choose her new heir.*

Wait, what?

Kairos turned away, but I'd heard the truth in his words. *If I don't succeed here, my mother gets to choose her heir? Is that what you said?*

Forget that. She didn't eat you, so I guess I'm stuck chaperoning you around for another two weeks.

I ignored his words. My mother had another heir in mind. That made sense. No wonder she had been surprised to see me. That was why she thought that I was some gift from her God. She hadn't expected me to ever show up, so she'd had a backup plan.

I looked over Kairos's face, noting the tense set of his jaw. Realization dawned. I jerked away from him. *It's you, right? You thought that you would be her chosen heir.*

His silence was the only answer I needed. I laughed, pulling away. *No wonder you are so miserable to be around. You thought you'd lined up the perfect gig, serving at her side then taking her job when she dies? Too bad the real heir showed up, eh, and now you have to babysit.*

The real heir? Kairos spun, finger pressing against me once more. *You have been here a week, Princess, and you believe you know what is happening in this kingdom. That's only more proof that you are not fit to lead us.*

I care about my people.

We are not your people. He was so close, his voice echoing in my mind. *Don't think I don't watch you. Don't think I don't know that you are far more concerned with saving your Adrialians than you ever were about getting to know us. You do not know us, so you do not get to speak for us. You do not deserve that honor.*

And you do? You hate everyone, but I think it's just a side effect from hating yourself.

His eyes narrowed. *You are acting like a foolish child who doesn't understand that the whole world doesn't revolve around them any longer.*

My chest heaved, and I pushed against his chest, only succeeding in pushing myself back away from him in the water. *I would know more if anyone actually told me what's going on. Ever since I came here, it's been one closed door after another. I am not stupid, Kairos. I know I don't belong. But something brought me here, and until I can find a way back, you are stuck with me.*

Kairos grabbed my arms, towing me along, back to the arc. The sharp bite of his temper didn't distract me from the subject at hand. Because now that I had him talking, I wouldn't be content to let this horrible waiting game continue. It would take my mother years to confess things little by little.

But this male, I could rile him up more.

Tell me why I piss you off so much. Why do you hate everything about me? Is it because of the throne? Did I take it from you? Poor baby.

He snarled, tail thrashing as he pushed us through the water. *I don't want the throne, Princess.*

I'm finding that hard to believe.

I don't want it, but if it meant him not having it, I would take on that weight. For Ceanus and for my people, I would do that.

Him?

And I'm going to fill in some blanks for you, because I do believe you deserve to know more. Kairos looked around the empty ocean before focusing on me, his eyes wide and dark. *Ceanus is killing your mother.*

What did you say?

It's draining her. Every breath you enjoy, every pulse of coral you live under, that is your mother's power. But Trayon is the giver of gifts, and he continues to lose interest. That means your mother's gift is wearing down, just as it did her father and her grandmother before her.

My heart thudded in my ears. *That can't be right.*

It is, Miraceti. Your mother suffers daily. I am by her side as a General, but also because of my power. He took a deep breath then reached out to touch the edge of my face, where the hippocampus's tail had flicked open a tiny wound. I could feel his fingers brush over the injured skin. Then a spark of heat.

I jerked away, surprised, but he growled and did it again, holding tightly to my chin as he drew my body flush with his, my toes brushing against the heavy muscle of his tail. A moment later, there was a coolness, like the first breath of cold air on a winter's morning, that filled my chest.

And then he released me. My fingers found my chin, skimming along the skin there, the flesh that was now perfectly knitted together as if it had never been cut at all.

I stared at him. *You're not just any healer. You're* her *healer.*

He seemed to flinch on the second part, his head dropping. *I'm doing what I can do to slow the damage Ceanus is doing to her body.*

That's incredible, Kairos. I—

It is my duty as a General. My gift, my strength is for Ceanus. And while your mother and I may not agree on everything, I will do what I can to keep her healthy.

I nodded. *Thank you, Kairos. Does that mean—*I swallowed—*Ceanus would do the same thing to me?*

He shook his head, dark hair drifting around his shoulders. *I don't know. We don't know. Cirein-Croin is convinced that Ceanus is rejecting its leaders because they are not the correct Mer to lead it. But the documentation of the times when Trayon was more involved with Ceanus leaves a lot to be desired. There are gaps in time, information that was lost. But the arc is shrinking. Each month there are fewer cursed. And among us, even fewer legacies who are training. They need someone to blame, a reason to change leadership.*

And now the council wants me out so they can campaign for their own House's power.

Exactly.

Will they kill me?

He snarled, fangs flashing. *Not while I am here.*

I blinked, surprised once more, *That's why you're my sponsor.*

And Akram is your guard.

What about Mehri? Why her? Akram and Kairos made sense. They were both powerful allies of the crown, House Leviathan choosing to back my mother in nearly every one of her pursuits. But the half-siren didn't make as much sense.

She was specially chosen to be able to protect you from a variety of attacks. Akram is my best soldier, and his gift makes him nearly unkillable. Mehri's resistant to nearly any form of gift, and her own can impact attackers with a brush of her fingers. And they both understand how court politics work. We will keep you safe.

We'd arrived at the portal, and while Kairos's words in my mind were chipped, frustrated, the hands that guided me down to the edge of the arc were gentle. Just before I breached the magic, my hands wrapped around his on my waist, stilling both of us.

I had to know.

Have they already tried to kill me?

His black eyes hardened. *The question, Your Highness, is not have they, but how many times?*

I swallowed hard, wishing I hadn't asked at all.

Chapter Twenty-Eight

Mehri was humming again as she moved around my room, straightening things that were already tidy. I could feel the subtle energy of her power swirling around my room, but today it wasn't going to change much.

I hadn't been able to shake my bad mood since my attempt to talk to the hippocampus. That failure meant that I'd needed to improve in the water, on my own. And I needed to do it quickly. I was planning on doubling my swim times, extending my time in the water and under the protection of the Claw of Cetus. I would either get faster on my own, or being exposed to the magical necklace would spark my own gift.

I wasn't very optimistic about the gift. Not after these weeks with little to no progress, unless I counted the ability to make the coral lights glow. But then, I'd seen one of the rare Ceanian children in House Kraken do that the other day in the market.

So when Mehri had let it slip that my seemingly all-knowing sponsor would be gone tonight, I knew I had to take advantage of the training time. With Kairos away with my mother and her council, I knew the guards around the portals would be stretched thin. My heart pounded. I would sneak out. I had to find a way to get better.

"Mehri, really, I'm fine."

The female slowed her movements, that waterfall of soft-pink hair falling over her shoulders as she gave me a reproachful look. "My lady, you know that I can sense emotions just as much as I can alter them, don't you? And even if I didn't..." She came to sit beside me on the balcony. "Most of Ceanus has heard about your fight with the General. And then before that, your confrontation with Rhoe."

I cringed, watching Akram as he shifted in front of my open doors. "Is it that obvious?"

Mehri nodded, but her cheeks were flushed. "More bets were made today than just your sparring match with Pierse."

"What do you mean?"

"There are many who thought that perhaps you and the General were, well, more than just training together."

My jaw dropped, my hands coming up to cover my mouth. "No, no, no. You're kidding?"

Mehri laughed. "Is it such a wild assumption? He has been your mother's right hand. You are the mysterious outsider with ties to the throne he has sworn to protect. Throw in all this time that you are spending together—"

"While we train."

"—and you might see what people are thinking."

I dropped my head into my hands, speaking into them. "Let me clear things up, then. General Kairos cannot stand me. And I... I just, every time I see him, I just want to grab that thick, stupid neck of his and..."

Mehri leaning forward, eyebrows rising. "And..."

Akram grunted from the doorway, and I rolled my eyes. "You are both wildly off course. There is nothing between the General and me. Don't forget I'm planning on going home to Adrial soon."

"Hmm," Mehri said noncommittally , pushing up from the bed to go back to polishing the same spot on the spiraling columns at the corner of my room once more. I watched her curiously.

"You know you can take some time off, Mehri. You have to be bored, staying around here with me all the time. You're essentially a babysitter."

"It's not like that," Mehri said, but I could hear the softness in her voice. The lie.

"It's alright if it is. I would hate being cooped up in here all the time." I thought of my night's plans and how much easier it would be if I didn't have to slip past both her and Akram. "Why don't you take the night to visit your House? I'll be fine here."

Her brow knitted. "You want me to leave, Your Highness?"

"I want you to keep your life. Tonight I'm going to go on a short swim." I held up my hand at the beginning of her outcry. "In the safe zone, with the guards all there."

I knew Akram was listening from the doorway, so I opened my shoulders, letting my voice carry. "Is that alright with you too?"

His head shifted a fraction, which I now knew was as close to a nod I was going to get while the entire hallway had eyes on him.

Smiling, I turned back to Mehri. "See, nothing to worry about. You go see your friends, Akram will walk me down the safe zone, and everyone will be happy."

Akram grunted, and I snorted. "As close to happy as that one gets."

Mehri giggled, pressing a hand to my forearm as she brushed by. "Let's get you fed, Princess, so you don't starve while I'm gone."

I rolled my eyes but let her drag me down to the main hall, where we'd recently begun to eat the later night meal on nights that I didn't eat with the queen. It was one of the few places that Akram and Mehri sat beside me, Mehri talking about her day and the other various castle gossip while Akram sat and watched the siren with rapt attention, only breaking his stare to take bites from the food served in large central platters on each table.

I watched one of the other tables, filled with laughing Mer, with interest. "Why are there not more children? All these people all stuck together in a bubble… I assumed the place would be crawling with them."

A passing servant nearly dropped the pitcher they carried, muttering frantic apologies as they hurried away.

Raising my brows, I turned to Mehri. "Did I say something wrong?"

She giggled, light eyes dancing as she selected something off of her plate. "They are not used to royalty discussing such things so openly."

I shrugged, rolling a bit of fish in a large kelp leaf and dipping it into the spicy sauce that was served aside nearly everything here. "My father would be horrified as well. Glad to see some things are the same in any court."

Akram spoke, surprising me. "Young Mer are difficult to come by in Ceanus. Only true mates can produce them, and those pairings are becoming fewer and fewer."

"True mates?"

"Fated to be together, destined for love. It's an old magic—God magic. Something you don't see much anymore. I'm not sure if that's because there are fewer cursed coming to Ceanus or because the magic itself is wearing thin." Mehri leaned her chin to her palm, eyes soft. "The mate bond is unlike anything else. They can feel each other's moods, affect each other's health… Some can even speak through their minds."

"Like how you do in squalls and through blood bonds."

"Yes, but it is more intense than that. Those bonds wear and change and eventually disappear. Mate bonds, those between true mates, do not." Mehri was suddenly very quiet, her hands dropping to her lap as she regarded Akram. After a long beat, she finally spoke again. "True mates cannot live without each other. If they complete the bond and one dies, so will the other."

"And only they can have children?"

They both nodded. "That means both of your parents were true mates?"

Mehri looked uncomfortable. "Sirens are a little more unique. There are laws against bonding outside of the Mer population, but my father was so in love with her, he didn't care. He bonded to her, but I'm not sure she bonded back. I think that was part of the reason people suspected her of using her magic on him. But I don't think she could. I mean, I don't know if it was possible for her. But then, I won't be able to ask her now. I will forever be the daughter of Esme, banished siren of Ceanus."

"She was banished?" I had not heard that part before.

Mehri nodded. "She wanted to leave anyway. I always felt like she did it on purpose, to be caught, and when the situation presented itself, she took it."

"What was she doing?"

"She was sneaking people in and out of Ceanus."

I took a sip of my tea. The kelp flavor still wasn't my favorite, but it did always make me feel better. "That doesn't seem like a crime."

"It was in your grandfather's time. After your mother ran away to Ceanus, my mother started a bit of a rebellion. Ceanians wanted to see what the surface was like. Some had mates they were desperate to see. She facilitated them sneaking ashore."

Akram planted his elbows on the table, leaning in. "Your grandfather was terrified of Ceanus being discovered, and her exploits began to cause interest on shore. He made a spectacle of her being banished and of all the siren people who were still in the arc."

"We lost my mother, our status, as well as any friends we had managed to keep all in one fell swoop. Even when I first came to the castle to work, people recognized me as the siren's welp, the one who sparked all of these laws about seeking out the surface."

Akram suddenly reached over, his hand settling over Mehri's in a move that left my mouth hanging open. "How we begin life does not dictate how we live it."

"You always know what to say." Mehri sniffed, letting her head fall, just for a moment to Akram's heavy shoulder.

I grinned at the two of them, letting the subject slide. "You don't say things often, but when you do, Akram, you know what you're saying."

Akram's eyes finally pulled from Mehri and looked to me, the smallest crinkle at the corner of his eye. "Imagine if I spoke all the time. You wouldn't be able to keep up."

I stared for a long moment then broke into deep, chest-heaving laughter at his words, at his humor. Companionable silence followed as we all finished our meal. Mehri handed off the last of our dishes to the same red-cheeked servant who'd overheard me earlier. I stood and faced the windows, staring out at the shimmering arc as it glowed with my mother's power.

"You know what? I'm going to go from here."

Akram stood, but I held up a hand. "No, Akram, please. Make sure that Mehri gets to where she needs to go in Kraken district. I'll be within range of the royal guard the entire time. She has a lot farther to go to see her father, and it's getting late."

I knew I was playing on Akram's emotions a little as far as Mehri went, but I didn't mind. I really wanted some time on my own to think things over. Especially after this morning's visit to House Leviathan.

"That's an order," I said finally, sensing they were both working up to telling me no. "I'll be safe, I promise."

Mehri and Akram shared a glance and then dropped respectfully into bows, their fists planted over their hearts.

"I'll be there first thing in the morning, Your Highness, as usual."

"I'll be fine, Mehri," I laughed, shooing her towards where Akram waited. "Go and see your family."

Nodding, she tossed her pink locks over her shoulder and hurried to join Akram at the end of our long table. Mehri barely came up to his pectorals, and the minute she got close to him, Akram's body shifted, moving as it wrapped around her, his hand even hovering in the air at her spine.

For all his no-nonsense attitude and gruffness, Akram was obviously enamored of the petite siren, and while the Houses clearly had rules about who they were or were not allowed to be with, I hoped he would be able to push past that.

Because they deserved to find each other.

The pair disappeared around a pillar, exiting the hall and leaving me to do the same, going the other direction and following the largest and most trafficked walkway to the portal. As I moved towards the portal, the crowd thinned until there were only a few

Mer remaining. The stationed guards eyed me with interest as I hesitated in front of the archway.

I took a deep breath and tried to ignore them. I stretched one arm across my chest, pulling the muscles taut before doing the same. I knew I was just buying time, dreading the moment I had to step through into the water alone.

There was no reason that the claw of Cetus shouldn't work for me. And yet, still, I had not managed to shift like the rest of my training squall. And I was the last in the group to manifest any type of gift. While she would never admit it, I felt that Ionia watched me often these days. Her eyes were sharp and curious, as if I might suddenly combust right in front of her.

But nothing.

At this point, I would gladly take the combustion. At least it was something.

I was the heir to the throne, a direct descendant from the founder of House Cetus. I was half-Mer, but so were many in Ceanus. None with this issue. There should've been nothing holding me back.

I moved to the archway, knowing that the guards were now watching me with rapt attention. They knew who I was. They probably knew before I did. I scoffed at my own thoughts, and I was getting within reaching distance to the portal when a deep, familiar voice reached my ears.

"Going for a swim, Princess?"

My blood ran cold, and I was already crossing my arms over my chest when I turned to face a smug-looking Kairos.

"What does it look like, General? You know, I had heard you were a brilliant strategist, but now I have my doubts."

His smile waned. "Just think… I was about to head out when I had this little inkling. And now, it looks to me like you're about to cause your mother more stress." He tilted his head, running his hand through the black locks. I tried not to sigh as it exposed more of his sharp collarbones and the spiraling ink there. "And based on your body language, you know it too."

He tutted at me, stepping close enough that I had to tilt my chin up to look into his dark eyes. Gods, I loved the way he smelled. I swallowed, focusing hard on the little scar at the corner of his jaw. "I am allowed to practice my training, just like anyone else."

"Not alone you aren't," Kairos said, his eyes leaving mine and into the darkness of the portal just beyond. "And not at night. There are things in these waters that you couldn't imagine."

"Which is why I'll be joining her."

Kairos's nostrils flared as he dropped a shoulder to glare over at Rhoe, who now stood by one of the guards.

"You," Kairos said, his tone rumbling as the other male moved towards me.

"General," Rhoe said with that casual, relaxed way he always had at home. He stopped up to my side, forcing the General to step back and away from me as he slung an arm over my shoulder. "Are you ready, Mira?"

I knew the use of my name is a brag on his lips, but I didn't care. I needed Kairos to go away. I really needed them both to go away, but I would start with the more difficult male first. Then I would remind Rhoe that he no longer had permission to call me by my given name. That was reserved only for my friends.

"I'm ready." I nodded to Kairos, a dismissal. "As you were, General."

He growled, actually growled, the flash of white teeth against his lips a surprise as my heart rate rose. But before another word was uttered, he was gone, boots hard against the stone walkways on the path back to the castle.

Rhoe whistled. "I knew you always had a way of pissing people off, but I don't think I've ever seen the General more rattled."

I tossed my head, effectively making Rhoe's arm fall off my shoulder. "He's the problem here, not me."

"I would never dare assume otherwise," Rhoe said, and against my better judgment I felt the corner of my lips curl. Rhoe's crystal blue eyes snapped to my lips, and he answered that small gesture with a broad grin of his own.

"Do I want to know why we're going on a late-night adventure into the Great Sea?"

"We," I emphasized with the flourish of my hands over his form, "are not going anywhere. You are going to go home to your father in House Cetus, and I am going to…train for a little while."

Rhoe's brows were nearly hidden by his hair, they were so high. "That's where you're wrong, Mira. Other than the issue about secret identities, I am still in the employment of the crown of Adrial. Therefore, I am still, at least in part, responsible for your safety."

I stared at him in shock, dumbfounded that he'd even mentioned this. I'd been avoiding him on purpose, making sure Mehri planned my day around avoiding him, but this was too much.

"Perhaps I wasn't clear. There was a lot going on when I found out that you had only been masquerading as my best friend for years, while simultaneously fighting against your own people and damning mine to an eternity of madness. Obviously a message wasn't made clear. So allow me to do that now." I looked him right in the eyes before speaking again.

"I do not want anything to do with you. Not now, not ever. You, Rhoe Karasea, chose to trick and betray me when I was at my worst. You let me believe that you loved me"—Rhoe's mouth opened, but I jerked a finger up— "at least in some capacity. And when the truth was revealed, instead of owning up to it like a real friend would, you followed your father out like a little duckling." His slight wince shouldn't have affected me, but it made my heart thump hard once.

"In summary, no, you will not be coming with me."

Rhoe's silence was deafening, and even the guards were frozen in place as my words curled around us. Then, at long last, Rhoe's eyes dropped to the necklace.

"Alright, Your Highness. You have my apologies." He backed away two steps then bowed deeply, hand over his heart. A well-trained courtier. "Enjoy your swim."

Something below my ribs shattered as I watched him straighten and turn away, moving slowly towards the Cetus district.

As soon as he was out of earshot, I let the tiny whimper of frustration and sadness slip out of my mouth. Then I turned and, before anything else could happen, dove through the portal.

The water was cool against my skin, a caress of calm while my blood churned with confusion and emotions that I didn't want to put a name to. The necklace felt heavy as my mother's House's gift began to circulate, making it possible for me to take in a deep breath, kicking out with my feet as I slowly made my way into the ocean water.

Swimming down, I found a bit of discarded coral and held it up in front of my face. The one thing that I *could* do was set up coral light. I wasn't sure whether it was the necklace that allowed that or if I'd finally soaked up some of Trayon's magic from being in

Ceanus. I still had to keep in contact with these smaller ones, but even so, it was helpful in the darkness of the sea.

The angular piece I held lit up in welcome, my palms tingling as magic was pulled into the coral and illuminated the area around us. I looked around the soft glowing area I now treaded water in.

I wanted to go see the hippocampus tonight. I hadn't told anyone because they would not be happy that I'd gone to the kelp forest without them, but this was necessary. We had combat training tomorrow, and without help, I was going to be a horrific failure. I couldn't keep counting on Kairos to help me at every turn.

My muscles had grown stronger, more adept at pulling myself through the water, but I could not compete with the rest of my squall. Each of them were able to move and position themselves with such ease and confidence in the water. Without a tail, I was virtually useless below the surface.

I was making good time, staying close to the arc for both additional light and direction as I made my way across the sea floor. Huge schools of fish and other sea life fluttered to life around me, surprised by my light in the darkness of the water. One red eye, belonging to an eel, gave me a long look when I dove lower to look at him, but thankfully I didn't have to use Kairos's dagger I had pushed into my waistband.

Finally, I followed the natural rise in the seabed as I pushed myself towards the kelp forest. I reached the edge, my muscles twitching a bit as I tried to remember the last time Kairos and I had been here and how we'd found the herd the first time.

But then I heard it. Sounds were always odd underwater, but this defied all of those odds, the strange grating noise filling my mind as I cringed back away from the floating greenery.

For a moment, there was silence, and then a shriek cut through my mind with such ferocity that I dove into the kelp branches without a second thought. Someone was hurting. I withdrew my dagger, pushing strand after strand of kelp aside until I swam into a small clearing, the kelp all uprooted and destroyed as a pair of creatures battled at the epicenter.

A long, black sea snake, its head finned and eyes a shining gold, was obviously the aggressor, and coiled in its tail, nearly unidentifiable, was a child. But it wasn't a human child. Nor was it Mer. I didn't know what he was, but I could see the tiny delicate lines of his hand as he pushed and shoved at the tail that had wrapped him in a death grip.

The serpent's gaze slid over me, and then, clearly dismissing me, curled back to the child. To my horror, its mouth parted, revealing row after row of shimmering teeth set in a nightmarish mouth.

I screamed, the sound coming out in bubbles, and lunged forward, swiping the dagger down the serpent's scaled hide. For a moment, the creature's muscles slackened, and I saw the child's head move, eyes finding mine in the dark, wide and terrified. I reeled back, slicing again, this time revealing a puff of blood that darkened the water in front of me.

Any chance of surprising the creature was gone. The serpent darted towards me, those terrifying teeth still visible as they snapped the air where my hand had just been. Awkward as I was in the water, the serpent's length made it more difficult to keep up with me as I moved lower, under the child, slashing and stabbing parts of the serpent that were farther from where the child still dangled.

The serpent was furious now, its massive length twisting and turning as I hid underneath its bulk, shifting and moving as I sliced and prayed to Artio that once I got the child loose, I could get us both away fast enough. There was no way these cuts would kill a creature like this. But it might just buy us time.

Suddenly, perhaps realizing that its grip on the child was what was allowing me to hide underneath it, the serpent released the child. The boy—who had very long legs, pale-green skin, and subtle striking across his bare chest and arms—was stunned, blinking at me as his webbed fingers spread wide in the water.

The serpent whipped out of the clearing, disappearing behind some of the intact kelp in a flash of dark scales. I had dropped the coral during the initial altercation and swam frantically to reclaim it from the sandy floor. I needed to make sure there was nothing wrong with the boy.

I held up the coral light and then my other hand in what I hoped was a sign of peace. Now that I held the coral, I could see more about the boy, from the soft webbing of his hands to the lidless eyes that stared at me with a mix of horror and fascination. He was a siren. A full-blooded siren.

He was beautiful and strange, and from what I could tell, he appeared unharmed. I half expected him to swim away as we stared at each other. The other half of me wished he would. I couldn't guarantee that the serpent would stay away, and I wasn't strong enough to take him back to Ceanus. And once there, would anyone even be allowed to help him? Dread curled around my throat, making it tight as I swam closer.

The boy didn't move, his fingers and long, webbed toes barely moving as his body floated in the deep-blue waters. My brows lowered as I realized that not only was he barely moving, but he acted like he couldn't.

I met his piercing blue gaze, and as I did, he jerked his gaze pointedly to his forearm. I followed his line of sight and felt my stomach drop. A perfect half-moon-shaped bite mark was still bleeding slightly from his forearm.

Oh no, I thought. That was not good. Carefully I gripped his arm, bringing it into the brightness of the coral light. The bite wasn't deep, but the muscles underneath were twitching. I looked at the boy, watching as I moved him through the water without any resistance.

We had snakes in Adrial too, some that infected their prey with a variety of venom when they attacked. In fact, farther up the coast from the capital, there was one that was nicknamed the lazy killer because it only really had to get in one bite. Then it would come back hours later to consume its prey after they'd already expired.

Ice cold awareness slid down my spine.

This serpent had poisoned the boy, fought to protect its prey, but when I got there, it had abandoned its meal when I had nothing but a little dagger. There was only one thing that made sense, and it sent a fresh wave of adrenaline flooding into my system. I gathered the boy close, feeling his slick skin against my chest as I curled my arm around his belly.

We have to go, I said, even though I doubted he could hear me.

The serpent wasn't gone.

It was waiting.

My swimming strokes had grown even more choppy as I juggled the boy, the coral light, and the dagger. When we reached the edge of the kelp, something in the water changed. Pushing the boy behind me, I turned, teeth bared, dagger out and ready to buy the boy any time he could have. Maybe the venom would wear off. Maybe he would be able to make it home.

The serpent was a dark coil, golden eyes sharp as he darted through the kelp, fixated on his next prey.

And that was me.

I drew in a deep breath and waited for that strike.

Chapter Twenty-Nine

Only, it never came.

Instead, a blur of green and blue streaked between us, silver light from my coral filling the space as an enormous body pushed me back into the kelp. I found the boy easily, again hugging him to my chest as I watched the female hippocampus that I'd met here before take on the serpent. The serpent was nimble and fast, but it was no match for the sharp barbs on the fins or the flashing teeth of the hippocampus. As soon as she got her jaw snapped into the neck of the serpent, I knew it was over.

To my surprise, she didn't bite down, just held the black creature there, his tail barely moving in submission.

Not here, creature. You do not come here. Her voice echoed with command and authority in my mind.

And then with one last vicious shake of her swan-like neck, she released the serpent, who slunk off into the kelp once more. When I tore my eyes from where the serpent had disappeared to, I found the hippocampus drifting towards us.

Unsure of her intentions, I gathered the boy closer.

Stay back.

You think I would hurt him?

I don't know. My chest rose and fell as she finally paused, her fins relaxing as she drew up nearly eye to eye. *I don't know. I need to get him help. It bit him.*

The sea serpent's venom is quite potent.

I racked my brain. I could take him to the portal and ask one of the guards to help. Surely there was someone from the castle healers who would come take care of him. I looked down into his eyes, which stared unblinking back at mine. No one would resist helping a child, right? Siren or Mer, you could not, not help him. My heart squeezed as his fingers closed a fraction around mine.

I need to get him back to Ceanus.

The hippocampus huffed, her long neck curling as she glared at me. *He is a siren, you know. He isn't allowed there.*

I don't care. Unless you have magical healing abilities, we are out of options, and he needs help.

The hippocampus was silent, her elegant head tilting as he observed me. After a long moment, frustration welled up in my belly.

Thank you for sending it off. And then, dragging the siren boy, I began the long trek home.

Stop, stop, stop, the hippocampus said. Then, in what sounded like she was speaking to herself, she added, *I'm never going to live this one down.*

I looked back over my shoulder as she approached again, this time bringing her body alongside the boy and me. I stared at her dumbly.

Get on. The words were an order.

What?

You heard me, Princess. Get on.

Blinking, I glanced at the boy, and then before she could change her mind, I guided his legs over her shoulders and then slipped a leg over behind him, settling myself across her broad back. Unsure of how this would work, I tightened my legs around the barrel of her chest.

Thank you.

She huffed. *Hold on.*

And then we were flying, or at least that's what it felt like, cutting through the ocean with a powerful sweep of her fins and tail. The powerful movements under my legs had me scrambling to find a place to hold on to her, pushing the boy between my chest and her neck as we slipped through the darkness. She was so slick, smooth, that I could do nothing but clamp my legs around her middle, hands tight around her neck as her fins fluttered, soft as silk against my lower half.

The boy was still largely unresponsive, and that was the only thing I could focus on for the remainder of the rush to get him there. I knew what I would have to do, but I still hated it.

Do you have a plan?

I do. It was a fucking awful one.

There was a sharp laugh. *You don't seem very pleased.*

It doesn't matter. I will do what needs to be done.

As the softly glowing arc grew closer and closer, I secured the boy one last time, and then I closed my eyes and focused hard on the wisps of remaining blood bond between Kairos and me.

Grasping it, I tried focusing on him, on how I remembered him. And when I spoke again, I knew it wasn't something that the hippocampus could hear. I was speaking directly to him.

I need your help.

He answered immediately, his deep voice rough with what sounded like concern. *Where are you?*

Almost to the portal. Can you come? Please, I begged to myself. Please come. I don't have anyone else.

I'm on my way.

Hurry. I need the guards to disappear. Relief flooded my body as the archway became more visible. The boy shook for a moment against me. I rubbed a hand over his back, making sure to not jostle his arm any more than I had to. *We're almost there, little one,* I whispered to him. Even if he couldn't hear me, it made me feel better to say it.

The hippocampus slowed her strokes. The soft rise and fall of her front fins kept us moving gently as we slowly slunk closer to the portal until I could see the moment that the guards were called away. A breath later, I pushed away from the hippocampus, turning to cradle the siren against my chest.

I can take him the rest of the way. You can stay clear of anyone looking.

The hippocampus's expressive eyes caught mine, wide and calculating. *Good luck.*

I kicked hard, propelling us through the water and towards the portal. Just as the magic seeped over my skin, I felt the dry air of the arc brush my hands first, then my cheeks and my face. The boy was suddenly heavy in my arms, and I stumbled, straight into Kairos's arms.

"Princess, what is going on?" His dark eyes were staring down at the child. "Is that a siren?"

I pushed up on my knees, "He is a child, and he was bitten. He needs your help."

Kairos went still, his palm pressed at the back of the siren boy's head. I wasn't sure what I'd expected, but it hadn't been this.

Kairos's hands moved over the young siren, his touch gentle. And when his fingers brushed over mine, sparkling heat danced over my skin. I gasped a little, and Kairos quickly moved his hands away.

Kairos leaned over, picking the boy up and out of my arms. My brows furrowed as the male stumbled a little as he stood. "Let's take him to my rooms. We'll get him sorted out there. The guards will be back in a few minutes."

Kairos began walking, leaving me to trail along at his side. The siren's eyes were still dim, but I'd seen them widen when Kairos took him from me. He didn't need to speak to tell me he was scared. I slipped his much smaller hand into mine once again, jogging to keep up with Kairos's pace.

"Do I want to know how any of this came about?"

"Probably not. How did you get rid of the guards?"

The male started walking up the deserted walkways, taking a new path that I hadn't used before. "I have eyes and ears everywhere, Princess. Moving two guards is the least of my worries about this evening."

I rolled my eyes, trotting after him as we made our way through the dark corridors and into the base of the castle. A few staircases later, which Kairos did all while holding the boy, and suddenly we were slipping into a chamber off the stairwell.

"Where are we?" I turned in a circle, the dim coral light illuminating a bed at the center of the room, the neat shelving that lined the walls. Salves, jars, stacks of blankets, and what might have been bandaging were all neatly lined up on the shelves.

"One more." Kairos moved to a door and, using the edge of his foot, propped it open. Just beyond, I saw the vast rooms that I recognized as Kairos's. Kairos took the boy straight to the chairs that formed a circle at the front of the room and placed him there, sitting up. The boy's body moved like clay, holding the pose, with none of the usual movement that came from a living thing.

Fear turned in my belly. "Is he going to be okay?"

"I'm going to take care of him first, and then we can talk about your little swim."

Kairos leaned over the siren, his palms siding over the boy's face for a moment and then down to the bite, which was still red and angry.

"Or we could talk about your secret. What is that? A healing room?"

He didn't look up. "I am a healer. That shouldn't surprise you that I have access to a healing room."

"But we have an entire ward for that. Why the secret room?"

Kairos hummed softly. "Princess, I am working."

I huffed, turning to pace up and down the stone floors. A chill broke over me, and after I began to rub my arms, Kairos spoke out one more time. "There's a blanket on the…"

I had already grabbed the blanket off the back of one of the chairs and wrapped myself into it, the warmth sinking into my bones. I resumed pacing and pressed my nose into the edge of the fabric for a moment. Kairos's scent invaded every part of my brain as I watched him lean over the boy.

Another pass or two, and I saw it. The boy's arm twitched in Kairos's hands, then his leg, his toes curling on the rug. My heart leapt to my throat, and I rushed to kneel at his feet.

"He's going to be okay?"

"He is," Kairos said softly, his arms brushing mine as we sat in front of the boy.

The boy's eyes were clearer now, and his mouth worked for a moment. Then he spoke, the musical lilt of his voice enough to make the hair rise on my arms. "You are the princess of Ceanus."

"I'm Mira," I said simply.

The boy looked at me, his eyes looking where I'd gripped his hand in my own and then where I kneeled in front of him. "You saved me."

"No." I shook my head. "This male did. He's a healer."

The boy didn't even look at Kairos. "No, he didn't. Sea serpent venom wouldn't have killed me."

"What?"

"The serpent… They paralyze their victims. If you'd left me, he would've eaten me. I am grateful to your healer, but you are the one who saved me." His voice was so unusual, melodic and beautiful, and it rolled over me. I couldn't believe it belonged to a child.

I blinked a few times then looked at Kairos. "So the venom wasn't going to kill him?"

Kairos shook his head. Feeling a little foolish, I rocked back on my heels. As if sensing this, the boy grinned at me, showing off a mouth with near-human teeth, save the two sharp fangs on top and bottom.

Kairos released the siren's arm, and immediately the boy pulled it close to examine the freshly healed skin. "It is quite uncomfortable, though."

"I'm just glad I got to you."

The boy nodded, agreeing.

I patted his knee, standing. "Do you know where your family is?"

The siren nodded again, and I turned to Kairos. In my panic to get him here, I hadn't thought of how we were going to get him back into the water. "How do we get him out of here?"

Kairos stood, swaying slightly. I smelled a slight, sweet scent that surrounded him as he did.

I dropped my voice to a whisper. "Wait. Are you drunk right now?"

Kairos didn't even look at me, instead moving across the room to open the door to the main hall. Akram, stoic as ever, stood there waiting. The guard slipped into the room, standing tall next to Kairos.

"You can take the boy down to the portal, the one we spoke about, and get him out to his family. The venom has been cleared from his system."

Akram nodded. "Of course, General." And then he moved across the room, standing in front of the boy. Siren and Leviathan guard eyed each other. Then Akram held his arms out. "Let's go, minnow."

The siren curled up on the chair, pushing so that he was standing on the seat, and then with cat-like lithe, he crawled onto the guard's chest. Akram immediately set off, his wide steps carrying the boy away from us. Those wide blue eyes met mine over Akram's inked shoulder, and there was a shy smile on his lips.

"Wait, Akram." I rushed after them, reaching up to grip the siren boy's hand when he reached out for me. "What's your name?"

"Bowe."

"I'm glad I met you, Bowe."

The boy's webbed fingers tightened one mine for a long moment, and then Akram was moving again, gently separating us as he moved back through the healing room and out the secret door.

My shoulders slumped the moment the door closed, exhaustion—
both emotional and physical—threatening to overtake me.

"We need to take care of you too."

I shook my head. "I'm fine. I just want to go to bed."

"No, Princess, you're not going anywhere."

"Excuse me?"

"You are wounded."

Sighing, I looked down, not seeing anything on my person.
"Where?"

"Come here," Kairos said, moving back to the chair Bowe had
just vacated. "Sit down."

I crossed my arms. "I don't feel anything."

"You will soon. Their scales leave tiny cuts anywhere they touch,
especially on human skin. Since you insisted on going against a
serpent…"

I bristled at his words but sat down beside him. The chair wasn't
large, and our thighs pressed together. "There was no other choice.
I…"

Kario's fingers brushed my shoulder, turning me away from
him, and my words died on my tongue. "I didn't mean it in a
negative sense, Princess. Just that they will need to be healed."

"Oh." My skin tingled as his hands slowly closed over my
shoulders. The heat in his palms, a balm against the exhaustion,
made my muscles quake. My head rolled back as what could only
be his gift seeped from his palms to my skin, pushing past my flesh
and racing through my blood, making my muscles quiver as they
stretched, shifted, healed. The heat then moved on, seeking out the
tiny marks on my hands and forearms, even my belly, that must've
been left by the fight with the serpent.

"That feels so good," I said, the words slurring as I stretched languorously under his grip.

"Almost there," Kairos said, but his words were rough.

Forcing my tired eyes to open, I could see him beside me, his jaw clenched, eyes closed. The pulse at his throat fluttered, nearly as wild as mine.

Disappointment warred in my veins as that wonderful, tingling pressure slowly retracted, climbing back up my body until Kairos took a sharp breath in and leaned back. The moment his gift left, I felt the disconnect, the pain down the now fragile bond between us. I assumed that's why he now backed away, wiping a hand over his face as he shakily stood and moved to make himself a drink.

In the weeks since I'd arrived, I'd never witnessed Kairos eat or drink anything. He was always on guard around me. Except tonight, things felt different. The sagging shoulders, the way his feet dragged against the floor of his room.

Something had happened, and it had nothing to do with Bowe.

"You *are* drunk," I commented, watching him swirl a decanter for a moment before selecting a small glass off the shelf by his wardrobe.

"Not nearly as much as I want to be."

"What happened?"

Kairos snorted then threw back the dark-brown liquid with a grimace. "I had a meeting tonight with Ionia. It did not go well."

"With Ionia? About what?"

"Some things must remain secrets, even between us."

I watched him circle me, a hand running through his hair as he moved.

"Enough about me. Are you ready to tell me about your adventure tonight?"

I crossed my legs, drawing shapes into the silky black training fabric of my pants with my finger. "You already know the answer. I needed to be stronger. I'm falling behind, and I don't want to be an embarrassment to the crown."

His steps slowed. "An embarrassment?"

"I can't shift, I can barely swim, and I'm a constant liability." I crossed my arms over my chest and sent him my best glare, focusing hard on keeping the lurking tears of frustration at bay. "Or so you remind me nearly every day at training."

Kairos resumed pacing, cutting a path down the center of his room. Eyes downcast, he spoke again. "You don't need to do any of this, and yet you keep pushing. I don't understand it."

"Is it so unbelievable that at the end of training, I want a House to bid for me not because of my bloodline or a yet-to-be-discovered gift, but because I'm worthy of it?"

Kairos stilled once more, but I kept going, letting the words slip free. "My entire life, I've been trained, practiced, and promised to do exactly what I needed to keep my people safe. They told me I was good at it, that I was the best. But how honest could they have been when they were all paid to say those things? Here, no one wants me to succeed, and that's not damning. That's powerful. Because I want to show that not only am I worthy to be here, but I earned my place the same way they did theirs. Their hatred will be my validation when I do this, on my own."

I swiped at my cheek, at the single hot tear that had slipped free. "Well, kind of on my own. Does that make it more clear, General?"

"Princess, I—"

Exhaustion was creeping back in, the weariness in my muscles matching the one that held over my heart. I made for his door, my head held high as I did. But just as my hand reached the handle, there were hands on me again. Turning me, pushing me back until my spine bumped into the thick wooden door. I gasped, staring straight into Kairos's onyx gaze.

"You weren't supposed to be here. You were supposed to be safe and happy without this burden. That was the plan."

I nodded, the intensity and heat in his expression making my body pulse. I didn't know exactly what he meant, but I could feel his frustration, the need to protect that throbbed around us. The blanket I'd still been wearing slipped down my shoulders, and Kairos's gaze dropped to the sliver of skin exposed.

"You have done nothing but make my life a living hell since you showed up, do you know that?"

His point was valid. "Yes." My voice was a ragged whisper that made his lids droop.

"Do you know why?"

I shook my head.

"Because I want to hate you, Miraceti. I want to hate you with every fiber of my being. But instead…" He took a rattling breath, his head falling a little. "Instead, you haunt my every waking moment. I cannot stop thinking about you. I cannot stop wanting to be close to you. This close…" He leaned in, his forehead nearly touching mine. "And closer." His breath was hot on my face, the need in his words making my thighs clench.

Chapter Thirty

"But you said..."

"I would've said anything and everything to keep you away."

"Why?"

"Because we can never be together." Kairos pushed back, and the air was suddenly cold around me. Numbly I gripped the blanket tighter. His blanket. "I know why you're here, Princess. I've known from the beginning."

I couldn't be sure what he meant. There were so many options. "What do you mean?"

"You seek an audience with the God of the Sea, and you plan on asking him to remove the curse."

I was speechless, staring up into those dark eyes. There was only truth there, watching me, waiting for me to confirm. Giving me a chance to be honest with myself and with him.

"Yes, that was my plan."

"Did you not think of what might happen to our people, to *your* people?"

I nodded. "Yes. Yes, of course I did. I'm not trading in Ceanus for the chance to save Adrial—I wouldn't do that."

"You wouldn't?"

"No, never. This place… This place is important to me too. There are things here, *lives* here. I would never put anyone in danger." *I would never put you in danger.* That was what I was about to say. But even uttering those words out loud made my anxiety spike, my fear leaching from my skin as I considered it.

What would've happened if my original plan to dive in here, to demand to see Trayon and convince him to remove the curse had worked? Would I have damned this entire kingdom?

"What did you say, Princess?"

"I said that there are people here who are important to me."

His smile was smug. "People?"

I shoved at his chest. "Fine. Mer. There are Mer who—"

And then I couldn't speak anymore because Kairos's lips were on mine, swallowing the rest of my declaration with the softened groan I'd ever heard. The noise flew straight to the junction of my thighs. And as Kairos continued to kiss me, I found myself sliding up the door, my hands moving to his shoulders, then his neck, then against the satin curls that spiraled down his back. His rumble of approval echoed in my body as his hands left the door to rest on my hips, hitching me up against his larger frame.

I gasped at the feel of him against me, and he used that moment to part his lips, his tongue seeking mine and moving against it in a slick slide of heat and need as I flexed my belly, pulling myself up against him for more.

The taste of him, the way his fingers splayed against my side, his thumbs brushing over my ribcage as my shirt rode up, exposing more than just skin to his touch… He was magnetic, addicting, and when he shifted against me, I moaned, pulling him closer, savoring the delicious pulse of joy and need in my chest.

He pushed away with a sharp gasp. No other part of our bodies moved. His hands were still holding, his body still hard and needy against mine.

"Don't you see, Princess, how much I hate you? Can't you feel it?" He rolled his hips against the cradle of my body, and I whimpered against the rough scrape of his jaw. "I hate you so much, I can barely breathe."

"In a hundred lifetimes, I never would've guessed that…"

And then we just stayed there, frozen with our own words, our breath mingling between us as I tried to make sense of this life-altering shift in my word.

He hated me.

But he didn't. He hated me because he wanted to. And I could understand that. He thought I was going to sacrifice his people for my own, and well, hadn't I first thought of that? Had it really been so long ago that I'd considered a plan to surrender Ceanus to Trayon in order to save Adrial?

That seemed so long ago now. But there was more I needed to say. I wanted him to understand. I wanted him to know me for more than just this driving pull that tugged us together.

I was changing. I *had* changed. I had more chances to do it. And I wanted to show him that. I wanted this infuriating male to see what I was really made of.

Kairo's tongue slipped out and wetted his bottom lip, and my mind cleared of all thoughts, leaving behind a dense fog of need to get close once again. I wanted to kiss that mouth, to run my tongue along the edge of his full bottom lip before I bit into it.

I breathed in, my mouth moving for his when something impacted the door at my back. I jolted, tightening my hold on Kairos and wrapping my legs around him for good measure.

"Shh," Kairos said, his hand moving up to my lower back where he cradled me there. "That's Akram returning from taking the boy."

I nodded, feeling a sharp stab of disappointment as the moment dissolved around us. Carefully, I untangled my legs from his body and let them drop to the door. Kairos released me, his hands lingering on my sides as he took a deep, rattling breath in before curling an arm around me and pushing me back behind him.

I rolled my eyes but allowed him to position me safely behind his bulk as he opened the door. It was not Akram who stood there, but Mehri, wringing her hands nervously in front of her.

"Mehri, what's wrong?"

"I'm sorry to bother you, General, Highness." She gave a brief bow in my direction before fixing wide, scared eyes on me. "You mother… She is coming to your room. She will be there any moment."

My brows lifted. I was an adult and had grown tired of explaining my location to anyone, let alone the mother I'd met only weeks ago, but something in her voice made me pause, the words stuck in my throat.

Kairos's hand brushed my elbow, making my skin heat in a flash, but his voice was also low, soothing as the half-siren at his door fidgeted in her sandals. "Are the halls clear?"

"Yes, General, all clear."

"You should go, Princess," Kairos said, stepping away from me and holding the door open wide. "Thank you for your help tonight."

I cocked my head a little, confused at the change in emotion and direction he'd just taken. But Mehri now gripped my wrist, tugging me through the doorway and up the first few stairs. I stumbled after her, forcing my eyes from the male who stood in the doorway, his eyes burning with something that I didn't understand.

Whatever had just happened, we wouldn't have time to deal with it tonight.

Chapter Thirty-One

Mehri practically shoved me into my room, her hands working frantically over my body as she tugged off my still-wet clothes, replacing them with a soft, billowing white gown. After she sat me down on the chair overlooking my balcony, Mehri's long fingers quickly wound my hair back and up until she could slide a sharp-ended pin into my hair, holding the wavy mass back from my face. Pearls dangled from the fin-tipped end.

"Mehri, what is going on?"

Mehri sighed. "Fear, anger, so much of it. I can feel it all around us."

"Who, though? Can you tell?"

Mehri shook her head, her fingers gentle as she fixed a strap on my shoulder and then dusted my skin with some kind of sweet-smelling powder.

"I can't tell. I just know that it comes from inside the arc" —her eyes found mine—"and outside."

Mehri then sped across the room, disappearing into her adjoining room. When she didn't return, I swung my legs around to look for her, only for a sharp knock to sound against the door. A moment later, Akram opened the door, stepping inside like the imposing door stop that he was currently acting as.

My mother's personal guard swept in, his face suspicious as he looked around my room. I rose, feeling my chin rise as the male took a long look at me. Mehri was right. Something was wrong. A pang in my belly told me it had to be something about the boy. Gods, I hoped he had gotten safely away.

Suddenly relieved that Mehri had given me back my dagger, I glared at the invasive guard, who now had a partner joining him in his search of my rooms.

"What is the meaning of this?"

But he didn't answer. He didn't have to. My mother, followed by Timor, stepped into the room. Her sapphire eyes were dark, bloodshot, and when they found mine, I felt something tug in my chest, because it didn't matter if I didn't know my mother.

I knew that look.

It was the one my father gave me moments before locking me in my room. The same one he'd given to me when he told me I had to marry by the end of the year.

It wasn't a parent's gaze, but a ruler's.

I bristled, every nerve in my body preparing myself for what might come next. The coral light around us brightened.

"Mira, my dear. I'm so glad you're safe." My mother's voice was rich with concern.

"What do you mean?"

"There was a squad of sirens spotted near the arc. They were fully armed and prepared to attack," Timor announced.

I watched him move into my room with bold strides. My mother followed, and I desperately wanted to ask why he was here.

"A squad?"

"A family," my mother said, dropping to the edge of the bed with a soft sigh. "They have rather large ones, and this one was no different. Warden Atlana and House Leviathan have been mobilized and are sending out the first wave now."

"And they attacked us?" I hid my shaking hands in my skirts. I threw a quick look at Akram, but he was staring straight ahead, an unmoving mountain as usual.

No one answered. My mother had found a seat in one of my small chairs and leaned against the armrest. Their silence held just as much accusation as their words. "I don't understand. Why are they here?"

"They come close at times, but never this close. We're guessing that someone must've lured them closer."

"And you're in my room because you think I did it? I'm sure by now you've heard of my lack of swimming prowess."

Timor broadened his stance, thick arms tightening at his sides. "No, Princess Mira, we don't think you did."

Akram and I understood his meaning at the exact same moment. I flew across the room, positioning myself between Timor and Mehri's door. Akram was my shadow, a living, breathing muscle behind me.

Something in the way his breath left his mouth reminded me of a growl, and I wished I could echo it with the same ferocity.

Timor spread his hands wide, an attempt to appear disarming. "We just need to question the girl, that's all."

"That 'girl' is a castle handmaid and my personal companion. Mehri will be given a declaration of innocence until proof is provided to me that she was involved in whatever crime you are accusing her of."

Timor sighed, looking at my mother. "Sirens haven't come here since they were removed from Ceanus in your father's time."

"Maybe they came here for a reason," she said, voice tired.

I swallowed. I swallowed. It had to have been Bowe's family. That's the only thing that made sense. But I couldn't tell them about Bowe, not without risking Akram's and Kairos's lives as well. What would they do to Ceanians who helped a noncitizen? The sirens were banned. Would that be their future as well?

"They have no reason to be here, and she is the only half-siren in the kingdom," Timor said, and I bit back the sharp retort that waited on my tongue.

"I read about them in your history books. You know, the sirens used to live here too. Maybe they wanted to talk."

"Ceanus was much larger then. Things were different."

"Different because they didn't willingly bow to every whim of the Houses? Or perhaps because you were scared of their abilities?"

Timor glared. "Stop, Mira."

I stepped up against him, my skirts swirling around my legs. "You may call me Your Highness."

"*He* doesn't." It came out a hiss.

"Who, exactly, are you speaking of, Timor?" a deadly cold voice spoke from the door, and the physical reaction that it had on my body was shocking. Kairos moved into the room in a new set of clothes, his hair tied up at the crown of his hair. I mentally shook myself, forcing my gaze back to a now pale-looking Timor as the General moved into the room to stand, face impassive and cool, between my mother and me.

Easy, barracuda, he said softly through the bond.

Timor blew out a loud breath. "Your Majesty, I demand that I be given the ability to do what I need to protect Ceanus."

I laughed, the sound cold, even to my ears. "Protect Ceanus from Mehri?"

"You were not here when the sirens lived among us. You don't know the things they are capable of."

I stepped forward, watching the thick vein in the Warden's neck pulse. "You're right, I don't. Why don't you tell me all about these monstrous things they did."

Timor's eyes went wide, and I knew I had him. There were nearly no records of the time when sirens had lived among the Mer, but from what I could gather from my conversations with Mehri, it was fear that kept the Mer from embracing their neighbors.

And this male in front of me, he smelled of fear.

"Your Majesty?"

"Timor, she has every right to protect her companion. And as I said before…" My mother got off the couch, her movements sluggish. "I hired Mehri especially for her bloodline's tendencies. I do not think the female would repay that gesture by bringing a siren attack to her own doors."

Damona gave me a thin smile, which I didn't return. "It is late, Timor, and I desperately need to go to bed."

"Queen Damona," Timor pleaded, his teeth still gritted as my mother's guards followed her to my door.

"Enough, Timor."

"I will station the best of Leviathan at the portals tonight." Timor threw a withering glance in my direction as my mother disappeared from the room. A moment later, he growled low in his throat and made to step around me towards Mehri's room.

Akram moved before I could open my mouth to say something, his hand snapping out and around Timor's neck before the male could get step closer to the subject of his inquiry.

Timor's face darkened as his hands scratched hopelessly at Akram's unfailing grip. When he did speak, the words were chipped. "You forget yourself, Akram of House Leviathan. You risk everything by touching me."

"Some things—" Akram's eyes burned into Timor's face for a beat before finding mine "—are more important than House alliances."

Heat rushed behind my eyes as the man repeated my words back to me, my mind flashing through the memories of this stoic, silent man carrying the siren boy back to his family. I met his eyes and nodded.

"Akram, please release Lord Timor." Kairos was leaning against the doorway of my room. "He's needed down by the portal."

Akram released the other male, who wiped angrily at his mouth, staring at me long enough to make my heart speed up once again, before whirling out of the room. Kairos held the door for him, never looking at me or acknowledging me. The moment the door swung shut behind him, Mehri burst out of her room, tears on her pretty face. She threw herself first at me, squeezing me, before gasping and pulling back to bow at me, and then turning, she stared up at Akram.

"He will tell your Warden. You are going to be punished." Mehri wrung her hands, approaching the male slowly.

Something in her movements heated my cheeks, and I dropped my gaze and took a step away.

Akram let out a slow breath. "I know what he is capable of. I couldn't let him get close to you."

Mehri smiled, more tears sliding down her cheeks as she rose up on her toes, stretching her arms up and around his shoulders. With a little grunt, he bent down and allowed her to press her slim frame up against his. He didn't pull away, but he also didn't return the hug. His arms hung at his sides still.

But when she took a rattling breath and stepped back, I could see his hands curl into fists. I hid a smile.

"Well," Mehri said, a tremulous smile on her mouth, "I'm going to bed, and then in the morning you two can tell me exactly what kind of trouble you were getting into tonight."

I blinked. "What?"

"Your Highness, you both reek of guilt. And I don't need to be a siren to know that." Mehri stopped at her doorway, her finger tapping her lips. "We will need to work on your facial expressions, Princess Mira, if you plan on being queen of anywhere."

Her head tilted. "Or if you plan on surrounding yourself with my kin more often. And I do not mean the Kraken."

I huffed out a soft laugh, my shoulders sagging as Mehri closed her door.

Akram had already stationed himself at my doorway once more, his frame filling the door as the coral light from outside framed him.

"Akram?"

He stilled.

"Thank you."

"There is nothing to thank me for." And then he closed the door, leaving me alone for the first time since before I'd found the boy.

How had so much happened? First there was the confrontation with Rhoe, and then the serpent and the hippocampus and almost losing the boy, and then Kairos's revelation that he hated me because he wanted me and...

I choked, a barely audible sob slipping from my mouth. I clamped a hand over it, surprised and embarrassed by the noise. My feet took me to the bed, where I stripped off the gown, leaving

myself in just my underwear. The hairpin went last, my fingers
noticing for the first time just how sharp the ends were.

I laid it on the stool beside my bed carefully.

When my head hit the pillow, exhaustion took over, and I fell
asleep holding the Claw of Cetus at my neck and hoping that
tomorrow might bring more clarity.

Chapter Thirty-Two

Mehri wasn't in our rooms when I woke up the next day. Akram replaced by another soldier, and I tried not to panic as I made my way down towards the portal. My stomach, too anxious about what Timor may or may not have found last night, couldn't handle breakfast. Instead I walked quickly towards our meeting space, hopeful that Kairos might be there and could tell me more.

Just before I left the shelter of the castle, Akram was suddenly at my side. He matched my pace, his face as serious as usual. "Your highness."

"Akram," I whispered back, looking around. There was no one listening, "What happened? Did Timor find anyone?"

He shook his head. My heart lifted, relieved to hear that my actions weren't going to be affecting Mehri, or even Akram. "Thank the Mother."

Akram sighed, "I don't think the Mother has been interested in our affairs for a long while, highness."

My mouth opened, but before I could say anything else, Akram had stepped back into the crowd of waiting trainees. Any conversation was effectively over. At least for now.

Delta was quiet today. Her face, usually so lit up in enthusiasm, was set and determined. And I knew why. Today we would be doing our longest swim yet, in formation with a small group of Leviathan in order to do a supply run.

I stood beside Delta, unsure if her unusually quiet demeanor boded poorly for our outing. I knew from Ionia that we were going to be using Delta's gift today.

She could shield people. And not just from weapons, but her energy could be projected into a sheer blanket or invisibility. Not just for her, but for whomever had contact with her. My mother had admitted at dinner one night that she'd never met a Mer with this specific ability and that several Houses had begun to show interest in courting Delta to join. Leviathan, for one, was very interested in the military implications of adding her to one of the squalls.

My stomach clenched as I thought about the very real possibility that this sweet-spirited young female would very possibly spend the rest of her life fighting. Her heart had been so pure, but since her gift had emerged, she had become dull, closed off.

I leaned down to her, hoping to jolt her out of her thoughts. "Hello, Delta. Are you ready for our swim today?"

She blinked up at me then dropped into a quick bow. "Of course, Princess." She then resumed staring blankly at the portal in front of us. Even the vibrant color of her hair and skin seemed duller than usual.

She actually flinched when we both heard the heavy footsteps that signaled more than just our small training squall was arriving. A group of Leviathan entered the portal space, each wearing training gear similar to ours, but these soldiers were armed as well. Most carried only small daggers or short spears on their person.

Kairos wasn't with them, and I tried to look like I wasn't scanning the space for him. Disappointed, I noted that Warden Timor had also joined us. Dressed for the first time in his own training gear, it was a sure sign that he'd be joining us in the waters.

"Great. Just great," I mumbled. I hadn't forgotten the look in his eye as we'd met in front of Mehri's room. The male was dangerous.

"You'll be fine, Princess," Kairos said from behind me, startling me, "They are just here to watch. It's normal at this point in the training. Virtually harmless."

"Easy for you to say. They don't want to roast you over an open flame."

Kairos was quiet for a moment, and I took the time to soak in the lines of his face, the sharp peak of his cheekbones. My traitorous heart thudded. That kiss… It had been incredible. Had it really only been last night?

"I mean, I'm sure at least one of them would like to try that with me."

I snorted out a laugh, and out of the corner of my eye, I saw a corner of Delta's mouth lift.

Ionia stepped to the center, and all eyes moved to her. "You all know what today is. We are going to go on our first supply run, the first for Ceanus in many months. Due to the fact that we can't trust you not to drown on your own out there, Warden Atlana has generously donated a small squall to assist us."

A group of six Mer, made up of both males and females, moved to stand next to Ionia.

"We are looking for supplies relating directly to household items. Blankets, bedding, even clothing that can be repurposed." Ionia pointed a crooked finger at the male in front, with close-cropped blond hair and a myriad of gold earrings along each of his lightly pointed ears.

"This is Sinot. He, as well as our Princess Mira, are the only two true sandwalkers in the group. The rest of you are at high risk if you were to become kidnapped—or worse, trapped on shore. If there is any need to breach the ship or come into contact with any of the merchants, it will be up to one of them to do it." Ionia threw a broad grin my way. "Of course, we don't anticipate any of that happening. The plan is simple. The ship will be waiting for us. Delta will bring groups of us up from under the sight lines to take crates from the merchants."

"Directly from them?" Pierse's voice spoke out from somewhere over my left shoulder.

"Yes, Pierse. These merchants are well paid to pretend that they are raided by the ferocious monsters of the sea."

"See," Kairos whispered for my ears only, "We aren't so bad."

Ionia held her hands wide. "Let's get started, trainees. Trayon bless and keep you, may the waves break upon you."

"Amen," we answered automatically. As a group, we followed Ionia toward the portal, watching her hand off her cane to one of the guards stationed there as always. Without a backwards glance, Ionia dove into the portal.

Delta, I noticed, hung back to walk through at the same time as Sinot. The blond Leviathan gave her a kind smile, and then together, they stepped into the ocean. Kairos and I stepped directly after, with the squall and the Wardens at our backs. I closed my eyes, sighing at the bliss the water always brought as the Claw of Cetus's magic engaged and my body normalized survival in the ocean.

At my side, Kairos's tail flicked, and then his hands were on mine, pulling me close. I gasped, eyes flying open. Shock filled my entire being. Because nothing could've prepared any of me for the chaos that was waiting for us just beyond the arc's magic.

Everyone was completely still. Even Ionia, as all eyes were turned to the blue and green creature that preened herself at the head of the group.

She came back, I whispered to myself, forgetting that Kairos probably still could hear most of my thoughts. But even so, I realized how it might look and began to swim forward frantically, pushing myself through the water with urgency. While the hippocampus clearly wasn't concerned about her audience, all I could think about was that she was now exposed to not just the trainees, but the powerful soldiers and Wardens who would be here any moment.

I swam past Ionia, kicking and turning until I could face the training leader, my hands raised. At the back of the group, the Wardens were standing behind a wall of worried-looking squall soldiers.

Please, don't hurt her, I practically screamed down the bond, hoping that most of them could hear me.

Ionia's eyes were wide, but her gnarled hands reached out. *Hurt her? We would never dream of it, Princess Mira. The hippocampus... They are sacred.*

I could actually feel the smug way the hippocampus swirled her immense green-scaled tail at those words.

Ionia looked from me to the creature and back again. *You know her?*

We had an agreement, I answered, unwilling to disclose any more about my experience with the hippocampus.

Ionia's hand moved to her mouth, rubbing it a little as she muttered into our minds. *I knew they once served the crown, the squalls, but I never imagined, not since before the first queen.*

You may tell her I am the first of my kind to allow a rider in nearly three hundred years, the hippocampus spoke directly into my mind, her voice clear as a bell. *And while she looks like she may be close to that, she's never met one of my lines.*

I nearly choked at her words. *She said none of her kind have been ridden in over three hundred years.* I left out the last part, because there was no way I was going to get on Ionia's bad side. Especially not today.

Coward, the hippocampus mused in my mind.

Ionia's eyes were still wide. *And you rode her?*

I did.

Is she here for you again?

My chin turned to observe the hippocampus. *I think so.*

Could I be any more obvious? Now get on. I'm getting bored.

I turned to Ionia. *I think we're on a timeline, right?*

Ionia shuddered, as if shaking herself free from the hold, and then nodded. *Princess Mira, you will be mid-pack, prepared to take the ship by leg if necessary. Your…mount…*

Krem, the hippocampus spoke into my mind.

Her name is Krem.

You two just stay together.

With as much confidence as I had in my wheelhouse, I turned and slipped a leg over her back.

For a moment, I felt around, listening to the soft voices in my head, the bonds from my training group, the pulsing blood bond that still tied me to Kairos, and now something new, tingling and bright behind my eyes.

Her.

Just casually showing up here... I asked her, Are you sure that's a good idea?

It's a horrible idea, Krem said, her front fins moving together to turn us, while the massive back fin that spiraled from the base of her spine flipped, moving us forward quickly through the water. *My kin won't let me live this down for a decade at least.*

My legs trembled on her sides as we hitched forward and back in the water, easily keeping pace with the rest of the group of mer. *I'm glad you're enjoying yourself.* I leaned forward, gripping her neck with my hands. *Are you going to do this every day?*

She snorted out a wealth of bubbles. *I am not a taxi service. We hippocampus have carried some of the most powerful and gifted Mer in all of the oceans. Trayon himself blessed my great-grandfather.*

Then why did you stop?

The hippocampus was silent under me, the water whooshing over my skin as we changed our route, turning to the shallower water, where the morning light was filtering through the blue waves.

That's a long story, sandwalker, and one I'm not ready to tell you.

I swallowed. *That's fair. I'm sorry that I pushed.* There was silence for a long moment, and I could see Kairos moving up closer to us, his eyes dark on mine. But I didn't want to end the conversation, not yet.

Krem is a lovely name, by the way.

Krem is a pet name I just made up for you. My real name you couldn't pronounce to save your life. Let's save both of our ears and sanity by letting them call me Krem.

I couldn't stop the laughter that spilled from my mouth, my head falling back as we continued on our path, and for a brief moment, it felt like maybe things would work out exactly as I hoped after all.

***

The entire operation went off without a hitch. The merchants were waiting, and Delta shielded the carriers as they loaded squad members' arms with great crates and barrels. After feeling more awkward than ever before, I had asked Krem to get closer to the waves.

She hadn't answered me, keeping me below Kairos's watchful gaze as the rest of the squall went through the process. But when Sinot and another Leviathan soldier named Roeck brought down a particularly heavy-looking group of crates, the hippocampus wordlessly held out her tail.

Remind him I am not a common pack pony, she hissed into my mind. I grinned at Sinot.

She wants to be sure you know she's not a pack pony.

Sinot looked startled. *She talks to you?*

I shrugged. *Sometimes.*

The Mer's brows rose, and with a quick shake of his shoulders, he resumed strapping the crate over Krem's spine just behind my seat. *She doesn't have to remind me. My grandfather lived in the days where we rode the bonded hippocampus. I've heard stories.*

You have? I nearly reached out for his hand to make him stay. *Like what?*

Just that a bonded hippocampus is a dangerous, emotional creature.

Krem snorted his direction, and his fingers stumbled on the knots. Without thinking, I smoothed a hand down the colorful scales of her neck.

No wonder you get along so well, Kairos remarked dryly above us, his dark tail flicking a little when I stuck my tongue out at him. *Dangerous. Emotional.*

Krem's purring voice filled my mind again, louder now. *Tell the dark-finned one that if he is jealous, he can just say so.*

I smirked at Kairos, relaying her words. *You're just jealous.*

It was Kairos who blew out a short breath now, shaking his head and joining Jahya and Delta as they continued emptying the merchant's ships of all our cargo. Crate after crate of items continued past us.

Not stealing, I thought to myself. Buying. And of course the merchants would support this. They were getting subsidies from the Adrialian crown for their loss of items *and* getting paid from the Mer.

I wondered briefly if my father knew this, would it change anything? Would he halt the laws against the merchants passing certain routes? If I went back, could I cultivate a trading situation between the Mer and the Adrialians and create more unity between the two kingdoms?

Shock made my heart skip a beat when I realized what I'd said: *if.* I hadn't said *when.* I swallowed the rocks in my throat as I stroked my hand down Krem's neck once more. I couldn't stay here. My entire life waited in Adrial. It was everything I had ever planned on.

This wasn't the kingdom I was needed in. My mother was young, powerful, completely capable of ruling Ceanus for decades to come. My father was human. He needed me.

I was going to talk to Trayon at the end of this training. I would find out what they needed from us in order to undo the curse and leave the Mer and the humans to rule their kingdoms as separately or as together as they liked.

Kairos would forget about me. Or, more than likely, he would go back to hating me, just like before, like he wanted.

Resolution filled my body as the squall finished their trade and began to make their way back down to the arc, each Mer carrying their own load, and Kairo, Krem, and me bringing up the end.

That went smoothly.

They usually do.

I rolled my eyes at him. *Are we going to talk about last night? Is he safe?*

You can't ask me those types of things, not here, not now.

Can you tell me later? Akram wouldn't tell me anything.

I'm supposed to stay away from you, Princess. I need to stay away from you, he said, voice steady,

Right. I nodded, Krem's casual strokes carrying me to the now familiar glow of the arc beckoning us home. *But are you going to?*

I could practically hear Kairos's sharp intake of breath.

Princess, he growled, his voice a rumble across my mind, making my legs tighten around Krem. Whether I wanted to run from him or run towards him, I wasn't sure.

As I went to respond back to him, Barrio called the team to a halt. Her silvery scales were dull in the coral light. The squall proceeded past her and began to unload the supplies, loading them through the portal to another contingent of Leviathan who were standing at the other side of the portal.

Pushing off Krem, I untied the crates, fighting the buoyancy of the wood the supplies were encased in. Kairos's hands surrounded mine, tightening his grip as he joined me in towing them to the line of people unloading. A friendly looking Mer took them off my hands, passing them along with a flex of his muscles.

Once my hands were empty, I traced the edge of the Claw, looking back to Krem to say thank you and to express my gratitude for her coming today.

But she was already swimming away, her sleek body cutting through the current with a squish of blue fins.

But just as I lost track of her in the water, a grating chuckle popped into my mind. *You're welcome, sandwalker.*

I grinned, propelling myself through the water and towards the portal as the trainees all situated themselves and pulled their way through.

Chapter Thirty-Three

I had barely stepped onto the sleek walkway when my mother's face appeared before me. I jumped, surprised at her appearance.

"They said you rode a hippocampus." Her blue eyes were wild. "Is it true?"

"I…uh… Yes, I did."

My mother's hands found mine, curling them in palms that felt scorching against my still-damp skin. "I want to hear all about it. Did they give you their name?"

"Yes—well, part of it. She said I wouldn't be able to pronounce her full name."

"She said?" Her voice dropped to an excited whisper. "She talked to you."

I nodded, still trying to understand why my mother was so excited about this. Ionia had been shocked, others afraid of those dagger-sized teeth, but no one had been nearly this excited. I glanced over at Kairos, who was watching me while inclining his head to one of the squall members. There was something in his eyes that made me gently remove my hands from my mother's grip. SHe wasn't detoured and linked her arm through mine.

"Let's go up to my chambers. I want to hear the whole story."

Once inside her room, my mother ordered her handmaiden out and closed the door, sealing us away from her guards. Sitting at one of several chairs set up in clusters for conversations around the room, she offered me the seat directly across from her with a delicate sweep of her arm.

"Sit, Miraceti." It was an order, disguised by good manners.

I obeyed, gritting my teeth as I sat, feeling the wet droplets from my hair trekking down my spine to soak the fine fabric under my legs.

"What do you want to know, Your Majesty?" The words came out chipped, and guilt squirmed in my belly. But I didn't apologize.

She leaned forward, her chin on her palms. "I know you aren't as familiar with our ways, Mira, but when Ceanus was new, the hippocampus welcomed us, coming out of the sea to serve Trayon at our sides."

"I've seen some of the artwork."

She gave a nod then pushed on. "But then, a little over two generations ago, the hippocampus slowly began to move back into the deeper oceans. Some of the Cirein-Croin believe they have moved back to the siren homelands farther into the Great Sea."

I was briefly distracted by this new fact. "The sirens live deeper?" Why had that young siren been so close to Ceanus?

My mother swatted the air. "Yes, they can live lower than us, closer to the original crest of Trayon. They were some of his original creations. They have different abilities than us. Like the hippocampus, sirens are his creatures, but they don't necessarily serve him as we do."

"Because of the deal the original queen made."

"Yes, exactly." She scooted forward. "What I'm most interested in, though, is how you were able to convince her to let you on her back. We've had many warriors over the years attempt to approach the hippocampus herd that lives by the forest. None of them were even able to get close."

Something made my skin cool, my temper flaring at the way she spoke. "I didn't convince her to do anything. They aren't like other animals—at least, no animal I know of."

My mother watched me closely. "I didn't mean to offend you. Why don't you tell me the story, and I'll just stop chattering and let you?"

My temper eased immediately. Clearly she hadn't meant anything by it. She was simply excited about something her people had once considered impossible. I shifted in my chair, more sea water rolling down my skin. "I am still not able to shift, and I am not able to keep up with the other trainees outside of the arc. General Kairos was very kind to help, but I couldn't keep relying on him. On one of the scrolls that Mehri brought me, I saw that in the past, hippocampus had been partners with the Mer."

I knew I needed to watch what details I told her—the story of Bowe didn't need to come into play. "This one, she thought I was interesting and approached me during a late-night swim. I asked for her help. She called me a sandwalker but clearly wanted nothing to do with me after a few moments. When she left, I assumed she was rejecting my idea. At least until she showed up today to help me."

"Do you think she'll come back?"

I shrugged. "Your guess is as good as mine. Sinot, one of the squall soldiers, mentioned that hippocampus used to bond with their riders. But it seemed like the way he said it meant it was different than a squall bond or a blond bond or a mate bond." I threw her a desperate glance. "You have a lot of complicated relationships down here."

My mother laughed. "They are not so complicated if you think
of it. Those you keep the closest are the only ones truly allowed in."

"Who can you speak to?"

The smile on her face disappeared in an instant. "That's none of
your business."

I recoiled, surprised by the wave of tension that bloomed all
around us. "I'm sorry. Is that something private? Kairos said—"

"General Kairos is easily swayed by your questions, daughter.
Those who share a bond with you is a deeply personal matter. At
least, it is for me." She rose, her face still and serious as she moved
towards her door. "It seems that this hippocampus has bonded to
you. Are you planning on riding her again?"

I nodded, and then, realizing the queen hadn't turned back to
see my answer, quickly stuttered out a response. "If she lets me."

My mother's stiff back was the only thing I could see. "I'm
proud of you, Mira. A hippocampus has not let a Mer ride on their
back in a very long time. The fact that she chose you is a testament
to your strength. You are blessed by Trayon, daughter."

"Thank you." I rose to my feet, feeling like I'd been dismissed.

Still reeling from the whiplash of her emotional shift, I moved
towards the door. A few steps from it, it was opened for me. On the
other side, Akram waited. His dark-brown eyes moved over me
from head to toe before fixing themselves on the wall just beyond
me.

"Ready, Your Highness?" he asked, eyes still avoiding mine.

I sighed. "Yes, Akram, thank you."

Together, we wound our way back to my rooms. Just before the
door was shut, Akram stepped in, blocking me from closing it.

"Akram, I'm tired. I was going to lie down."

"A message for you, Princess Mira."

Brow furrowed, I said, "Proceed."

"The general has been asked to settle a dispute near Trayon's temple. He will not be back for several days."

"Oh."

Akram didn't move away, and finally he continued. "I will be your sponsor until he returns."

"For training? I'm not sure that's necessary."

"The day after tomorrow will be dueling." His throat worked. "Outside of the arc."

My heart sank. I might be able to hold my own inside the arc or on the shores of Port Sol, but I was going to be a mess in the water. "Fuck."

"My sentiments exactly."

I groaned, my body sagging at the prospect of getting my ass handed to me by another trainee. "I'll see you in the morning."

"See you then, Your Highness."

"Akram, please, no one else is here. And if they are, I don't care. You can call me Mira."

"Princess," he repeated, closing the door and sealing me in my room.

For once, I was relieved for the quiet. And before I'd even had a chance to mull over everything that happened today, I was asleep.

Chapter Thirty-Four

I bounced from foot to foot and back again, watching the murky shadows of the Mer who had already passed through the portal get into position. We'd had a morning full of learning about Ceanus, and while I now knew ten different ways to bring joy to Trayon, this was the part that I was actually worried about. The dueling, especially the dueling underwater.

Without fins.

I fingered the claw, watching the trainee ahead of me step through with an excited toss of their arms. Akram stood beside me, dressed in his casual swimming uniform, and as if sensing my thoughts, he gave me the slightest bump of the shoulder.

"Cheer up, Princess. They can't throw you out," he said quietly. "At least not until after you meet Trayon."

My jaw was hanging when Akram took an enormous step forward and passed into the water. In all our time together, it had only been yesterday that I'd finally seen the stoic Mer in his natural state. Dark, bloodred scales covered his lower half as he propelled himself out of the way of the other Mer then gave a condescending brow raise in my direction.

Noted.

I stepped forward and bounced on my toes then dove through the portal and out into the waters. The cool water slipped over me like a familiar blanket. Distantly, I could hear Ionia's voice in my mind, encouraging us to follow her closer to the sea floor. Blinking, I realized Akram must've been here partially to drag me around since Kairos wasn't here to do so.

The idea of Kairos hauling me around the ocean was embarrassing enough, but having Akram do it? My face heated. I definitely should've warned him beforehand. There was no way my prickly bodyguard wanted to wrap me up and carry me around.

I did have one option, though, even if it was slim odds.

Krem? Are you here?

You have two eyes, sandwalker. You should use them someday.

I couldn't stop the short laugh that bubbled into the Great Sea. Krem, complete with narrowed eyes, hovered in the water near Akram. The latter of which was twitching faintly, as if unsure whether he should flee or fight. When I reached out to talk to Akram, I realized another step we had missed during our initial conversation about this.

Akram and I didn't share a blood bond.

Kicking my feet, I swam closer to Akram, laying my hand on his forearm. He nearly flinched away from my touch, which made me roll my eyes. Ignoring him, I pointed to the side of his head then to mine. His jaw tightened visibly.

Groaning internally, I glanced around, hoping Ionia would be close and I could ask her how to set up a bond like the one that she had invoked between the training squall. But no luck. She was far ahead, and I knew from experience that slowing her down would only lead to a tongue-lashing.

Your problem-solving skills are lacking, Krem commented. I glared at the hippocampus before gripping Akram's arm again. This time, he seemed to have come to the same conclusion I had. He raised a hand and, with a swift, effective swipe, sliced a tiny cut open across the back of my hand. He did the same to his own then pressed the wounds together.

The blood instantly diluted as it entered the ocean, but I felt the pull of a new bond in my mind. It entered like a moment of déjà vu, a tremulous prod of a memory. I knew it instantly as Akram.

Does this mean I can talk to you all the time now?

Akram sighed. *Please don't, Your Highness.*

I grinned, releasing his arm and kicking my way towards Krem. *This is going to be so much fun.*

Enjoy it now… Blood bonds, especially ones like this, only last a few days.

A few days?

They wear off more quickly the farther from our hearts they are set in skin.

That doesn't make any sense. Ionia bonded this group over two weeks ago. Same with Kairos when he found me cursed.

Ionia's gift is the power of bonds. She is uniquely capable of setting up long-term bonds. It is her gift that equips the magic that ties the House bonds together. The same with squalls and other training groups.

What about Kairos? Has his just stuck around because he bit me?

Akram's face was hidden as he pressed his hand to my side, moving me farther onto Krem and away from him. *I did not realize… You will have to ask him. Monitoring the General's gift and the reach of his abilities is beyond my role requirements.*

Krem swished her back fin, and I slipped a leg over her back then wrapped my arms tight around her neck. I wanted to ask more questions, but Akram was already diving, powerful red tail propelling him after the group.

He didn't answer my question, I pouted as Krem sprang after him.

He did not. Krem turned a green eye back to me as she swam. *Perhaps he believes you already have the answer.*

What do you mean?

Sometimes, sandwalker, the answer is right before us but cannot be revealed by anyone other than yourself. And time, perhaps.

I stroked a hand down her neck, the scales shining dark as the water around us grew colder. *I'm so tired of people not explaining things to me here.*

Are you? Because I would harbor a guess that not knowing is much safer than knowing. And you, Miraceti of Port Sol, do so love to be safe.

Chapter Thirty-Five

"When did you get back?"

"Just now."

"Aww." I couldn't help myself. I grinned, leaning back against the wall of my balcony. Below me, the sounds of nighttime in Ceanus drifted up. "Did you come straight here to check on me?"

"You?" Kairos scoffed. "Not at all. I heard you thrashed my finest warrior. I wanted to make sure Akram was alright."

Kairos crossed the room to lean against the wall directly across from me. He looked out of the city with me, the soft coral light casting shadows across the stones at his back. He looked tired, lines under his eyes and a tightness to his mouth more pronounced than before.

"Did your trip go well?"

Kairos didn't speak, but a half shake of his head told me everything I needed to know. No, it hadn't.

"I'm sorry." And I really was. Seeing him upset like this triggered something in my belly that was new, confusing.

"Why? You don't know what I was doing."

"Would you tell me?" I asked softly, surprised when he actually looked like he considered it.

Finally, Kairos took a long breath in and then let it out. "I wish I could."

"What do you hope to gain with all of your secrets? Is it my mother's business? Ceanus? Or is it because you cannot trust me?"

Footsteps, and then he was leaning over the wall at my side, his forearm so close to mine I could see the sharp pinpricks of his ink against the line of his warm tan skin. "She doesn't think that she can maintain the city very much longer, not with the amount of power Trayon requires from her."

"Requires?"

"Ceanus may be his creation, but we are a vessel for his power, a center to keep and maintain. Each soul's contribution directly affects his power."

"And the queen?"

"She is the funnel. Her gift is powerless, if you can believe it. But she can borrow abilities, funnel power. Further proof that she was designed to be our queen."

"But you said it's killing her?"

"Because he demands too much." Kairos wiped a hand down his face. "He is a greedy creature by nature—all of the Gods and their children are. But now that he knows he can get it, he wants to keep the power for himself. Especially if he means to wage war on his brother Artio."

"And so he takes from Ceanus to power his other projects? What is he building?" I stared out at where the pieces of Ceanus had most recently been surrendered to the sea, just outside of the arc's protection. The arc, of course, that Trayon threatened with his greedy hands. How many more homes would be lost? Mer who would be in danger if he continued to steal from his own people to power his war?

"That, Princess, is what we must find out."

"How do you serve him?"

"Who? Trayon?"

I nodded once.

Kairos looked at me, onyx eyes soft as velvet tonight. "It is a complicated answer and not one you are ready to hear."

"Fair. But what do I do in the meantime?"

"Exactly what you are doing." His smirk reappeared. "Your shenanigans with the hippocampus distracted your mother for days. I've not seen her that powerful in ages."

I rolled my eyes, turning to lean over the wall, giving him my back as I did. "You're welcome, then, healer."

Kairos snorted, which made me smile.

I stared out into the soft glow of the coral-lit city, goose bumps rising along my skin as I felt him move closer. His front to my back, his hand beside mine on the balcony. He was so tall that I actually fit into the smooth lines of his body. My shoulders brushed his chest, and then he drew back, but ever so slightly. His head craned down, breath hot against my neck. "She seeks another power source. Something to make her more powerful than him."

What would be more powerful than the God of the Sea?

My heart raced—from the sharing of this secret, or the fact his pinkie lay over mine on the railing, I wasn't sure. "Another source? Like what?"

He shook his head, dark hair slipping forward to brush over my upper arm. I shivered as his other hand moved down to rest against my side, splayed and bold. "That part is yet to be determined. But remember this. For all his power, there are places that he is not able to go to. Things he does not know."

Taking a deep breath, I turned in his arms my back now to the balcony, my hands forced to rest upon his chest. My forehead was at his chin, and I tilted my head back to meet his gaze once more. All softness gone, he stared down at me with a fiery determination that made my thighs tighten.

"You think we can offer him the source and he would leave Ceanus be," I said in question.

His jaw ticked and my fingers twitched, longing to follow that overused muscle.

"What he wants is his favorite weapon. Trayon has asked Her Majesty to find it for him many times. To send her sandwalking Mer to the lands to find it, far beyond what Trayon is capable of traveling to on his own."

"What is it?"

"Nidian and House Cirein-Croin believe it is his beloved trident. The same one he gave to the first queen and king to create Ceanus."

I wrinkled my nose, my fingernail sliding up the seam of his shirt, the silken fabric parting and showing more of that perfect tan skin. "In the stories I've heard, Queen Divina hid it from Trayon."

"That's the same story we have here. But she didn't hide it from him. She asked the original four House monsters to guard it. The House monsters do not abide by Trayon's laws or ruling. Father Earth created them long before humans or Mer were even a concept. They are older than the most ancient records we can find."

"It seems to me that you really have two options. Find the weapon or find another way to power Ceanus. One that doesn't put its ruler at risk."

"To put it simply, yes."

Without thinking, I trailed my hands farther up the curling lines of his tattoo, over the sharp line of his collarbone. "And what happens now?"

I heard his sharp inhale and held completely still, my fingers hovering over the base of his throat.

"Princess…"

"Can I ask you a question?"

"Of course." His voice was tight, and something about it made me smile.

"I see the way the Wardens watch you. The way the Leviathan squalls avoid you. Why are they so scared of you?'

For a long moment, I thought maybe he was not going to tell me, to avoid telling me this truth about himself. I could've asked Mehri or even Akram, but for some reason it was important to hear from him.

"I'm a healer. You know that." He cleared his throat, and this close, I could feel the soft rumble under my hands.

I nodded.

"I also have a secondary gift, one that mirrors my healing."

"What does that mean?"

"It means that unless you've had the direct privilege of never healing from anything, then with my gift, if I so chose to use it this way, I can essentially undo it."

"Undo healing?"

"Open old wounds, release illnesses, undo broken bones or torn ligaments. I can do it with a whisper of a thought." Kairos's eyes were hooded as he watched me absorb this information. "Relieving pain is only the beginning of what I can do. And the dark side of my gift can be quite disorientating to watch, even worse to experience."

My heart pounded. Or was that his?

"I didn't know." I swallowed. "I mean, I had no idea."

One heavily inked shoulder rose in a shrug. "It is not something to brag about. Where there is darkness, there is light."

I looked back over the city. "Do you think I'll ever get a gift? Everything is so different here. I may be the queen's daughter, but I feel like a stranger most of the time."

I sighed, "Every time I turn around, someone is mentioning that I'm a sandwalker or the daughter of Artio. They have to know that my father is a flesh-and-bone man, right? I mean, half of them came from the city. They know who I am."

"They know who you *were*."

Silence fell. "Who I was…?"

"Now you are heir to a dying kingdom trapped at the bottom of the ocean and full of Mer who not only have abilities, but powers. That's a lot to take in. It's alright to not know everything all at once."

I stared at him. "Couldn't you have said that to me those first few days? You know, after you bit me?"

His lips curled slowly. "No, I was still busy trying to hate you."

My heart thudded. "And now?"

"Now, Princess, I'm finding that you might just be worth the pain."

I breathed out slowly.

"I have to know something, though," he continued.

"Yes?"

"Rhoe Karasea… Do I need to kill him?"

My breath caught. "What?"

"I do not take lightly to competition." Kairos's hand brushed my neck, his fingertips embedding into my hair as he tilted my head up to look into his face. "And he is still going to attempt to make a claim…"

"I handled it myself." I cleared my throat. "He was my best friend, my companion. It was a natural progression at that point. But…" My eyes stung. "But I'm not that girl anymore."

Kairos's eyes went black. "No, you are not."

"Kairos."

"Mira."

"What are we doing?"

"Hmm," Kairos hummed against my throat as his other arm snaked around my waist. "Breaking all of my rules."

"Why?"

His breathing was ragged against my throat. "Because I can't live with the thought that you go to Trayon in only a week's time and I spent the entire time furious at you for existing when I could've been showing you at least a little more about myself."

"About yourself? The secretive general speaks?"

His eyes softened. "I was only doing what I felt necessary to keep you safe."

"I know. Now tell me something else."

Our breaths mingled as he pulled me close, tucking me against the hard lines of his body. "I am deeply jealous that the hippocampus lets you ride her."

I burst into laughter, and his arms snapped tight around my waist. "I knew it," I whispered into his chest, my body heating at the pull and press of his hands on my back. "Tell me something else."

"That day I saw you fall into the ocean, it was the worst moment of my entire life. I couldn't think of any way I would be able to reach you fast enough."

"But you did."

"I did."

"And now we're here."

"Don't give me those eyes, Princess. You have a dueling lesson in the morning, and I am a responsible sponsor." His nose brushed down mine.

My heart pounded. "Oh, are you now?"

"Yes."

"What happened to breaking all your rules?"

"Mira…"

"Stay." The word burst from me, surprising both of us. His hands stilled against my clothing.

"If I stay here any longer, Mira, there is no way I will be able to resist touching you. Feeling you against me."

"Did I say no?"

"No." Kairo's voice was a low growl. "But you should. I'm not the hero in your love story, Miraceti. I'm the villain."

"Isn't that up to me?"

Settling my hands high on his shoulders, I pushed up on my tiptoes and brushed my lips over his neck. He was so warm there, his skin smelling of salt and somehow the sun. Intoxicating. He was intoxicating. I paused to bite into the flesh gently with my teeth. When his breath caught, I knew I had him.

"Fuck, Mira."

My entire body vibrated with the knowledge, the power of him against me. "General…"

His arms clenched tight, forcing the air from my lungs. "Don't call me that. Not now, not like this."

Sensing the tension in him, I couldn't resist turning my face into his throat once more, nuzzling that pulse point that fluttered so quickly. "Why not? I've always called you General."

"Not like this, though. When I'm holding you like this? With your legs around me, and your lips wet from my mouth, I want you to call me by my name. That way I could—"

His grip softened, but only enough that I could pull back to look him in the eyes. The black velvet was soft now, the cut of his jaw tense as he struggled to find the words. I waited. "I could almost forget about who you are and who I am."

I brushed my nose against his. Heat still bubbled in my veins, spurred on by his words. The male who barely spoke to me, who refused to share his truths. Now he spoke truth to life, let it hover just between us. He knew I could keep this secret safe.

Just like I knew he would keep me safe.

"We can't change who we are, Kairos, but maybe, just for a little while, we can pretend that the only thing that matters is how I feel when we are like this."

Kairos's harsh exhale heated my face, and then his lips were on mine. The soft pull was not nearly enough. I could almost feel his hesitation still. Frustration welled up. Digging my heels into his ass, I curled my body towards him, driving my hands into all that thick black hair.

"Don't do that. Don't go."

"I'm not going anywhere," he whispered back, chest rising and falling as his hands shifted until they cupped my cheeks, cradling me against his body and kissing me again. This time harder. This time letting me feel his rampant need, the hard length of him pressing against my inner thighs.

My body rejoiced in this, more exposure, more of the Kairos I craved. I wanted to make all of his pieces fall apart so I could see them for what they were. No longer that stoic, sour General. I wanted the male underneath.

But then, my heart thudded in my ears.

I would have to let him go again. But instead of cooling that heat burning in my belly, it drove me only higher. Because I couldn't not experience him. It felt like I'd been waiting a lifetime to experience this.

I would never allow it to pass without indulging. Because here I could be selfish—*with him* I could be selfish.

I would worry about my people, my life, my crown, another time.

Now there was only me and only him.

Thank the Gods.

His hands were moving, one sliding up my side until he brushed against the tight black top I still wore from training. I moaned, rolling my hips against him, when he brushed his fingers against the aching peaks of my nipples.

Lightning flew through my body, making my fingers dig deeper. His tongue played with mine, dancing and stroking as his fingers continued to play, to tease. But I needed more. Gods, I wanted more.

When I broke away with a growl of frustration. I swear the male actually laughed, pressing his face into the side of mine. "Such a demanding thing, aren't you, Princess?"

"Only with you," I said back, trying to pull his mouth back to mine. "Everyone else just does what I want."

Kairos laughed, the sound so startling that I froze, savoring the rumbling sound's origin just under my hands. Beautiful. He was so

Gods damned beautiful that in that moment, I almost forgot what was on the line.

That it was my future on the line.

I kissed him then, sweet and hot and desperate to taste the sound of his laughter on my lips. Rarer than Emenian wine, and twice as heady.

"Mira…" His voice was ragged, tortured, when I finally pulled away, catching my breath as his hand moved low again. It found the perfect spot against my thigh, where the long tips of his fingers were wrapped around, ending up just a breath from the very core of me. "I can't."

"You can't? Can't do what?"

His forehead ground into mine, his breath ghosting over my face. "This…what you want from me… It's different here. It means something different here."

For a moment I wanted to cry, to plead for this one time for someone to explain this to me. But then I remembered something Mehri had told me.

"I've heard that the Mer don't do casual relationships."

Kairos sighed. "We don't."

I couldn't help but smile against his throat as his fingers still moved gently against my thigh. "And so you're saying that we aren't casual?"

Kairos growled. "We are the furthest thing from casual."

My heart leaped in my chest, the happiness blooming there mixing with the heat from his kiss, creating a storm of emotion that I could barely contain. "So what do you propose?" I reached out to playfully bite at the flexing muscle of his shoulder.

Kairos shuddered against me, one hand holding me while the other moved to thread into my hair, pressing me there. I hummed against his skin, loving the burst of power that filled me with every movement the usually stoic General made against me.

"Gods, Mira, there are so many things I want to do to you." His hand pulled me away from his throat, pressing me back against the wall so that my heavy-lidded eyes could find his black ones. "But I know where we will start."

My head fell back, his mouth tracing the lines of my throat. First with his lips, then with his words.

"Let me feel you come, unravel and fall apart. Just for me. Just because of me."

My hips bucked up against him. My neck was suddenly weak as I nodded. Again and again.

"Let me hear it, Princess," Kairos murmured. "Let me hear how you want me to make you come hard enough to see the stars, even at the bottom of the sea."

My heart was pounding, but even so, my words came out sure. Bold.

"Yes, Kairos, please. I want you to make me come."

Chapter Thirty-Six

Even saying the words made my entire body vibrate with a
renewed flush of heat. And by the time the words had left my
mouth, we were already moving. The next thing I knew, he was
untangling me from around him. My knees brushed my bed, but I
couldn't stand not to see him. I turned and a moment later, the
pressure of his hand at my back pushed me down until I stepped
forward, kneeling on the edge of the mattress.

Kairos rumbled his approval as I spread my thighs a little to
stabilize my position on the bed. The mattress dropped me a little
lower than if I'd been standing, so now I could feel the length of
him pressing hard and aching against my lower back.

"Good girl," he murmured, his hands moving from the small of
my back, up to my shoulders, where one moved back down my
arm. The other snaked around and gently bracketed my throat. "Do
you trust me?"

I didn't think. I didn't need to. "I do."

His mouth rushed over the back of my neck, the hand on my
throat loosening as his grip moved low to find the hemline of my
top. With a quick, smooth movement, Kairos yanked my top over
my head.

I shivered then. I wasn't sure whether it was because of the cool air that ghosted across my flesh or perhaps it was because his hands immediately covered my breasts, his rough, calloused skin hot against mine.

"Oh Gods," I murmured, my head falling back to rest against his collarbones.

Wordlessly he ground into me a little before uttering, "No Gods here, Mira. Just you and me." His hands kneaded my breasts, and I bit down on my lip to muffle the sounds coming out of my mouth.

But then he stopped, his hand moving higher to run his thumb over my bottom lip. "Don't hide those noises, Princess. I want to hear them all."

He bowed his head over me, pressing into my hair, where he inhaled hard. "I want to hear every moment of your pleasure and know it is me making you sound that way."

I instantly released my lip, letting the moan I was hiding slip free as his hands returned to my breasts. Rougher now, he tugged at my nipples then cupped the mounds and pressed them together. Wanting to hear more from him, I arched my back, letting my breasts fill his palms, even as my ass rubbed against the base of him.

"Fuck, Mira. Even like this, you know how to test a male's patience."

I let out a sharp laugh, quickly muffled as his hands dropped, one splaying across my belly, the other moving to my waistband.

"Is this what you want?"

I moaned a little.

"Let me hear it," Kairos urged, his fingernails tracing the edges of my waistband. "Mira…"

Gods, I loved the way that he said my name. "Say it again," I whispered.

"Mira." His fingertips turned sharp against my skin. "Let me touch you, Princess, and finally know what I've been missing out on."

"Yes, yes, yes," I whimpered, my own hands going to his, pressing them lower, pushing them under the magic-imbued fabric. He breathed out a short laugh, which quickly became a groan as his fingers traced lower, finding the heat of me there.

"Fuck," he groaned into my hair. "So slick, Princess. Gods, I had tried to imagine, my dreams tried to replicate, but there is nothing, *nothing* like feeling you." His fingers traced lower, finding the seam of me, dragging his fingertips over me until my hips were rising and falling against his hand.

I was so close to what I wanted. And while I wasn't experienced, it didn't seem to matter. Whatever this was between us…my instincts had plenty of ideas. And when Kairos finally leaned in, the pressure of his front to my back, his fingers carefully circled the most sensitive part of me.

"Kairos!"

"Is it there, Princess? Is this where you want me?"

I nodded against his chest, my fingers still clamped around his forearm. I could feel the muscles there bunching as he tortured me with this bliss.

"Or do you want me lower?" Kairos purred, his body grinding against mine as if he couldn't help himself. I delighted in that need in his voice, my body curling up against his grip.

"Lower… Oh Gods, lower please."

Kairos hummed, his fingers slowing around my clit to slide lower. I gasped as one thick finger dipped into me. The slick heat of my body gave no resistance as he sank deep, flexing where no other male had ever been.

His head dropped back over my shoulder, and the muscular forearms draped around my body flexed as we both let out a collective groan.

"Too much?" he murmured a few breaths later.

I shook my head. "No, just give me a moment. Your hands are…" I didn't need to tell him, and something about saying these words, out of all the things we'd said and done so far, seemed too intimate. The confession was simply too much. At least for now. I prayed to Artio that he would understand.

And he must've, because he remained still, merely turning his palm towards my body to rub gently against my clit as we both breathed loudly into the room's silence.

"Alright." I bobbed my head against his chest. "I'm ready for more."

The hand on my ribs tightened, holding me in place. Bracing me for more. And then slowly, that thick finger began to work me, slipping in, out. My body lit up, making the blood in my veins spark to life, My lungs were tight, the muscles in my thighs quivering as I arched rhythmically into his pumping hand.

The slick sounds of his hand cupping me, moving into me, should've made me blush, but I was past that now.

One of my hands surrendered his forearm, climbing my own body until I could comb my fingers into his hair, pulling his face closer. Breath hot on my neck, Kairos moaned a little as my nails dug into his scalp.

"Let me touch you too. Gods, I want to do that."

Kairo groaned, his teeth briefly biting, holding on to my neck, just above where he'd first bitten me, just weeks ago.

Gods, how much had my life changed since then?

"Mira, if I let you touch me, there's no way I'm leaving this room without my cock buried deep, deep inside you." His finger gave a deep pump, making my breath whoosh out.

"What's wrong with that?"

Kairos laughed, but the rough was rough/ "I'm having a harder and harder time remembering right now. But not today, Mira. Not until you know what being with me would mean."

"Tell me now," I whimpered, rotating my body against his hold.

"No, Princess, not while we are both too far from our own reality," Kairos said. When I whimpered, he said, "Don't think I'm not just as disappointed, Mira. But like I said, I refuse to have half of you. When you are mine, there will be no doubt in anyone's mind the truth of that. Including yours."

"Yours?"

Kairos turned my head, kissing my mouth hard. "You have always been mine."

I bumped his nose with mine. "Then show me those stars."

His hips moved, rubbing against my ass. "As you wish, Your Highness." That finger pumped deep, the second hand moving to my breast, where it teased and played with the hard, puckered peak.

Lightning soared down my spine, making me move and arch and grind back against him. His warmth was a delight. His cock only made me more desperate, aware of the fact that this male, this beautiful male wanted me just as badly as I wanted him.

And when he circled that aching nub once more before adding a second thick finger, plunging deep, I couldn't stop my hips from stuttering against him.

"Right there," I pleaded, my body curling around that damning, beautiful touch. "Oh Gods, right there."

Kairos repeated the movement, swirling around then pushing deep. This time, though, he curled his fingers, dragging them across those slick, desperate interior muscles. And just there, he pressed hard against a part of me that made my body sag. I cried out, my head falling back against his chest as I rode the fierce line of my pleasure. Wave after wave, driving me headfirst into pleasure that made my mouth hang open as I whispered his name over and over again.

His fingers left me, brushing over my now sensitive clit as he stroked me down from my high. Kairos moved his hand from my hair, capturing my waist and hitching me up until the pair of us could tumble onto the bed together.

Then, and only then, he extracted his hand from my leggings. I let his body wrap around mine. His arms remained around me, his breathing just as ragged as mine. I reached back, hoping to find him, to return the favor. But my hand was caught, captured, brought to his lips.

"No, Mira."

"Why not?"

His voice dropped low. "I meant what I said earlier. The only place I'm going to come is inside you, and I don't think either of us are ready for that tonight."

I paused, blinking. "I…um…"

"Exactly," Kairos said, a hint of his usual smirk in his voice. "Just let me hold you, Princess. You've already given me more than I ever imagined."

I let my head fall back into my mattress, the soft pillows. Looking down, I traced one vein that ran down his forearm. "Will you stay?"

"The night?" Kairos asked.

I nodded, unsure if that was really what I meant.

"A thousand soldiers couldn't drag me away."

I linked my fingers through his, knowing if he got up now, I would notice in an instant. With his scent and touch surrounding me, I tucked myself against his side.

Sleep came easily.

Chapter Thirty-Seven

I'd half-expected to wake up and find that Kairos had snuck out. Or perhaps he was never there and I just had a fantastic fever dream of some kind.

But that wasn't the case at all.

When I woke up the next morning, I was tucked deep into my blankets. And Kairos's arm was still curled over my waist, holding me tight up against his chest.

I stared down at the arm, at the twisting elaborate ink. Sometime in the night, he must've ditched his shirt, because I was able to follow the designs up high onto his shoulder, where the lines thickened, spread to where the sign of Leviathan swirled over his heart. The texture was ever so slightly different there. I frowned at the design, pressing firmly enough that his muscles leaped under my touch.

That made me smile.

"You," I whispered loudly, "are a horrible actor."

Kairos's lips twitched, although his eyes remained shut. "You would be surprised, Princess."

I snorted, flopping back into the pillows once again.

"Are you done examining me?"

"Why? Are you uncomfortable with that? All those years examining others as a healer… Must feel odd to have the roles reversed."

Kairos rolled onto his back, tugging me down across his chest. "In case I wasn't clear, I will always be glad to have anything of yours on mine. Even if that is only your eyes."

I worried my bottom lip. I hadn't pictured him being charming, but like this, strong features relaxed, his fingers stroking the small of my back, I could actually picture this.

This was something new. Something I wasn't sure I had felt before.

Happiness.

And not the happiness that came with sparring with Rhoe in Port Sol. Or playing cards with my father. This was different. It was dangerous, thick and heady in my bloodstream, infecting every part of me, system by system.

It wasn't long until he would be in my heart. Buried there, deep and permanent.

Fear pricked the back of my eyes, but it wasn't what I had felt the first time I'd pictured my future in Ceanus.

It was something else. Fear of losing this happiness.

Of losing *him*.

"Mira? Where did you go?" He reached up, cradling my cheek in his palm.

I shook my head, turning into his touch and pressing a kiss against his skin. It allowed me to hide my face for just a moment, to gather my thoughts as the male under me breathed, slow and sure, against me.

"Come back to me."

I smiled, my throat still thick. "I'm here."

Kairos's brows lowered, but instead of pushing, he simply used the hand holding my face to bring me down to his level. The kiss he left on my mouth was too brief, too light to wash away the residual fear.

"Akram will be here soon."

I leaned back. "How do you know that?"

"Blood bonded. Before he was your guard, he was my right hand."

"Is that why he's my guard?"

"He is the best, and while he isn't the best at keeping you in your room, I'm pretty sure he's still doing a better job than anyone else."

I grimaced. "I am sorry about all of the sneaking out."

Kairos laughed. "No, you're not."

"No, I'm not." But now I was smiling too. And when I swung my legs over the side of the bed, one arm moving to cover my naked chest, I couldn't resist looking back at Kairos. He watched me with unabashed interest.

I swatted at him. "Stop looking at me like that."

"Just returning the favor, Princess."

I giggled then quickly covered my mouth to hide the sound, choosing instead to push off the bed and let my arms swing loose and long.

Kairos growled at the sight of my breasts, and another surge of happiness thrummed its way into my chest. Without another look back, I moved to the wardrobe and carefully selected my clothes for the day. No training meant I could wear something less conforming. And, most importantly, less monotone.

But as I straightened, a multitoned blue dress in my hands, a thick chest bumped into my back, arms wrapping around my waist to cradle me close. Kairos's mouth brushed my ear. "You have to know that the only thing that's keeping me from picking up your saucy little ass and dragging you back into your bed for the day is the fact that your bodyguard is already outside. And likely hearing all of this."

I flushed but didn't pull away.

"Please…" Kairos bit down gently on the lobe of my ear. "Have a heart, or at least be gentle with mine."

And then he released me, stepping away and moving across the room to retrieve his clothing. Trying to pretend I wasn't awkward, I slipped my training pants off, pulling the dress on before slipping into my bathing chamber to take care of necessaries. Returning back to my bedroom, I found Kairos dressed, waiting and watching me.

I opened my mouth, somehow needing to say something. To cling to this idea that this wasn't a one-time thing before we left this room. Because that fear still lurked deep in my chest. The one that screamed at me to see reason. That there was no way this was meant for me.

Even if I wanted it.

But he spoke first. "Akram is at the door. He's been asked to bring you down to House Cetus's headquarters."

I nodded.

"Timor wants to talk."

I crossed my arms, aiming for nonchalance. "He can talk all he wants. It doesn't mean anything."

"He means to confirm you are going to pledge Cetus."

I moved closer, watching the tight flex of his throat. "Is that what my mother wants me to do too?"

Kairos's dark brows lowered. "Why would I know?"

"You're her General, her healer."

"And you are her daughter."

"You and I both know it is more complicated than that."

Kairos sighed. "You should pledge to the House that makes you feel like home."

I blinked at him, something scratching the back of my mind. "Is that what Leviathan is for you?"

A strange sort of tension bloomed between us, and I knew that I'd just surrendered my chance at the confirmation of whatever we were with this question. "My House is everything, Princess. I am truly Trayon-blessed."

That black gaze bored deep into mine, my heart still pounding in my ears, as a loud knock sounded against my door.

"Come in," I whispered, both aloud and down the still thinning bond between Akram and myself.

The bodyguard answered by swinging the door wide. He entered without saying a word, moving to stand over by the door to Mehri's apartment. Mehri herself had still not shown up, but I wasn't worried. There was no way she and Akram didn't know that Kairos and I had spent the night together.

Heat flooded my cheeks at the reality of those words. How long until more people knew? And how did I feel about that? I didn't have any time to consider it as Kairos moved off, patting Akram's shoulder as he headed to the door.

The guard said nothing, but I detected an additional layer of stiffness to the Leviathan male.

If Kairos noticed, he didn't say anything. At least not until he reached the door, when he turned back to me.

"I don't care what house you choose, Princess." He smirked. "As long as you leave a little room over your heart for me."

I huffed and turned back to my wardrobe, but not before a fierce grin stole its way across my face.

After Kairos left, I made my way down, with a slightly pink-cheeked Mehri, to the arena. She told me that after some discussion they had decided to move this meeting to neutral territory. And while I had rolled my eyes initially, I found some comfort in the arena's cool stone, the open platform, and the way that when I tilted my head back, the arc above me shimmered down at me in what was becoming a familiar sight.

It wasn't the sun.

It wasn't the moon or stars.

But it was something just as beautiful, just as unique. A smile tugged at the corners of my lips, and I found the tiniest spark of something deep in my chest. The feeling raced from my heart to my fingertips, where they hummed with life.

I stared down at them. From the outside, they looked just as they always did. But something was different. I felt it in the marrow of my bones.

I raised my hand up to the light of the arc's shimmering, transfixed by the feeling of something so new suddenly a part of me.

And yet, something just beyond my hand moved.

Something bright enough that briefly, the veins and bones in my hands glowed as the light illuminated the interior of my structure down to the core.

Everything slowed. Time. My heart rate. Even the way I blinked against the flash of that something…no…someone who moved towards me.

I lowered my hand, my heartbeat a dull roar in my ears. I knew that face, the one that had followed me through the halls of the Ceanus castle. It stared back at me from my mother's chambers.

Its likeness stood only feet away, cemented forever in marble, beautiful and bright and terrifying.

But it did nothing to prepare for me how it would feel to stand face-to-face with the God of the Sea himself.

And he looked furious.

***

There were priests and priestesses the world around who would've given their souls to meet the Gods they served. Or any God at this point.

But the moment I laid eyes on the God of the Sea, all I could feel was dread.

He was a work of art, that much was true to legend. His form, which strolled across the base of the arena, was that of a male. But it was oversize, dwarfing Timor as the Mer male bowed continuously from one side. He wore a robe of the darkest blue, and as I stared at the fabric, something moved there, as if the fabric itself was patterned into life.

Trayon's flesh was so pale, it was nearly transparent, and I shuddered as my eyes swept closer to his face, more afraid than before to look upon this face—his face—and to know the God behind the curse.

I ducked my chin, flushed with shame at my fear, staring at the smooth polished ground until a pair of large, pale feet stepped into my line of sight. So close that I knew by raising my chin, I would be forced to look into his eyes.

"Daughter of the sun," Trayon spoke, his voice a deep throb in the back of my mind. "You are far from home, little sundrop."

"My lord, Trayon," I whispered, dropping into a curtsy and holding it, my thighs shaking. "You honor us with your presence."

To my surprise, Trayon took a step back, out of my perspective. "Rise, sunling. I have little time and much to discuss."

I straightened, watching as the male moved back and forth before me. He appeared as if he were waiting on someone, like a parent waiting up for an errant child.

"What can I do for you, my lord?" I asked, straightening.

Trayon paused, one long finger pointing my way for a moment. "A great many things, I fear, but we will start with the most simple. After the rest of our party arrives."

I noticed for the first time that Trayon was not alone. At his back, there were…creatures. At first I thought they were Mer, the next maybe they were sirens. Their skins were shades of blue and green, overly large dark eyes fixated on me and their lord.

Trayon must've noticed my gaze. He swatted at the air then resumed his pacing. "Do not worry about my creatures. They serve only me."

In my shock and confusion, I gave up on propriety. "What are they?"

Trayon gave a low laugh. "They are all the best pieces of my creations, pulled together and fused with my own magic."

The one closest to me tilted his head to observe me, making my stomach clench at the very animalistic way the creatures acted.

"What do you call them?"

"I do not name them," Trayon said, his strange voice filled with humor. "They do not require anything other than a desire to serve me."

I didn't know what to say, but Timor did. He suddenly appeared at the shoulder of the God, his hands spread wide, as if he'd planned to stroke the God's coat and then thought better of it. His hands, one wearing the seal of Cetus, hovered over Trayon's chest. Too terrified to touch.

Or perhaps Trayon had stopped the male's movements. I had no idea the depths of magic with Gods.

And yet, I observed the way that he recoiled from Timor. Gambling on my observation, I steeled myself. "Why are you here?"

Trayon looked at me, for the first time taking the time to really survey my form, strange glowing eyes taking in every bit of me before settling a smirk on his lips. "You dare to question a God?"

"Curiosity favors the bold."

Trayon chuckled, just the one, the sound piecing in the arena's auditorium. "It does indeed. I am here, my little imposter, because you have something I need."

"What could I possibly have for you?"

Trayon began to circle me, his hands tucked behind the small of his back, his robes billowing around him. "I'll tell you the entire story once your mother arrives."

"Then you can begin now, my lord Trayon," my mother said smoothly, entering through the side entrance and walking up to where Trayon stood before me. "I apologize for making you wait."

To my surprise, she did not bow, merely inclined her head as she reached us. Her subtle show of power did not go unnoticed.

Trayon smiled at her, all teeth. "Queen Damona, dramatic as always. Thank you for finally joining us."

"Like I said, I apologize for making you wait." She gestured to the side of the arena, where three of her guards as well as Kairos filtered in. My silly heart leaped in my chest as the General settled against the waist-high arena wall. "I had business to attend to."

Even from here, I could see the way Trayon eyed the crown on her head. "Perhaps you were getting a quick treatment from your healer."

Her silence was answer enough for all of us.

Trayon laughed again, colder now. "No wonder you seemed so spry. I was half expecting to come here and see you willing to surrender your burden. Especially since an heir so conveniently showed up."

My mother sniffed, coming to stand by my side. "You would know; it was your will that brought her here."

Trayon tilted his head, looking sharply at me then at someone behind me. A moment later, that uncanny gaze found mine again. "Do you want to be queen of Ceanus, sundrop? Do you want to stay here in my underwater kingdom for all time? Your mother's crown would look magnificent on your head." Trayon selected a glass of wine from the table to the side, taking a long drink. "Even if it was only for a short time. Your blood will always work against you in that way. You may look like one of us, but inside"—his mouth twisted—"I see your ordinary, delicate…mortal soul."

His words were sharp as a blade, carving into my chest. Not only because I felt the truth of them, but because I could tell my mother did too. Her chin dropped, her shoulders rounding.

Ordinary.

Delicate.

Mortal.

I would never be like them.

I opened my mouth, desperate to defend myself. To say anything, a pitiful attempt to defend myself since no one else would.

But Kairos spoke first, his deep voice a snarl. "Be careful, ancient one. I don't like your words' meaning."

Trayon rolled his eyes then moved ever closer to my mother and me. "How long can he keep this one alive, Damona? Will you share the destruction with her? Or let her bear it for you?"

"Trayon, I beg you," Damona said. At my side, her hand gripped my wrist, hard. "You are spinning tales, Sea God."

"Tales are all just truths at the beginning. Before the common chattel of this world dilute them. My ears tell me that you have spent most of this Adrialian's time here confusing her. I am merely offering the final pieces in a puzzle that was started and scattered long before she arrived. Which clearly she is not catching onto." Trayon wrinkled his nose. "Next time choose a brighter one, eh?"

"This one?" I stepped away from my mother. "What is he talking about?"

Damona was pale. "You don't understand, God. This is my daughter, my real daughter."

The god moved away again, his shoulders giving a casual shrug. "It makes no difference to me what you call them. Only that you continue to serve me in the way of our agreement."

My heart was racing again.

"She is my daughter, Trayon. That means that…" Damona faltered. "That means the deal will change."

"What proof do you have?"

"You are a God. Can't you tell?" She was hysterical now, her voice pitchy, filling every breath around us. And still I stared.

Trayon shrugged. "I have been burned too many times, Mer queen."

"Don't. I beg you. She is the one. I can prove it." Damona was pleading now, her words slurred, promises and reminders of past memories of them together. But my eyes were only on him, my ears waiting for his words. The recognition that my entire existence here in Ceanus has been building to this moment, that it could be explained by exactly this moment.

Trayon must've understood too, his face so serious as we stared at each other, him savoring this moment, the joy of knowing and holding it above me like the bait at the edge of the hook. And yet, I would bite anyway. I would never be able to resist.

And he knew it.

His tongue rolled over his teeth, the pale-pink appendage flicking over the dangerously sharp teeth.

"Who are the others?" The words were stilted as they fell from stiff lips.

"Why, the other sacrifices of course." Trayon smiled broadly at me.

I blinked, confused. He raised one long, clawed fingertip and tapped against my bottom lip. "You must have realized by now that the number of cursed Adrialians would have pushed my kingdom past the agreed-upon boundaries."

"Trayon, please."

"Where… Where are they?"

Trayon snorted, pointing one finger between my mother and me. "So many times, she came to me, claiming this Adrialian or another had more of a gift than the others. That they had earned their stay." He shrugged. "I finally agreed to let them train, under the pretense that they might get to join our world."

"But that's not true."

"We do keep a few, don't we, Damona? But the unpledged, the ones that not even my bickering children would select, those individuals become the most important assets to my queue."

Trayon moved behind my mother, his body dwarfing hers as he draped his fingers over her shoulders. "You must have figured out by now that every gift has an opposite. Many of my Mer have harnessed these gifts. None so well as your mother though."

His fingers caressed her collarbones in a touch that meant no affection. "Surely she has shown you her fascinating ability."

Her ability to power things. She gave power to the arc, to the coral lights, to every part of Ceanus. Without her, the kingdom would literally fall.

She was a giver of power.

My throat stuck. Pain filled my chest at such a fast rate that I thought I might explode from the pressure of it. Kairos had said that his gift, his healing gift too, had a dark side, that it would remove the healing. That it would physically undo all the good that had been done.

Mother's gift was to give power.

That could only mean one thing.

Trayon's head tilted, a predator waiting for me to take the bait, knowing that the blood in the water was too much for me to resist. I looked to my mother, swallowing the bait whole. A tear slipped down her cheek.

"You can steal power."

"Mira, please."

"Do you steal the Adrialian's powers? The ones who go unpledged?"

"I couldn't keep the entire city intact. It was impossible to protect so many. I had to make a choice. The best choice for the kingdom—the sacrifice of the few to save the many."

I could hear my breathing in my mind, my fingertips numb as I clenched my fists together. "You stole power that was not yours, from my people, to save your own. And yet you had the audacity to pretend you wanted to help me, that you would help to lift the curse."

"Please, daughter." My mother's—no, Damona's face was tortured, her eyes filled to the brim. "I did what I had to. But when you arrived, I had so much hope. My child, finally returned, the only one in my bloodline who could inherit the throne. I thought maybe things could be different. That together we could push back the boundaries, make the city bigger and safer once more."

"And then I didn't have any power."

The silence was her answer. I had had nothing to steal. That was why I had been safe. I had been useless to her. Her heir without any power. No chance that I could truly inherit the throne. Just a placeholder until she could find another alternative.

My breath rattled in my chest. "How many other 'daughters' did you attempt to sell to Trayon as your heir?"

Trayon stepped away, strolling around my mother until he approached me once more. "No other heirs, at least not in so many words. She brought many to our doors, hoping to partner with them. This one…" He pointed over my shoulder, at where I knew Kairos was. "He actually fits the bill. But while he is a healer, his power does not translate well into any type of power source. Therefore, all he does is keep her alive. Without him, she would have been forced to consolidate the kingdom even further."

"Why do you let that happen? I thought this was your creation."

"Oh, yes, of course. This was one of my favorite ideas I've had. But you see, a God such as myself, I spend my ways defending my boundaries from my family's constant warring. I do not have time to keep you all alive individually. It is why I designed the gifts. It is why I cannot come to your rescue every time something becomes precarious. I have already been generous enough to take only what I need to maintain the war with Artio. And nothing else."

"What happens if my mother's magic fails?"

"You mean if she can no longer drain enough undesirables to keep the kingdom intact? Then my Mer become permanently water-bound. They will find a way, I'm sure."

"You care so little for your own people… I don't know how I ever thought that you might help me save mine."

Trayon huffed. "Why would I ever help my brother's people? More Adrialians pray that Artio helps only him. At least my curse provides Queen Damned…I mean Queen Damona with more gift and life to drain to keep Ceanus and me in power." His frown deepened. "I will win this war and prove to my parents that they gave Artio too much. And then I will be given my birthright. The land of salt, the land of sand. United under my hand."

"You would do that? You would damn thousands just to get a little more power."

"Do not pretend to understand my intentions." Trayon's lip curled, and I felt Kairos's heat at my back. "You are a speck of sand upon the sea floor, and I am the wave that moves you."

Tears were sliding down my face now, a slow, steady stream. Trayon stepped past me, beginning to circle Damona and me once again. I did not want to hear any more. I wanted to go home. I wanted to curl back up in bed with Kairos, to pretend that there was nothing playing with me like the string on a puppet. I wanted to believe that my mother truly had wanted me here, to know me, gift or no gift.

But that time had passed. Gods, how I wanted it back.

The futures swirling around me made my eyes burn harder. To my surprise, Kairos spoke out again, moving to stand against my arm, his bare skin brushing my own.

"There must be another way to best Artio." Kairos's voice was confident, sure. "They say there is a weapon, your preferred weapon."

Trayon made a face. "If you have looked into it that much, then you know that it has been lost for generations. Likely stolen by Artio himself and either destroyed or out of reach."

In the pause there, I looked at Kairos, shocked to find him staring down at me. Without breaking contact, he spoke again. "What if I told you we had found guaranteed proof of the existence of the dagger? Your dagger."

Trayon's posture changed ever so slightly. Then his words, sharp and frustrated, sliced across the arena floor. "I cannot defeat my brother with just the dagger."

"But you cannot reconstruct your trident without it."

His brow rose. "You speak boldly healer."

"Because we both know that you need her to find that dagger. Only a true heir to the throne, a daughter of Ceanus, could call to Cetus and find the dagger. If you weild the dagger, made from the heart of the trident, then you would not need as much of the power from Queen Damona."

"Perhaps. Continue."

Kairos's fingers brushed mine, "If we can find the dagger and return it to you by pledging, then you must promise to release the Adrialians from your curse." He paused for a breath then continued. "Permanently."

Air filled my lungs, relieving some of the pressure. Awareness of all the ways Kairos was trying to touch me, to keep me close, reminding me that the game we were playing was much grander than a simple hook and bait.

Trayon was serious for a long beat, then two. Finally, a slow, sharp-toothed smirk slipped across his face. "You find my dagger, bring it to me in my home, and I will remove my curse."

I opened my mouth to answer, but Kairos cut me off. "You must give your word."

"Always the smart one." Trayon looked to Damona. "You were wise to keep him alive, even if he's the reason for this entire debacle anyway."

Before I could think of his words, or anything else, he gave me a short bow. "You have my word, Princess Mira. Bring me the dagger, and I'll trade it for your kingdom's freedom from my curse."

I looked at Kairos, who nodded. I let out a shaking breath. "I accept your word."

Trayon smirked deepened, and he whirled on Damona. "Giftless as she is, I like her. Would it not be such irony if the one person you never considered an option to be the one person capable of saving you all?" He took a deep breath in. "It is exactly my favorite brand of chaos. I cannot wait to see if you survive, sundrop."

With that, Trayon raised a hand, his fingers snapping. In an instant, his body appeared to lose its color, its vibrancy, turning transparent. Another half a moment, and he disappeared from in front of us, splashing to the marble floor, which dried immediately.

He was gone.

Leaving behind a chasm of pain and knowledge that sat on my skin like the chaffing of salt. I wished to brush it off, to forget everything.

But I couldn't. Because even amongst the pain, there was the smallest hope that bloomed there. It blossomed, warmed by Kairos's continued presence at my side. And even the dull silence that surrounded me, I found myself unable to look at my mother.

But that wasn't stopping her.

"Mira, please, look at me."

I didn't, but her words continued to fall, dripping further into my mind with every pump of my severed heart.

"I can explain everything. You just have to—"

I snapped then, my tolerance evaporating. "No, Mother, not anymore. You have had weeks to explain, a hundred instances that would've been perfect moments to inform me that not only was I your giftless, helpless mortal daughter, but while you pretended to listen to me discuss saving my people, while you allowed me to dream that I might succeed at saving them, you knew the entire time that I was nothing but a failed plan. One who was standing idle around, training with the same people who you were planning to suck the gift and life from when the time came."

Damona opened her mouth, and I raised a finger to halt her. "Let me correct myself. The same people you are *still* planning on sucking the gift and life from." I hated how high my voice was, how it came out a whisper.

I looked up at the top of the arc, desperate to stop the prickle of tears that scratched at the backs of my eyes.

"Mira…"

Lowering my head meant the tears that were hiding there slipped free, making the crown's silver sheen a blur in the glowing light that shone down on us.

"I'm going to get him his dagger. Even if it kills me, I will. Because a true royal, a true queen, would sacrifice everything for her people instead of sacrificing its people to hide the truth: that this throne, that damned crown on your head, are alive only because others are not."

"You think you are so much better than me? Wait until you do feel the weight of the crown. Then you will know. You would understand what a torture it was to make that choice."

"The choice to murder thousands so that you don't have to tell people you aren't as powerful as they believe? Oh, you poor thing." My blood pumped through my body, adrenaline making me twitch. The Claw of Cetus at my throat hummed faintly.

Damona stepped forward, eyes flashing a brilliant, strange silver as they did.

Kairos stepped between us in one quick move of his body. To my surprise, Akram did the same, solidifying the wall of angry male Mer between Damona and me.

"What do you think Trayon will do when he gets his dagger, Mira? Do you think he will do good with it? He will wage that war with his brother, the one who rules over your other home. And when it comes down to it, will Artio ever forgive you for giving his brother a weapon against him? You will remove a curse but damn an entire continent. Are you prepared to do that? To weather that burden?"

"I will solve that problem, after I stop the slow and methodical destruction of my people's sanity. And if Artio chooses to blame me, then who am I to stop him? But the bottom line is that I am done playing games with Gods. I am done begging for help. I will do what is best for my people, and I will do it myself. Alone if necessary."

Damona was very still, or at least the sliver of her that I could see from behind Akram and Kairos. Pressing my hand over my heart, I lowered my chin.

"With your blessing, Your Majesty."

But I didn't wait for her blessing.

Chapter Thirty-Eight

The hallways were a blur, my steps hurried as I made my way back up to my rooms. I didn't need to look back to know that my twin Leviathan shadows followed in my wake. I wasn't sure whether news of Trayon's visit had passed or whether Mehri was simply blessed with immaculate timing, but the doors to my room swung open just as we approached.

The three of us stepped through, and Akram turned, sealing the door behind us.

Mehri's chest was rising and falling rapidly as she stared at each of us. "Your Highness, are you well?"

"I'm fine, Mehri," I said. Although I wasn't sure I was. There was something sharp, painful wedged beneath my heart. I raised my hand to press my palm there, distracted briefly by the fluttering heartbeat that pounded in my ears.

My mother. That crown. They were powering this place, giving life to everything within it by draining the gift and life from others. It was impossible, yet at the same time, it made sense. The lack of population growth. The extended lifetimes of those within it. Damona was stealing life to give life. Not just to Ceanus, but also to Trayon.

Oh Gods, the Sea King was not going to make this easy on me. But I had to stay the course. I had gotten my deal. Now I had to fulfill it. The dagger—Trayon's weapon. I had to get it for him. I needed to pack. I could leave now, just as soon as this pain passed.

"I..."

I pressed harder, searching for the source of the pain. It was only increasing, growing harsher, the stabbing pain further inside. My fingers found nothing, but I couldn't stop, pressing my other hand there too, searching for the source—the reason I felt like I might slump to the floor at any moment.

"Princess." Kairos was there, his dark shirt blocking my vision as his hand sealed over mine. The long arm he cast around me pulled me flat against his chest. My hands stilled, trapped between our bodies. The pain persisted. Gods, maybe it got worse. I couldn't tell now.

"It hurts," I whispered against the fabric. "Why does it hurt?"

Kairos tightened his grip on me. "You're safe now. It's okay."

His words irritated me, making me struggle to pull away. "I'm fine, Kairos."

"No..." Kairos spoke into my hair, the hand on mine slowly guiding my grip off of the nameless pain until I was gripping the small of his back. And then we were pressed completely together, no space, no air, no falsehoods between us.

"I'm not alright," I tried to say, but the words come out only as a strangled sob. And then I couldn't stop, the sounds ragged as my knees bent. Kairos bore my weight without a word, another rumble of soft words as the sobs burned their way to life.

There was silence then, apart from the soft noise that I tried in vain to muffle against Kairos's chest. I didn't know how long we stood like that, at the center of my chambers. When the pain in my chest eased enough, I raised my hands to press against Kairos.

"Mehri?"

"I'm here, Your Highness," Mehri said, her usually bright, smiling face serious.

"We are leaving." I glanced to Kairos then Akram. "I'm assuming that someone knows where the dagger is?"

Kairos nodded. "We have reason to believe it is at the cusp of Trayon's Trench, the source that split land from sea during Artio and Trayon's original disagreement."

"How long until we can get there?"

"If we leave today…"

"Yes, if we leave today." I hoped my words sounded more confident than I felt.

Akram and Mehri glanced at each other, Akram finally answering. "One day, perhaps part of a night if we run into weather."

But I was already moving, pushing Kairos farther away, making sure my mind would clear with his absence. Mehri was a flurry of skirts, her slight form moving around my room with an effectiveness I couldn't hope to compare to. So instead I moved to the small drawer alongside my bed, letting my fingers trace the edges of Kairos's own dagger, as well as the sharp edge of my hair comb.

On a whim, I picked them both up, tucking the hairclip into the bodice of my top. The dagger I palmed, finally opening a drawer to select a harness that would keep the dagger strapped against my thigh. I didn't know what we would be facing. I didn't know enough to be throwing myself into this venture. I had no idea why it had to be me to go get the dagger. I had no idea why Trayon needed it.

But I didn't have time to dwell on this anymore.

I had to go.

I had to focus.

Get the dagger. Give it to Trayon. Save my people. Then I could go home.

My real home.

"Here, let me," Kairos said, leaning to fasten the strap of the leg harness. Then he held out his hand for the dagger.

I placed it into his hand, letting the touch of his fingers calm my fears, if only for a moment.

Kairos held the dagger for a moment, his broad chest rising and falling as he focused hard on the weapon in his hand. The air hummed, and I swallowed my surprise. He was imbuing the dagger with more of his gift. I almost told him to stop, suddenly afraid of having someone give me any part of their magic. It seemed too close to what my mother had been doing.

"I'm giving it to you. Just for now."

"Kairos."

"A gift, to use as you would like." His dark brows lowered. "You did not ask or take it from me. I give it willingly."

Swallowing hard, I nodded, and Kairos quickly slid it into the sheath on my thigh. "Are you ready?" he asked, not meeting my eyes.

"I don't know if I'll ever be ready for this. But that never stopped me before."

Kairos patted my leg. "That's my girl."

Standing, he moved towards Akram. "Do you know what to do?"

My guard nodded, but I didn't miss the way his eyes strayed to Mehri for a moment before returning to his superior. "Of course, General. I will leave immediately to tell them."

I frowned. "To tell who what?"

Akram's serious face tightened as he ducked his chin and headed for the door.

Kairos turned, giving me a small glimpse of worry in his expression as well. "I don't know for sure that your mother won't send someone after us, to run interference. Akram will stay here, guarding her in my place so that we are aware of her actions."

"You think she would do that?"

"You may very well be severing a cord that links her to a God," Kairos said. "There is very little people won't do for power."

"Oh." I stared across the room at Akram. Suddenly I wanted him to do something, to say something to me about this. I needed confirmation I wasn't trapped in some kind of nightmare that I couldn't get out of.

My mother was murdering people. My people. The kingdom I was heir to was only alive because of the loss of those lives. Well, that and the arrogant desires of a once-great God.

Mehri touched my arm, a soft hum in the back of her voice. Akram's gaze dropped from mine to Mehri's. I could practically feel the words there, the softness that passed between them like the ghost of a caress.

My throat felt tight again.

Akram pressed his hand over his chest, bowing to me. "Your Highness, I will always stand by those who do what is best for the people. My pledge is to Leviathan, but my friendship is pledged to you."

Don't cry, I chanted internally. Princesses didn't have time to cry.

Akram straightened and then vanished through the doors, sealing us in once more.

"Mehri," I whispered. "Can you make it hurt less?"

Mehri sniffled, and I saw her hand dart up to her face. "No, I don't think I have that kind of power."

"Why does this feel like goodbye?"

Mehri's hand squeezed my wrist. "Because after today, everything will be different, Your Highness."

"Am I selfish for wishing it wouldn't?"

"I think it makes you human, one of my favorite things about you," Mehri said, letting out a breath. "You are my friend, Miraceti of Adrial, and I believe you will succeed."

A watery laugh slipped free. "Can't you just call me Mira?"

"Never." Mehri grinned, twin tears slipping down her face. "Now, tell me, what else do we need to pack?"

She released me to rub her hands together eagerly.

Kairos answered for me. "Nothing. We must pack light and move fast. We have to get you back for pledging, don't we?"

I shrugged, unsure how to tell him that once I had Trayon's dagger, I had no idea where I would go. How did something that had mattered so much just a few hours ago suddenly feel so hollow?

Or perhaps it was me who was empty.

Either way. I embraced Mehri, pulling her slight frame against mine and whispering into her ear. "Thank you for being my friend."

Her fingers clutched my shirt, and I knew she'd heard me. I didn't wait for her to speak again. Instead, I swiped at my eyes and

allowed a heavy hand at my back to guide me out of the rooms and
into Ceanus.

Perhaps for the very last time.

Chapter Thirty-Nine

We stood by the archway into the Great Sea. I should've been surprised that the guards there were no longer present. I was sure it was just another thing that Kairos had already taken care of. My feet felt heavy as we slowed there. Kairos seemed content with just the two of us going, and while this morning I would've sold my soul to spend some alone time with the General, I had a distinctive feeling that the previous night we'd spent together wouldn't be happening again anytime soon. Not with this new knowledge pressing into me.

Not with my people's future—my future—hanging in the balance.

"Are you ready?" Kairos asked, his hands moving over his black uniformed training suit. He had added several more weapons to it, all shorter and better for close quarter combat.

He anticipated running into trouble.

I blinked, unable to even muster the fear I should be feeling at his words.

"Princess?"

"Are you planning on carrying me all the way to Trayon's Trench?"

Kairos's dark eyes narrowed. "I thought you wanted to make good time. It's the best way."

"It is… Just…" Just that it was a constant reminder of just how out of place I was here. And his carrying me only cemented in my mind that I was still a damsel in distress, even when he didn't meant to treat me like that.

There's no need for dramatics, sandwalker. I'm here.

I gasped, stepping toward the sea. *Krem?* I was rusty from speaking mind to mind with the hippocampus.

As I already mentioned, Krem says dryly, *I'm here. Now get your unfinned ass in this water so we can get moving. Trayon's Trench is a long journey.*

How did you know? About the trench?

Krem approached the portal, her scales glowing a dark green in the coral light from the archway. *You ask too many questions for someone who can't swim.*

I laughed, brushing my fingers over the Claw of Cetus and stepping into the arc. A moment later, the tingling pressure of the sea swept over my skin. *I missed you, Krem.*

Of course you did, sandwalker. The hippocampus's enormous head lifted and seemed to stare down Kairos as he came into the water as well. She sighed, flanks expanding and contracting dramatically. *I refuse to slow down for your pretty male. He will have to ride too.*

Finally reaching her side, I pressed a hand against the scales of her arched neck. *You would do that?*

I would do a great many things in order to get this over with more quickly. Krem's forefins flexed, moving her forward a little. *Get on, sandwalker. You two, black scale.*

Kairos looked at me, confused.

I giggled, bubbles slipping out of my mouth as I did. Directing the conversation down the bond that still tied the General and me, I spoke to him. *She wants you to ride too.*

Are you sure? Kairos looked unconvinced.

Yes, she's excited to have you.

Sandwalker, please, you're embarrassing us both, Krem said, her nose expelling a great amount of bubbles.

Kairos gave me a long look.

I shrugged. *Alright, so she's not excited. But she said she won't be waiting for you. So you best join me.*

Kairos, interestingly enough, pressed a hand down against his dark fins. As if catching fire, his scales changed, moved, allowing his legs to reemerge. They maintained the scales that he donned as a Mer but with the dexterity of a two-legged human.

I stared, slack-jaw.

You're drooling.

You can't drool in the ocean. But nonetheless, I closed my mouth quickly, directing my question to Kairos. *Can every Ceanian do that? The…half-Mer-half-human look?*

Kairos shook his head, dark waves catching in the ocean and surrounding his face. *No, not every Mer.*

He didn't elaborate, and I could actually feel Krem's vibrating need to get moving. *Alright, I'm letting this go for now, but you're going to have to explain more sometime soon.*

Kairos grinned at me. *Or what?*

Or else, I will torture it out of you. Moving close to Krem, I slipped a leg around her smooth, scaled middle. After giving the hippocampus a long look, Kairos did the same. His hips bumped mine as we slid together, and his groan was rough in my mind.

You already are, Princess.

Grinning, I leaned forward to stroke Krem's neck. *We're ready.*

The hippocampus's front finned legs stroked the water lightly. *I highly doubt that, but there's no changing your mind, is there?*

Nope.

Alright then, sandwalker. Hold on tight.

I had believed that Kairos was fast. That thick black tail of his propelled him through the water as quickly and easily as a hot blade through butter. But Krem, she was something else entirely. Her body cut through the currents, riding the waves and curling low and high over various paths that had my mind blurring. There were several times we were low enough in the dark that I could feel the Claw of Cetus tingling at my neck, my ears threatening to pop with the pressure of it. But each time, just before I would've had to say something, Krem would change course and bring us higher once more. It was thrilling and terrifying at the same time.

Kairos must've felt same, because while his body at my back was tense and tight, he said nothing.

I'm afraid to distract her, he whispered down the bond at one point as we swooped through a particularly rocky outcropping, barely visible with the dull coral light that Kairos held aloft.

I nodded, agreeing completely. The hippocampus was moving too quickly for any predators, and in the back of my mind, I wondered if she would even circle back if we fell off.

No, came the response in my mind.

I frowned at the long, snakelike neck in front of me. *Rude.*

Efficient, she countered, this time with an edge of humor.

I let one corner of my lip curl as we smoothed out, her fins slowing ever so slightly. I found my eyes closing, lingering that way, exhaustion and confusion over recent events making me drowsy.

I must've leaned into him, because a few moments later, a hand was there, pressing higher up on my belly. In another world, another place, I might have pushed him away, told him that I was fine.

But he knew what I had experienced. He understood what was at stake. I allowed my body to relax, to cuddle back against his powerful torso as Krem's powerful strokes continued to drag us through the ocean. One of his hands stayed there, stabilizing my middle against him. The other reached up, smoothing my hair away from my face, turning my face in the same movement.

His eyes were so dark, hungrily taking in every inch of my face. I let my own hand wander up to grip his wrist.

Is everything alright?

Kairos nodded. *Just let me hold you. Trust me, Princess. Please.*

I smiled, weariness settling back over me. *Of course, Kairos. I trust you.*

My eyelids were heavy, but I was only able to sleep a short time. Krem's movements were not as still and stable as a horse, and I found myself anxiously looking around our odd little group as we made our way into lighter, warmer waters.

We are close, Krem said softly. *I cannot take you the whole way. I already provoke my herd's ire by helping you. Taking you that shallow would be ill-advised.*

I translated to Kairos, who helped me slide off Krem's side before he also slipped free of the hippocampus.

Thank you so much, Krem. I don't know how I can repay you.

You can't, but there is something I want you to remember.

I tilted my head, swimming close enough I could see my reflection in her fist-sized emerald eyes. *What is it?*

Krem's snout dropped slightly then pressed against me. *You have a hard road ahead of you, sandwalker. May the waves break upon your back, and may the sun light your way.*

I blinked at her, and then, giving in to a longing I'd had since I first met her, I reached up and stroked down her face. *Will you be here when we get out?*

I will.

Thank you, Krem, for everything.

Kairos appeared beside me, and I allowed my hand to drop to my side. With a soft nod of gratitude, the Mer General, now will full tail intact, swept me up in his arms.

How much farther? I asked him, my eyes scanning the serene blue waters around us. His arms tightened, and for a moment, I felt a stab of panic hit deep in my chest. My fingers traced the pain for a moment, and then I shook my head, unsure of where that particular emotion had come from. I was overwhelmed, perhaps, but not panicked.

Only a short distance.

Tell me again how the trench was formed.

When Mikel believed that his brother had killed his love, his wife, he went to Trayon for revenge. The Sea God was eager for a deal and shared his most powerful weapon with the Adrialian prince. The trident. Mikel went ashore, walking on Artio's territory, where he declared the curse, and infused by Trayon's magic, he thrust the trident into the courtyard. The magic severed the land right there, splitting down to the very core of this cliffside and dragging the old part of the city straight into the water.

I couldn't even imagine a power like that. And all because of love. *And the trench is there because…?*

It is said that the trench is the line that Mikel drew, and when Ceanus was created, a line of magic remained. For a generation or two, many

Ceanians would come here to honor Trayon. But eventually we moved the statue they had built to the arena and other offerings to the temple in the Deep. There was no more need to come here.

I shivered at the thought of the Deep. The darkest part of the ocean held no interest for me, especially after meeting the God who resided there, so close to the dead realm. *And you think the dagger is there?*

Yes, likely hidden amongst the old temples and offerings. There were many at the time. It would've been easy to lose track of just the dagger.

And we are looking for the dagger, not the trident.

The dagger was simply one point of the trident. Trayon has to begin somewhere, I suppose.

I opened my mouth to ask more questions, when I saw Kairos's face change. A broad smile lit up his handsome features.

Look, Princess.

There, just a short distance ahead, was the sharp incline of a cliff, the edges decorated with jewels and carved with artwork. At the base, darkness creased, as if a sliver of the earth opened just below.

My heart leaped in my chest, and the Claw hummed upon my chest. It was here. I knew it.

We had made it to Trayon's Trench. The key to my future, to my people's safety, lay just below us. My heart felt lighter than ever, my entire body tingling with joy as I slipped out of Kairos's arms and kicked hard.

I wanted to see the sun.

I *needed* to see the sun, to let myself celebrate this minute victory. There was more to come, more battles to fight, more tests to pass before I would be holding that dagger in front of Trayon.

But for the first time, it felt real.

The end of the curse of Adrial was nearly upon us.

Kairos seemed to know what I needed. He slid his arms around me, and then with a swirl of that powerful tail, we were flying up, my arms reaching overhead, laughter bubbling in my chest.

Tomorrow. Tomorrow we would go into the trench, find out what we needed to do to acquire the dagger. Then together, we would conquer it.

The light of the sun filtering through the water showed off every beautiful inch of Kairos's face as he swirled around me, his tail gently propelling us upwards as his hands sat first on my waist, and then slowly, one rose to cup my face.

We made it. I can't believe we're so close, I said, even my thoughts breathless with the joy of it. My mother's necklace hummed at my neck. We had done it. A deal was set, one that would let me save my people—all of them.

I was going to help my mother. I was going to be what my people needed me to be. For once in my life, I was at the right place at the right time.

We did, Kairos answered, his voice warm as he rubbed his thumb against the edge of my jaw.

We were nearing the surface now, but I couldn't look away. I couldn't stop staring into his gaze as he twirled us higher and higher, the joy in my chest threatening to explode completely as I held on to him.

Mine. He was mine. The dagger was mine. The throne was safe. And so was my mother. We would be back in plenty of time to tell her to not make the deal with Trayon. The city would have its queen, and I would have my mother.

Do you remember what I said when your mother assigned me to you?

I smiled, nodding. *You would protect me.*

There was a stillness to him that made me pause, my joy diminishing ever so slightly. Kairos's throat worked. *That I would protect you at all costs.*

I huffed out a short laugh, letting my hands claw up his shoulders to knit with the slick wet curls of his hair. *I don't remember the exact words. I was a little distracted.*

Kairos's chest rose and fell quickly, his eyes holding mine with such devotion that I didn't dare look away. *At all costs, Miraceti. I would do anything to make sure that you were safe.*

Something unfurled in my chest, making my fingers pause in his hair. The light from the sun was bright around us now, the sea glittering like jewels all around. *Kairos?*

Since the moment I saw you on the docks, I suspected it. I requested every bay area pursuit, each merchant raid, hoping to catch sight of you again. But when you dove in, exposed yourself to the curse, I knew I was right.

His hand settled at the nape of my neck, holding me still as his words tumbled wildly between us. *I tried to stay away, to make sure that you weren't dragged here, into this war you didn't even know existed. I wanted you to remain ashore, if even just to keep yourself safe. I would gladly accept a world without you if it meant that you would not suffer like you would as the queen of Ceanus.*

Kairos, you're making me nervous.

He held on even tighter. *I lied, Mira. I lied over and over to both myself and you, trying to deny what no creature alive has the power to deny. I even tried to see if Ionia would undo it. If she could. But she refused. It was too strong, she said. Which I knew from the moment I saw you, but hearing it from her, it only confirmed what I already knew.*

No, I whispered. *Could it really be that simple?*

Kairos nodded, clearly sensing my thoughts. *Yes.*

Why didn't you tell me? I thought you just…wanted me.

Kairos's laugh was sharp. *I do want you, Mira, but not just your body. I want all of you. I want to see your every smile. I want to experience every laugh. I want to be the one who wipes away your tears and the male who strikes down anyone who dares to upset you in the first place. I am beside myself for you, driven to the point of insanity over the mere mention of you. You were meant to be mine.*

My heart was hammering in my throat. *Kairos…*

His mouth took mine, aggressive in its desperation, in the pleading way at which his lips begged mine to return the affection. But he didn't need to worry about me not responding to him. It was impossible not to. I feared that it always would be. I arched into him, my fingers diving into those thick, dark locks. His tongue dragged across mine, making my heart leap and my belly quiver. I moaned, chasing his tongue with my own, as his fingers dragged down my sides until he could clasp me against his body. I reveled in the sensation, the strength of his torso, the movements of his tail below us as he kept us afloat in the waves.

Time stopped, my future speeding towards me as I smiled into the last of the kiss, letting my eyes flutter open. The eyes I had always mistaken for cold burned into mine, full of passion and want and…something else.

Kairos's lashes lowered, and his nails turned sharp against my side. *Which is why, I hope someday, you will be able to forgive me.*

My heart pounded in my ears. *For what?*

He pressed his mouth to mine again, but it was different now. A soft ghost of our earlier kiss. The heat that had been burning so hot in my veins shifted, cooled.

For this.

Hands wrapped around my arms, and I was yanked—no, pushed from Kairos's grip until my head broke the surface and the blinding light of the morning sun forced my eyes closed. I fought harder, calling out his name, trying to rip myself free of this grip.

"Kairos! Kairos!"

For a moment, I broke free, slamming back into the water. I screamed into the blood bond, begging Krem to be close, to come back. But the bond was silent. When I surfaced again, I was gasping, fighting the grip of what I could now see were a group of soldiers on a boat.

An Adrialian boat.

I relaxed, but only for a moment. They held me, half in the water, half out, as I struggled against them. Kairos surfaced in front of me, his eyes so dark and pained that another wave of panic threatened to overcome me. "Let me go! Kairos!"

"I'm sorry, Mira, but we can't do that."

Shock made me still as Rhoe, flanked by Homer, stepped forward.

Rhoe remained silent, but he looked back to the ocean. Why wasn't Kairos fighting for me? He could drag them under in a moment. His gift would render each of them useless in a single breath.

But he wasn't.

Instead, he moved forward, his long, dark tail rolling in the water of the Great Sea.

"Kairos? What are you doing?" I whimpered. Suspended between Rhoe and another guard, their grip tight on my arms, I hung halfway out of the water. The kiss of the sun and the cool caress of the ocean made my mind whirl.

"Forgive me," Kairos whispered one more time. Then he reached out, and with the same hand that he'd held me just moments before, he ripped the Claw of Cetus from my neck.

My body shivered as the magic washed away, the chill of the sea becoming unbearable in a moment. And yet, Kairos looked down at it, at the necklace that had kept me alive all of these weeks. The only thing that allowed me to survive in Ceanus.

The only gift I'd ever received from my mother.

Kairos looked to Rhoe, giving the other Mer a long nod. "Go. You're wasting time."

And he released the necklace. The heavy silver chain sank, a living thread of magic and metal that slithered beneath the surface. The Great Sea swallowed it in an instant.

"At all costs," he whispered just to me.

And then he, too, disappeared under the waves, the current removing any traces of the world he'd shown me.

The future I had believed in.

Or the magic that allowed me to have either.

The End

Mira, Ceanus and Adrial will all be back in soon in the next installment of The Kingdom Below series. You can find out more details about this next release, as well as other books by Maggie White by visiting Maggiewhitebooks.com or locate Maggie on your favorite social media.